Don't Let Me Go

Don't Let Me Go

J. H. TRUMBLE

KENSINGTON BOOKS
www.kensingtonbooks.com

KENSINGTON BOOKS are published by

Kensington Publishing Corp.
119 West 40th Street
New York, NY 10018

ISBN-13: 978-0-7582-6927-0
ISBN-10: 0-7582-6927-7

First Kensington Trade Paperback Printing: January 2012
10 9 8 7 6 5 4 3 2 1

Printed in the United States of America

For Danny and Anna

ACKNOWLEDGMENTS

A huge thank you . . .

To my agent, Stephen Fraser, for saying yes, for his belief in this story, and for his ready words of encouragement when I most needed them.

To my editor, Peter Senftleben, for pushing me to rethink elements of the story and making it so much better as a result, and for the laughs. And to all the others at Kensington Publishing who contributed their talents to make this novel happen.

To Roland Smith for buying me a pocket Moleskine, and telling me to fill it with crap and then turn it into something beautiful, and then for making me believe I could do just that.

To James Howe, whose own story and gentle courage validated my belief in happy endings. You are a true inspiration, my friend.

To Sarah Ittner, my first reader, who received my manuscript via an errant e-mail, read it, and then generously shared her enthusiasm for these characters.

To Susan Cox, Patty English, Teresa Guerrero, Karen Guest, and Alissa Wood for slugging through that very early draft and for not telling me it sucked, even when it did. And to Don Stirman for his continued willingness to answer my legal questions, personal and otherwise, and for never charging me.

To Brent Taylor for his passionate running e-mail commentary as he read, for telling me he hated this novel because it made him want a boyfriend so badly. I appreciate you more than you know.

And most of all, to Danny and Anna Trumble for all those nights there wasn't a clean dish in the house and for all those dinners that consisted of, pretty much, whatever. And for the vacant looks when you tried to engage me in tales of your teenage lives. I owe you for that.

Chapter 1

Saturday, July 26

Two things:

One. I lied. All that crap about me wanting you to go, about me needing to know who I am without you. Lies. Every stupid, lying word of it. I don't want you to go. God, I don't want you to go. And not only do I not need to know who I am without you, I couldn't care less. There is no me without you. The yin and the yang. You, yin; me, yang. Adam and Nate. Two parts of a whole. Existing together in beautiful harmony. Without you, I'm just a broken piece.

Two. You had to know that.

I veered my car sharply into a Shell station a few blocks from Adam's neighborhood.

"You're kidding," he said, glancing at the time on his cell phone. "Nate . . ."

"What?" I maneuvered the car next to a pump and hit the brake a little too abruptly. "You want to get to the airport? We need gas."

He huffed, one of those irritated and irritating noises he'd been making all morning. "Why didn't you put gas in the car yesterday?" he said, turning down the stereo. "We don't have time for this."

"We don't seem to have time for a lot of things lately." I killed the ignition and popped the handle on the door.

"Come on. That's not fair. We spent the entire night together."

"Sleeping," I muttered and dropped my head back against my seat. This was the part where he was supposed to console me, whip out his ticket and rip it up into a million pieces right in front of me, toss it out on the concrete, beg me to turn the car around, profess his undying love, confess he couldn't live without me.

Instead he lit up his cell phone. "Shit," he said softly. He dropped the phone in his lap and growled, which might have been sexy if I hadn't been so angry and if he hadn't been so freaking anal. "Are you trying to make me miss my flight?"

So much for love. "I don't know why you're in such a damn hurry. At the rate we're going, we'll have time to wax the stupid plane before they board passengers."

"You're being a brat," he said. "You know that?"

Brat? He called me a *brat*? He'd called me a lot of things in the last ten months and nine days, a lot of sweet, beautiful things. But brat? Never brat. Not even close.

He opened his door. "I'll get the gas."

"I'll get it," I said, and got out.

I jabbed the nozzle into the tank and locked the trigger, but I kept my hand on it. The other hand I shoved deep in my pocket. I watched the air shimmer around the pump handle.

Adam leaned against the car and watched me. When I didn't look up, he tipped his head low and fingered my T-shirt at the waist. "Just to set the record straight," he said, "we didn't sleep all that much either." The tiniest of smiles tugged at the corners of his mouth. My eyes locked on his and my heart lurched in my chest. It was an unexpected moment of intimacy standing next to a gas pump on a stifling July morning, sweat trickling down my back and the smell of gas strong in the air, the moment so brief that in the days and weeks ahead, I would think I had imagined it. But for three, maybe four fleeting seconds, I saw in his eyes the guy who loved me, the guy I loved back so much that it scared me sometimes.

His eyes shifted past me to the spinning dial on the pump, and as suddenly as it had arrived, the moment was gone.

He took the handle from me and released the trigger with a

thunk and seated it back on the pump. I stared at the dial, not quite believing what I was seeing—five gallons. *Five* gallons? That was all he could give me this morning? A five-gallon delay? I stood, stunned, as he secured the gas cap and smacked me on the butt. "Let's go, handsome."

As I pulled back onto the road, he checked the time on his cell phone again and then tucked it back in his pocket and resumed patting his thigh to the song. I thought if he pulled that freaking phone out one more time, swear to God, I was going to pitch it out the window. The gas gauge nudged just past a quarter tank, but my internal gauge was quickly slipping toward Empty.

"You won't miss your flight," I said, the hurt coating my words, weighing them down so that they tumbled out, heavy and muted.

He put his hand to my ear and rubbed my earring with his thumb. "I'm going to have to send you a new pair of earrings."

I kept my eyes on the road but shifted my head and my shoulder to trap his hand just for a moment. "I don't want another earring." I swallowed hard past the lump in my throat. How could he even think I could part with this one? When I'd woken up in the hospital, one of the first things I'd noticed was that they'd taken my earrings, the ones he'd brought me from New York. He'd taken a black stud from his own ear then and put it in mine. I hadn't taken it off since that day. I didn't intend to take it off ever.

I glanced at him. He smiled and dropped his hand and looked back out the window. I could sense his thoughts slipping away again as he picked up the song and the beat.

"We're pulling apart," I said.

"Hm?" He looked over at me.

"The line. It's *we're pulling apart*."

"What?"

I looked back at the road. "Never mind."

He smiled distantly and turned back to the window. Up ahead, the freeway split. I slid into the right-hand lane and made the wide sweep onto the toll road as Adam butchered yet another line.

It was stupid, *stupid,* getting pissed off over something I did myself all the time. Who cared whether he got The Fray's lyrics right or not? Except that he'd been doing more and more of that in the past few weeks—feigning attention, smiling vaguely when I said something or asked a question. Sometimes it felt like he was already gone, like his brain had been unplugged from the here and present and plugged back in to the there and future. Maybe I was to blame. I'd pushed him to take the job. *This is your time. Please, go to New York. Be fabulous.* I just never thought he'd go for it with such gusto.

"You're wearing the green underwear," I said.

"What?" He turned down the AC.

"I said, You're. Wearing. The green. Underwear."

"What? You're complaining about my underwear? You want me to take them off?"

"We don't have time for that, remember?" I said, sullenly.

He rolled his eyes. "Why does it matter what underwear I'm wearing?"

"Because I bought them for you in Key West."

"I remember. I like them. A lot. I promise, they're clean."

"I just don't know why you're wearing them today," I mumbled.

Okay, *now* I was being a brat.

I popped the cover on the storage compartment in the console and felt around until I found a thin jewel case. One-handed, I flicked it open and popped out the CD. The case clattered to the console, then dropped into the space between the console and Adam's seat. I hit the eject button and switched the CDs, then dropped The Fray back into the storage compartment sans case and smacked the lid shut. Three Dog Night wailed about some stupid bullfrog named Jeremiah.

"Is there something we need to talk about?" Adam asked.

The heat was creeping back into the car. I turned the AC back up and stared at the toll booths up ahead, considering the penalty for crashing through the gates. We'd get pulled over for sure. I'd probably have to take a sobriety test—walk the line, breathe into some little tube. I'd get a citation for failure to stop and pay a toll and probably a hugely inflated bill for replacing the gate. And then Adam would miss his flight. And for just a little while longer he'd stay. But there were other flights. There would always be other flights.

I hit the brakes and fumbled in the tray at the base of the gear shift for quarters. I counted out five. "Dammit, I should have gotten some quarters before we left." The tray held some loose change, mostly pennies and a stray nickel or dime. I slid the coins aside until I found two more quarters. I pinched one and added it to the five in my hand, then flung all six at the basket. Three overshot and fell to the concrete.

"Great." I got the last quarter out of the tray. "Do you have any quarters?"

"Just back up and go to the full-service lane," he said, clearly annoyed.

"I can't just back up." A horn blared behind us. I glanced in the rearview mirror, then popped the door handle and gestured to the dickhead behind us as I got out. He leaned out his window and called me a faggot. I found two of the coins and made some suggestions to the guy about how he might amuse himself while he waited for me to move, then got back in the car, slammed the three coins into the basket, and hit the accelerator, almost taking out the gate anyway.

I couldn't stand any more *joy to the fishes*. Gag me. I jabbed the track button. After a pause, an electric guitar ripped from the speakers. I'd burned this CD of rock anthems years ago when I first decided guitar was more than just a way to blow a few hours after school each day. I might have lost myself in the music if it hadn't been for the stupid lyrics.

Well, I'm hot-blooded . . .

Oh, hell, no. I hit the track button. From the corner of my eye, I could see Adam staring at me, but I kept my eyes on the road. The airport exit was just ahead, three-quarters of a mile. I considered staying in my lane, driving until we ran out of gas. (How far would five gallons take us? Galveston, maybe? I could finish my senior year at Moody High. Surely there was a theater company Adam could perform with. It didn't even matter. We could be beach bums, sell T-shirts to tourists in a beach shop, live on love. That's all we needed, right? The toll road to I-45, then Galveston. It would be so easy.)

A jet screamed overhead. The noise—the jet, the AC blowing

full blast, the music, the roar of traffic around us—it was all too much. I turned off the AC again and flicked on my blinker and slid into the exit lane.

Fame (fame) lets him loose, hard to swallow.

I jabbed the button again, twice, then a third time.

"What's wrong, Nate?" Adam said.

I shook my head, not trusting my voice. The heat was creeping back into the car. This time it was Adam who turned the AC back on.

And then "Free Bird" was playing and my fingers ached with the urge to hit the track button again, but I could feel Adam's eyes on me, so I didn't. Death by Lynyrd Skynyrd.

"Hey," he said, running his hand up and down my thigh. "Let's do Key West again next June. It'll be my graduation gift to you this time. No parents."

I gripped his hand tightly and hoped to God I could make it to June. Key West was magic. And I was afraid I was going to need some magic by then.

Chapter 2

Two months earlier
Graduation party and Key West

"Open it! Open it!" Mea cried, bouncing impatiently in her chair.

Adam grinned. "I'm opening it." He painstakingly worked the envelope flap loose just to tease his little sister. Adam's parents had waited until the party guests had gotten out of the pool, dried off, and gone home to give him their graduation gift.

Clearly, the wait had been almost too much for his little sister. "It's an airplane ticket," she blurted out before he could finish the job.

"Mea!" Mrs. Jensen said, putting her hand over the six-year-old's mouth.

Adam stuck his tongue out at her and removed not one, but two tickets from the envelope. He looked at them, said, "Wow," cleared his throat, then held them up for me to see.

"What?" I said, surprised, because one of the tickets was issued to Nathan Schaper.

"Family trip," Ben said before we could get the wrong idea, which was approximately two seconds too late.

Mrs. Jensen slinked her arm around her husband's waist. "We've already cleared it with your mom, Nate. We have a lot to celebrate and, well, we're really hoping you want to go."

A week in Key West with Adam? Was she kidding? Even with

his family, it was still a week in Key West with Adam. Just a week and a half ago I'd been girding myself for a second trial, a repeat of the painful and humiliating experience that had been the first trial in March. Facing the second assailant in the courtroom, reliving that horrible night five months ago, laying out the most intimate details of my relationship with Adam, and feeling like I was the one on trial. And then, at the eleventh hour, a plea deal.

Just like that, it was over.

I hadn't felt this free, been this happy since last New Year's Eve, until Mea innocently blabbed half an hour later, "Adam's going to be a star."

I was helping her get her toys out of the pool while Adam helped his mom and Ben carry the food back inside.

"Adam's already a star," I said, hooking a yellow raft with a net and dragging it toward the edge.

"No, he's going to be a for-real star. In a play and everything. In New York. He even said I could visit him. And he's going to take me to the zoo in Central Park. And let me feed the pigeons and . . ."

New York? New *York?*

Over the next week, I kept waiting for Adam to hit me with New York, my excitement over the trip to Key West marred by a new impending sense of doom. But he said nothing. And by Friday afternoon I was beginning to think that Mea had gotten it all wrong.

Adam was rummaging through my suitcase when I got out of the shower.

"Why do you have so many books packed?" he asked, flipping through the pages of a novel I'd picked up at a used bookstore after work a few days earlier. "When do you think you're going to have time to do all this reading?"

"I always read at night before I go to bed."

"Not this trip. You're sharing a room with me."

"What?" I froze in the middle of towel-drying my hair and stared at him, shocked.

He laughed and tossed two books over his shoulder. "Mom and Ben finally gave up trying to figure out room arrangements. They could only get two rooms at such a late date, so they were going to have me sleep with them and Mea. And then that seemed ridiculous when there was an empty double bed in the room right next door. So . . ."

A slow smile spread across my face. "So I'm stuck with you for a whole week? In Key West? Me and you? Together? Like alone? All night?"

He laughed and held up a pair of pajama pants. "You won't be needing these either." He tossed them over his shoulder too. I threw a box from my nightstand into my bag and he read the label. "Trojan natural lamb. For a more sensual feeling." He held it up to me, smiling. "A twelve pack? Are you kidding me? I hope there's a First Aid kit in here somewhere too."

Key West—the southernmost point in the United States, a mere six square miles, the last in a string of keys off the tip of Florida, and a place where, as one Web site claimed, closets have no doors. But thankfully, the rooms did, with locks. Ben handed over the key with a slightly amused grin.

"I expect you two to behave."

Fortunately, our room wasn't next to theirs after all.

The week was pure magic. We filled our days with long walks on the beach and lazy swims in the ocean. We explored the island on bicycle, taking in the nineteenth-century architecture, dodging the free-roaming chickens, and chatting up barefoot hippies with tiny dogs nestled in their bicycle baskets. We wandered through Ernest Hemingway's house and speculated about Tennessee Williams's life as we stood, hand-in-hand, outside the bungalow he'd lived in decades ago. And when we got hungry, we ate Cuban sandwiches or conch fritters at a sidewalk table or sitting on the curb and watched other lovers in fearless public displays of affection.

Our nights we filled with passion and long soft gazes and sweet words. We weren't behaving ourselves, and we didn't for one moment feel guilty about that.

On Thursday evening, I paid a street performer twenty-five dollars to borrow his guitar for five minutes. It was the first time I'd played Adam his song, the song I'd written for him as a Christmas present, the song I'd not had the heart to play for him before then.

And it seemed right that I'd waited. I played it for him sitting cross-legged under a street lamp in Mallory Square with the crowds and tightrope walkers and jugglers as a backdrop. He cried.

Too soon it was the last day, the sun on the beach just as intense as it had been on the first, but the water cooled our feet as we walked through the surf. Adam took my hand.

"Can I ask you something?" I said.

He smiled and strengthened his grip.

"When were you going to tell me about New York?"

The look on his face confirmed what I'd been dreading. The smile disappeared. He stopped and stared off at the ocean for a long time, then turned to look at me. "How do you know about New York?"

"I know."

"I've been waiting until we got back to talk to you about it."

"When do you leave?"

"I haven't even agreed to take the job yet."

I looked away, down the beach. Two guys who looked like body builders were making out on a striped blanket under a palm tree about ten yards away. A lone woman tossed a Frisbee into the ocean and stood with her hands on her hips while a black-and-white dog bounded through the surf to catch it.

"Come on," he said, pulling me after him into the deeper water.

We rose and fell with the swell of the ocean, and finally he told me about New York.

"It sounds like a great opportunity," I said.

"Mom's not too happy with the idea. She wants me to go to Austin."

"You have to do what's right for you."

He stared back toward the beach. "Just say the word, Nate, and I won't go."

I couldn't do that. As much as I wanted to, I couldn't. "I don't want you to stay," I said.

His face told me he hadn't expected that. A wave tossed me into him and then pulled him away.

"I don't believe you."

"You know what I mean. This is your time. If you don't do this, then I'll always feel like I robbed you of your dreams. I can't live with that."

"I'll be a hero for you, Nate. Let me be that. I can chase my dreams here."

I shook my head. "No, you can't. Please, go to New York. Be fabulous."

"I don't want to leave you."

I drew in a slow, deep breath to steady myself. He'd saved me when I couldn't save myself. And it was my time to return the favor.

"I don't know who I am without you anymore." True. And then the untruth that I knew would release him. "I need to find out. For me, for you, for us."

What could he say? We were somber as we headed back up the beach some time later. He dropped my hand and slung his arm around my neck and pulled me snugly to him and sniffed.

Chapter 3

I waited off to the side as Adam took his place in line at passenger check-in. The line wasn't as long as he had feared, and he seemed to relax a little. He adjusted his backpack on his shoulder, then slipped his cell phone out of his pocket and put it to his ear. He smiled as he talked, then glanced at me and winked.

If I leave here tomorrow . . .

I jostled my leg and drew in another shaky breath, then closed my eyes and tried to end the "Free Bird" death track loop in my head. Adam did that to me sometimes—he'd hum a song until I picked up the tune. It was an annoying little trick he liked to play on me, but one that he found endlessly amusing. There was this one song—"Wichita Lineman," an oldie by Glen Campbell. I used to play it for my grandmother. She loved the song and she loved hearing me play the guitar, but when Adam told me it was about someone who strung telephone lines, it totally killed the romance. At odd times, he'd start humming the song and the next thing I knew I was humming it too (*I am a lineman for the county . . .*), looping it repeatedly in my head until suddenly I'd realize what I was doing and stop. He got such a kick out of messing with my head like that. I actually would have welcomed "Wichita Lineman" right then, but "Free Bird" played on.

A little kid bumped my hip with her SpongeBob backpack as she bounced past me, her hand tightly gripped in her dad's. The line behind Adam had lengthened, and I was reminded of how quickly time was running out.

It wasn't too late. I could tell him the truth. But, God, what was the truth? That I was still so pathetically needy and selfish that I'd let him throw away his dreams just so he could continue playing nursemaid to me? And for how long? He deserved better. He was my hero. But surely even heroes grow weary lugging around the burdens of their heroism.

The ticket agent handed a boarding pass to a man in a suit. Adam glanced back at me, then stepped up to the counter and set his backpack on the floor next to him. One at a time, he heaved his suitcases onto the scale while Lynyrd Skynyrd continued to tear at my heart.

What a waste. Ronnie Van Zant, Steve Gaines, and Cassie Gaines were dead. Gone. Forever gone. The 1977 plane crash had claimed six lives, six hearts that would never know *sweet love* again. You didn't get any freer than that.

A few feet away, SpongeBob girl pulled a butched-up Barbie from her backpack. The doll's hair had been cut almost to the scalp and she was wearing Ken's clothes. I smiled to myself. The little girl caught my eye and smiled back, then buried her face in her dad's pant leg. *You go, sister,* I thought. I turned to watch Adam.

But like fingers to an itch, my mind returned to the song, changing *girl* to *boy* like it did in all love songs now.

Sometimes I wondered, though, at his complete willingness to believe whatever I threw out there. *I'll be fine. I want you to go. I don't know who I am without you anymore. I need to find out.* Did he believe the lies because he wanted them to be true? My stomach clutched at that thought, and I fought the urge to heave right there on the scuffed tile floor.

"Mom wants you to come to dinner one night soon," Adam said when he'd finished checking in. He tucked his boarding pass into a side pocket in his backpack and hitched the strap back on his shoulder.

"Do you have any gum?"

He stuck the piece he was chewing between his teeth. I took it and stuck it in my mouth. He grinned. "Come on, I'll buy you a pack."

He checked the time on his phone as the newsstand clerk made change.

"Who's picking you up?" I asked.

"Justin, I think." He slid the change into his jeans pocket and the gum into mine, letting his fingers linger on my hip for just a moment, and looked at me with those deep blue eyes.

I looked off toward the crowds making their way from check-in to security and blinked a few times.

"Oh, Nate. If you cry, I'm gonna cry too."

Would you, Adam? Would you still cry for me? Does this come anywhere near doing to you what it's doing to me? "I'm fine," I said.

He shouldered his backpack again and hooked a finger through my belt loop. "Come on. I have something for you."

We found a spot just outside the newsstand. He slipped his hand into his backpack and brought out a black Sharpie. "If Juliet gets to write on you, then so do I."

"That was a long time ago." A lifetime it seemed, before there was a Nate and Adam. A time when his best friend had hoped her name would soon be linked to mine.

"Not so long," he said.

I rolled my eyes. "I already know your cell number."

"I'm not writing my cell number." He held the Sharpie poised in the air, and waggled his fingers at me in a come-on gesture. I held my arm out and he pulled it under his own, blocking my view with his back. "No peeking until I'm done."

The Sharpie tickled, but I held still until I heard him snap the cap back on the pen. He released my arm and turned back to me and smiled. He had drawn a big heart on the inside of my arm. Printed inside in neat block letters: AJ + NS 4Ever.

I looked at him, then at the security agents clearing passengers about fifty feet farther down, then at my arm again, then at Adam. My chin started that awful quivering again.

"It's just a month, Nate. I wouldn't miss your birthday for anything. It'll be here before you know it. I'll feed you cake and then we'll get you all tatted up."

I nodded and blinked.

He cleared his throat and stepped in a little closer. When he spoke, his voice was low, conspiratorial, his breath warm against my ear. "And then I'll let you do nasty things to me."

"Promise?"

"Mr. Schaper. I. Am. Shocked," he said with mock horror.

"You are not."

He laughed, then pressed his mouth to mine. When he pulled away, I scanned the check-in area—a simple knee-jerk reaction I still couldn't shake.

"Are we being watched?" he asked.

"Always the freak show."

"Consider it a public service."

I studied his face for a moment. "Is that what we are now? A flesh and blood PSA?"

He frowned, and a crease formed between his brows the way it did anytime he was worried or confused.

Adam glanced at the monitors hanging from the ceiling—Continental 1079, Houston to New York LaGuardia Airport, On Time—then at the passengers lining up at security. My stomach turned over, and again I thought I might throw up. My nose burned. I stared down at my feet.

Adam pressed his forehead to mine. "Don't let that tramp Juliet steal you away from me."

I laughed a little and blinked back tears, but one rolled down my cheek anyway.

"Oh, Nate." Adam let his backpack slip to the floor and pulled me to him. I planted my face in his neck. "I'll call and text and Skype every day," he said. "You're going to be sick of me before the month's over. It'll go fast. You'll see."

I sniffed, then he sniffed, and that made me sniff even harder, especially when he drew little circles on the base of my neck with his finger. "I don't have to go, Nate," he whispered. "Maybe it's just too soon. If you need me to stay, I'll stay. I can work at one of the community theaters and take classes at U of H and—"

"No." I shook my head. "No. This is your dream. Broadway."

"Off Broadway. *Off* off Broadway."

"You're going. And you're going to be fabulous and amazing." I swallowed hard. "I'll be okay. I'll start that blog or something."

"Save the world for the queers?"

"Yeah, something like that. Maybe I'll sleep with Juliet."

"You'd never."

I smiled weakly and blinked away fresh tears.

"I'll stay, Nate."

I shook my head, and when he asked if I was sure, I lied and said I was. He made me promise to write more songs for him. And then he pulled me to him one last time, kissed me, and let me go.

He held on to my fingers until he couldn't anymore and took his place in line. I stayed there and watched him until he was lost in the crowd and the distance.

In the parking garage I turned the ignition key, ejected the CD, leaned it on a pencil behind my left back tire, and backed over it.

My hero was gone.

Chapter 4

Last March 14
Things that scared us

ADAM: *Where r u?*

ADAM: *Answer ur phone, dammit! Ur mom is worried sick.*

ADAM: *Nate, pls call me.*

ADAM: *Im coming to look for u.*

NATE: *Im fine ok ☺ im fine no need 2 worry . . . just nd some time alone k ☺ im fffiiinnneee!*

ADAM: *Just tell me where u r.*

ADAM: *Answer ur fucking phone!*

ADAM: *Nate, pls, baby. Its 2 in the am. Tell me where u r. Ur scaring me.*

NATE: *I HAV 2 GO! DAMN! IM FINE!*

ADAM: *Im calling friends to help look for u.*

NATE: *if u call . . . I will never forgive u.*

ADAM: *If something happens 2 u I'll never forgive myself.*

NATE: *NO DO NOT CALL. I ND 2B ALONE FOR A REA-*
         SON! NOT TO WORRY THEM!!! DO NOT
         FUCKING CALL! PLEASE DON'T CALL. I DON'T
         WANNA WORRY ANYONE.

ADAM: *Then tell me where u r.*

Long pause.

NATE: *Football field.*

The moon was full and my eyes accustomed to the dim light, so I could see him when he climbed up into the bleachers and sat down, center field, six rows up. I hadn't told him what football field. But he was here so quickly, it was obvious he'd guessed right. What other field would I have gone to but the one where I had suffered so many humiliations? The one where Coach Schaper, dear old Dad, had taunted me relentlessly—*You're throwing like a pussy. No son of mine is running like a homo. Don't you dare cry. I didn't raise a faggot*—turning what might have been my field of dreams into his killing fields.

I dropkicked another football toward the goal. It veered to the right and dropped just a few feet inside the end zone. My bare toes stung from the impact. "I always wanted to be placekicker on the team," I shouted. "Kickers have to have good form, nerves of steel. I would have been a good one too, you know. If I'd kicked, I might have even liked football. Maybe I'd still be on the team." I sniffed and wiped at my dripping nose with my dirty, sweaty forearm. The pads on my shoulders were too small and pinched. I adjusted them again. "You wanna know why I wasn't?" I picked up another ball from the six or seven lined up along the forty-yard line and dropkicked it cleanly through the goal posts. "Because my dad said placekickers aren't real football players. And if you're not a real football player, you're not shit.

"Especially if you're the coach's son," I muttered.

I picked up another ball and planted it on my hip and look at him through the darkness. "You want to play?"

Adam got up, slipped under the railing, and dropped to the ground.

I nudged the other footballs out of the way and met him at the fifty. "One on one," I said. I showed him how to hold the ball, tuck it up snug in the crook of his arm where it was less apt to get loose, and then how to get in line position. Even in the semi-dark, it was obvious what a mess I was. He took it all in, but he did what I said without a word. When we broke, he dodged me and sprinted for the end zone, but I flung myself at him, just catching his left ankle with my outstretched arms. He went down with an *umph*.

"Shit, that hurts," he muttered.

The next time, I carried the ball. I went down on my knuckles at the forty-five. When we broke, I faked right and easily slipped past him on the left and ran for a touchdown, then jogged back. "Let's go," I said, gutting him with the ball.

He planted the ball on his hip. "Nate, you can't keep doing this."

"Come on," I said. "Again."

I got down on my knuckles, but he didn't budge. "This didn't just happen to you," he said. "This happened to me too."

I scoffed. "Nobody yanked your pants down and shoved a wagon handle up your ass in front of a couple dozen people."

"You know what I mean."

I stormed back over to him, snatched the football from his hip, then stormed back and jabbed it down at the fifty again. "Let's go," I said furiously. I got down again, mentally preparing myself for my next move should he decide to call me on it. Instead, he hesitated for just a moment, then got in position and locked eyes with me. "This has got to stop, Nate. You can't do this by yourself."

"Snap the fucking ball."

"You have to—"

"SNAP THE FUCKING BALL!"

He snapped the ball and dropped back a few steps. I threw myself at him and he went down again, on his back this time. He groaned and then grew quiet. And still.

"Adam?" I grabbed his leg at the calf and shook it a little. "Adam? You okay?"

Nothing.

"Adam?" I crawled up him. "Shit. Adam!" I laid my hand on the side of his face and slapped it lightly. "Oh, please, God. Be okay. You can't leave me. Adam?" Panic swallowed me up whole.

"I am never fucking doing that again," he said abruptly.

When he opened his eyes, I was smiling. He smiled back.

"You scared the crap out of me," I said, wiping my damp eyes with the heel of my hand.

"I may never walk again, but other than that, I'm good." He closed his eyes. "This game is barbaric. No wonder you don't like it."

"It's not so bad when you're padded."

He opened his eyes again and fingered the mesh practice jersey I wore. "Speaking of which . . ."

"The equipment room was unlocked."

"Hmph."

I laughed a little and rolled over onto my back next to him. We didn't talk for some time. But the silence felt good, easy, simple. On the field, away from all the trees, the sky seemed so much bigger, so much deeper. The moon was low in the sky. If I tipped my head back, the sky was blacker, the stars more numerous. I picked out the Big Dipper and followed along the handle to the North Star.

"Why a dragon?" I asked. I had run my fingers along the tattoo on his lower back many times but never thought to ask about it.

"That was random."

"What does it mean?"

"I'm not sure it means anything. Dragons are mythical creatures—powerful, free, evolved."

"Like you."

He laughed. "I'm glad you think so."

"When did you get it?"

"Not too long ago. Early November. It was my birthday present to myself. Remember that first day you sneaked a look at me over your shoulder in government class? That was the first time I thought you might actually play on my team. You gave me a reason to come out of the closet, Nate. And the tattoo, well, it was my way of taking control of my body. My way of saying I decide who I give it to. And I wanted to give it to you."

"Do you want to give it to me now?"

He turned onto his side and propped himself up on his elbow. "You're kinda scary all padded up like that," he said, tugging at the pads around my hips.

"They're removable, you know."

"I know." But he made no move to remove them. I felt the subtle shift before he even spoke again. "What happened tonight, Nate?"

I looked away from him and fixed my eyes on a cluster of stars. How could I tell him that my own father, a man who hadn't even bothered to visit me once in those weeks after I got out of the hospital, had suddenly shown up at the door, implying that I was somehow responsible for my own assault?

I want to know what you were doing in that backyard with those boys.

I don't want to find out in front of an entire courtroom full of people that my son's a whore, the way I found out in front of all those people at the hospital that he's a fag.

The humiliation, the hurt. I couldn't repeat his words, not even to Adam. I wouldn't have told Mom either, but I didn't have to. She'd walked in on the tail end of it, her shock and anger distracting Dad just enough for me to escape. I ran—no car keys, no shoes. God, why hadn't I let her get the door? What chance did I have in court if my own dad was so willing to believe the worst?

"The defense attorney is gonna try to make us look like perverts," I said finally. I took a deep, unsteady breath. "He's gonna try and convince the jurors that I wanted it."

"He's just doing his job, Nate. You're not on trial here."

"They're going to ask about us. You know that, don't you?"

"I know. I have to testify too."

"What will you tell them?"

"The truth. I'm not ashamed of anything we do. 'I will wear my heart upon my sleeve. For daws to peck at.' "

"Shakespeare?"

He smiled. *"Othello."*

"Do you think the world is ready for the truth?"

"It's not immoral to tell the truth, Nate. It doesn't matter if the world is ready or not. Truth is truth." He fingered the rubber bracelet on my wrist, the one he'd had made for me last fall as a reminder to stay true to myself. Stamped in the rainbow-colored band were the letters WWND?—What Would Nate Do? "You're wearing it again," he said.

"I want a tattoo."

"A tattoo, huh? People are going to think I'm a bad influence on you."

"Yeah, you're so bad."

Later, in the musty-smelling equipment room, which was really just a temporary building outside the field house, we made love. Afterward, he cleaned up my bloodied toes with some antiseptic wipes he found in a cabinet. "It's just superficial," I kept telling him.

Chapter 5

I knew that night had scared him. I looked at his text again.

Seatmate: u look sad. Me: Leaving boyfriend. No more seatmate. LOL.

God, I loved him. I took a deep breath and fisted my hands around the phone, trying to quiet the trembling. I still needed him, but I was on my own now. There'd be no Adam to talk me off the cliff the next time I danced with self-destruction. The key was to stay off the cliff.

I cut the engine, and the temperature in the car immediately began to rise. In the front window of Ratliff Music, the *Open* sign glowed. My shift didn't start for another hour and a half, but I had nowhere else to go. I tucked my phone in my pocket and went in.

"Hey," Juliet said as she hooked a little plastic bag of guitar strings on a wall peg behind the counter. She flashed me a grin. It faded quickly. "Oh, Nate." She dropped the rest of the bags into a box on the floor and hurried around the counter.

"He'll be back," she said, throwing her arms around me. More than anyone, Juliet knew what Adam's leaving was doing to me. But I can't say I welcomed the embrace. It gnawed at what little self-control I'd managed to amass on the drive over. Fortunately, it didn't last long.

From the office doorway, Juliet's dad cleared his throat, and she let go. I swiped at my eyes with the collar of my shirt, embarrassed, but Mr. Ratliff pretended not to notice.

"You're early," he said.

"Yeah. I dropped Adam at the airport and didn't really have time to go home, so I just came on in." I stepped behind the counter and retrieved the bags Juliet had dropped.

Mr. Ratliff slapped me on the back as he slipped past me to the scheduling book. "Great. I could really use a guitar sub today. Gary can't make it in until noon, and he's got a new student scheduled at eleven. Danial Qasimi. I was planning to cancel, but since you're here . . ." He looked up at me cautiously. "You up for it?"

I told him I was and then glanced at the clock on the wall behind him. Ten twenty-three.

He told me to grab a guitar off the shelf—acoustic. I chose a Takamine I'd had my eye on for a while.

While we waited for the new student, I sat on a bench and tuned the strings and filled Juliet in on how things went at the airport, leaving out the more embarrassing lapses of control. She laughed at the homophobic seatmate. "Was she afraid she might get zapped by some flash discharge when God sent the lightning bolt down on the gay guy?"

I laughed a little. "Yeah, I guess."

"Getting pretty bold, aren't you?" she said fingering my T-shirt.

It was a simple black shirt, printed across the front in white letters: *Closets are for brooms, not people.* "Every crusader needs a slogan." That's what Adam had said when he gave it to me that morning before we left his house. I smiled, remembering how he'd helped himself to one last appreciative look as I switched shirts. I shrugged.

"He dressed you, didn't he?"

I pressed my finger just behind the fifth fret on the D string and strummed both the D and the G strings, then tightened the tuning peg until the notes echoed each other.

Juliet watched me, a grin pulling her lips wide.

"What?" I said, looking up at her.

"He's marking you, you know."

"I resemble that remark." I showed her my Sharpied arm. She shook her head.

When the door opened a few minutes later, Juliet tweaked my shirt and got up. "Showtime, hot stuff," she said.

The name hadn't registered with her earlier, but her eyes lit up when the new student stepped into the shop and pushed the door closed behind him.

"Danial Qasimi? I thought that name sounded familiar." She gave him a good once-over with her eyes. "Whoa. You've grown up."

"Whoa, yourself," he said, grinning widely. "Juliet, right?"

He was tall. Middle Eastern—Pakistani, I found out later. His skin was a rich brown, almost the color of burnt bacon, but beautiful. His hair black. A dimple on the right side gave him a boyish look when he smiled. Juliet explained that they'd been office aides together in seventh grade, back when Danial was a scrawny nerd. Apparently he'd grown up a whole lot since then. He looked like a linebacker.

I watched with amusement as the two caught up with each other, Juliet animated and brazen as always, Danial more reserved but clearly charmed.

I glanced at the clock after a bit, sorry that I had to interrupt their little reunion. "You brought your guitar," I said, nodding at the case he gripped loosely in his left hand.

"My brother's. Are you my instructor?"

"Just a sub." I reached out to shake his hand and introduced myself. Juliet followed us with her eyes as I showed him to a lesson room. I glanced back at her.

"Wow," she mouthed.

I stifled a laugh.

"Gary's your regular instructor," I said, turning back to Danial, "but he's running a little late today, so you got me." I closed the door and sat opposite him in the closetlike space. There was just enough room for the two chairs and a small table with a CD player. On the door, Gary had hung a poster with guitar chords. On the wall behind Danial was my contribution—a poster of Bob Marley in concert. Danial sat down and flipped open the well-worn case, then pulled out a beautiful Taylor guitar.

"Can I see that?" I asked.

He handed it over. The back and sides were a rich, finely grained dark brown. "What kind of wood is this?"

"African mahogany, I think."

"Pretty."

The fretboard had a beautiful pearl inlay that looked like calla lilies. I strummed the strings, then adjusted the tuning and strummed again, enjoying the rich sound. "Does he still play it?"

"My brother? No. Not anymore."

"So," I said, handing it back, "show me what you got."

Danial knew his way around the guitar and could play some chords. After encouraging him to mess around a bit, I taught him a riff that required only three power chords he was already familiar with and a few single notes. I played along, improvising once he got the hang of it. He stopped periodically to massage his fingertips with his thumb. Before we finished, I wrote out the notes of the riff on a musical staff so he could practice at home. I thought for a moment that it would be nice to have him as a regular student.

"Where are you from?" I asked as he laid his guitar carefully in the case.

"Chicago."

"I meant, where did your family come from?"

He laughed. "I know what you meant. My parents were both born in Pakistan. They moved to the States after my brother was born. First Chicago, then Clear Lake, then here." He snapped the latches closed and stood up. "Nice shirt."

I bristled but ignored the comment. I picked up the Takamine and opened the door.

Danial blew on his fingertips as he stepped out.

"Sore?"

"You could say that."

"Keep your practices to about ten minutes at a time until your fingers toughen up a bit more."

He nodded, then dropped his eyes once again to my shirt and smirked.

"Is there a problem?" I asked, an edge in my voice.

He grinned a little and scratched at the back of his head. "No problem."

I left him at the counter with Mr. Ratliff so he could pay, thinking maybe I didn't want him as a regular after all. I replaced the Takamine and found Juliet restocking band lesson books in a wire floor rack. With summer band camps starting in a couple of weeks, there'd been a run on them. Mr. Ratliff had had to restock twice. I picked up the scissors from the floor and sliced the paper tape on a box of books and ripped it open.

"How did it go?" she asked.

"Okay."

"Okay? That's it?" She looked past me to get a glimpse of Danial at the counter. "He's really grown."

"Yeah, I know. You already said that."

"Shut up." She gave me a little shove that threw me off balance, and I dropped onto my butt. "I'm telling you, when we were in seventh grade, he was like this little boy computer geek. I mean, he's a freaking genius on the computer. He was posting articles on Wikipedia before a lot of kids even knew what Wikipedia was. He was always getting into some kind of trouble for it."

"Oh yeah? What did he do?"

"I don't know. A little creative editing on some religious articles or something. I think he put some school stuff on there that they made him take off." She grabbed a stack of books from the box and slid them into their respective slots on the wire rack. "You should get him to help you with that blog you want to write."

"Maybe." Maybe not.

Shortly after Danial left, Mr. Ratliff caught me yawning and checking the time on my phone. "Nate, go home. And do me a favor and take this one with you," he said, giving Juliet's hair a playful yank. "Gary will be in shortly; we can handle the store the rest of the day."

I was not about to argue, not today, because (1.) I was an emotional wreck, and (2.) Adam had spoken the truth—we hadn't slept that much.

Juliet poured us sodas and popped popcorn in the microwave. And then we just stared at each other over the bar. I needed sleep. I needed to go home. She reached over and tapped a kernel of corn in my mouth and watched me chew. I made a pouty face and she made one back, then came around the bar and hugged me from behind.

"What's that for?"

"Just for being you."

I smiled and turned to hug her full on. "I don't think Mike would like this."

She tilted her chin down and looked at me, a mischievous grin on her face. "He knows I'll always love you best." Which made me laugh because not only was Mike Rutgers crazy about Juliet, but I was no threat to him, and he knew it.

My eyes flicked up to the wall clock next to the kitchen sink.

"What time does our boy arrive?" she asked.

"Another hour and a half."

In Juliet's room we pulled up the airline's flight info on her computer. The flight animation showed a little black plane hovering over a map of the United States. According to FlightView, Adam was flying over southern Illinois at 530 miles per hour at the moment. We watched the flight tracker for a while, updating the results every few seconds, but it was like watching the seasons change.

"What do you think he's doing right now?" I asked her.

"Sleeping. Listening to music. Staring off into space. Thinking about you."

I stared at the black plane and tried to envision Adam kicked back with his earbuds in and bopping his head slightly like he always did. And then I envisioned an explosion ripping a hole in the fuselage and the plane nose-diving toward the ground and people screaming and shit flying everywhere and—

"Can I ask you something?" Juliet said. "Why did you make him go?"

And now it was just a piece of clip art again. "I didn't make him go. This was his dream. His big opportunity. He wanted to go."

"He didn't want to go."

"Did he tell you that?"

"He told me he was scared," she said.

"Of what?"

"Of leaving you."

"That's *not* not wanting to go."

She watched me for a moment like she was trying to unravel my brain, but I didn't want it unraveled, so I looked back at the screen. The plane had scarcely moved a nanometer. "He called me a brat," I said.

"He did not."

I scoffed. "This is a lot harder than I thought it would be, Jules. I gave him a really hard time on the way to the airport." I flopped back on her bed and she cozied up next to me. A long strand of her red hair slapped me across the face.

"Don't beat yourself up. He loves you. This is hard on both of you."

"Is it?" Because it sure didn't look that way to me.

We lay quietly for a moment.

"We're pathetic," she said finally.

I stared at the ceiling. She had no idea.

Juliet sighed and giggled, and when I asked what was so funny, she leaned over me, her face just inches from mine, and said, "I just realized that I finally have you alone, in my bed." She raised an eyebrow. "If I were that kind of girl, I would so take advantage of you right now."

"Oh you would, would you?" I laughed and gave her a quick kiss on the lips. But the laugh didn't come easily, and it disappeared as quickly as it had appeared a moment before. I bit my lip and focused on the ceiling, the bits of dust that clung to the sharp texture and swayed in the draft from the cold air blowing from the vent.

"It's okay to cry," she said.

That was all it took. She pulled me to her and held me tight while I emptied myself of all the fear and frustration and hurt that had been building over the past weeks. When the shaking finally subsided, she held me away from her, her eyes all soft, which should have been a warning. She kissed me on the corner of my mouth, then again full-on. I pulled away. "Jules, don't."

She looked hurt and embarrassed, the same look I'd seen the first time she saw Adam and me *together* together.

"Jules." I felt like I should say or do something else, but I just didn't have the emotional energy. So I just said her name again.

She got up, just like before, and left, pulling the door shut behind her. I closed my eyes and tried, for her sake, to forget that momentary failure to observe a well-established boundary. I fixed my eyes again on the ceiling, but my mind was on a memory loop from last night. We hadn't slept that much, but we had slept, our bodies and our minds exhausted by the intensity of the days and nights leading up to his leaving, sleep dragging us under like a strong tide. I kept trying to remember what it felt like having him next to me, but I couldn't, because he wasn't.

I debated going after her. It wasn't entirely her fault, this awkwardness between us.

Chapter 6

Last October 5
New boundaries

Juliet grabbed the front of my shirt and hauled me through Adam's front door. I lost my balance and stumbled hard against her. I think that was the idea. She threaded her fingers into my hair and pulled my face to hers. She wasn't going to make this easy.

We'd known we had to tell her sooner or later. It wasn't fair to let Juliet keep throwing herself at me while Adam and I explored our feelings for each other behind her back and flirted with the desire—the need, even—to explore each other in a more physical way, something more intimate than an occasional brush in the hallway or a touch when one of us handed the other a pencil or a book. I'd opted for later, but Adam had known her longer and trumped my later with his sooner. This bit of subterfuge we'd just embarked on had been his idea.

From the kitchen doorway, Adam cleared his throat loudly and she let me go.

"So, what's going on?" I asked like I didn't know.

"Cupcakes," Juliet said brightly. "For Mea's birthday party tomorrow, and you're going to help."

Of course I am. Keeping my face neutral, I trailed her into the kitchen, slipping past Adam, who had stepped into the doorway just enough to force some full-front contact, not that I was complaining. Like Juliet, he was wearing a silly apron, and I lost myself for a moment in a little indulgent and rather sexy apron-only fantasy.

Juliet smacked me in the stomach with a muffin tin. "What are you smiling about?"

I shifted my eyes to her and said, "Cupcakes. What else?"

She gave me a *hmph* and put us to work. We did her bidding, exchanging quick glances when she wasn't looking, trying to find an opening, a natural door that we could swing open and let her in, or rather us out. But she babbled on about every little thing under the sun, seemingly oblivious to the fact that we weren't much engaged.

"This is never going to work," I mumbled to Adam as Juliet reached into the refrigerator for cold drinks.

He glanced toward Juliet, then tweaked my side. "I know. I feel like we're ganging up on her."

"What are you guys whispering about?" Juliet asked.

Adam looked at me and winked mischievously. "I was just telling Nate how much I wanted to get in his pants."

"I actually believe that. Can I watch?"

"Uh-uh. Private party."

Talk about ganging up on her.

"Well, that's just selfish." She dipped a wooden spoon in the bowl of batter and tipped it back with her forefinger.

"You wouldn't dare," he said, laughing.

And that's when the batter war started. She did. Then he did. Then they dragged me into it. When it was all said and done, the kitchen looked like a bomb had exploded in a Hershey factory. We collapsed into a slippery chocolate heap on the kitchen floor.

"I think we're going to have to start over," Adam said.

Juliet cracked up and leaned her head back against the cabinet. "What a mess!"

"Yep, you made quite a mess here in my mom's kitchen, little girl."

"Shut up." She punched him playfully in the ribs and then examined the sticky ends of her hair. "Can I borrow your shower and a change of clothes, kind sir?"

"Absolutely, milady."

She hopped to her feet and sashayed to the door. "I expect this kitchen to be spotless when I return. And stay out of Nate's pants."

Adam gave her a salute.

We sat quietly on the floor for another half minute. I think we were both suddenly, awkwardly, and disturbingly aware that we were alone together.

Adam looked sideways at me and grinned. "That was fun," he said.

"Do you really want to get in my pants?"

He laughed. "That was just a diversionary tactic, you know, hiding in plain sight. Maybe it'll give her a new way of thinking about us before we spring the news on her."

"So you don't want to get in my pants?"

"Hell yes, I want to get in your pants."

"Do you want to get in them right now?"

He narrowed his eyes playfully. "Are you flirting with me?"

"Uh-huh."

"I haven't even kissed you yet."

"Yeah, about that. Why haven't you kissed me?"

"Why haven't *you* kissed *me*?" he came back.

"I'm playing hard to get. My grandma says guys like that."

"She does? Well, you were hard enough to get already."

I was? "So why haven't you kissed me?"

"I was waiting until your face was splattered with chocolate so I could lick it off because that would make you mine forever."

I swallowed hard.

"There're raw eggs in there," I said stupidly.

He raised a brow.

"You can get E. coli from raw eggs."

He grinned. "I'll take my chances."

"Then what are you waiting for?"

He leaned in close, his lips almost touching but not touching. "You are so asking for it."

You have no idea, I thought.

His lips brushed lightly against mine. I held perfectly still, my lips slightly parted, breathing in the smell of him and chocolate, all mixed up together. I wondered if I'd always associate the smell of chocolate with him and this moment.

"Hey, you guys think you could . . ."

We sprang apart like magnets that had suddenly been flipped like-pole to like-pole.

She looked from me to Adam, needing only a split second to take it all in. The color drained from her face. It was a moment before she could even speak. "Wow, uh, I'm sorry, this is kind of awkward." She closed her eyes. "Uh, I'm, uh . . ."

I got to my feet. "Jules."

She waved me away. "Don't."

"We need to talk."

She laughed a little and started to say something, but then turned and fled the kitchen.

Adam banged his head against the cabinets.

"I'll talk to her," I said.

"What are you gonna tell her?"

I stared off at the door she had slammed shut behind her. "Hell if I know."

"The truth is always a good place to start."

I found Juliet out by the pool. She was sitting on the side with her feet dangling in the water, but when I approached, she got up to leave.

I grabbed her arm. "Wait, Jules. Don't go."

She yanked her arm away, but I grabbed it back. "I don't want to talk to you, Nate." She sniffed and wiped her nose on the collar of her shirt.

"You have to talk to me."

"The way you talked to me? Huh? *Huh?* How long has this been going on between you two?"

"I don't know. A couple of weeks maybe." Eighteen days to be exact, more if you included how long I'd been thinking about it.

"You've been letting me make a fool of myself and the whole time you wanted my best friend. And YOU—" She was yelling now so Adam could hear her inside. "YOU *WERE* MY BEST FRIEND! *WERE!*"

"It's not you, Jules."

She snorted. "You think I'm upset because you prefer Adam over me. You're a fucking idiot. YOU'RE A FUCKING IDIOT TOO, ADAM! I'm not mad about that. Okay, maybe I am a little bit. But mostly I'm fucking pissed as hell that neither one of you trusted me enough to tell me."

She yanked on her arm, but I didn't let go. "No wonder you wouldn't ever kiss me back. I just thought you were scared. And I made you touch my *boobs*. Shit. That must have really freaked you out."

She looked back at me, and I shrugged. "Not too much."

She rolled her eyes. "Thanks a lot."

This time when she yanked her arm away I let her go. She climbed to the top of the rock ledge on the far side of the pool and stuck her feet in the waterfall. I stared after her, caught somewhere between needing to make things right between us and wanting desperately to get back in that kitchen and create some suction between my mouth and Adam's. We'd been so close. I glanced back at the door, then followed Juliet.

I rolled up my jeans and dropped my feet in. We sat side by side and stared at the water for a time, neither of us speaking.

"Why didn't you tell me you dig guys? I would have totally understood." She wiped a smear of chocolate from my cheek, then dropped her hand. "You didn't even give me a chance. God, I feel so stupid." She looked away.

"I don't dig guys," I mumbled.

Her head snapped back, her eyebrows practically in her hairline. "I think that train has already left the station, baby."

That stung, but I deserved it. Old habits die hard.

"You still don't trust me." She laughed a little again and shook her head. "I guess I shouldn't be surprised. It's not like the clues haven't been right in front of my eyes."

I frowned and looked at her. "What do you mean?"

"I've seen the looks between you two. Your eyes get all melty whenever you look at him. They don't melt when you look at me. I wish they did, but..." She shrugged. "And Adam talks about you a lot, more than I do even." She bit her lip and shook her head from side to side, then laughed lightly. "I never really believed you were coming to rehearsals to see me, you know. You're not that good a liar."

He talks about me?

She captured one of my feet with her own and held it up out of the water and studied my toes. "You and Adam. Shit. God, I should have known when he kept asking me questions about you. He's never talked about a guy like that before."

Something locked into place. "Wait. You mean, you knew about Adam?"

"Well, yeah."

"Why didn't you tell me?"

"I guess I thought you knew, and"—she shrugged—"it wasn't mine to tell anyway." She flung a small rock into the pool. "I still can't believe you didn't tell me."

"If it makes you feel any better, that's what we planned to do tonight. We were just trying to find the right time."

"Well, you blew that. I guess when Adam said he wanted to get in your pants, he wasn't kidding."

"I hope not."

She shot me a look.

"Sorry."

We were quiet for a few minutes as Juliet came to terms with the changing boundaries in our relationships. I listened to the water splashing into the pool below and let her have whatever time she needed.

"Nate."

I looked up.

"Have you told anybody?"

I leaned back on my hands and looked at the black sky, then closed my eyes, and took a deep breath. Finally I shook my head.

"Why now?"

"I never had a reason to until now."

"He's a great guy, Nate. The greatest. I wouldn't trust him to just anyone."

"You'd trust him to me?"

"I already have."

"Can I tell you something, Jules? I'm scared to death. I'm scared to death of what's going to happen when everybody else finds out. I keep thinking maybe they don't have to. You know, and maybe you knowing . . . maybe that's enough."

"I can't tell you what to do, Nate. But I have to say that all those people you're worrying about, they're not worth you losing yourself. You can't live your life walking on eggshells so you won't offend other peoples' sensibilities, or in this case, *insensibilities*. Don't pretend your happiness isn't important. It is. And at the end of the day, that's all you got."

I dropped my head back and stared into the moonlit sky. "I don't know. It could all explode in my face. It's not like I can change my mind later. Once it's done, it's done."

"It's done already, Nate." She laid her hand on mine and stroked my fingers. "Give yourselves permission to live and love on your own terms. There are a lot of people out there who will support you. Me, for instance." She smiled, a little sadly maybe, but she did smile. "You can count on that."

We locked eyes. "You don't have to figure this all out tonight," she added. "Take baby steps. It'll all work out."

"Thank you," I said.

"For what?"

I thought for a moment before I answered. "For making it okay."

She smiled again. "Ain't nothin' but a thang."

"A thang?" I grinned back for a moment and then grew serious again. "I love you, Jules." And I knew at that moment that I meant it.

"What's not to love," she teased, giving me a little push. I reached over and pulled her to me. This time the kiss was real— chaste, but truly genuine.

Adam opened the door. "Is it safe to come out?"

Juliet flung a rock at him.

He closed the door behind him. "Good. I thought you might still be mad."

He climbed up and sat down behind us and draped his arms around our shoulders.

"I still hate you," Juliet said.

"No, you don't." He kissed her cheek and then he kissed mine.

Chapter 7

My ringtone startled me awake. Groggy and confused, I fished my phone out of my pocket and pressed the answer key, my eyes still closed, sleep tugging me back toward sweet oblivion.

"Hello," I croaked.

"Nate?" A laugh. "Did I wake you?"

Immediately I was up. "You're there!" I sent up a quick prayer of gratitude.

"I just stepped off the plane. I'm headed down the escalator right now to baggage claim. Were you asleep?"

I looked around me, then ran my fingers through my hair. "Yeah, I fell asleep on Juliet's bed."

"Juliet's bed, huh." I could hear the smile in his voice. "I'm not gone four hours and you're already in bed . . . with a *girl?*"

"Yeah, I'm thinking about expanding my options while you're gone, maybe procreating a little."

"Uh-huh."

"You know I don't roll that way. Mr. Ratliff sent me home early. I just hung around here to wallow in my misery."

He got quiet on the other end.

"I'm okay," I assured him, then changed the subject. "Is Justin there to pick you up?"

He hesitated, obviously deciding whether or not to pursue that *okay* bit. In the end, he let it go. "He said he'd meet me at passenger pickup after I get my bags. I'll call and let him know I'm in in just a minute. I wanted to call you first."

After some small talk about the flight (long, uneventful, boring, lonely) and the airport (crowded and lonely), he promised to Skype when he got to the apartment. I wanted to keep him on the line, maybe until forever, but he'd forgotten to charge his phone the night before ("Busy, remember?") and the battery was running low. Reluctantly, I let him go. I closed my eyes and tried to hold on to the sound of his voice in my head, letting it soothe me back to sleep like a lullaby.

I woke almost three hours later and panicked for a moment, thinking I might have missed Adam's Skype. But he'd said they were going to the theater first, then probably dinner. It would be early evening before he could get to his computer.

I found Juliet in the kitchen with her mom, drying lettuce in a salad spinner. Mr. Ratliff was home too. He was draining a metal basket of fried shrimp over a pot still popping with hot oil. It was only about four thirty, so I figured he must have left Gary to lock up.

Mrs. Ratliff gave me a one-arm hug when I came in. "Juliet told me you were having a nap in her room. Better?"

Not really, but I nodded anyway.

I watched Juliet empty the water from the spinner, then put the basket of lettuce back in the bowl for another spin. "Here, I'll do it," I said, taking the bowl from her. I pumped the button on the lid, and when the lettuce was spinning, I looked at her. "Are we okay?" I mouthed. She grinned sheepishly and mouthed back, "We're okay."

"Here, try this, Nate," Mr. Ratliff said, and popped a sizzling fried shrimp in my mouth. I had to suck in some air and blow it out a few times before it cooled enough to chew. Juliet giggled and I smiled back. "Yum."

"I'm glad you like it," Mrs. Ratliff said. "You're staying for dinner. We're eating early tonight. Mr. Ratliff and I are going to see a movie."

I tried to beg off with some lame excuse about my mom and

grandmother expecting me, but she insisted I give them a call. I glanced up at the clock and then helplessly at Juliet.

"I heard your cell earlier. Was that Adam?"

"Yeah. He got in right on time. He's gonna Skype when he gets to the apartment this evening." I tried to send her a meaningful look, a look that conveyed how desperate I was to get home. But she blew me off, and since dinner was almost ready, there was no arguing.

"Nate's starting a blog," Juliet said brightly as she filled four glasses with ice from the dispenser in the refrigerator door.

"Do you need some help?" Mr. Ratliff asked. He handed me a pitcher of tea. I took a glass from Juliet and poured.

"I don't know. I haven't even looked at it yet. I was thinking about asking a friend of Juliet's to get me started."

That wasn't exactly true; I hadn't been thinking about it at all, but it was a thought, and one that caused Juliet's mouth to widen in a very big grin.

As we sat down to dinner, Juliet's parents exchanged a look, and then Mr. Ratliff discreetly pulled the blinds closed, thus shutting out the back patio. I pretended not to notice.

Chapter 8

Last New Year's Eve

Things we want to remember; things we try to forget

There were a lot of things I'd pretended not to notice since last New Year's Eve—the looks, the whispers, Adam's subtle maneuvering to shelter me from the worst of the gawkers after I returned to school, others carefully shielding me from anything that might remind me of that night, including views of the scene of the crime.

That last day of December, as well as my belief that the worst thing that could ever happen to me was being degraded by my own father, both had ended for me on the Ratliffs' patio.

But it had begun in Adam's room. What had ended as one of the worst days of my life, had begun as one of the best.

Because Adam was home from his first trip to New York. A Christmas vacation with his family, and an excruciatingly long week for me, one that I thought would never end. But it did end.

"We'll be in my room," Adam called out to his mom and step-dad as he bounded up the stairs with his bags and me in tow.

"Keep the door open," his mom called back from the kitchen.

He threw me a look over his shoulder that said, "The hell we will."

When we got to his room, Adam tossed his stuff on the bed and kicked the door closed.

I raised my eyebrows and laughed.

A week hadn't cooled our passion for each other one bit. Fortunately, no one came upstairs to check on that door thing. I wondered for a moment if maybe his mom and stepdad knew what they would find and opted for the ol' head-in-the-sand method of parenting: What you didn't see, didn't happen.

Once we'd quenched the fire, somewhat, there were a million things to talk about. That tattoo that I had seen almost immediately on Adam's side for one. I made him hold his arm up, and I raised his shirt again so I could get a good look. I traced my fingers across the graceful black letters inked into his sunburned-looking skin: *Gnothi seauton.* He shivered.

"It's Greek," he said, looking at me looking at him. "It means 'Know yourself.' It's kind of a coming-out present to myself."

"It's awesome," I said. I was completely fascinated by the artistry of the tattoo. His body made a beautiful canvas. I traced my fingers over each letter again. "Know yourself," I said softly as I did.

"Okay, enough." He laughed and pulled down his shirt. "Keep that up and I'm going to have to disobey Mommy Dearest again. Besides, I have a present for you."

He slipped a small black box from his pocket and handed it to me. Inside were two tiny silver hoop earrings.

"Do you like them?"

I swallowed hard around the lump in my throat. "Yeah. They're great."

He reached up and removed the standard new-pierced-ears studs from my ears (my response to his do-something-crazy-while-I'm-gone suggestion) and deftly replaced them with the hoops. I watched his face as he did, ignoring the dull pain in my earlobes and feeling like my heart would burst. His eyes flicked to mine when the last hoop was in place.

"I missed you so much . . . it scared me," I said.

His face grew serious and he fingered one of the hoops in my ear. "We went to the World Trade Center site one day." He kept his eyes focused on my ear. "I was standing at the edge of the memorial—really just a big hole in the ground—trying to imagine how it must have felt to lose someone you loved that day." He bit his lip and shook his head, his eyes sliding back to mine. "I couldn't bear losing you, Nate . . . ever."

I reached up and took his pendant in my hand—the yin, a white, comma-shaped figure, surrounding a black eye. The yang— black with a white eye, his Christmas gift to me—hung from a thin leather strap around my own neck. He'd given it to me, wrapped in snowman paper, before he'd boarded the plane a week ago, with instructions not to open it until Christmas. I opened it in the parking garage. I turned his pendant to look at the back: *Nate.* I looked into his eyes. "Why do you get to be the girl?"

He laughed so suddenly that he blew spit in my face. He wiped it off, then pulled the pendant from around his neck. "Here, you want to be the girl for a while?"

I smiled and pushed it back over his head. "Nah. I'm good."

"Do you like it?"

I decided to take a chance. "It means we complete each other. Together we make a whole."

He nodded.

"I googled it."

"I thought you would. That's how I feel about us, Nate."

Tell him. But I couldn't get the words out.

It was such a relief to be out. At school, we'd stayed on the down low. But Juliet's New Year's Eve party wasn't school. It would be the first time we showed up somewhere as a couple and no one's jaw hit the floor. I had never been happier or felt more whole in my entire life. There wasn't anything more I wanted from the world at that moment, except maybe a few more minutes alone with him. But there'd be time for that.

By nine the party had ramped up and Juliet's parents retired to their room to wait out the New Year. We kept everything indoors since the weather had finally turned cold. We'd put on our jackets later, after midnight, and shoot off some fireworks.

"Come on, lover boy," Juliet said, cutting me from the crowd and hustling me to the kitchen. "You can help me with the margaritas."

"Virgin?" I asked.

"Of course," she said, then pulled a bottle of tequila from a brown bag in the cabinet and unscrewed the lid.

"Quite the little rebel, aren't you?" I smacked her lightly on the ass.

She pinned me to the cabinet with her body and laughed. "No teasing the redhead tonight."

"Pleasant . . . but not my type."

She sighed wistfully. Then she shook her head as if to clear it. "Come on, let's rock these margaritas."

"Are you trying to get me fired?"

"My dad loves you. It's just a little tequila. Pace yourself and nobody will know."

She showed me how to rub the rims of the plastic cups with fresh lime slices and then dip the cups in salt she'd poured into a little dish shaped like a donut sliced in half. I rimmed and she blended, and then I held the cups while she filled them. We loaded them on a tray. I took two and followed Juliet into the family room.

Adam was telling Mike all about New York. I slipped in behind him and handed him a drink over his shoulder. He took it and turned his head back for a kiss. Once my hand was free, I wrapped my arm around his waist and pressed close to his back. He reached around with his free arm and held me to him. He felt so good, so solid, so real, and so here. I held on to him and sipped my drink and soaked up the sound of his voice.

Eventually Juliet had passed out all the drinks and came to claim Mike. She gave me a wink as she dragged him off to dance with her.

"I still can't believe you're really here," I said, once they'd gone.

"I'm really here." He laced his fingers with mine. "Will you promise me something?"

"What?"

"Promise me when I take you home tonight, you'll get your guitar and play me my song?"

I nodded, my heart swelling at the request. I had envisioned playing it for him in a room lit by only candles in a house occupied by only the two of us. Tonight wouldn't be ideal. We wouldn't be alone. In fact, with Grandma just across the hall, I wouldn't even be able to play without waking her.

We'd figure something out.

We walked over to where the other kids were dancing and he pulled me to him. We danced, holding each other, experiencing each other all over again. After a while, he pressed his mouth to my ear. "I love you, Nate."

Before I could respond, Juliet had me by the arm, dragging me back to the kitchen to mix up another batch of margaritas. He watched me go with a combination of frustration and longing.

"Are you having fun?" she asked, unscrewing the cap on the margarita mix.

"Yeah."

"Adam looks tired."

"He better be."

"Stop!" she whined, shoving a stack of plastic cups in my chest. "Now you *are* flaunting it."

I laughed a little and separated the cups and set them out while she poured the mix then filled the blender with crushed ice from the freezer door. "I can't help it, Jules. I'm in love with him."

She seated the blender jar onto the base and looked at me, her face a question I understood perfectly.

"I'd be declaring myself right now if you hadn't interrupted."

"Really? Well, what the hell are standing in here for. Go! Finish the job. Tell him."

I laughed. "In a minute." I pressed the button for her and the blender crunched, then whirred, drowning out any possibility of conversation for a minute.

"Are you still here?" she said when the ice was crushed and smooth.

I removed the jar and poured. "I'm going to get him all liquored up so I can have my way with him."

"Like you need alcohol for that."

I started to make some clever remark, but loud voices in the living room stopped me. "Nah, man. We just came to party."

"What the hell?" Juliet said.

We hurried back to the living room. In the entryway, Juliet's dad was holding his ground against three boys. They pressed up against him, chests puffed out in some primal display. I recognized Andrew Cargill immediately. The two others I knew only as troublemakers. Juliet's mom hung back, clutching a phone in her hand.

"Leave now or I'll call the police," her dad threatened in a voice that commanded a lot more respect than his slender, pale, and freckled frame. He was hardly a match for the three thugs looming over him. Still, he blocked their passage, his jaw clenched, and he wasn't moving.

"Aaah, come on," Cargill slurred, "we just want to party with our faggy friends here." He locked eyes with me.

I stood next to Juliet and felt the temperature rise in my veins. Adam, Mike, and a couple of the other guys Adam knew from theater arts—Warren Calicutt and Traveon Smith—positioned themselves behind Juliet's dad. I joined them. Cargill took it all in, then seemed to reconsider. He let loose a string of homophic slurs, then backed out the doorway with his little band of thugs. Mr. Ratliff calmly closed the door and locked it.

After that, we all needed a little tequila. The drinks were melting on the kitchen counter, and any guilt I might have felt about the alcohol—Mr. Ratliff would not have been happy—was forgotten. Adam leaned against the edge of the counter and handed me a drink. My hand trembled slightly as I took it. He wrapped his fingers around mine for a moment, then he picked up the tequila bottle and topped off my cup. I looked at him.

"I'm the designated driver tonight."

"What is it with those creeps?"

He shook his head and pulled me close. "Don't worry about them."

I leaned against him, enjoying the feel of my body pressing against his in all the right places. I drank half my margarita, set my cup on the counter, and put my mouth close to his ear. "Do you think anyone would notice if we disappeared for a while?"

"Do you care?" he asked, grinning.

Not even a little bit.

We left the chatter, and the laughter, and the music behind and locked ourselves in Juliet's room. My pulse still raced, but for another reason altogether.

It was close to midnight when we slipped back into the living room. Juliet was passing out hats and horns and poppers that shot out long paper streamers. "Did you bring the sparklers?" she asked Adam.

"Yeah. I left them in my car." He gave me a quick kiss on the neck and fished his car keys out of his pocket. "I'll be right back."

Juliet watched him go, then looked back at me. She drew in a deep breath, then let it out in a loud sigh, shaking her head slowly back and forth.

"What?" I asked.

She raised her eyebrows. "Enjoy my room?"

I blushed. "You saw that?"

"You're not exactly stealth."

Adam had been gone too long. I expected to see him immediately when I stepped out onto the front porch, but I didn't, even though his car was parked in front under a street lamp. I walked toward it. "Adam?" The car interior was dark, but I peered in through the window anyway. Nothing. A prickly sensation crept up the back of my neck.

"Umph."

What the hell? The noise had come from the backyard. I started toward the side of the house. "Adam?" Another *"Umph,"* and I broke into a run, icy fear closing around my heart, blood pounding in my ears, my fingers tingling from the adrenaline screaming through my veins.

The gate was slightly ajar. There were voices now, low but menacing. Another grunt.

Adam.

I burst through the gate and into the backyard.

Chapter 9

It was after midnight when Adam Skyped. I'd fallen asleep with my head on my arm. I wiped the drool on my shirt and clicked the Answer with Video button. Adam's face appeared on the screen. He looked tired and disheveled. It had been less than twenty-four hours, but already I missed him so much it physically hurt. I grimaced a smile. "Hi."

He smiled back, then raised his eyes to his webcam so he was looking directly at me through the camera.

It sounded like a party in the background. I lowered the volume, then changed my mind and raised it again.

"I'm sorry it's so late," Adam said.

I checked the time in the lower corner of my screen: twelve thirty. That meant it was one thirty in New York. I'd been sitting at my desk since seven—five and a half hours. I shifted around to get the blood flowing.

As if answering my unspoken question, he went on: "We dropped my things at the apartment after the cast meeting, then dinner, then back to the director's apartment for drinks. It's been crazy."

"I've been waiting for you."

"I know, baby. I'm sorry. My phone died."

"Couldn't you have borrowed one?"

He bit his lip and that crease formed between his brows again. Before he could respond, a shirtless guy slipped an arm around Adam's shoulder and leaned close to the screen. "Is this your boyfriend? Hi, boyfriend." He waggled his fingers at me, then picked up a drink I hadn't noticed on the desk next to Adam and took a sip. "Come on, baby," he said to Adam and tugged at his arm.

On the screen, I watched Adam laugh and push shirtless guy away.

My skin prickled.

Adam turned back to the screen and said, "Ignore him," still smiling.

I was not smiling. "Who's that?"

"*That* was Justin." He rolled his eyes.

"That was *Justin? Roommate* Justin? I'll-pick-you-up-at-the-*airport* Justin?" I guffawed and looked off into a corner of my room. "You've got to be fucking kidding me."

"Nate." He glanced around, then told me to hold on a minute. The image on the computer jarred and blurred, and I could tell he was moving the laptop somewhere else. When his face appeared on the screen again, he told me he'd moved to the bathroom, then turned the screen around so the camera could catch the fixtures.

"It's the only place I could find," he said, a little apologetically. "This apartment is small. *Small* small. Everything in here is like miniature. You should see the kitchen. It's half the size of my closet back home. The refrigerator looks like one of Mea's toys. And my side of the closet—"

"You're sharing a closet too?" Just the thought of his things brushing up against someone else's felt all kinds of wrong.

"A closet, a room, a bathroom, and everything else in this matchbox." He sighed wearily and looked right at the webcam. "Nate, you know I have three roommates."

"Looks to me like Justin might want to be more than just a roommate."

"Whatever. You know I love you."

"Are you still wearing the green underwear?"

He must have known from the sound of my voice that it wasn't one of those sexy what-are-you-wearing questions. "What is it with the green underwear?" he said. "Yes, I'm wearing the green underwear. I've been wearing them all day. More than eighteen hours. I thought you liked them on me."

"I do. I just don't like them on you . . . there."

He huffed. "I'll burn them if it makes you happy."

"I don't want you to burn them."

"Then what do you want?"

"I wanted you to call me earlier. It's one thirty in the morning there, Adam. One fucking thirty. I've been sitting at this desk for hours. And then you finally Skype and some half-naked guy is hanging all over you. Do you know how that makes me feel?"

He ran his hands through his short hair and sighed again. "I'm sorry. Okay. You're right. I just got caught up in all the craziness. Will you forgive me? I promise I'll make it up to you when I get back home."

"How?"

"You're gonna be like that, are you?" He laughed, just a little. "Well, hmm, I'll give you one of my lava lamps."

"Uh-uh. I already stole one anyway."

"I'll paint your toenails again."

"Sexy, but not good enough."

"I'll take you parking again at Ridgewood Park."

Ah, Ridgewood Park. The place where our first fight had ended, and our first makeup session had begun. And Adam was very good at making things up to me.

"Tempting," I said, "but you know sudden flashlight beams still send me into a panic."

He laughed again, more like the Adam I remembered, then came up with an idea so graphic and naughty that I actually blushed.

Chapter 10

Last November 10
Making up and making out

The cast party was held in the Black Room behind the stage, the small room packed with family and friends who waved flowers and shared hugs and kisses with the heavily made-up cast members. Juliet dragged me around and introduced me to everyone. I discreetly tried to keep my eye on Adam, but he was always surrounded by friends I'd never even met, especially girls.

The atmosphere was charged with both excitement and relief. Juliet held on to my hand, letting go only briefly to give a hug or accept one. I don't know how many of her friends I met before I realized she was carrying out her own subterfuge. While she wasn't actually introducing me as her boyfriend, she was providing me that cover. I felt guilty that I appreciated it so much. She'd been doing that a lot in the five weeks since we'd let her, and only her, in—playing girlfriend to me in public, while I played kissy-face with Adam in private, of which there had been precious little.

We finally joined Adam's group. Juliet flung her arms around his neck. He dipped and grabbed her below the butt and hoisted her into the air, her belt catching the edge of his shirt, flashing some skin. Juliet beamed at the sudden attention, but for me the moment was all about that flash of tanned, smooth, bare skin. I looked away and forced myself to think about oil-covered pelicans.

He put her down and reached out to bump my fist. "Hey, man. I'm glad you came." He looked at me for a brief moment until someone called his name, and he was off to be adored by someone else.

Hey, man? I'm glad you came?

Juliet had been swallowed up by the crowd, so I found a soda and sat in a plastic chair against the wall. I read Adam's text again—*Stay for the cast party. Pls? GGLA*. It taken only minutes to break the code: *Gotta Go Love Adam*. I nibbled on a cookie and checked the time. When the party finally wound down and parents headed home and cast members headed off to change, Adam made his way over to me. I handed him my soda and he took a sip. "Is that all I get?" he asked.

"What do you want?" I challenged him.

Before he could answer, his leading lady, Chloe, slid up behind him and wrapped her arms around his waist, her hands flat against his stomach. "Hey, we're all going out for burgers to celebrate," she said into his shoulder. Then she deftly slipped her hand under the edge of his T-shirt, an indiscretion that annoyed the hell out of me. "Coming?"

"Sure." He looked at me with his crazy blue eyes. "Nate's coming too."

Nine of us crammed ourselves into a large booth at the restaurant. I was hoping to sit next to Adam, but Chloe dragged him in next to her and I found myself on other the other side of the table, sandwiched between Juliet and a girl named Amanda. I don't think Amanda had gotten the message that I was "with" Juliet judging for the way she kept leaning into me and twirling her hair.

I inched closer to Juliet and she squeezed my thigh, understanding.

Adam was focused on Chloe and that was pissing me off. I knew when he listened to people, he listened all the way. He made you feel like you were the only person in the world, that what you had to say was more important than any other words uttered since the dawn of time. And I loved that about him, but right now, I didn't give a shit because Chloe had what was mine, and he was giving it to her, and I didn't appreciate it one damn bit. He'd hardly glanced my way since we'd sat down. I hadn't even told him yet how great his performance was.

Amanda said something, but I missed it.

"What?" I said.

Juliet nudged me and I realized how rude I'd sounded.

Amanda repeated her question and I responded with a "Hmph." Finally she gave up and turned to talk to whoever was sitting on her other side.

"You're staring," Juliet whispered in my ear.

Adam looked up and caught my eyes, held them for a moment, then excused himself and headed to the bathroom. I toyed with the idea of following him, but Juliet must have read my mind. She would have had to move for me to get out, and a quick shake of her head made it very clear that was not going to happen.

Moments later my cell phone vibrated.

You're leaving with me!

In the parking lot, Juliet offered to drive back to school with everyone who needed to pick up their cars. Adam would drop the rest—Mike and Natalie—at their homes. Amanda seemed pretty disappointed about the whole arrangement but went peacefully enough. Not so Chloe. She pouted and clung to Adam's elbow until Juliet gunned the engine and put the car in drive and let it roll a few feet.

It was nearing eleven by the time we'd dropped everyone off.

Adam pulled away from Natalie's house and reached for my hand. I folded my arms and looked out the window. He put his hand back on the steering wheel.

"What time do you have to be home?" he asked.

"Midnight."

"What happens if you miss curfew?"

I shrugged.

He pulled up to a traffic light and looked over at me. "Nate, what's going on?"

"I don't know. Why don't you tell me?"

"You're mad?"

"You think?"

"Don't play games with me. Just tell me what's wrong."

"Maybe you should ask Chloe."

"Chloe?"

I finally turned to look at him. "You had quite the little party going there tonight. Too bad she had her car at school. You could have dropped me off first and made her your last stop."

He stared at me for a long moment like I'd lost my mind. "You cannot be serious."

"The light's green. Go."

He took his foot off the brake and made a left turn. "Nate—"

"You practically ignored me the entire evening."

"I thought that's what you wanted. You flinch every time I get anywhere near you when other people are around." He made a frustrated noise in the back of his throat. "I don't know what you want."

"I want you."

"You've got me."

"Chloe thinks *she's* got you. Do you know how that makes me feel?"

He glanced over at me. "How does that make you feel?"

I couldn't answer. I picked at my cuticles. Up ahead, a deer darted across the road. I watched it disappear into the dark. "Can we go to your house for a while?"

"Mom and Ben invited some friends over after the play. I don't want to get caught up in all that adult-adoration crap tonight." He glanced at me. "I want to be alone with you. Unless you don't want to—"

"No," I interrupted him. "I mean, yeah. I want that too."

He turned into a small parking lot in a wooded area and pulled the car far up under a stand of trees. He cut the engine and turned off the lights without waiting for the auto shutoff. The quiet was sudden. I used my sleeve to wipe the condensation off the window.

"Where are we?"

"Ridgewood Park. There's a pool and tennis courts and a basketball court right over there." He pointed, but it was too dark to see anything.

He shifted in his seat to look at me. I could hear his breathing and my breathing, unnaturally loud in the quiet car.

"It makes me feel like it's not real," I said, looking out my window at the blackness, "like we're not real. Everybody looks at you and Chloe, and they think she's what you want."

He reached across the console and found my hand and pulled it to his lips. "What I want is right here. What's real is right here."

"Sometimes it doesn't feel that way."

"What do you want me to do? You can't have it both ways. You want me to act like there's nothing going on between us when we're in public, and then you're mad when that's what you get. What do you really want, Nate?"

"You can't always get what you want," I mumbled.

"But if you try . . . you might get what you need."

I sniffed. "You're quoting The Rolling Stones to me?"

"Mick Jagger must have known something. The Stones stayed together for decades."

"I always thought he had a thing for Keith Richards."

"He wasn't singing 'I can't get no satisfaction' for nothing."

I laughed a little. It faded quickly. He pulled me to him. "Oh, Nate. I don't know how to make this right. I don't like pretending around our friends. I wanted to be celebrating with you tonight. I wanted you running your hands under my shirt and sitting next to me and squeezing my leg under the table."

"She was squeezing your leg under the table?"

"Stop." He pressed his forehead against mine. "Look. Either we go on pretending we're something we're not, something we've never been, and keep on getting hurt and angry and frustrated, or we . . ." He stopped.

"We what?"

He didn't answer. He closed his eyes and looked away from me for the first time.

"Is that what you want?" I asked.

"What I want is you. All of you. All the time."

I took a deep breath and let it out slowly, an image of Chloe leaning against him, giggling, touching him sharp in my mind. "Okay."

"Okay?"

"No more pretending."

"Do you know what you're saying?"

"I know. And if that bitch Chloe ever lays another hand on you, I'm going to break her fingers."

He chuckled. "I'll hold them out for you."

A silence descended upon us as we tried to figure out where to go from here.

"You know," I said, "I think we just had our first fight."

He laughed a little and said, "Hmm."

"I think this means we get to have makeup sex now," I said, my voice slightly hoarse.

"I thought you were playing hard to get?"

"Yeah, well, I got over it."

"Does that mean I can do this now?" He slipped his hand up under my shirt and flattened it across my chest. My heart pounded against the warmth of his palm. I watched his face watching mine. "How about this?" His dropped his hand and grazed it across the strained zipper of my jeans.

I swallowed hard. "I have a curfew, you know."

He grinned, and then we were all over each other. Our mouths, our hands. I wanted him, and I had no patience with buttons and zippers and things. And we didn't let the console keep us from pressing our bodies together, his on mine and mine on his.

Suddenly, Adam pushed against me with his hands. "Nate. Nate. *Nate.* Slow down."

"What?"

He was breathless. "Damn, you know, you really should come with a black-box warning. You're going to hurt yourself . . . or me."

"You lit the fuse, so don't complain if you get a little gunpowder on your fingers."

"Gunpowder?" He laughed and pulled me back to him. "I'll show you gunpowder." He released the seat and it flopped back, then he twisted me around in a maneuver I thought impossible in such a small space.

Suddenly, a beam of light. My eyes snapped open.

"Shit." I scrambled to get my jeans up and zipped.

The light shone through the fogged-up window, and then a fist pounded the glass. "Step out of the car, please."

"Dammit." I groped around for my shirt. "Where's my fucking shirt?"

"Here, I've got it." I grabbed for it, but he held it behind him, just out of my reach. "Nate, calm down. Kids get busted messing around in cars all the time. It's not that big a deal." He handed me the shirt and I yanked it over my head.

"You know this isn't the same thing," I whispered.

More pounding on the window, this time heavier, more demanding. "Step out of the car *now*, please."

"Okay?" Adam made me look at him until I nodded my head. "Okay." He zipped up his jeans and calmly opened the door and got out, throwing his shirt casually over his shoulder. "Can I help you, sir?" I heard him say.

"I need your girlfriend out too." The cop shone his flashlight back into the car, peering through the open door, probably hoping for a peek at some sexy teenage girl huddled half naked in the front seat. "Well, well, well," he said when he got a good look at me.

I got out and walked around the car to join Adam, my fists shoved deep into my pockets. He was leaning against the hood of the car and winked at me when I shuffled up next to him.

The cop played his flashlight down and back up, taking in our disheveled look and Adam's bare chest and makeup that he hadn't bothered to remove after the show. Adam had to be cold.

"Uh, uh, uh. Do your parents know you're out here diddlin' each other?"

"Diddling?" Adam said.

I shot him a look. He seemed amused by the whole thing.

Adam smiled. "We hadn't exactly gotten to diddling yet. We were just warming up to that."

The cop eyed Adam, looking a little more pissed than he had at first. He shook his head slowly. "I don't know what this world is coming to." He let that sit there for a moment before continuing. "Listen, you're a couple of good-lookin' boys. Why don't you find some nice girls to screw and keep your hands off of each other's dicks?"

Adam furrowed his brow. "I don't think I can do that, sir."

Jeez. Why didn't he shut up? He was gonna get us shot, or worse, hauled into jail, where they were sure to call our parents. As if reading my mind, he glanced at me and winked again.

The cop examined Adam's driver's license with his flashlight. With the light off us, Adam found my hand and gave it a squeeze. "You boys are pretty lucky I'm the one who interrupted your little party," the cop said as he handed the license back to Adam and shone the light in our faces again. "Another officer, or even some of these kids who run around causing trouble, might have busted you up a bit." He stared at us to make sure we understood the point he was making. "This is a family community, boys. Go home."

"A family community. Right," Adam said, slipping his wallet back into his pocket. There was no longer an ounce of humor in his voice.

I hadn't spoken a word and didn't even realize I'd been holding my breath until I got back in the car. As soon as Adam closed his door, I hit the locks and sucked in a deep breath. My heart was still racing from the adrenaline. If I survived this evening without a coronary, it would be a miracle.

I couldn't believe it when Adam leaned over and kissed me passionately on the lips. "Have you fucking lost your mind?"

He laughed, turned the key, and pulled on his shirt; then he adjusted the heater before he put the car in drive. "He was totally checking you out. Didn't you see?"

"No, he wasn't." I glanced uneasily at the cop car still idling at the edge of the parking lot.

He stroked the stubble on my chin. "Are you kidding me? I thought I was totally going to have to defend your honor." He backed the car out into the parking lot. "All right, Clyde," he said, putting the car in drive and turning the wheel sharply, "let's get you home before our man in blue there gets carried away by the green-eyed monster. Because I'm *not* sharing."

Chapter 11

The rest of the month passed in agonizing, heart-rending, mind-screaming seconds, minutes, and days. There were too few phone calls from Adam and too many from me, most of which ended in a one-sided conversation with Adam's voicemail, and with me trying desperately but failing miserably to not sound needy and a little pathetic. He Skyped at night, always late, and almost always from the bathroom. There were those nights that he was so tired, he just said good night, then headed off to bed. I sometimes waited all day to talk to him, and that was all I got—a few seconds with the guy I loved sitting on a toilet.

The job helped.

A little.

Actually, not much at all.

August 22

His flight arrived at the gate two minutes early at 10:32. I met him at baggage claim, but he had only a carry-on, so by 10:47 we were all over each other in my car in the parking garage. I couldn't believe he was here. I wanted to look at him, touch him, kiss him. No. That wasn't quite right. I wanted to devour him.

"Can we go someplace?" he asked, breathless.

I groped blindly for the key already in the ignition, anxious to get him alone but reluctant to let him go long enough to get him there. "My house," I breathed into his mouth, allowing my hands to travel across as many parts of him as possible before I let go. "Mom left right after I did. She's taking Grandma to visit her sister."

I pulled up to the curb, and we raced each other to the front door. I fumbled with the key even as we kissed. He bit my ear and pressed me against the door, his eagerness for me and mine for him grown so obvious that we should have been plastered with a warning label like they put on aerosol cans. *Caution: Contents under pressure.*

"Hurry up," Adam breathed, his hands under my shirt now, his fingers raking across my chest.

"I'm trying, but you're distracting me."

"It's just a key."

"I know it's just a key, but I can't get it in the damn hole."

He giggled and turned me so I was facing the door. "Now concentrate," he said, then slipped his fingers beneath the waistband of my shorts, making it impossible for me to carry out my mission, except that somehow I did. I pushed the door in with my shoulder and we stumbled across the threshold, still groping at each other and panting.

"SURPRISE!"

HONK.

I gasped as Mom and Grandma, Juliet and Mike, and Gaby and Warren (another former leading lady slash mistaken romantic rival and her talented actor boyfriend—Adam's friends, and now mine too) suddenly appeared from around the corner, all with party hats and horns poised at their lips. And then just as suddenly the room went utterly silent. Adam quietly removed his hands from my pants and slid behind me.

Mom blushed and turned away, but Juliet took a good long look at my lap and laughed. "Looks like the party started early."

"Do you mind?" I said.

"Not at all," she said.

I gave Mike a pleading look and he covered Juliet's eyes. Not exactly what I had in mind, but, okay. Thank goodness Gaby had the good manners to look away.

"All right, everybody, show's over," Grandma said, herding everybody toward the dining room. "Time for cake." Turning back and in a voice that bubbled with amusement, she told us she was lighting the candles and we had about one minute to put those things, as she called them, away.

Adam snickered behind me and kissed my neck.

"Just kill me now," I said.

He laughed. "Here, let me help you put that away. Grandma's orders."

"Quit that," I said, twisting away and trying not to be too loud, but laughing anyway. "Shit."

"I guess your mom didn't leave after all."

"The liar." I shook out my shorts and tried to get everything back in its place. Adam looked down and stuck his lower lip out in a pout. I strummed his lip with my finger and grinned. "You are so getting some of that later."

He shook his head as if to clear it. "Come on. Let's get you all birthdayed up so I can get you alone. You're spending the night at my house."

I made a wish (*Go home, people!* Honestly, my mind was firmly in the gutter.), I blew out the candles, I opened a few presents, and then I willed them to leave. I tried to at least look like I was listening to the conversation, but Adam's eyes kept flicking to mine from across the table, making me squirm. I nudged Juliet under the table. She pretended not to notice, so I nudged her again, harder. A grinned played at her lips.

Finally, just when I was about ready to scream my wish—GO HOME!—Juliet stood up and announced it was time to leave.

Adam was on his feet so quickly his chair teetered, threatened to fall over behind him, then settled down with a *thunk*. "What's your hurry?" he said sarcastically.

Juliet just winked. We said our good-byes at the door, then fell all over each other trying to get the table cleared. He buried his nose in my neck while balancing the leftover cake in one hand and plates in the other. "Tell her," he whispered and then stuck his tongue in my ear, which sent a shiver up my spine so severe that I almost dropped the soda cans I was cradling in my arms.

Grandma took the cake from Adam in the kitchen. He grabbed one last pinch and popped it into his mouth. "Yum," he said, flicking his eyebrows and charming the pants off my grandmother all over again.

She grinned and hugged him to her one-handed.

"Mom." I cleared my throat. She was filling the sink with soapy water and glanced back at me over her shoulder. "I need to get Adam home."

"Okay," she said, turning off the water. She dried her hands on a towel.

"Um, I'm going to crash at his house, tonight."

That stopped her. *Crash* hardly described what we'd be doing at his house. But I already knew she'd let me go. She had to have known it was coming, and there were some battles she knew she couldn't win.

Upstairs I threw a few things in my backpack while Adam lounged on my bed. "I miss this room," he said, looking around and sighing.

Not half as much as I missed him in this room, I thought. I dropped my backpack and crawled onto the bed, over him, and settled on his lap. "When do I get my birthday present?"

He cocked an eyebrow and laughed. "Are you referring to the tattoo I promised you, or the one where you get me naked?"

"The second one."

He threw his head back and groaned. Then I kissed him and he kissed me, and soon it became pretty clear that somebody was going to have to show a little restraint or we were going to break house rules again. And it wasn't going to be me.

"Come on, tiger," Adam said finally, sliding out from under me. He slung my backpack over his shoulder. "We have an appointment at the tattoo parlor and Mommy Dearest still has to fuss over your birthday." He grinned and adjusted himself again.

I groaned. Couldn't I just be alone with him? Jeez.

At the door, Mom embraced Adam, and he kissed her cheek. She pulled away and held his face between her hands and then launched into a whole list of banal mommy questions—*Are you eating enough? Sleeping well? Not working too hard? Seeing some sights?* Finally, she released him and swatted me on the butt with a "Go. You boys have fun." Then she reddened when she realized what she'd just said. After all, it wasn't like it was the first time.

Chapter 12

Last November 20
The first time

It was Juliet who came up with the coming-out plan. First stop, the counselor's office, the day before Thanksgiving break, a move designed to give us both support and time before the big reveal the last week of school before Christmas break. It went...well. Ms. Raney was surprised, shocked even, titillated maybe, amused, who knows, but she hid it well. She'd offered both her support and her advice: *Tell your parents.* Hmph. Not likely.

The halls were empty when we left Ms. Raney's office. We took our time walking back to our respective classes.

"Why don't you come crash at my house tonight?" Adam said.

I stopped and looked at him. "Are you crazy? I can't spend the night at your house."

"Why not? We're two guys." He laughed another of those mischievous laughs. "That's the beauty of dating someone from your own gender...until you come out, you can share a room and nobody thinks a thing about it."

For the rest of the afternoon, I tried to dismiss the idea as mental, but the seed had been planted and my overstimulated imagination had been growing it until the idea had fingered its way into every nook and cranny of my thought processes.

I felt completely transparent as I pulled up a chair at the bar for dinner. Grandma handed me a plate as Mom poured tea and caught up on the day's news on the TV situated in a corner of the bar. "Okay if I stay over at Adam's tonight?"

I probably should have left it at that, but panic and guilt made me want to justify the question. "We've got a government project due before Christmas. A couple of the guys and I thought we'd get a head start. I'll be home in time to help with pies and stuff tomorrow afternoon."

I sounded like a moron. A guilty moron. I expected suspicion at the very least, but Mom didn't even look away from CNN.

"Okay," she said. "Be sure and take your toothbrush."

"Um, sure," I said.

"When are you going to bring that nice boy back over for a visit?" Grandma asked. "He's a great dancer." She did a little Fred Astaire move in the kitchen.

I kept my head down. "I'll tell him you said that."

I tried to look unhurried as I cleared my dishes and headed upstairs to throw a few things in a bag, sure that at any moment I'd do something that would give me away, but it was ridiculously easy. I scrubbed in the shower, brushed my teeth twice, flossed, and ran some product through my hair, then thought twice and washed it out again. Any more primping would have been too obvious. I crammed a few things in my backpack and hurried to the stairs. I was halfway down when I remembered my government book. I'd planned to carry it under my arm for visual cover. I wanted to take the stairs three at a time and then jump the last half, but I forced myself to a less-eager pace.

"I'm going, Mom," I called out.

She stuck her head around the corner, a dishtowel in her hand. "Have fun. Be back by four o'clock, okay?"

"Okay."

I'd never given my mom any reason to distrust me. I was working on a whopper right now.

* * *

My partner-in-crime met me at the door.

"Oh, hey, you brought your government book." He rolled his eyes and laughed.

"Yeah, well..."

"Hi, Nate!" Adam's mom called through the house from the back porch.

"Come on," Adam said and led me through the family room. His mom and stepdad were stretched out on lounge chairs next to the pool, cocktails in their hands. They looked relaxed and content.

I wondered for a moment what it would be like to sit out here with Adam, like a real couple, tiki lamps flickering around the edges of the patio, tiny lights twinkling among the tree branches.

"How are you?" Mrs. Jensen asked. "It's nice to see you again."

I stuffed my hands in my pockets and shuffled my feet. "I'm great, thanks," I said.

"Nate's going to crash here tonight," Adam said. "That okay?"

I couldn't believe he hadn't even asked them yet. I felt like an idiot standing there with my backpack slung over my shoulder.

"Of course! You're always welcome, Nate."

"Uh, thanks. My, uh, Mom is, uh, out of town tonight. And we have a government project."

I held up my book. *Oh, brother.* I realized how lame that sounded as soon as I said it. But what was I going to say? *Thanks. I'm here to bang your son. Is that okay with you?* I felt their eyes on me and was relieved when Mea turned their attention away.

"Hi, Nate!" She waved. She was sitting on the edge of the pool, swinging her legs back and forth, making little splashes that fell just short of getting her Little Mermaid pajamas wet.

I waved back.

Adam pulled my sleeve toward the house. "We're going to watch a movie or something upstairs."

I was trying not to imagine what that *or something* might be, but that wasn't really working out for me, so I prayed I'd be swallowed up before I embarrassed myself further.

"And your project?" his mom called after us.

"Yeah, we'll get to it eventually."

She smiled. "Okay. Would you take Mea with you? I'll be up to put her to bed shortly."

"Sure. Come on, brat."

Adam scrolled through the On Demand listings. "How about *Othello?*" he asked. "Forbidden love." He flicked his eyebrows at me.

"*Othello?* What's *Othello?*" Mea said.

"It's a sedative for little girls," Adam said.

"Huh?"

"Shouldn't we be watching football or something?" I asked.

"Football?" He laughed. "Surely you jest. If my parents caught me watching football, they'd know something was up for sure," he said quietly. "No, *Othello*'s got it all . . . love, passion, danger . . . and he gets it in the end. It's perfect."

I was pretty skeptical still, but I didn't think I'd be watching the movie anyway. It was hard to focus on anything with Adam around. He was still the sexiest thing I had ever seen. I blushed, thinking about the night ahead. What would midnight feel like? Two A.M.? Four? I made a mental note to google the inventor of door locks and light some candles for him (or her).

I was sprawled out on one side of the wraparound sofa in the media room. He must have noticed the effect he was having on me. He winked and tossed me a leopard print throw. "Children," he mouthed.

I caught the throw with one hand and draped it over my lap, embarrassed.

Mea insisted her big brother braid her hair so it would be "full and bouncy" in the morning. I divided my attention between the movie and the salon activity unfolding in front of me. Adam pulled Mea's hair up into a ponytail on the top of her head, then meticulously divided her hair into three sections, which he then carefully braided down to the very tip and secured that with another smaller band. When he was done, she kissed him on the lips and then snuggled in his lap. Her thumb made its way into her mouth.

He kissed the top of her head as her eyelids grew heavy. My

throat tightened. He caught my eye and smiled sweetly. I would have been content just to watch them like that all night long. Well, maybe not *all* night. Okay, I couldn't wait for Mea to go to bed.

Adam's stepdad came up to tuck her in a short time later. She was sound asleep by then. He stuck his head in again on his way downstairs.

"Your mom and I are going to bed soon, Adam. Be sure you turn off all the lights before you go to bed."

Adam assured him he would.

"Don't stay up too late, boys."

And then we were alone. I started to get up and move closer, but Adam shook his head.

"Not yet," he said softly.

After *Othello* stabbed himself and died, Adam grabbed some random movie without even looking at the case and shoved it into the DVD player. It didn't matter what played next. We leaned on our elbows facing each other across the expanse between couch ends and passed the time with small talk and long silent gazes.

"Your feet are warm," he said, folding his toes into the arch of my foot.

"You know what they say about warm feet."

"What do they say?"

"Warm feet, warm heart."

He grinned. "I believe the saying is cold hands, warm heart."

"Hmph. Then what do warm feet mean?"

"I have no idea, but I intend to find out."

I sucked in a shaky breath. I desperately want to touch my lips to his, to explore all those secret places. My whole body ached with holding back.

He seemed to understand. "I'll be right back," he said.

In less than two minutes he was back in the doorway. He motioned for me to come with him.

My heart hammered against my ribcage as I cast the throw aside and reached to take his hand. This was it. Terrified hardly described what I was feeling.

* * *

The last time I'd been in his room—the first time—I'd been too self-conscious about getting naked with him, in the same room, at the same time, naked, together, to really notice the space he occupied every night. I'd just had my first date with Juliet, a disastrous couple of hours that had ended in a not-so-disastrous romp in Adam's pool, fully dressed. I'd stood in almost this very spot, dripping on his carpet, when he'd tossed me a pair of sweatpants and a dry T-shirt. I took about two seconds to look around now. Neat. Orderly.

I found it odd that he hadn't brought me up here again in the nine weeks now that we'd been together. But it had been my idea to stay on the down low. With two confidantes under our belt, and more to come soon enough, I guess we weren't so down low anymore.

I took in a deep breath and blew it out as Adam secured the door lock. I checked it with my free hand, just to be sure. He shook his head and laughed quietly, and then his laugh dissolved into a shy grin, and he let go of my other hand and crossed the room. "When I count to three, you turn off the light, okay?" he said.

Intrigued, I did as he said . . . on three. And suddenly the room was awash in the soft light of a dozen or more lava lamps. They lined a high shelf that ran the entire width of one wall—different sizes, different colors, glitter, no glitter. Adam stood on a chair and unplugged one of the smaller ones and removed it from the shelf. He put it on the table next to his bed and plugged it back in.

With his back still to me, he shuffled through playlists on his MP3 player until he found one he wanted. I watched him from the door. He settled the player into the speaker system and adjusted the volume so it played softly in the background, then turned back to me.

My entire body thrummed like a taut steel guitar string. "Do you want to play Internet poker or something?" I asked.

He laughed and deftly pulled his T-shirt over his head. "Uh-uh." He tossed it to the side.

I started toward him, but he shook his head and told me to wait. I drew in a ragged breath and held it, keeping my eyes locked on his as he unbuttoned his shorts. "You're not sneaking peeks in the first grade boys' bathroom anymore, Nate," he said gently. "It's okay to look. No shame. I want you to look at me."

I wanted to look. God, I wanted to look, but my eyes were fused to his. When I hesitated, he rolled his eyes playfully and reached into his bedside table drawer and pulled out a sparkly pink mask rimmed in pink fluff, the kind girls wear over their eyes to block out the light when they sleep, although I'd never known anyone to actually wear one. Across the front it read *The Princess Is Sleeping.*

"What else did you steal from Mea's room?" I asked.

He smiled sheepishly and fished a pair of toy handcuffs from the drawer.

"Kinky."

He dangled them from his finger. *Oh, hell yeah.* I came closer and took them from him with a trembling hand. He pulled the princess mask over his eyes, then turned and put his wrists together behind his back and waggled his fingers at me. Suddenly I understood what this was all about. I locked the toy cuffs around his wrists. The fit was tight and I had to be careful not to pinch his skin. He turned back. When the rest of his clothes lay in a crumpled pile on top of his T-shirt, I finally allowed myself to take him in, my eyes to linger where they'd never been allowed to linger before, my hands to touch what they'd never been allowed to touch before. And I wanted to tell him thank you . . . for this amazing gift, for not mocking me for wanting you so badly, for making it okay to be me.

The lava was warming up, rising and stretching into elongated blobs, creating colorful shadows that were easing across the ceiling, when Adam said hoarsely, "Nate, get these fucking cuffs off of me. Now!"

Chapter 13

"You still have Mea's handcuffs?" I asked as we headed down the sidewalk to my car.

He laughed and slung his arm over my shoulders, then looked back at my mom still standing on the front porch and gave her a wave.

"I see where you get that cute blushing from," he said, turning back to me.

"Yeah. Luckily she's got a strong heart." I turned back and waved too.

"Let's just skip the tattoo," I said once we were in the car. "Let's go straight to your house."

"No way! You've been waiting for this for months. And this is my birthday present to you. We are *not* skipping it."

"God, you're killing me." I pulled into the street and cast a glance at him, then sighed heavily. "Tattoo, and then I get my other present."

"Absolutely." He grinned.

"And tomorrow it's just you and me. I've been thinking maybe we could drive to Galveston. Juliet's dad has a little pop-up camper we could take. We could sleep on the beach."

He was quiet for a moment, then, "Nate—"

"If you don't want to sleep on the beach, we could get a room. I'm sure the last weekend before school starts is crazy, but I bet there are still—"

"Nate—"

"I don't *care* where we stay. We can throw a couple of blankets on the ground. I just want to be with you. Alone. Just me and you." I turned the fan up on the air conditioner. Why was it so damn hot in the car?

"Nate—"

Don't. The muscles in my chin started to twitch before he even said the words.

"I have to leave tomorrow."

I stared at the road ahead. A Ford F150 with a bumper sticker that read *I'll keep my guns and my religion; you keep the change* slid into the lane in front of me. I pressed on the accelerator. "You said you were staying for the whole weekend."

"I know. I wanted to. That was my plan. But the director said no. The show opens next weekend, and there's some event tomorrow afternoon and I have to be there. He didn't even want me to come down for one day. But I wouldn't have missed your birthday for anything, baby."

"Who cares what he wants."

"I'm under contract." In my peripheral vision I could see his legs tense, his feet braced against the floorboard. "Get off his ass, Nate. You're gonna kill us."

"Asshole," I muttered and eased up on the accelerator.

Adam relaxed his legs. "Look, I'm here right now, and I promise you we're going to make the most of it."

I took the corner at Lake Forest way too fast and then asked, "Just how much *it* do we have to make the most of?"

He was quiet for a moment, then said softly, "I'm on the eight o'clock flight tomorrow morning."

I mentally calculated the time we had left. Too little. Almost nothing at all.

"Come on, let's get that tattoo, then we'll ditch the family, and it'll be just you and me."

"I don't want it anymore."

"Don't say that. We've been planning this for almost five months. I want to do this for you. Please let me do this for you. It won't take too long, I promise."

He was making a lot of promises, but the promise of time, the one thing I really wanted, he couldn't give me.

Mea met us at the door an hour or so later wearing an animal nose strapped to her face and blowing a sparkly silver horn. "Happy Birthday, Nate!" She threw her arms out and I picked her up. Her long curly hair tickled my nose as she clung to me like a crab. "I'm a warthog!"

I smiled. "I can see that."

I carried her into the kitchen with my unbandaged arm. I knew the second I saw Adam's mom in a cat nose that party hats were way too cliché for this family.

"Elephant or *rhiiino?*" Adam said, his eyes glinting. The way he emphasized rhino, I knew the choice had already been made for me. I rolled my eyes at him, but he just laughed and strapped the horned snout to my face. He pulled an opened-mouthed shark snout over his own.

Adam's mom grinned at me and finished lighting the candles. "Hope you haven't had too much cake yet," she said.

There was only one thing I wanted to put in my mouth at that moment, and it wasn't cake. "No way," I said with every ounce of fake cheer I could muster. "It looks great."

"Happy Birthday, Nate," Adam's stepdad (in a pig nose) said, handing me a present wrapped in sparkly silver paper that matched the horn Mea was still blowing. I looked at the gift in my hands, really moved that they were doing this for me. They felt as much like my parents as my own mom, and more so than my dad. "You guys really didn't have to do this," I said, a little embarrassed.

"Open it," Mea said. I perched her on the bar and peeled off the paper. "It's a picture," she announced before I could completely finish the job.

"Thanks a lot for ruining the surprise, brat," Adam teased her. She pushed out her lower lip, looking a little hurt until I winked at her. Then she beamed.

I set the paper on the counter and turned over the eight and a half by eleven frame. I recognized the photo immediately. It wasn't one I'd seen before, but I knew the image. It was a candid shot of the two of us walking on the beach in Key West. We were holding hands and looking at each other and laughing. I couldn't remember about what.

Adam's mom must have taken the picture. It struck me how beautiful we were together—tan, Adam in his white trunks with the black hibiscus print that I knew so well, riding low on his hips as always, me in solid black trunks. I bit down hard on my lower lip.

Beside me, Adam exchanged a look with his parents, then wrapped his arms around me and pulled me to him. I planted my face in his shoulder, still not believing he was here, still afraid I'd wake up and it would all be just a dream, and knowing that this time tomorrow, he'd be gone again.

"Mom's been dying to give you that picture since we got back from Key West, but she wanted to surprise you with it for your birthday." I sniffed and he squeezed me tighter. "I have one just like it. Every time you came over, I had to hide it in my closet. It's by my bed in the apartment now." He grinned into my hair.

I clung to him and eventually he had to force my arms from around him so he could look at me. "Okay?"

I nodded, not entirely trusting my voice just yet. His parents and Mea had left us alone, knowing it embarrassed me to lose it in front of them. The candles had burned down to little puddles of blue wax on the chocolate icing. Adam blew them out and led me upstairs.

Chapter 14

"Nate, baby, take it easy. You're hurting me."

I rolled to my other side and flung the condom across the room. My chest heaved from the exertion, and from anger and hurt.

Clueless, Adam turned and pressed himself to my back and trailed his fingers lightly up and down my arm. He kissed my shoulder. "You didn't have to stop. I just meant you were getting a little, um, overly enthusiastic, and passionate, and——"

"I wanted to hurt you."

He grew still behind me. The lava lamps along the high shelf were warm now and active. The lava swelled and stretched toward the top of the lamps, creating thin threads that eventually snapped, bouncing the lava up into fat globules that rose and slowly settled again. Red, purple, and green shadows floated across the ceiling. After a few minutes he got up and I could hear him dress. Then he quietly let himself out of the room.

I found him lying on his back on the wraparound couch in the media room down the hall, a throw pillow hugged to his chest.

I picked up his feet and sat down, pulling them back in my lap. I pressed my thumbs into the arch of his foot and slowly drew them toward his toes. He stared at the ceiling, but when I kissed his toes, he closed his eyes. "I didn't know this would be so hard," I said.

"I understand that, Nate. But you don't seem to understand that this is hard for me too. There are times when I feel like I can hardly breathe I miss you so much."

"Then don't go back." I didn't plan to say it, but once I'd started, the words just tumbled out. "I don't want you to go. Stay with me."

"I can't." He made a growling noise in the back of his throat. "I've made commitments. I signed a contract. I have to go back. I know that's not what you want to hear. But I wish you had told me this before I left for New York."

"I didn't want to hold you back. I knew this was important to you."

"And now you don't care?"

I winced. "No. It's not that."

He draped his forearm over his face. "I know it's not," he said, his voice thicker and softer than before. "Come here." He tossed the pillow over the back of the couch and reached his hand out to me. I stretched out next to him. He shifted up against the back of the couch to make room for me, then fingered the bandage on my arm.

"We have to take this off."

"Later." I molded myself to him, desperate to keep him close to me.

"Not later. Now. Come on."

In the bathroom he peeled off the bandage, then gently washed my arm with Mea's baby soap, using his hands to clean the area and rinse it. I felt like a little boy with a scraped knee.

"I'm sorry," I said.

"I know." He reached for a hand towel and patted my arm dry. "Me too. I forget sometimes how much you've been through. You're stronger than you think, Nate. A lot stronger. I don't have half the courage that you do. And I couldn't be prouder that you love me. You can do this."

If that was supposed to make me feel better, strong, it wasn't working so great. I looked at my arm. *Fear is temporary. Regret is forever.* The skin around the black slanted lettering looked and felt sunburned. "Just leave it alone until tomorrow," Adam said, "then you can use some baby lotion or maybe some A and D ointment if you don't use too much."

I nodded, and then probably because I looked as shitty as I felt, he pulled me to him. "It's just until Thanksgiving," he whispered into my hair, but again, if he thought that would make me feel better, well, I had already checked the calendar—ninety-five days. I'd barely survived twenty-seven. The air conditioner kicked on. I hadn't put a shirt on and the cool air made me shiver. I folded myself more snugly into him.

"Mmm. I kinda like this," Adam said.

"Can we try again?" I said. "You did promise I could do nasty things to you."

He grinned. "I did, didn't I? Well, I'm a man of my word."

I couldn't let go of the hurt and resentment. The rest of the evening was like a bad song, set on repeat. Him, playful and sweet; me, not playful, not sweet. And all of it interspersed with moments of passion that at times felt more like fighting than loving. And even though he was next to me and he was warm and he was here, I didn't have to look at the clock to know how little time was left before warm and here became warm and there. I scooted even closer to his back and felt the regular rise and fall of his breathing and tried desperately to memorize his smell, the warmth of his skin against mine, the feel of his fingers wrapped around my fingers. I couldn't help thinking it would have been easier if he hadn't come back, because letting him go again was so damn hard. I pressed my nose into the short hairs at the nape of his neck and whispered, more to myself than to him, "I don't know how to let you go."

He twisted around under my arm, surprising me, and settled again, facing me now, his mouth so close to mine I could feel his breath. "Then don't, Nate." He ran a thumb across my brow. "Look, I don't care if I break my contract. Let them sue me. It's not worth having you feel like this. We all have our limits. Just say the word and I'll stay."

It occurred to me that I had said The Word. And now he was asking me to say The Word again? And when he put it in terms of broken contracts and lawsuits, he made it all sound so immature and childish.

"I thought you were asleep," I said.

He found my hand in the semi-dark and held it to his heart. I opened my fingers and lay my palm flat against his skin. He pressed his hand over mine.

"School starts Monday," I said. "It's gonna be so weird without you there."

"I'll stay, Nate. If that's what you want, I'll stay."

What I wanted was to never have to let him go, to crawl inside his skin, to be one with him, every second of every minute of every day. Forever. That sick kind of wanting that rips at your soul while making you look like some kind of psycho to the rest of the world. I had no doubt I could say The Word, and he'd stay. But he didn't want to. I could hear it in his voice. He wanted me. He wanted to be with me. He wanted to be here for me. But he wanted New York too. And I knew I had to let him go. Isn't that how it's supposed to work—if you love something, set it free? If it comes back to you, it's yours. If it doesn't . . . I didn't want to go there.

"No. I want you to go," I said, "and then I want you to come back to me."

We sat facing each other—me on the edge of the bed, Adam on his desk chair. His thumbs traced circles in the palms of my hands. He looked at the still angry-looking skin around my tattoo. "Put some lotion on it later this afternoon. And no scratching."

I nodded.

He smiled. "Good. Be sure to follow all the directions, okay?"

He glanced past my shoulder at the clock on his bedside table, then back at me. My breath caught in my throat. He pressed his lips together and swallowed hard.

"I'm gonna finally start writing that blog, I think," I said. I hadn't had the energy to figure it all out over the past month. I didn't have it now either, but God knows, I had to do something to fill the long days ahead.

"Good. You can help a lot of kids." He glanced at the clock again. "Baby, I'm gonna miss my flight if we don't get going."

"Can I have another lava lamp?"

"You can have anything you want."

I wanted the one he'd put on the bedside table last night. He unplugged it and wrapped the cord around the base and handed it to me. By the time I got him to the airport, it was so close to flight time that I had to drop him at the curb so he could check in while I parked. When I got to passenger check-in, he was gone. I hadn't even said good-bye. I groped for my cell phone, but it wasn't there. I must have left it in his room. I made my way back to the parking garage, alone.

Chapter 15

I picked up my phone at Adam's, then on impulse headed over to the music store. I wasn't working today; I'd taken the day off to spend it with Adam. But I did need a phone number, and a life, I thought wryly. I called Danial on the drive back to my house, and he agreed to help me set up a blog the next afternoon. The rest of the day I spent in an emotional freefall as I came to terms with the lonely months ahead.

Adam called the moment he got off the plane—at least I assumed it was the moment he got off—and the first thing out of my mouth was, "Why didn't you wait for me?"

"I'm sorry, baby, there was no time. I would have missed my flight."

As if that would have been the worst thing in the world. He was breathing heavily like he was running through the airport. Before I could respond, there was another voice, more distant, but near enough that I could hear every word: "There's my sexy Adam." A laugh—Adam's—and then some muffled noise that I interpreted as Adam's phone on the back of Justin's neck as he embraced him.

"Hey, baby," Adam said in the phone again, "I'll Skype you this evening." Then to Justin, "Yeah, I'm all set."

"Don't bother," I mumbled.

"What?" he said, having clearly missed my sarcasm in his juggling of two conversations.

"Nothing. Yeah, sure."

When he spoke again, his voice was low and close to the phone. "Let's make it late. *Late* late, after everyone's gone to bed. Wear your football jersey. That mesh one. And lock your door."

I relaxed a little and grinned into the phone. "And what are you wearing?"

"Whatever you want, baby. It's just you and me."

Only, that night on cam, it wasn't just him and me.

It was him and me and Justin.

The Skype had started out great, beautiful, and then in the background, there was Adam's creepy roommate, parading around the apartment like the damn emperor, seemingly oblivious to the fact that he wasn't wearing a stitch of clothing.

Adam had on his headphones, so he didn't notice him slither into the room behind him until I muttered a "What the fuck?" He turned just as Justin placed his hands on Adam's shoulders.

"What are you doing up in the middle of the night, hot stuff?" He dipped his head down next to Adam's. "Oh, I see. It's little Nate. That's sweet." He smiled one of those creepy smiles that seemed to say, "Enjoy it while you can," and walked off.

Adam turned back to the screen. "I'm sorry."

"I have to go."

"Don't."

"He's naked, Adam. Na-ked."

"I know he's naked. What do you want me to do about it?" His voice was short, impatient, irritated.

"Nothing. Not a damn thing."

I ended the Skype, then shut down my computer and turned off my cell phone.

"Nathan? Are you still asleep? It's one o'clock." Mom jiggled my leg. I groaned and pulled the quilt over my head. "Wake up. You have a guest downstairs. A Danial Quasimodo or something."

Oh crap. I'd forgotten all about Danial coming over this afternoon. "Qasimi. It's Danial Qasimi," I said, getting up and stumbling to the closet. "He's helping me set up my blog." I yanked a T-shirt off a hanger. "Will you tell him I'll be right down?"

"Okay." She turned to go, then paused and turned back. "Why were you sleeping in your football jersey?"

You don't want to know.

I switched shirts and pulled on a clean pair of shorts. Danial was at the base of the stairs chatting with my mom when I got down. I reached out to shake his hand, suddenly self-conscious about my disheveled look. He just seemed amused.

In my room, I pointed to the computer, then excused myself to brush my teeth, wash my face, and rake my fingers through my hair. My head ached thinking about last night. Adam hadn't even been gone twenty-four hours and we were already fighting again. I knew Justin's come-ons weren't his fault, and yet I couldn't help feeling like they were, just a little. But I couldn't deal with that now.

Danial had my computer booted up and was kicked back in my chair surveying my room—the unmade bed, yesterday's shorts and T-shirt wadded up on the floor. My football jersey crowning the pile.

"Sorry for the wait."

He grinned. "Rough night?"

"Yeah." I grabbed another chair from the desk in my grandmother's room and pulled it up next to him. "So, what do I need to do?"

"Do you know what blogging service you want to use?" Danial said. He shook his head and laughed at the blank look on my face. "Let me just show you some. The three biggest ones are free services. They each have a different look, different features." He showed me some blogs that he followed, mostly geeky stuff, but I really couldn't have cared less and yawned more than once. I was just going through the motions.

I decided on one (well, technically he decided on one, and I just said okay). Danial pushed his chair aside so I could complete the signup screen. It took only ten minutes to choose a template, configure the blog posts, add a few gadgets, and decide all the other minutiae of setting up a Web log. The biggest hang-up was coming up with a name and a tagline.

"So, what are you going to blog about?" he asked, clicking on another template just to see the effect.

Before I could answer, Skype signaled an incoming call.

"Do you want me to reject it?" Danial asked, moving the cursor in that direction.

"No!" I reached for the mouse. "Sorry. This will only take a minute."

He shrugged and sat back but didn't move. I clicked Answer with Video without thinking twice, and then when I thought twice, I quickly turned the screen to me, but not before Adam saw Danial in the video window. I could tell by the surprised look on his face. He didn't ask who he was. I didn't know why that pissed me off, but then I chided myself for being so sensitive.

"I've only got a few minutes," Adam said, looking right at the webcam as he spoke. "I had to run back to the apartment for a new shirt, but I've got to get back. I tried to Skype earlier, but your computer was offline."

"I slept in."

He looked like he could have used some more sleep himself.

"We need to talk," he said, to which I said, "I know." In the background I could hear someone call his name.

"Who's that?" I said.

"Can I Skype you tonight? It'll be late."

I looked at the camera and swallowed hard. "It's okay. I'll be here."

He pounded his heart with his fist twice.

"Me too," I said. He disconnected the call without answering my question about the voice in the background.

"Your brother?" Danial asked.

"No. My boyfriend."

His eyebrows shot up. "Your boyfriend? Really? I mean, I noticed the T-shirt, but I figured it was just some political statement, not something personal."

I shoved the screen back toward him. "Do you have a problem with that?"

He put his hands up like I'd pointed a gun at him. "Hey, don't get your panties in a wad. I'm just, uh"—he grinned—"surprised."

"Why should that surprise you?" I sneered. I was itching for a fight.

Danial scratched behind his ear, still grinning, and cleared his throat. "Well, for starters, you're not very girly."

I glared at him. "Maybe I should slip on some stilettos."

He shrugged. "Suit yourself."

The jerk was mocking me. I slammed the screen down on my laptop and stood up. "Forget it. We're done."

He calmly reached over and reopened the screen, scooting his chair back up to the desk. "You need a name for your blog and maybe a tag," he said again, ignoring my outburst. "A line or two that tells people what your focus is." He looked up at me. "So, what do you want to blog about?"

I maintained my defensive stance. "What else?"

He studied me for a minute, then turned to the keyboard, a grin tugging at his mouth again. "Okay." I sat down, feeling foolish and relieved at the same time.

He paused, drumming his fingers lightly on the keys without actually pressing them. "How about *Gay Nate talks Straight*."

"Gay Nate?"

He shrugged. "I thought it was kind of catchy."

I rolled my eyes.

He laughed. "So let's hear your ideas, Shakespeare."

Adam did that. Quote Shakespeare. Danial wasn't quoting Shakespeare, but the reference . . . God, I was pathetic. I struggled to focus. Thoughts of Adam would have to wait.

"I don't want to use the word *gay*."

He looked at me. "Let me get this straight. You want to write about being gay, but you don't want to use the word *gay*. Brilliant! A from-the-behind sneak attack," he said, which wasn't half as funny as he apparently thought it was, judging from the grin on his face.

I glared at him. "*Gay* is gender specific."

He snorted. "So I hear."

I ignored him. "I want to use *queer*. It means non-gender conforming, but it's a broader term that includes lesbians, bisexuals, and transgenders."

"Really?" he said, sounding sincere for a change. "So . . . you're really queer?"

I wasn't sure if he was simply verifying the term or my actual status. Either way, I decided it didn't matter. "Yeah. Get over it."

"That's it!"

"What's it?"

His fingers raced over the keys, and then he turned the screen for me to see. There was my blog page. And spanning the top was my new tagline in bold, blue sparkly lettering: *I'm queer. Get over it.* I stared at it, dumbfounded. It certainly went right to the heart of the matter.

Danial misinterpreted my silence. "Ah, you don't like it." He grabbed the mouse and moved to edit the line.

"No," I said, placing my hand over his to stop him from clicking on Delete.

He looked down at my hand and then up at me with a look that said, "Are you holding my hand?"

"Uh, I'm flattered," he said, "but you're not exactly my type."

I released his hand, embarrassed and irritated at the suggestion, and stuck it under my leg. Then, thinking that made it look like I was trying to keep myself from touching him again, I laid it in my lap.

He watched me, amused. "If you're done acting gay—excuse me . . . *queer*—I gather you like the tagline?"

I sneered.

"Oh, come on." He bumped my elbow with his. "Don't tell me *queers* don't have a sense of humor."

"We do when someone's actually funny."

"Oh, smack!" he said, laughing. "Come on. Do you like it or not?"

I shrugged. "It's good."

"All right!" He slapped me on the back. "You're in business."

He showed me how to create and publish posts, add links, and other bloggy stuff. I followed along, nodding, asking questions occasionally, knowing all the while I'd forget half of it the minute he left. Fortunately, the site looked pretty user friendly. I'd figure it out.

"You probably want to moderate comments. You know, have a look before you let them show up under your posts."

"Why would I want to do that?"

"Well, for starters, there are a lot of crazies out there. Censorship can be a good thing."

"No moderation. People should be able to express themselves freely."

"You don't get out much, do you?"

I glared at him. He shrugged and turned off the comment moderation feature. When he ran out of stuff to show me, he slumped back in his chair. "Questions, sweetheart?"

I can't say I was getting used to his barbs, but they seemed good-natured enough, and I was starting to enjoy his company. Unlike a lot of kids, he didn't seem threatened by me. More amused than anything, and that was okay. I could do amused.

I gave him an air kiss. "I'll let you know if I think of any, darling."

"You could have done this on your own, you know. It's not that complicated."

"You could have told me that on the phone, *you know*."

"Yeah, maybe so." He grinned and reached up for the picture Adam's mom had taken. It was sitting on a shelf above my computer. "Your boyfriend?"

My jaw tensed. I cleared my throat and took the picture. "Yeah." I put it back on the shelf.

"Where is he?"

"New York."

Danial raised his eyebrows but didn't ask any more questions.

Adam called me from the hallway instead of Skyping.

"It's the only place I can get any privacy around here," he said. "Even the bathroom's taken."

I gave him points for sounding almost as frustrated as I felt. "How was your day?" I asked, wanting to know every last detail and not wanting to know at the same time. It still bugged me that he hadn't answered my question earlier, and it bugged me that he hadn't yet asked who the guy was sitting at my computer.

"Long, tiring. How was yours?"

"Long, lonely. I got the blog up. *I'm queer. Get over it.*"

He laughed. "Well, that pretty much says it all, doesn't it?"

"Danial suggested *Gay Nate talks Straight.*"

He laughed again. "Gosh, Nate, I've only been gone a day and already you've got some cute guy in your bedroom? Are you trying to make me crazy?"

I forced myself to smile because he didn't sound crazy at all, and I wanted him to. "He just helped me with the blog. There's nothing on it yet, but you can set up an e-mail subscription. The URL's just nateschaper.com."

"I will. So, who's this Danial?"

Finally. I filled him in with what I knew, which wasn't much.

"Don't you ever get a day off?" I asked when I was done.

"Doesn't seem like it, does it? But, yeah. Everything is such a different pace here. I feel like I'm running all the time. Even on Sunday. Can you believe it?"

I was starting to. "Who was that calling your name?" I asked, unable to hold back the question any longer.

"When?"

"When you Skyped earlier."

"Oh. That was just Alec. He'd left his iPhone and came back with me to get it." He laughed. "He whined all morning because he couldn't check his Facebook status."

I mentally kicked myself for being so suspicious.

An awkward silence stretched out between us.

"Nate, talk to me about last night. I couldn't sleep knowing you were upset. I thought we had this all sorted out. I don't know how to make this right. You knew I was going to be living with three other guys. It's too expensive here to live alone. They don't pay me that much."

"He was naked, Adam."

He got quiet.

"I mean, what is that you're living in? Some kind of freaking commune? Free love and all that crap?"

"It's not like that, Nate."

"Then what is it like? Because from where I'm sitting it looks pretty damn—" I choked up, unable to finish the thought. I took a deep, shuddering breath. "He had his hands on you."

"They were on my shoulder."

"Why was he naked anyway?"

"He sleeps that way."

"He *sleeps* naked? And I suppose you're going to tell me next that he's the one you share a room with?"

Again, he got quiet.

"Great. That's just great."

"Nate." He sighed heavily. "I can't control what any of my roommates do. But you're the only one I'm interested in. You're the only one I want to look at. You know that."

I scrubbed my hand over my face. I couldn't stand the idea of Adam living with three other guys in such close quarters, but to see Justin strutting around naked and touching Adam . . . and now hearing that this was likely a nightly occurrence . . . it was too much. No wonder he usually Skyped me from the bathroom.

"Oh, Nate, this was a mistake. I shouldn't have come back. I shouldn't have come at all. It's too much, too soon. Look, I'll get a flight. I can be home in a few days."

"No. No." I gritted my teeth. "I don't want that." I swallowed hard. "I just want to know that you miss me as much as I miss you."

"You know I do. I'd never do anything to hurt you. We established that a long time ago. Right?" When I didn't answer he repeated that last word until I finally admitted what I knew in my heart—he would never hurt me. At least, not intentionally.

Chapter 16

Last February 14
An unintentional hurt

Two weeks after I was released from the hospital, Adam and I had our first post-trauma date. Appropriately, it was Valentine's Day. He stubbornly refused to tell me where he was taking me. "I want it to be a surprise." I was intrigued when he pulled the car into a parking lot in front of a small, nearly windowless building behind a strip center and cut the engine.

"What is this, some kind of underground gay bar?"

"Nope."

I squinted at the unassuming sign hanging above the single door. "Westboro Playhouse?"

"It's not Broadway, but I thought you might like it."

"What are we seeing?"

He chuckled and pulled the keys out of the ignition before answering. "*Alice in Wonderland*. You're going to love it. Trust me."

I raised my eyebrow, skeptical.

"You're so cute when you do that," Adam said. He traced my eyebrow, then allowed his fingers to continue down my face and brush across my lips. I closed my eyes and tasted his fingers, running my tongue over the tips, feeling the smooth edges of his nails. A familiar tingle began to work its way through my body.

"Stop that," he said, his voice husky and close to my face. "I paid fifteen dollars each for these tickets and we're using them."

The playhouse was small. We wormed our way through the crowd inside the lobby, stopping here and there so Adam could hug or kiss someone. He'd obviously been here before, a lot of times. I understood moments later when he led me through a crowded narrow hallway. The black walls were plastered with pictures from past productions. He stopped and pointed to an eight by ten glossy of a kid dressed in a medieval costume. I studied the picture. "That's you," I said.

He grinned at the surprised look on my face and nudged me down the hallway, pointing out other pictures. A twelve-year-old Adam dressed as a lion. A fourteen-year-old Adam as a ragamuffin. Even a fifteen-year-old Adam as a girl. "You do a very sexy girl," I said, pinching him a little on his side. There were pictures of him everywhere.

"I've been performing here since I was a kid," he said.

I pointed to an older Adam in green leotards, then looked over my shoulder at him and raised my eyebrows.

"Peter Pan," he said. "Just a couple of years ago. I was sixteen."

"I like the leotards."

He leaned in then and whispered in my ear, "I still have them. Maybe I'll wear them for you later tonight."

My insides did a little flip.

He laughed and pulled me by the hand into a small, semi-circular theater with seating for maybe two hundred. Every seat was practically right on the stage.

The play was cool, I guess, but I was distracted. My mind was like a rubber band—I kept stretching it to focus on the stage, but without warning it would snap back to images of Adam in those green tights . . . and out of those green tights. So when the lights went up, I grabbed his hand and headed for the door. "That was great. Let's go."

"It's only intermission. There's still half the play to go."

"I've seen the movie. Alice eats some bad mushrooms, grows,

shrinks, wakes herself up. End of story. Let's go." Adam laughed and stumbled after me.

"Where to, Clyde?" he said when we were in the car.

"Still got a lock on your bedroom door?"

"Hm. I think I can do better than that."

The house was dark when we pulled up to the curb. "Where are your parents?"

"Out."

"How long?"

"Long enough."

He let us in the front door, closed it, and turned the deadbolt. I had my hands in his pants before he could turn around. We hadn't been together like this in a month and a half. I was desperate to see him, to touch him, to have him touch me. He laughed and turned back to face me, dislodging my hands. I dropped to my knees and grappled with the button on his jeans.

"Shouldn't you buy me dinner or something first?" he said.

"You ate yesterday."

I watched out the window as his neighborhood retreated and mine advanced, the profound lack of conversation buffered only by the low whine of gears engaging and disengaging. Adam pulled up along the ditch in front of my house and cut the engine. I popped the door latch and started to get out, but he reached a hand over to stop me.

"Don't go."

I dropped back in my seat and stared out the windshield at the empty street. A possum nosed out of the shadows and trundled into the lamplight, where he paused to sniff the air, then continued in his nightly scavenge for whatever discarded crap he could find. I white-knuckled the door handle, but I didn't get out.

"What happened back there?" Adam said.

Breathe. In. Out. One. Two. Three. Four.

"Talk to me, Nate. Whatever it is, just say it. Whatever it is, we'll work it out. But you've got to talk to me. We've waited so long, and now . . . I don't understand what happened."

Five. Six. The possum disappeared into the shadows on the other side of the street.

"Did I hurt you?"

I scoffed.

"What did I do, Nate?"

He reached to touch me, but I deflected his hand with my forearm. He recoiled in surprise. "It's not what you did," I said through gritted teeth, my voice all sharp edges. "Don't you get it? It's what you didn't do!"

"No, I don't get it."

"I wanted *all* of you tonight. *ALL* of you." I fought the burning in my nose and the pricks in my eyes.

His voice was soft when he spoke, and confused. "You had all of me." He reached for me again but I flinched and he backed off.

"I didn't have all of you. I *wanted* all of you, but I most definitely did not *get* all of you."

"What?"

And then I could feel the aura around him change. "Is that what this is all about, because I wouldn't . . ." He swore just under his breath. "Nate. You know how much I want you. All of you. Every inch of me craves every inch of you. But, I can't, Nate. It's too soon. I won't hurt you, no matter how badly I want you."

"If I disgust you, you could at least be a man about it and say so. You owe me that."

"Disgust me? *Disgust* me? Have you lost your fucking mind?"

Maybe I had. I was tottering on the cliff of hysteria, but I couldn't pull back.

"You want me to beg? Then I'm begging." I fumbled for the button on my jeans, but he grabbed my hand.

"Stop it."

I jerked my hand free and got out of the car and slammed the door. Adam was out of the car too. "Nate." He grabbed my arm as I came around the back, but I broke into a jog. He lunged for me, grabbing me from behind. We stumbled and fell to the ground. I struggled to break free. He was no match for my fury. I got to my feet, but he was there again. I spun around and shoved him. Then I took a step toward him and shoved him again, harder.

"Stop it, Nate."

"You stop it. Stop pretending like nothing's changed. Everything has changed." I shoved him again. I wanted him to fight back, to hit me, to do something to stop me from spinning completely out of control.

He pinned my arms to my sides in a tight embrace. "Don't," he whispered in my ear.

But it wasn't enough. I twisted and writhed in his grasp until I broke free. Then I swung, my fist connecting with his jaw. It wasn't a hard blow, but the surprise of it knocked him to the ground.

I stood over him, breathing hard and sweating profusely.

He pushed up on one arm and looked at me, stunned.

And then, as if someone had cut my strings, I slumped to the ground and covered my head with my arms and let go. "I don't know how to do this," I cried. "It hurts so bad sometimes."

He crawled over to me and wrapped me in his arms.

I woke sometime during the night fully dressed, my head in Adam's lap. The bedside lamp was on, and he was asleep, sitting up against my headboard, his head slumped at an angle that was sure to mean a sore neck when he woke up. I felt guilty about that, but I let him sleep. I eased out of bed and made my way quietly to the bathroom and shut the door.

I peed and then brushed my teeth, avoiding my reflection in the mirror. The shakes started just as I was about to spit and my stomach clenched. I dry heaved into the sink a few times before emptying the remnants of an early dinner from my stomach. When there was nothing left, I rinsed my mouth and the sink, brushed one more time, then slid down the wall and grabbed my knees and held on.

Some time later—maybe a minute, maybe an hour—Adam knocked softly on the door. "Nate?"

When I didn't answer, he opened the door a crack. "Can I come in?"

I scrambled to my feet and made a show of washing my face. In the mirror, I could see his mussed hair, red eyes, and creased brow. I had no idea what he saw, but he slipped his arms around me from behind and leaned his chin on my shoulder. Our eyes locked in the mirror. He ran his fingers lightly up and down my arms and watched me for a minute.

"You're trembling," he said.

I shut off the water and scrubbed my face dry with a hand towel.

"What do you see when you look in the mirror, Nate?" he said.

I chewed on my bottom lip but didn't answer.

"Let me tell you what I see." He squeezed me tighter. "I see a boy who's been hurt. But that hurt is what happened to him, it's not who he is. What I see is the same beautiful, loving, outrageously sexy boy that used to sneak looks at me when he thought no one was looking."

I wanted to believe him.

"I'm not going anywhere," he said to the me in the mirror.

"I wouldn't blame you if you did."

"You'd have to hit me a lot harder than that."

My lips twitched into an almost smile, but it faded quickly.

He watched me in the mirror, his eyes so intense that I could hold them only a moment. I closed my eyes and focused on the feel of his arms around me. Strong arms.

"I know you want to pretend like everything's okay, baby. I know you want to pretend like that night never happened. But it's not, and it did."

I stiffened. *Shut up.* But he didn't shut up.

"You have to face it. Don't let them do this to you. Don't let them do this to us. If you do, the creeps win. Please, for us, call Dr. Par—"

"No."

I jerked away from him and left the bathroom. I did not need a shrink. I just needed him. *All* of him.

Chapter 17

August 25

The first day of school. Senior year. It should have been exciting. It wasn't. But at least I didn't have to rip a *Go #77* and a silly megaphone cutout off my locker before I opened it this year.

Juliet leaned against the locker next to mine. I grabbed my English and calculus books and elbowed the door closed.

"Interesting choice of clothing for the first day of school," she said, eyeing me with a mixture of amusement and disbelief.

I gave her the stink eye and fished my schedule out of my shorts pocket.

Even Mom had been a little annoyed that I'd chosen to wear the *Closets are for brooms, not people* T-shirt Adam had given me. If she'd known I was going to wear it today, I doubt she'd have washed it for me yesterday. Maybe annoyed wasn't the right word. I think she was just scared. "Do you really want to draw that kind of attention to yourself?" she'd said.

I think that's exactly what I wanted to do. I wasn't even sure I could explain why. In part, I was still irritated with Adam over the whole roommate thing in New York. And in part, I was just sick of people acting like I wasn't right somehow. Maybe I was just itching for a confrontation. Or maybe it was just a way of keeping him close. In any event, wearing the shirt had been strictly impulse. It was there. It was clean. It felt right. I wore it.

I shouldered my backpack, and we headed down the crowded hallway together.

"Let me see," Juliet said, grabbing for my schedule. She glanced over it. "Crap," she said, slapping me in the chest with it. "Not a single class together. We've got lunch, though. I'll save you a seat." She pattered on about something, then waved a hand in front of my face. "Hey, big boy, are you listening to me?"

I wasn't.

"Attracting attention already, I see," she said.

Most of it innocuous, I noted—some giggles, some stares, some whispers here and there. I wasn't sure if it was my notoriety as a crime victim, the TV interviews I'd done, or just the fact that I was the school gay. Or maybe it *was* the political statement on my T-shirt. Who knew? But the attention was there. A year ago I would have shrunk away from that kind of scrutiny. A lot can change in a year. A lot had. I drew myself up to my full height and practically dared someone to challenge me.

We ran into Danial at the base of the main stairwell. When he saw me, his eyebrows shot up and a slow smile crept across his face. He shook his head and kept going.

Juliet watched him go, stretching around me to keep him in her sights. "So, um, did Danial get you all set up?"

"Yeah, and then I screwed his brains out."

"Nice. Have you posted anything yet?"

She shifted to look over my shoulder again, presumably to catch a last glimpse before Danial disappeared around a corner.

"Obvious," I said.

"What? I can't help myself. Damn. Have you seen that cute butt?"

"I hadn't noticed."

"Liar."

I laughed. "What about Mike?"

"Mike, Mike, Mike. I like Mike. I don't know. He's just so . . . so—"

"—boring, one-dimensional, short—"

"—not you," she said and gave me a look that said, "You asked." "There's just no passion there. Hey," she said, changing the subject, "fall rehearsals start today. Why don't you stop by the auditorium sometime?"

"Sure," I said, but I think we both knew I wouldn't come. Without Adam there, I didn't see the point.

At the next intersection I gave Juliet's hair a playful yank and told her I'd see her at lunch. Then I turned and ran smack dab into another kid who told me to watch where I was going, and just because he wasn't a big enough asshole, he called me a faggot. I was the wrong guy to be messing with right then. I shoved him and he stumbled into a passing group of freshman girls.

"Hey. What the hell's wrong with you?" He sneered, bringing up his fist and moving in toward me. Coach Carr stepped between us before he could throw a punch. I was relieved, though I'd have taken it and given it back.

"Get to class, gentlemen," Coach said. He stood there, his arms spanning the distance between us, until the testosterone ebbed and the kid huffed away. Coach took a look at my shirt and shook his head. "Your dad okay with this?"

"I don't talk to my dad anymore."

He scoffed. "Get going, Schaper."

"Damn, Nate," Juliet said over my shoulder. "Take it easy."

I glared at Coach as I walked away. Those days of taking it easy were long gone. And Coach Carr was just as much to blame as anyone, including me.

Chapter 18

Last August 27
Another first day of school

Junior year. I navigated the crowded main hallway with schedule and locker number in hand, which quickly proved completely unnecessary. Up and down the hallway, select lockers—football players' lockers—had been covered in Knight blue paper and foil-covered megaphone cutouts that screamed *Go #82, Go #7, Go #53* in sparkly silver lettering. I knew the other guys liked the attention, but I never understood why this school, or any school for that matter, thought that a bunch of egotistical Neanderthals deserved to be singled out for such elite status when other kids busting their butts in academics or the arts or even other sports were virtually ignored. It felt wrong. And if anyone had bothered to ask, I'd have said, "No thanks."

I found my locker, and after a quick glance up and down the hallway, ripped the paper off and the obnoxious megaphone with it and stuffed it all inside. A streamer broke free and drifted to the floor. I picked it up and shoved it in too. No paper this year. No megaphones. No sparkly lettering. No streamers. No *Go #77*. No football.

I wondered if Coach Carr had checked his updated rosters yet. He didn't like surprises, and he was about to get a big one. Even if he hadn't scanned his rosters, he'd know soon enough. I had him for PE—I glanced at my schedule again—fifth period. Right after lunch. Great.

A commotion down the hallway caught my attention. Andrew Cargill and a couple of his jerky friends—Carlos Cuevas and Butch Evans—were weaving and plowing their way through the crowd, making openings where there were none with sheer momentum and disregard for rules of civility. You moved, or they displaced you. Matthew Shin, a slight Asian kid I'd known since fourth grade, didn't move. Cargill muscled past him—"Out of the way, homo"—giving him a shove that sent him stumbling into me. I braced myself and grabbed him to keep us both from hitting the ground. He dropped his lunch bag and a banana skittered across the tiled floor. Five or six kids stepped on it and then freaked out at the banana mush on their new shoes before the rush of kids could part around the mess.

A tall guy with dark hair, earrings, and these long narrow purple and black plaid shorts that hit him just below the knee picked up the brown bag and handed it to Matthew. "You okay, man?"

"Yeah." Matthew took the bag, then looked at his ruined banana like he might try to salvage it. He shook his head. "Fuckers."

The guy laughed. "You can say that again." Matthew looked up at him and smiled a little, as if they shared some secret, then he moved off still shaking his head and muttering to himself.

His savior shouldered his backpack and turned to me, but I didn't notice immediately because I was focused on the gray Stones T-shirt that hung from his broad shoulders and ended loosely around his hips. He looked like he might have just come from a *GQ* shoot. "Matthew's a brilliant kid," he said, refocusing my attention and causing me to blush. "Someday he's going to grow up and own those jerks."

I cleared my throat and looked down the hallway after Matthew, but he'd already disappeared. "He has to survive high school first."

"This is true."

At the other end of the hallway, Cargill and his goons were flexing their physical prowess by jumping up and slapping the *Welcome Back* banner that stretched across the hallway.

"I think somewhere three villages are looking for their idiots," I said.

He laughed. I looked at him and thought that I very much liked the sound of that laugh.

"Adam!"

He turned back, so I did too. A pretty redhead hurried toward him.

"Your girlfriend?" I asked as nonchalantly as I could.

He made a *hmph* sound and smiled. She flung her arms and legs around him, and he staggered slightly against the onslaught, then steadied himself and propped her back on her feet. I busied myself in my locker and tried not to be too obvious about my eavesdropping. She spoke in excited little bursts about who was playing what role and costumes and something about a meeting in the auditorium. Then she grabbed his hand and they moved away. He looked back at me and winked. "I like your shirt. Watch out for the idiots."

"I will," I said, but the girl had already dragged him off down the hallway. Until then, I had barely been aware of what I had put on that morning. I looked down—Bob Marley—and smiled for the first time in days.

"Let me see your schedule," Liam said, reaching across the table at lunch.

Brett was seated next to him, their elbows crowding each other. The two linemen had their own schedules on the table, rumpled in the space between hoagie sandwiches big enough to choke a horse. I didn't ask to see theirs; I had no interest whatsoever in where they were at any given time of the day. I considered refusing mine, but it was going to happen eventually, so I fished the folded paper out of my pocket and handed it over.

"You have PE next period? What the fuck? Why aren't you in athletics?"

I shrugged.

He looked at me in disbelief. "You're not playing football." It wasn't a question. More like something he'd seen coming but didn't think I'd ever get away with doing.

"Nope."

"Why not? You just did two weeks of fucking summer camp. In one hundred ten degree heat. You don't die, you play, man."

For about three seconds I considered telling him the truth, just getting it over with. I was so done with lies and pretending and living for everyone else. I didn't care what anyone thought of me; it couldn't be half as bad as what I'd been thinking of myself for years. But when I opened my mouth, what came out was one more fantastic retelling of the Schaper-sidelined-with-shoulder-injury crap. Brett wasn't buying it and argued that I hadn't even dislocated my shoulder, just separated it.

"So you're a doctor now?" I said, unscrewing the lid on a bottle of water and taking a long drink.

He said he wasn't, but proceeded to give me a diagnosis anyway, which pretty much added up to a major case of pussy. I stared at him, but inside I was thinking, *Not bad, Armstrong.* Give that boy an honorary medical degree. Pussy? Oh, yeah. But not for the reasons he thought.

He glared back at me. "I guess while you're sitting in the stands nursing your little booboo, that dick Brookstone will be starting receiver."

I wouldn't be in the stands.

After lunch, I headed to regular PE for the first time since sixth grade. The athletes had athletics and the band kids had marching band. What was left was an odd assortment of thugs, creative types, emo kids, and nerds. And then there was Jake Winfield, too meek and nerdy for even the nerd kids to embrace. I spotted him on the bleachers as soon as I walked in the gym. He hugged the wall, his face half hidden behind the pages of a book.

"Schaper," Coach Carr barked. He was seated in a plastic chair facing the boys but not watching them. Instead, he was studying a clipboard. Without looking up, he held out a square of paper to me—a hall pass. "Take this to the counselor and get your schedule changed. You're supposed to be in seventh-period athletics."

When I didn't take it, he looked up. "Go."

I took the pass, and he went back to his clipboard, but I didn't go. I almost went. It would have been so much easier just to do what everyone expected me to do, but I couldn't, not even when Andrew Cargill came strutting into the gym with that smug attitude and the promise of a crappy year trailing behind him like toilet paper stuck to his shoe. Cargill had shown a lot of promise as a tackle in junior high. He wasn't afraid of anything, including consequences. He got permanently kicked off the team freshman year for being a vicious freak, which was why he was here. He took down anything that got in his way—on and off the field—including his own teammates. My balls still ached when I thought about the kick he'd delivered to my groin in eighth grade when I didn't complete a pass he'd cleared the way for. Coach Schaper—dear old Dad—sent him to the shower and then berated me in front of the rest of the team for missing the ball. As I held my knees to my chest, I didn't know what hurt more—the pain in my testicles or his words.

Coach looked up again, clearly annoyed that I was still there. "Is there a problem?"

"It wasn't a mistake," I said as evenly as I could. "I changed my schedule." He glared at me, a thin layer of confusion adding to his thick layer of annoyance, so I kept talking. "I asked to be switched out of athletics."

"You want to tell me why?"

Not really. I took a deep breath and hoped this was the last time I'd have to run this lame play. "The shoulder's still bothering me."

"So?"

"So I don't want to risk injuring it again."

"Just because you have to sit out a few games doesn't mean you ditch athletics. Go get it switched back." He looked back down at his clipboard, essentially dismissing me, and scribbled a note.

"No."

His head snapped up again. He studied me for a moment and then took off his glasses. "No?"

I glanced over my shoulder. Cargill flicked a tweetie at Jake. It pegged him in the back of the head. Jake didn't flinch. If anything, he hunched over a little more like a pill bug rolling up when it's molested. He stared at his book, but I doubted he was getting any reading done.

Cargill was sitting next to Carlos Cuevas now, who was laughing and holding his nose.

"I don't want to hold the team back."

I knew he wouldn't believe that. I hadn't even bothered to fake sincerity when I said it. What was the point? Go through the motions and get it over with.

Coach Carr leaned back in his chair and folded his arms. The angle seemed to defy gravity, and I half expected him to fall over. He didn't. "You don't want to hold the team back." He guffawed and shook his head. "You want to know what I think?"

Not even a little bit.

"I don't think you want to play at all."

I didn't respond. I looked back at the bleachers. Cargill flicked another tweetie, this time hitting Jake in the cheek. Jake angled himself so he was facing more toward the wall. The other kids were watching now. Some were laughing.

"Is your dad on board with this?"

When I didn't answer, he laughed softly and shook his head. "Well, that should make for some interesting dinner conversation tonight."

"We don't eat dinner together."

Coach shifted his weight forward and his chair hit the ground with a smack. "Find a seat, Schaper." As I walked away I heard him mutter, "What a waste."

I sat as far away from Jake as I could.

The Jake Winfield show hadn't ended there.

In the locker room the next day, Coach Carr barked out orders as guys stripped down and pulled on gym shorts and T-shirts. I averted my eyes and made my way to my locker to change. I hated locker rooms. I hated the noise. I hated the overwhelming smell of testosterone and underwashed bodies. I hated the sophomoric muscle flexing and penis jokes that always started when the coaches retreated to their offices or moved on to the gym or the practice field.

Coach finished his orders and disappeared, and the games

began. Some cosmic kick-in-the-gut had assigned Jake Winfield a locker in the same bank as Andrew Cargill's. Cargill had already stripped to his underwear and was intentionally intimidating the other kids with his loud laugh and raunchy displays of his questionable manhood. I suspected all the grandstanding was cover for a tiny dick. He damn sure didn't have anything I wanted.

Jake turned into a corner and unbuttoned his shirt, then tried to slip it off and pull on his PE T-shirt in one motion—difficult at the least and awkward at best. No surprise it proved to be too much of a juggling act for Jake. The T-shirt fell to the floor, and before he could cover his narrow, pale chest and pick it up, Cargill kicked it away from him.

"Did you lose something, pussy?"

Jake flushed and shrank in on himself as he grappled for the button-down, also on the floor and quickly snatched away from him by some random jerk and tossed across the room. Jake darted toward his T-shirt lying in a heap a few feet away.

Carlos Cuevas grabbed it off the floor. "Aah, the homo lost his shirt." Cuevas sniffed the shirt dramatically, then pinched his nose. "Ugh. This stinks. You been jackin' off on this shirt, homo?"

"No way." Cargill laughed. "Winfield doesn't have a dick. That's pure pussy."

Jake kept one arm firmly wrapped around his bare chest and grabbed for his shirt with the other, but Cuevas yanked it farther out of his reach. He had a good eight or nine inches on the smaller boy.

Tears sprang from Jake's eyes. A couple other guys near me laughed. I didn't know who I hated more at that moment—the jerks tormenting Jake, the cowards watching it happen, or the coward wearing my athletic shoes.

Cuevas shoved Jake in the chest and tossed the shirt back to Cargill. And Jake played right into their hands. After he got his feet back under him, he rushed Cargill. Cargill held Jake's shirt just out of his reach with one hand, and with the other grabbed Jake's right nipple and twisted as hard as he could. I winced. I knew that pain. One of the guys on the team was acting like a shit our freshman year and tried that on me. It hurt like a mother, but I knocked his hand away immediately. I knew the pain, but I had never known this level of degradation and humiliation.

Jake cried out, but Cargill didn't release him for another three or four seconds. When he did let go, he laughed and flung Jake's shirt in his face. Jake was crying openly now, but trying desperately to stop.

I turned away and left the locker room.

Someone narc-ed. It hadn't been me. And I regretted that.

For the rest of the week, Coach Carr stood guard in the locker room while we changed, but Jake looked only slightly less nervous than usual. The next week, Coach's appearances became more intermittent. By the third week, he'd quit showing up at all, and the games began anew, but they were more subtle now. There were no more raucous games of keep-away, just a daily nipple twisting that left Jake's chest a horrid blend of black, blue, purple, and yellow. I didn't even see it happen most days, and he didn't cry out anymore, but occasionally I got a glimpse of his chest when he changed, and I knew.

The one bright spot in my day came sixth period, right after PE. If a cosmic kick-in-the-gut had put Jake's locker in the same bank as Cargill's, perhaps it was some cosmic gift that had placed me in government with Adam and Juliet. By the fifth week of school, Adam and I knew there was more between us than just a spunky redhead. But knowing hadn't translated into action. "She's my best friend," he'd said to me, standing next to his car, the toads mating in the ditch next to us with raucous abandon. "I don't know what to do."

That Tuesday, Jake was absent. Same thing Wednesday. In the early morning hours on Thursday, Jake hung himself from the banister in his own house. The wood splintered, and he crashed to the floor. His mom found him lying there, unconscious, an extension cord still wound around his neck.

Word traveled fast. The subsequent joking and laughing in the locker room sickened me. I had done nothing to help Jake, but that afternoon, in my fury, I stuck out a foot and tripped Cargill as he dribbled a basketball down the court, sending him sprawling to the floor.

He got up and landed a punch in my jaw that snapped my head back. It smarted and tears sprang to my eyes despite my efforts to hold them back.

There was something about that moment, something about the fear and the cowardice that had brought us to that moment, that steeled my resolved.

I spent the next hour sitting in the nurse's office with an ice pack on my jaw, a chip on my shoulder, and a fire burning in my soul.

I caught up with Adam in the hallway just as Chloe was about to throw an arm around him. I ran interference without explanation. Adam looked amused and told her he'd see her later, but the smile disappeared when he looked at me.

"Where were you? What happened to your face?"

"I need to talk to you."

"Okay. Shoot."

"Alone."

He looked down the hallway, then at his feet, then back at me. "You want to get together this weekend?"

"No. Today."

"Today. Okay. I'll, uh, stop by after rehearsal."

I nodded and turned to walk away.

"Nate?"

I turned back.

"Are you sure about this?"

I glanced around at the crowd flowing around the island that had become us. Familiar faces, unfamiliar faces, happy, not happy, indifferent. We'd been tap dancing around the issue of *us* for over two weeks now, and I was sick of it.

"I'm sure."

"Why don't you know what to do?" I demanded.

He winced slightly as he closed the car door. Then he grabbed my chin. His thumb pressed lightly but painfully on the bruise on my jaw. "What happened?"

"Andrew Cargill happened. He hit me because I tripped him in basketball because he's a fucking asshole and I've been too much of a fucking coward to stand up to him or anybody else and I'm fucking sick of it. I might as well have wound that extension cord around Jake Winfield's neck myself."

"What are you talking about?"

"He tried to kill himself, Adam, Jake Winfield, this kid in my PE class. He tried to kill himself because he couldn't take it anymore, because I never did anything to stop them. They tormented him every day, every fucking day. And I'm as much to blame as they are because I let it happen. Just like I let my dad fuck with me for so many years."

He pressed his lips together and didn't try to tell me it wasn't my fault.

I slammed my fist into the side of his car and blinked back the stupid tears that were screwing up my vision. I sniffed.

"This isn't really about Jake or your dad is it?"

"Do you want me or not? And if you say not, I am going to fucking lose it because I haven't been able to think about anything but you for weeks and I can't even look at you anymore without wanting to touch you and I'm so afraid I'm going to do it and you're just going to walk away."

He studied me for a moment. "I won't walk away."

"Somebody here has to know what the fuck to do." I was on the verge of really letting loose the tears and I didn't give a damn.

Adam took a step closer. "Nate, I won't walk away."

Chapter 19

August 25

And he hadn't. Not then, not in those terrible months following my assault, and not now. I just had to keep reminding myself of that. And despite all the resentment I felt over his new life, I wanted to make him proud of me.

Maybe that's why I was wearing the T-shirt.

Dress code violations had to be pretty blatant before anyone was called out. I think in part that's because the line between acceptable and unacceptable had become so fuzzy that it wasn't worth the trouble. Ms. Clark in Calculus hardly looked at us first period. Second period, Mr. Lambert, Music Theory, actually grinned and gave me a thumbs-up. Judging from his appearance, I guessed we were kindred spirits. Not that he looked gay. He just looked like some Woodstock throwback, someone who might march on Washington, DC, carrying a protest sign, or walk in a Gay Pride parade wearing a loin cloth just because he could. Ms. Waxley, third-period English—not so much.

She stopped me before I'd gotten both feet in the door. "Mr. . . . ?"

"Schaper," I supplied.

"Mr. Schaper," she said, "go to the restroom and turn that shirt inside out, please."

"Why?"

"Because it's inappropriate for school."

"What's inappropriate about it?"

She dipped her chin and looked at me with equal parts boredom and irritation. I didn't budge as other kids jostled past me. "Look," she continued, a hard edge in her voice now, "I don't have time to argue with you. I have a class to get started. You can either do this on your own, or I can write an office referral and you can take this up with an assistant principal."

"Let me know when you have that referral ready," I said and took a seat.

Mr. Wolf slumped back in his chair. He drew in a deep breath and let it out slowly, tapping a pencil lightly against the arm of his chair. He studied my shirt and my defiant posture. His eyes paused on the tattoo on my forearm. We had faced each other across his desk before, and I could tell from his hesitation that my history gave him reason to be more flexible with me than he might have been with another student.

"I saw some of your interviews this summer," he said finally.

I nodded.

"I thought you handled yourself well. Your mom is really proud of you."

Mom? "You've been talking to my mom?"

"I've kept in touch."

I shouldn't have been surprised, but I was. I knew that Mr. Wolf had given a statement to the police after my assault. And he'd been in the courtroom for the trial. Just how much had they talked?

"That took a lot of guts to get out there and tell your story like that."

I shrugged.

He sighed audibly and sat up. "We could have worked with this, Nate, if you hadn't gone and pissed off Ms. Waxley." He held up the referral. Waxley's anger showed in the little tears on the triplicate form where her pen and her anger had gotten the better of the thin paper. It was a written and visual complaint, I thought. Poetic. Kind of like a concrete poem, but where meaning was added not with shape but with indentations and gouges and tears. I was actually starting to admire Ms. Waxley.

"There's nothing inappropriate about my shirt," I said, coming back to the issue. "Saying there's something wrong with it is like saying there's something wrong with me."

"Maybe. Maybe not." He slipped a sheet of paper from a vertical file on his desk and cleared his throat. "The following are some of the highlights of the dress code," he read in a weary voice. " 'Any form of dress or hairstyle that the principal or his designee deems to be disruptive to the educational process, a health or safety hazard, or inappropriate in any way will not be allowed.' "

"So which is it? Is my shirt disrupting the educational process?" I raised my eyebrows. "Or maybe it's a safety hazard. It that it?"

"Why are you doing this?"

"Because if I don't, who will?"

"Don't make a big deal out of this, Nate. Turn it inside out. Go enjoy your senior year."

"And if I don't?"

"I cite you for defiance and you spend the day in ISS."

"Ooooooo." I knew I was walking a thin line now. In-school Suspension? On the first day of school? He'd thrown down the gauntlet, so to speak. I considered it for a moment, then yanked my shirt over my head, pulling it inside out as I did, and slipped it back on.

"Am I safe for school now?" I smiled sarcastically.

He laughed. "I don't know if this school is ever going to be safe as long as you're a student here." He studied me for a moment, then took another deep breath and let it out before continuing. "But maybe that's not such a bad thing." He stood up and leaned over his desk. "Let me see the arm."

He read the tattoo out loud. "Fear is temporary. Regret is forever." He mused over it for a moment, then asked, "When did you get it?"

"Friday. It was a birthday present from Adam."

"Keeping it clean? Keeping lotion on it?"

"Yeah."

"Good. Looks like it's healing nicely." He dropped back into his chair and sighed again, then tipped his chin toward the door. "Get back to class."

"You're not going to make me cover it up?"

"Just don't make a big deal out of it, okay?"

He stopped me again as I was leaving. "Nate."

I looked back.

"This isn't over, is it?"

I smiled and left. I'd come too far to back down now.

On Wednesday I found a brown lunch bag secured to my locker with piece of masking tape. I peeled it off.

"What's that?" Juliet asked.

I shrugged, stuck my hand in, and pulled out a soft, gray T-shirt. I shook out the shirt to read the slogan. I grinned as I turned it around for Juliet to see.

" 'I can't even think straight,' " she read. She looked up at me, her mouth agape. "Who put that there?"

I looked inside the bag and all around it for some clue, but there was none. "I have no idea."

I handed Juliet the shirt and let my backpack slip to the floor.

"Nooo." She laughed as I tugged my T-shirt over my head to a few wolf whistles and shoved it in my locker. Juliet stared. "Damn, Nate. That's better than a triple-shot latte for getting the old heart started in the morning."

I grinned and pulled the gray T-shirt over my head.

"You are a troublemaker, Nate Schaper."

By lunch I was back to wearing my T-shirt inside out. After that, more T-shirts started showing up anonymously on my doorstep, in the mail, again on my locker, under the wiper on my windshield. They said things like *Your gaydar should be going off right about now* and *Yes, I am* and *Ask. Tell.* One of my favorites was *I see gay people.* I wore a different shirt to school each day, except for the one that read *The rumor's right. But, unless I'm fucking you, it's none of your business.* I thought that might be pushing Mr. Wolf too far.

It became a game. I'd usually get through second period before someone (Waxley) sent me to Mr. Wolf's office to turn it inside out. I could have gone to the boys' room, but I liked seeing Mr. Wolf fight back the smiles. After the first week, Ms. Waxley didn't even bother with the office referral. I just checked in with her then headed to the administrators' area. The day we had a substitute third period, I got to wear my *HOMO* shirt (the O's were actually pink hearts) all the way through lunch before some overzealous teacher caught me in the hallway.

The next week, a few kids showed up at school with their shirts turned inside out.

September 12

Friday afternoon I leaned back in my chair, laptop balanced on my lap, and stared at the screen. It had been almost three weeks since Danial had helped me set up the blog, and still I had no idea what I wanted to write about. A pop-up in the lower right corner of the screen alerted me that Adam had just logged on to his computer. Things were better between us. I liked to think it was because things had changed in the apartment, that Adam had given his roommates (Justin) the what for. But the idea that he was just more careful stilled nagged at the back of my mind. I shook it off. I was eager to talk to him, to hear his voice, to see his face. I Skyped him and smiled as his image appeared on the screen. The apartment behind him was quiet.

He grinned back. "Let me have a look," he said.

I held the computer back so the camera could capture my shirt. I was wearing one that read *I kiss boys*. "You are a naughty boy." He laughed. "How long did you get to wear it right side out?"

I settled the computer back on my lap. "I managed to get through the front doors, barely." I grinned. "Do you remember Denton Townsley?"

"*Denton?* What kind of name is Denton?"

I laughed. "You know, he wrote that column for the newspaper last year, junior class president . . . Anyway, he had his shirt on inside out today. It was really cool."

"Is he—"

"Nah, I don't think so. He just likes protests."

"How many today?"

"I counted seven."

"Sounds like you've started a movement."

Hmph. Maybe I had. It was his next statement though that set my imagination on fire: "Why don't you make it official?"

Chapter 20

I'm Queer. Get Over It.
Give me a T!
By Nate Schaper on Sept. 14
Yep. That's me. And this is my blog.
Anyway, I have an idea. I'm calling it T-shirt Tuesdays. Here's the
deal (and it doesn't matter where you fall on the orientation spec-
trum or where you go to school): Show everyone you don't fear
queer by wearing your T-shirts inside out every Tuesday. And take
pictures, send them to me, and I'll post them (if I can figure out
how to do that—Danial?)!
Somebody riddle me this. Why do people find pro-gay slogans on
T-shirts so threatening? Like one of my T-shirts says, What does
my being gay have to do with you (them)?
To Adam: Thank you. You know why.

As an afterthought, I posted the link to our school's unofficial
Facebook page. Before I hit the door the next morning, I checked
for comments, not really expecting any. I was surprised to find five.

Comments:

GodChild223
Sep. 14, at 11:20 P.M.
  God hates queers, asshole.
HappyBoy
Sep. 14, at 11:58 P.M.
  T-shirt Tuesday. Brilliant. It's on! Keep writing, Nate. I'll be following. Do u Twitter? And GodChild223 . . . ur a jerk! God hates hate, ignoramus!!!
Xyz123
Sep. 15, at 12:01 A.M.
  I think ur rly brave, Nate. Im a soph at wphs. Not sure I can do T-shirt thing yet. I'll b watching u tho.
RedHairedBeauty
Sep. 15, at 12:16 A.M.
  You did it! I gotta get sum sleep but wanted to say you rock. C U in the AM. XOXOXO
Adam
Sep. 15, at 1:16 A.M.
  Congrats! Look forward to discussing your comments in person. LOL. Post a pic!!!
Check your e-mail. I'll send one.

    I glanced at the time in the corner of the screen. I needed to get going or I was going to be late for school and miss my opportunity to get picked off for my *Shhh . . . Nobody knows I'm gay* shirt, but I couldn't resist a quick check of my e-mail. I felt a stab right through my heart when I opened the file Adam sent. It was a picture of us at a summer concert on Market Street. I vaguely remembered Juliet snapping it. Adam was standing behind me, his arms wrapped around me. I remembered thinking it was too hot out for that much contact, but not wanting him to let go either. I touched his face on the screen and struggled to swallow past the tightness in my throat, then shut down my computer and hit the door.

Chapter 21

Danial stopped by a few days later to show me how to upload photos to my blog. He took one look at the photo of Adam with his arms around me and said, "Cute."

"Jealous?"

"Uh-huh," he said in an exaggerated way.

"Just show me how to upload photos."

He grinned and settled the cursor on a small square on the menu bar above the editing screen. "Insert picture. Browse photos. Click. Done."

"That was it?"

He laughed and shook his head, then scrolled down to the comments below. "Who's GodChild223?"

"I don't know. Some creeper." Danial moved his mouse to delete the comment, but I stopped him.

"Just leave it. Let him spew his hate. How did he find his way to my blog anyway?"

"Well, either he's a student—you did post the link to Facebook, so a student and a self-righteous nerd—or maybe he's set up a Google Alert for *queer* or *gay teen*. I figure he's either a serious closet case or some right-wing nut job out to save the world from the gays, i.e., a serious closet case."

He propped his chin on his fist for a moment and studied the screen, then rotated his head to look at me. "Are you sure you want to do this? You know, you're not the only one running a campaign out there."

I knew. I'd seen the T-shirts too—the innocuous *Adam and Eve, Not Adam and Steve* and *Gay marriage is a sin.* But there was also the scarier *Gay Rights? Under God's law the only "rights" gays have is the right to die (LEV. 20:13).* The kids wearing those shirts had been intercepted as well, but instead of turning their shirts inside out, they hid them beneath hoodies, which were too hot to wear this early in the school year, but which allowed them to unzip and flaunt their crap in my face when no adults were around.

"Today I actually saw a bumper sticker in the parking lot," he added. " 'AIDS: God's cure for homosexuality.' "

"They're just a bunch of ignorant assholes. They don't scare me."

"Maybe they should."

Adam agreed.

"What's the body count today?" he asked me after the second T-shirt Tuesday.

"Thirty-five for. Against, hard to say."

We were talking by phone. Adam's show was in its fourth week, but he'd had the day off, sleeping most of it.

"We had some new visitors on campus today." I told him about the protestors outside. A small group of adults—parents, or maybe just some local religious kooks—had marched in a ridiculously tight little circle just across the street from the school entrance. They'd carried sad little homophobic signs with stuff like *Keep Our Schools Moral* and *Gay* with a red circle around it and a slash through it—the international symbol for prohibition, or oppression, depending on how you looked at it. The signs looked like they'd been made with old tempera paint on the side of a cardboard box.

"I don't like this, Nate."

Neither did I.

Chapter 22

Last December 10
Coming out

It hadn't taken long for Adam and me to draw fire after coming out. By design, we hadn't been overly affectionate that first day—Adam's hand on my hip, a whisper, a slight decrease in personal space. Juliet had suggested we ease into it, nothing overt, give everyone a chance to get used to the idea of *us*.

Adam waited for me at my locker after the final bell. I unzipped my backpack, shoved my pre-calc book in, then zipped it back up and shouldered it. "Not so bad," he said as I slammed the locker door and snapped the lock back into place. I grinned back at him. "Not so bad."

He hooked a finger in my belt loop as we headed to the door. When I saw Andrew Cargill approaching, I pushed Adam's hand away, a reflex I instantly regretted. He looked at me, surprised until he saw Cargill plant himself in our path. I clenched my fist at my side.

"Don't," Adam said, grabbing my elbow.

Cargill looked down at Adam's hand on my arm and sneered. "I always knew you were a fucking faggot, Schaper." His eyes were dark and full of trouble.

I took a step toward him, my face burning. "What's your problem." It wasn't a question.

Andrew shoved me hard and I stumbled back into Adam. "My problem is you cocksuckers. You make me sick. Why don't you faggots go suck each other off in some other school?"

Adam tugged at my arm, but I stood firm, angry and ready for a fight if that's what he wanted. A crowd gathered around us, eager for some blood.

Andrew spat on the hallway floor. "If I catch you faggots alone, I'm gonna fuck you up. That's a promise."

"Anytime, anywhere, asshole," I said, my voice hard and angry. "But you better bring your A game because I'm not little Jake Winfield."

A slow smiled spread across his face. "You'd look real pretty with an extension cord wrapped around your neck." He shouldered past me. I turned, prepared to tear that asshole limb from fucking limb. Adam positioned himself in front of me, his hands firmly on my arms.

Only after Cargill disappeared around the corner did I allow Adam to pull me away.

It went downhill from there. The snickering behind my back, the insults, the taunts, the threats. Adam tried to keep me grounded. "We knew this would happen, Nate. Don't let them get to you."

But by the Thursday before Christmas break, I was just one *faggot* away from an out-of-school suspension. So when Butch Evans blocked my way outside English class and demanded to know if I charged for my services, I snapped. I tried to muscle my way past him, but he shoved me. I stumbled back a few steps. When I regained my balance, I came back at him with all the pent-up fury of a lifetime of putting up with everybody else's shit. He stumbled into several girls who were trying to pass, setting off a flurry of curses. He recovered and tackled me, letting fly a string of homophobic slurs. We struggled for advantage, but before either of us could get in even a glancing blow, Mr. Wolf and one of the male teachers pulled us apart.

*   *   *

I sat across from him as he completed the forms. A uniformed police officer stood in the doorway. Mr. Wolf rubbed his temple. "All right, Nate," he said. "Normally fighting carries a three-day out-of-school suspension."

"I didn't *do* anything."

He kept his head down when he spoke. "You shoved Butch Evans."

"He shoved me first."

"You provoked him."

"I provoked *him?* How? By being gay? How is that provoking someone?"

Mr. Wolf looked at me, exasperated. He popped the cap on a bottle of Tylenol and tossed two back, then snapped the cap back on and slid the bottle into his top desk drawer.

"There were no fists involved, no weapons. I'm going to reduce it to a one-day suspension." He leaned back in his chair and scratched his eyebrow. "Consider it an early Christmas gift. Go home. Maybe when school resumes after the break this will all have settled down. You're gonna have to give people time to get used to the idea."

"And while they're getting used to the idea"—I said this with as much dripping sarcasm as I could muster—"are we supposed to just sit on our hands and let them trample all over our rights?"

"What did you expect?"

What *did* I expect? "Can I ask you something?" I said.

He indicated that I should continue.

"Where do you stand on this?"

He turned back to his paperwork. "It doesn't matter where I stand."

That's what I thought.

He looked at me thoughtfully for a moment. "Does your mom know?"

"Know what?"

Instead of answering he dipped his chin in a you-know-what-I-mean way.

"No."

"I'm going to have to call her. She has to come in and sign these papers and take you home. And I'm going to have to tell her about the threats. I can hold off on that for a day so you can have the talk. Unless you want me to be the one to tell her."

Oh, hell no. I'd tell her myself. I was so done with trying to make people comfortable.

Chapter 23

It was the third T-shirt Tuesday, and the *God Hates Fags* mob was back. I was determined that I would not let them rattle me. Another school suspension would defeat the purpose of being both *out* and *there*.

I found Danial propped against my locker, his T-shirt inside out. I preferred to wait until I was asked. I had a repeat on today: *Let's get one thing straight. I'm not.*

"I see you've got your fan club out there again today," he said.

"What can I say? I'm a Three Stooges magnet. Don't you have a locker of your own somewhere?"

He laughed and moved out of my way. I'd been seeing a lot of Danial in the hallways in the past couple of weeks, and I found it absolutely amazing how his schedule just kept intersecting with mine. I opened my locker and looked at him while I grabbed for my books. "Are you developing some kind of man crush on me?"

He snorted. "Oh, you'd like that, wouldn't you?"

"Taken. Remember?"

He laughed again. "Just keeping you safe for the rest of the queers."

"Oh, what? Now you're my bodyguard?"

I was kidding, but he shrugged, and I realized that was exactly what he was doing. "You can't be serious," I said. But I could see that he was. I wasn't sure if I was irritated or relieved. Maybe both.

Homosexuality was one of those polarizing issues, like abortion or Obama. You were either for it, or you were against it. There didn't seem to be much middle ground. From what I'd heard here and there, my little T-shirt campaign—okay, to be blunt, the fact that my dick wanted to reach and touch someone else's—was apparently threatening The American Way of Life. I guess all that stuff about life, liberty, the pursuit of happiness, and personal freedom was just a feel-good piece of rhetoric—nice for political speeches but suspiciously MIA when the rubber met the road.

"I don't need a babysitter," I said, not fully believing that to be true.

"Oh, come on," he said, punching my arm playfully. "I don't want anything happening to my favorite substitute guitar teacher."

"I gave you one lesson."

He ignored the comment and continued. "Then I might get stuck with Juliet, and"—he cleared his throat—"I can't guarantee *her* safety."

Well, well, well. Danial did have a thing for Juliet. Before I could pursue that thought any further, he smirked and held out something for me—another T-shirt?

"Really, you shouldn't have," I said, taking it.

"Not me. It was here when I got here." He laughed.

I held it up and grinned when I saw the slogan—*Sexy Bitch.*

"You are *not* going to wear that shirt. I might be able to fight off the bad guys, but I'm not so sure about a flock of flamers."

I shoved my backpack in his hands and yanked off my repeat shirt, quickly replacing it with the new one.

"You got some balls for a girly man," he said, shaking his head.

"Thought you said I wasn't girly."

Instead of answering, his eyes flicked over my shoulder and he jutted his chin in that direction. "Looks like your boyfriend might have a little competition."

I shot a glance over my shoulder, just catching some kid's eye before he looked away and hurried down the hall. He wore a UT shirt and had shaggy blond hair jutting out wildly from beneath a

baseball cap. I didn't recognize him. He was tall but looked younger.
I guessed he was either a sophomore or a junior.

Danial raised his eyebrows. "Come on, sexy bitch," he said,
shoving my backpack into my chest. "Let's get a move on. This
babysitting's really gonna kill my perfect tardy record."

Morning Announcement:

"Students, I'm sure you noticed that we have some protestors
outside our building again this morning. Those protestors are not
on school property and are exercising their constitutional right to
free speech. However, we will continue our school day just as we always do. You are here to learn. I expect you to focus on your work.
Protests inside the school will not be tolerated."

As Juliet had once said to me, that train had left the station.

Chapter 24

I'm Queer. Get Over It.
Don't hate me because I'm gay!
By Nate Schaper on Sept. 30
<u>God hates fags?</u> Really?
Does it make sense that God would love haters but hate lovers?
To the village idiots outside my school today: Get the fucking log out of your own eyes before you try to remove the splinter from mine.
And for those of you who claim to be okay with gay as long as you don't have to watch. Don't watch. Please.
To my fellow queers...where are you? The statistics tell me you're out there. Everywhere I go now, I watch for you. But I don't see you. Or do I?

Comments:

GodChild223
Sept. 30, at 11:22 P.M.
   Your an abomation. A freek of nature.

HappyBoy

Sept. 30, at 11:54 P.M.

I'm sending you a pic of our first TT! So awesome. UR a celeb here. And GodChild223—learn to spell! What an idiot.

Xyz123

Oct. 1, at 12:01 A.M.

I'm here. I'm just not as brave as you, Nate. Maybe someday. Maybe soon. Is that your boyfriend you hang out with at school? Who's the guy in the picture?

RedHairedBeauty

Oct. 1, at 12:16 A.M.

Can I watch? Please??

Adam

Oct. 1, at 12:30 A.M.

OIC. Get your own guy, RedHairedBeauty, you trollop. LOL. Please add a caption to our pic, Nate. You're giving these peeps the wrong idea! And who are you hanging out with at school?

PakistaniPal

Oct. 1, at 8:30 A.M.

We need to talk about comment mod.

Chapter 25

"It's just Danial," I told Adam when he Skyped that afternoon. "He's my self-appointed bouncer now, I guess."

I hadn't talked to Adam for two days. I hadn't seen his face for almost a week. Just a series of missed opportunities as our schedules got crazier. Or maybe the distance was taking its toll. I couldn't help but feel like we were losing our grip on each other, like we were in some cosmic ocean, the waves and the undertow pulling us apart and no physical hold on each other to keep us together. It was always one thing or another. Either one of us had forgotten to charge his cell phone, or a series of blackouts in New York had knocked out communication, or we'd just gone to bed too tired to connect. We texted, we left messages, but it wasn't enough.

"Danial, huh," he said. He rubbed his eyes. "Everything okay at school?" he asked, but somehow it was like he wasn't really interested in the answer.

"Yeah. I'm a one-man freak show, but other than that, it's okay. Where are your roommates?"

"Don't know, don't care." He laughed a little. "Actually, they're still at work. The show closes next weekend. They're trying to tweak a few scenes for the big finale. But I couldn't deliver a line if you put a gun to my head today. Too tired. The director sent me home." He rubbed his eyes again.

"You need a haircut," I observed.

He grinned. "I just got one. Do you like it?"

Saturday morning dawned bright, cool, and sharp thanks to a mild Canadian front that had passed through during the night. When I got to the music store, a caffe latte in hand, Juliet was propping the door open to let the fall air in. That usually irritated her dad; with the fresh air came the flies. He insisted if she let the little pests in, she had to get rid of them. Watching Juliet smack flies with a swatter, squealing and screaming when she missed and they buzzed her, was always a good entertainment value. Lucky for her, but to my disappointment, the front had blown all the flies away.

Mr. Ratliff greeted me with the news that Jessica was home sick today and asked if I wanted to fill in for her piano lessons. Was he kidding? I checked the schedule. She had six. The lessons paid a lot better and the guy at one o'clock was working on the Charlie Brown theme song, "Linus and Lucy"—I could hear him practice through the walls each Saturday. The first lesson, though, was a new student at eleven thirty. That gave me an hour and a half to re-stock and do a few minor repairs. I did a quick visual inventory, then got to work refilling the displays from boxes in the storeroom while Juliet waited on the first customers. When the racks were full, I grabbed a guitar that needed restringing and laid it gently on the counter in the workroom. I removed the broken fifth string, wiped down the area under it, and then uncoiled the new string and slid the ball end down a few inches into the hole on the bridge. I replaced the bridge pin, then gently pulled the string up toward the headstock and wrapped it around and fed it through the tuning peg. I turned the peg to tighten it.

Juliet came in and sat on the wooden stool next to me and watched. "You get any better at this, my dad is gonna retire and then I'm gonna get stuck with all the books."

I smiled. "You're dad is having way too much fun to retire."

I turned the tuner on the sixth string to slacken it and then uncoiled it from the tuning peg.

"You could do this a lot faster if you didn't take off the good strings too, you know."

"The strings are worn. Replace one, replace them all, or the sound won't be right."

She continued to watch as I replaced the sixth, then abruptly got up. "So what's your hunky boyfriend doing tonight?" she asked, getting a soda from a small refrigerator.

I shrugged then recoiled when she pressed the cold can to the back of my neck. A bridge pin slipped from my hand.

"Oops," she said with a coy smile, then got down on all fours to scavenge for the pin. "Found it," she said, handing it to me.

"Why don't you go to a movie with Mike and me tonight?" she said as I took the pin and slipped it back into the hole.

"No."

She uncoiled the next string and handed it to me but still held on. "Come on, you never go anywhere anymore."

I tugged on the string and she let go.

I picked up the wire snips and clipped off the loose ends. "All done." I settled the guitar in my lap and plucked at the strings, listening to the sound and adjusting the tuning pegs, not listening to Juliet's commentary on my pathetic social life.

When Danial arrived about ten fifty for his eleven o'clock lesson, she was still trying to talk me into a threesome.

"Look," I said, placing the guitar on a rack behind the counter, "I am not going on a date with you and Mike." I took a sip of my latte, steaming again from a quick nuke in the microwave, and set it back on the counter so my hands would be free to tag the violin a customer had just dropped off.

Juliet threw her arms up in the air. "It's not a date. We're just going out to a movie—three friends. You haven't been out even once since Adam left. You cannot sit around in your room and mope every weekend until Thanksgiving."

I rolled my eyes.

"Tell him, Danial," she pleaded.

"You cannot sit around in your room and mope every weekend

until Thanksgiving," Danial parroted. He picked up my latte and took a sip. I looked at him like "Seriously?"

"You don't have anything I can catch, do you?" he said, hesitating before he took a second sip.

I rolled my eyes at him now.

Juliet huffed and glared at him. "Why don't you come too, Danial? Then Nate won't feel like the odd man out, which he wouldn't be anyway," she added, and I could tell from the look in her eyes that the idea of having Danial around was much more enticing than having me.

Danial grinned at me and folded his arms on the counter. "Won't your boyfriend get jealous if you go out on a date with another guy?"

"We are *not* going out on a date."

He laughed. "What time is the movie? I don't get off until seven, so I'll have to meet you there."

Juliet gave an excited little clap.

Terrific.

While Danial had his lesson, I worked the front counter. Nice days always meant a steady stream of customers needing repairs, lesson information, instrument rental, and odds and ends like flip books and lyres for band instruments. It kept me busy. Maybe a movie wasn't such a bad idea.

I would have killed for a sip of my latte, but Danial had taken it with him. I found myself wondering where he worked. He didn't talk about himself a lot, and I didn't ask a lot of questions. When he emerged from the lesson room with Gary half an hour later, I gave him a tipping motion with my hand to indicate I wanted my drink back. He crossed the room to the counter, shaking the cup and grinning. "Sorry, man. Empty."

"Bring your own next time, moocher."

"Excuse me," a woman said, stepping up to the counter. "I'm Ms. Martindale. My son, Ryan, has an eleven thirty piano lesson with Jessica."

Ryan looked to be about ten. I reached out my hand to shake his. "Hi," I said, "I'm Nate Schaper. Jessica will be your regular teacher, but she's out today, so I'll be giving you your lesson." Then

I reached to shake Ms. Martindale's hand. But she didn't put it out. She was looking at my shirt.

Juliet's dad had been cool about me proclaiming my gayness on my chest every day. I think he was even a little amused by it and understood my need to be unmistakably O-U-T. But customers' reactions had been mixed. Those who were bothered by it, though, had the good manners to hold their tongues. At least, so far they had.

I dropped my hand and looked to Ryan instead. "Are you ready to go, Ryan?"

Ms. Martindale put her hand on her son's shoulder as if to hold him in place. "Is Mr. Ratliff in his office?"

I glanced through the plate-glass window of the small office off to the side of the counter "Um, yeah, he is, but he's on the phone right now. Is there a problem?" Of course, by then, I knew there was a problem. The disgust on her face couldn't have been plainer.

Danial leaned up against the end of the counter next to me.

"Look," she said, giving Danial an even more disgusted look, "I'm sure you're a very good piano teacher, but to be perfectly honest, I don't want my son alone in a room with you."

There it was. Homophobia at its finest.

Mr. Ratliff had stepped out of his office. He opened his mouth to speak, then seemed to think better of it.

"He's a little young for me," I said, fighting the sarcasm in my voice and losing, "but if it makes you feel better, we can leave the door open."

She ignored me and turned to Mr. Ratliff. "We'll just catch Jessica next week."

Mr. Ratliff studied her for a moment, then approached the counter. He picked up a pen and marked a line through something in the appointment book. When he looked back up, I could see flint in his eyes. "I don't think she has any openings."

She huffed and dragged Ryan out with her, casting a scathing look at Danial and me as she went.

"Mr. Ratliff, you really didn't need to do that."

He smiled. "You're family now, Nate." He clapped me on the shoulder and went back to his office.

"Well, that was humiliating," I said to no one in particular.

"What happened?" Juliet said. She'd been straightening the piano room and had missed the exchange.

"You want me to beat her up?" Danial joked.

"Beat who up?" Juliet asked.

"She thinks you're my boyfriend, you know," I said.

"Lucky you." He winked at Juliet and picked up his guitar case. "Wear something pretty for me tonight, sweetheart," he stage-whispered to me.

Juliet giggled.

"Get the hell out of here," I said harshly, but he knew I didn't mean it.

Juliet watched Danial leave, and sighed dreamily. "Too bad he's not gay. You two would make a cute couple."

I looked at her.

"What the hell am I saying," she said, grabbing fistfuls of her red hair. "Don't tell Adam I said that."

I helped Mr. Ratliff close up shop at five o'clock then ran home for a quick shower. The phone rang just as I opened the front door. I didn't see Mom or Grandma around. I grabbed the phone on the fourth ring, just before it went to the answering machine. "Hello," I said, a little breathless.

There was a pause, and then, "Nate?"

I didn't recognize the voice. "Yeah. This is Nate. Who's this?"

The caller cleared his throat. "Nate, this is Mr. Wolf."

When the assistant principal is calling your house on a Saturday afternoon, it can't be good. I mentally ticked off the events of the week: I hadn't been in any fights, I hadn't insulted any teachers that I knew of, no major school rules broken with the exception of the daily dress-code violation that I always rectified in his office. Nothing.

I asked him if there was anything wrong.

"No. But, uh, actually I'm glad you answered the phone. Uh, I guess I'll just be straight with you." He cleared his throat again. "Nate, I'd like to ask your mom out on a date. Would that be okay with you?"

Okay, now this was just too weird for me. Mr. Wolf? And my

mom? A date? Really? I didn't even know they knew each other beyond the couple of conversations he'd hinted at earlier. I wasn't sure exactly how I felt about them dating. But who was I to tell anyone who they could or couldn't be interested in. When I hesitated, he said, "If you're not—"

"No. I mean, sure. I think she'd like that."

"You do?"

He sounded so relieved I almost laughed. Mom was reading on the back deck with Grandma. When I told her Mr. Wolf was on the phone, she blushed. Uh-huh. She took the phone from me, and Grandma grabbed my arm, directing me back into the house. At first I thought she just wanted to give Mom some privacy, but then she handed me Mom's laptop.

"It's got one of those bugs," she said, shrugging and feigning complete innocence.

Bugs? Oh boy.

I sat the computer on the counter and booted it up. Before I could execute any other commands or open any programs, a pop-up appeared on the screen, followed by another and another. Each pop-up featured a couple of guys getting it on . . . on my mom's computer. Oh shit.

It had been a shock to Mom when I came out to her last December, but Grandma had embraced my identity. She even blackmailed me into showing her how to surf the Internet so that she could "understand" what being gay meant. I figured by now she must understand better than I did.

And now we had a problem. "I'll take care of it, Grandma."

She patted my arm. "Nice young men, though, don't you think?"

Nice, yeah.

I flopped on my stomach on Juliet's bed while she fiddled with her makeup in her bathroom. I'd texted Adam earlier this afternoon to let him know about my "date," but he'd had a matinee performance and had only just now responded: *LOL. Have fun!!*

I don't know, but that really wasn't what I was after. Okay, he trusted me. Good. Great. But couldn't he be just a little bit jealous?

I texted back: *Wut r u doin tonite?*

I wasn't sure which I dreaded more—hearing that he was just hanging out at the apartment with his roomies or out partying with his new look. Both left me uneasy and feeling like an outsider, like a little high school kid.

No show tonite. Museum party with some of the guys. Tell Danial to keep his hands off u! Srsly.

About time.

"Nate?"

"Hm?" I said, thumbing out another text to Adam.

"Nate? Hello?"

I looked up.

"What about this one?"

Juliet was standing at her closet door now, modeling a pretty cool Bob Marley T-shirt, thin, no bra underneath.

I cleared my throat dramatically. "Uh, jeez, Juliet. You might want to leave a little something to the imagination."

She smirked and yanked the shirt over her head and flung it at me. Okay. Juliet, topless.

The shirt landed on my shoulder. I pulled it off and turned it right side out. "Nice shirt. Can I have it?"

She dipped her chin and gave me one of her I-want-you-you-want-me looks. "Come on, Nate, doesn't this turn you on just a little bit."

I studied her half-naked self. Nice, if you liked that sort of thing, but I thought a hard, slightly muscled chest was much, much, much sexier. I smiled a little thinking just how much sexier. She smiled back and shifted her weight to her other hip, waiting, I guess, for me to get aroused. "Well?" she said.

"Well, what?" I looked back down at my phone.

"Oh forget it, asshole." She turned back to her closet.

I snickered and thumbed out another text: *Im that gay guy that girls get naked in front of now LOL.*

He texted back.

"Adam says to tell you to quit hitting on homosexuals or you will end up a bitter, frustrated, childless old maid with a closet full of battery-operated dildos, a lifetime subscription to *Playgirl*, and bad skin."

"He did not."

I held the phone out to her. She had on a bra now and was pulling another shirt over her head, this one a low-cut V-neck that showed off her cleavage but at least kept the girls tamed. She took the phone and read the text.

I grinned and she flung the phone at me.

Chapter 26

Tinseltown was always packed on date nights. I feared we'd be sitting in the neck-spasm section up front, but a party of three with an empty seat next to them got up and moved a few rows down. Danial loped up the steps and nabbed the seats for us by stepping into the row. Danial was a pretty hunky guy, and Juliet had to squeeze past him to her seat. I was thinking it would have been easier if he'd just sat down or taken the end seat or stepped into the aisle, but he didn't. Juliet took the next-to-last seat. Then Danial did sit down. Mike had to climb over both him and Juliet to get to the last seat. "Really?" I mumbled as I climbed over his long legs and took the seat next to him.

"What?" he mouthed, feigning innocence.

I handed him the bag of popcorn we were sharing and checked my text messages. I'd felt the vibration in my pocket as we were climbing the steps. Danial craned his neck over the armrest.

"Do you mind?" I said, turning the screen away from him.

"Actually, I do. I believe you're *my* date tonight, cupcake."

"In your dreams."

He laughed. "Uh, didn't you see the PSA? The one that said 'Please turn off your cell phones in the theater'?"

"The movie hasn't started yet," I said, thumbing in a reply.

He leaned forward to see what Juliet and Mike were doing. I cast a sideways glance at them too. Mike was whispering something to her. His hand fondled the pendant at her throat and looked like it would like to be fondling something else. I turned back to Danial. "Would you like to change places with me, *cupcake?*"

"Pass," he said, flopping back in his seat and bracing a foot against the seat in front of him.

My cell phone vibrated again.

"Oh my God." Danial groaned.

I smiled at the small screen. "Adam said to tell you to keep your hands off of me."

"Give me that." He grabbed the phone, and I let him have it. He thumbed in a long reply and hit Send, then handed the phone back to me.

"What did you do?"

He shrugged and stuffed some popcorn in his mouth.

I checked the outbox. *This sexy bitch is mine tonite. I plan 2 thro him up against the nearest wall after the movie and have my way with him. Danial*

Shit. The phone buzzed again. *Nate?*

I texted back an assurance that Danial was kidding, then elbowed him hard across the armrest.

"Ouch."

Juliet leaned over me. "Would you two children knock it off? People are starting to look." The middle-aged couple in front of us turned around. Danial tossed his arm over my shoulder and squeezed. The woman gave us a disgusted look, then whispered something to her husband before turning back to face front.

I gave Danial a withering look, and he took his arm back.

The movie was some apocalyptic flick. Between texts and Danial's spying, I had trouble keeping track of the plot. I kept my phone low and close to me to keep the screen light from bothering anyone. Adam's texts were getting increasingly amorous. *Someone's getting drunk . . . and horny,* I thought. Was he at the museum party already? I'd never seen Adam drink before aside from a few covert sips of a margarita or a wine cooler. Or was he high? Hadn't seen that either. Danial was reading each text over the armrest, so I decided to hold my questions until another time. I'd given up trying to hide the screen. Damn, he was nosy.

I miss u so damn much. I want to hold u, touch u. I want to run my tongue all over ur body, feel u inside me.

I blushed at that one. Danial cleared his throat and shivered violently.

I rolled my eyes.

I luv u, baby.

I luv u too.

"Oh, God." Danial groaned. "I hope they blow up something soon cause all this sweetness and love is making my teeth hurt."

He took one more look over me at Juliet, then slunk down in his seat.

I grinned and threw my arm over his shoulder.

He leaned into me and pressed his mouth close to my ear and said in a low breathy voice, "I want to feel you inside me." Then he snorted, causing Ma and Pa Jones in front of us to turn around again. Danial gave them a little finger wave. The Missus huffed and turned back to the movie.

I sneered at Danial and took my arm back.

A man sitting behind us leaned forward. "You boys need to take that homo crap some other place. We don't want to see you queers touching each other while we're watching a movie. There are kids in this theater."

My face flushed in anger, and I started to my feet, but Danial placed a firm hand on my arm and shook his head. I reluctantly settled down. He calmly turned to the man behind us. "Keep your eyes on the movie, asshole, and off my boyfriend." Then he put his arm around me again and muttered, "And it's staying here for the rest of the movie even if I get a fucking cramp in my shoulder."

The guy behind us didn't say another word. Danial shifted uncomfortably a couple of times, but he refused to put his arm down even after I whispered he'd made his point. I wasn't complaining though. I kinda liked his arm around me.

"What the hell is going on?" Juliet asked.

"Nothing," I told her, then smiled so she'd get that worried look off her face. Mike whispered something to her and she turned back to him.

Later in the movie, some redneck stumbled on his way back up the stairs, splashing some of his soda on Danial. It didn't look like an accident.

When the movie was over, Danial finally retrieved his arm and rubbed his shoulder, presumably to get his circulation going again. I laughed. "Serves you right." The jerk behind us left before the credits ran. The couple in front of us was quick to exit as well.

We took a few minutes to stretch before following Juliet and Mike down the steps. About halfway down someone stepped on my heel. "Move, faggot." I lurched forward and grabbed the handrail for balance.

But Danial had already whipped around and grabbed the guy by the collar, forcing him to back up several steps. I didn't hear what he said, but when he released him, the guy stumbled backward and landed on his ass. Danial's face was dark when he turned back and grabbed my arm. "Come on. Let's go."

The night was cool. We walked for a bit on Market Street, had a Starbucks, then sat on a park bench on the green and people watched. I hadn't heard from Adam in an hour or so, even though I'd texted several more times. That bugged me. I didn't like not knowing what he was doing, and I didn't like not liking not knowing. Finally, annoyed, Danial had taken my phone and stuck it in his pocket.

The party had gone out of me. Adam. The jerk in the theater. I'd had enough. "I'm gonna head home," I said. "Mike, you'll take Jules?"

I couldn't help notice that Juliet looked a little disappointed.

Danial left with me. We sauntered back toward the movie theater and our cars, not talking much. "I'm on the second floor of the garage," I said when we got there.

"I'm out in the lot, so I guess I'll see you Monday," he said, clapping me on the back.

I gave him a fist bump. "Yeah. Oh, hey, can you clean up a

virus? My, uh, grandmother has picked up something on my mom's computer. It's causing all these pop-ups."

"Sure. Bring it over tomorrow afternoon. I'll text you directions a little later."

I headed to the garage, then up a flight of stairs. Other than a young couple getting into their SUV, the second floor was empty. I hit the unlock button on my keypad and honed in on the flashing taillights.

I wanted to try Adam again. I reached for my phone; it wasn't there. "Shit." Maybe if I hurried I could still catch Danial. I was so wrapped up in my thoughts that the sound of slapping feet on concrete hadn't registered in my brain until I turned. I stumbled backward into the trunk of my car as something *whooshed* mere inches from my face. "You didn't think I was just going to let that go, did you?" a dark figure spat. He reared back again, and I considered the possibility that this was how I was going to die—alone, in a parking garage. This time the damage might not be fixable. I braced myself for the blow. Then a shout—"Hey!"—and Danial was there. A ninja kick sent the guy flying. He smacked the ground, rolled, and fled.

Danial hauled me up by the arm. "Let's get out of here. Come on. Go. Go." He had the driver's side door open and shoved me in and over the console, then got behind the wheel. "Keys!" Numbly, I handed them over. "Goddamn motherfucker. He had a fucking tire iron."

He cranked the engine and slammed the car in reverse, squealing the tires.

"You okay?"

I didn't answer. Because, no, I wasn't okay. I was most definitely *not* okay.

Danial looked over at me, concern in his eyes. He reached into his pocket and handed me my cell phone. "I forgot about your phone," he said. "Right after you walked off, you got a call."

I took the phone and shoved it in my pocket.

"Shit. I should have seen this coming," he said. "It was that jerk from the theater."

He pulled up alongside his car. "Can you drive?"

I nodded.

"I'll follow you home. You sure you're okay?" he asked again, but all I heard was the *umph* Adam had exhaled when Cargill kicked him in the gut.

Chapter 27

Last New Year's Eve
The party's over

Adam, doubled over, his face contorted in pain, blood dribbling from a busted lip. The big dirty-looking one gripped him in a stranglehold and forced him upright again. "NO!" I sprang forward. Cargill kicked him in the groin an instant before my shoulder connected with his chest, and Adam dropped to his knees.

We went down, rolled, and immediately scrambled to regain our footing. A pain shot through my shoulder. I hesitated just a fraction of a second, but it was enough to give Cargill the advantage. He was on his feet and kicked me in the head. I went down again. I squinted, struggling to focus and fighting back the blackness closing in around the edges of my vision. I got to my knees, but I was too dizzy and nauseated to get to my feet.

"Nate, get out of here," Adam called hoarsely to me.

"This little faggot's not going anywhere. You like it on your knees, don't you, Schaper?" Cargill nudged me with the toe of his shoe.

"Leave him alone," Adam begged. Then I heard him vomit.

The big kid forced Adam back to his feet but held him fast. "Looks like your little homo friend wants to play in somebody else's sandbox," he sneered.

Adam twisted and snarled, but he was no match for the Neanderthal.

I tried again to get a foot underneath me, but just as the sole of my shoe met the flagstone, Cargill grabbed a fistful of my hair and dragged me backward. I yelped out at the sudden pain.

I was off balance, unable to brace myself. I sank my nails into his hand, and he released my hair, spewing a string of curses. I fell backward and rolled to my stomach, but before I could get to my knees another blinding pain exploded from the back of my head. I heard a sickening crack, and everything went fuzzy.

I was facedown on the flagstone when Cargill yanked my hips up.

Chapter 28

I undressed in the dark and climbed under the sheets, still shaking, my cell phone clutched in my hand. I speed-dialed Adam's number, but all I got was some bullshit cell-customer-you-are-trying-to-reach-is-unavailable message. There was a missed call and a voice mail. I didn't recognize the number, but I most definitely recognized the voice.

"Hey, baby! Sorry I missed you. It's crazy here." In the background, horns honked and voices stumbled through some drunken version of Adam Lambert's tribute to gay sex: *You thought an angel swept you off your feet.* Adam shushed them, but no one shushed. "Another blackout. Can you believe it? The cell towers are down too. I'm borrowing a friend's landline." Laughter in the background. Someone calling Adam's name—*Come on, sing with us.* "They canceled the museum party, so we've just been hanging out on the stoop, having drinks." He giggled and said in a low voice, "Quit it." Then, "I'll call again as soon as we get power back. Gotta go. Love you."

I pressed the End button and flung the phone across the room.

My cell rang early the next morning—a miracle in itself, in that the battery hadn't popped out when it hit the wall night before. It was pathetic the way I sprang out of bed and groped around on the floor for it, like a junky needing a fix. I think I could have forgiven anything that morning just to hear his voice. I caught the call on the fourth ring, but it wasn't his voice on the other end.

"Hey, man. You okay?" Danial said.

Okay? That was an interesting word. Were all my body parts still attached? Yes. Was I bleeding from any orifice? No. Were there any empty pill bottles lying around? No. But okay? "Yeah. I'm fine."

"Good. Bring your mom's computer over this afternoon, and I'll take a look."

"Sure."

I jotted down directions, then ended the call and rolled over onto my back. I ran my thumb across the keys on my phone, my eyes fixed to the ceiling. After a moment, I brought the phone to my face and located the two, placed my thumb on it, then dropped my arm back to my side. *Don't think about it; just do it. Don't think about it.* I pressed the two and counted to three, then brought the phone to my ear. The towers were back up, and the phone rang one, two, three times. I was just about to hang up when Adam answered.

"Hey, you," he croaked, the words barely distinguishable.

"Hey. You sound terrible."

"I feel worse." He groaned. "God, I think I'm going to throw up. Hold on."

I held on. A few minutes later he was back. "I'm dying."

"That must have been some party on the stoop last night."

"Mmm. You got my message. Good." His voice was soft, breathy. "How was your date?"

My date. Wow. That rolled off his tongue way too easily, I thought. "It was okay."

He didn't respond.

"Adam?"

"Hmph."

"I really need to talk to you."

"Mmm. I'm listening."

No, he wasn't. I held the phone to my forehead. *Shit.*

"Adam?" It was quiet on the other end, and I knew there'd be no talking to him now.

"Go back to sleep. I'll call you later."

He disconnected with neither an acknowledgment nor a good-bye.

Chapter 29

"All right, let's see what you've got," Danial said, lifting the screen and pressing the power button. I stared at the screen as it booted up, but I could feel Danial watching me. It was uncomfortable.

"Where do you work?" I asked to divert his attention from the train wreck next to him.

"Geek Squad."

Best Buy. Figured.

I knew what was coming, but the pop-ups took Danial totally by surprise.

"Whoa," he said when the first one hit the screen. He had only a moment to take in the boy-on-boy action before a second pop-up overlaid it, then a third, then a fourth.

I grinned. I don't know how he did it, but things always seemed just a little less grim when Danial was around. He was like Lil Wayne, but without the dreads or the body art or the prison record. "Uh, as you can see, we have a problem."

"What the hell have you been looking at on this computer, Natey?"

"Not me, Danial-son. My grandmother."

He looked at me, his mouth agape. I watched the pop-ups. "She wanted to know what gay men did." I shrugged and laughed a little. "I guess she knows now. But, uh, TMI for my mom, if you know what I mean."

"Uh, yeah." He tapped a few keys to stop the pop-ups, then started closing them one at a time. With just a few left open, he stopped and peered more closely at the remaining pictures. "So, uh, does this stuff turn you on?"

I grinned sheepishly. "Yeah. Doesn't it turn you on?"

"Uh, not really." He gave me a sideways glance. "So . . . do you and your boyfriend do that?"

"My boyfriend has a name, you know. And, yeah, we do that." I pointed to the other pictures. "And that, and that."

He cleared his throat and shook his head violently. "Now that is TMI!"

"You asked."

He closed the rest of the pop-ups. "So what is it about guys that turns you on?"

"You're kidding right?"

He raised his eyebrows. "Not kidding. Okay, your boy—I mean, Adam. What is it about him that makes you all gooey inside?"

Gooey? I guess that was a pretty apt word. "You really want to know?"

Danial gestured that he did.

"It's a lot of little things. The way he feels when I hold him—all hard and muscled. But not too muscled, you know. Just . . . solid. I like the way his stubble scratches me when we kiss. The way he can't hide it when he's turned on."

Danial winced.

I laughed. "You did ask. What I don't get is what you see in girls. They're so . . . squishy."

"Yes, they are." He grinned, shaking his head. He inserted a flash drive in a USB port and looked at me sideways. "So, are you one of those guys who thinks he should have been born a girl?"

"What? No, I don't want to be a girl." I rolled my eyes. "Look, idiot, the only difference between you and me is what makes our dicks hard. That, and I'm a better guitar player."

"I have a better tan."

I laughed. "Yeah, you do. It's kinda sexy."

"Down, boy." He palmed the back of his neck and seemed like he wanted to say something else, but then dropped it. "Let's see if we can clean this up for Grandma."

I watched him work for a while, then let my eyes wander around his room. Stuck in the plastic outer sleeve on a one-inch binder lying on the floor was a strip of four black-and-white photos, the kind that you get in those booths in the mall or at Chuck E. Cheese's. I picked up the binder. I recognized Danial, but not the little kid. "You have a little brother?" I asked.

He glanced at the photos. "Nope. That's me. I was nine, I think. That's my big brother. He was ten years older than me."

Was? He looked so much like Danial. "Where is he?"

Danial took a deep breath and let it out slowly, keeping his eyes on the computer screen. "Dead."

He removed the flash drive and changed the subject. "Done. Tell your grandmother either ixnay on the Internet porn or she's going to need some better security on this thing."

"I'll tell her you said that."

"So, how's the blog coming along?"

"Pretty good if it weren't for all the whack jobs out there informing me with each post that I'm going to burn in hell."

"Oh, yeah?" He pulled up the blog and had me log in. "Wow!" he said, looking at the stats. "You've had some traffic, here. Pretty impressive."

He scrolled through some of the blog entries and comments as if he were reading them for the first time, which I knew he wasn't. "It sure didn't take long for the self-appointed moral police to set up camp, did it? My, my, my. I'd love to be standing at the pearly gates when these ambassadors of love try to check in. 'He that loveth not, knoweth not God.' "

I studied Danial's face as he read. He was something of an enigma to me. I had other guy friends, but we didn't hang out like this together. Being gay seemed to preclude close male friendships, even with guys who claimed to be perfectly okay with gay. There always seemed to be an emotional distance with other guys that I didn't feel so much with Danial. I didn't know if that was because guys in general were emotional wastelands or because subconsciously they feared I might want more than just friendship. Not that Danial and I were *close* close. But we were getting close. He didn't seem at all threatened by or awkward around me. I respected him for that.

"Did you read this?" he said, taping the screen with his finger. It was another comment by Xyz123 posted just last night in response to a post I'd titled "That's Disgusting!"

Thanks for another great blog, Nate! I agree totally!! I don't understand why people would think that it's disgusting when cute boys make out, but not when Donald Trump does the dirty with a girl 30 years younger than him. I mean, have you seen that hair? What's up with that? Anyway, all that should matter is that the two people kissing (or whatever ☺) are attracted to each other. Keep writing. Maybe someday I'll have the courage to come out too. Did you know October 11 is National Coming Out Day? BTW, I really liked the Sexy Bitch T. I hope you'll wear it again.

"Xyz123 has posted a comment to every blog you've written. Did you notice that?"

"Yeah. Apparently he's a sophomore at school."

"Do you have any idea who he is?"

"Uh-uh. But I really feel for him. He seems afraid of what his parents will do if they find out he's gay."

Danial got up suddenly and cracked the window, then fished a joint and a lighter out of his desk drawer. He leaned against the windowsill, lit the joint, then drew in a deep breath.

My mouth hung open for a moment.

"What?" he said, his voice tight as he held the smoke in his lungs.

"Nothing. I just didn't know you smoked." He offered it to me but I passed. Danial didn't seem the type to smoke pot. I didn't really know what that type was, but, well, I was just surprised. He seemed tense all of a sudden too.

He shrugged and sat back down at the computer. "Let's put some controls on here so you can screen comments before they post. Free speech is one thing, but you don't need to give these nut jobs a platform. Just delete the crap that's likely to scare small children and queer teenagers. Okay?"

He handed me the joint. I held it pinched between my thumb and forefinger and watched him work. "What do you think about National Coming Out Day?" I asked.

"What do you mean what do I think?"

"Maybe we could do something?"

He took the joint from me and took another deep drag. "We?"

"Me. The blog is great and all, but it still feels so closeted. I want to do something bigger, something more out there, something that says we're here, we're just like you, we don't want to eat your children. You know what I mean?"

"You do that every day, Natey, with your T-shirt protest."

"It's not the same. Seeing *homo* on a T-shirt is way different than seeing two live homos touching, God forbid. And you know it. When Adam was here, we'd hold hands, dance at parties, you know, stuff that all the other kids were doing. But it was all pretty covert. I mean, it was almost Christmas by the time we came out. And then . . ." I paused and shook my head a little to clear the *then*. "It just wasn't enough. The year was over and I felt like we hadn't really claimed a place. And now it's a new year and nothing's really changed."

Danial had never asked me about the details of my assault. I wondered, not for the first time, if he knew. Hell, everybody knew. You didn't get your face plastered all over CNN and have people not know. But he didn't ask, and I didn't tell.

"So now, I'm gay, I'm out, but my boyfriend is in New York, so I can't really act gay. Does that make any sense?"

He laughed. "So, you want me to pretend to be your boyfriend for a while?"

I stared at him, then smiled.

"I was kidding."

"No, no, it's brilliant. I don't mean pretending to be my boyfriend. You wouldn't have to go that far. But—okay, just think about this for a minute—be my date to the homecoming dance. It's October eleventh, the same day as National Coming Out Day."

He looked at me like I was cracked in the head.

"Come on. It's poetic, man," I pleaded.

"Your date?"

"You were my date for the movie last night."

"Good thing for you."

That stopped me in my tracks, but he didn't seem to notice. I waited while he thought it over. This wasn't like hanging out at the movies together. What I was asking was for him to do just the opposite of what I was doing—pretend to be something he wasn't so I could be something I was.

"Would I have to slow dance with you?"

"Uh, yeah. That would kinda be the point."

Danial just looked at me. I was working on my next argument in my head when he said, "Okay."

"What?" His answer came so quickly, it derailed me for a moment. "I thought I just heard you say okay."

He shrugged.

"Really?"

He got up and flicked an ash out the window, then leaned against the sill and grinned back at me. "Which one of us is wearing a dress?"

"I think you're missing the point about boys liking boys."

"I do have to draw the line at squishage. There has to be some mandatory straight-guy dick separation."

"But I'm not a straight guy." I winked and then felt like I was flirting, and maybe I was. I sat up straighter and cleared my throat. "You're either all in or you're all out. It won't work any other way."

"You're just trying to piss people off now, aren't you?"

"So you'll do it?"

"You are so going to owe me."

Adam was still in bed when I called later that afternoon. I had to beg him to get up and boot up his computer. I felt bad about that, but I needed to see his face.

"Wow. You look wasted," I said.

He propped his chin on his hand and smiled. "I feel wasted. So, you and Danial at the homecoming dance. That'll raise some eyebrows." He yawned.

Bored, Adam?

"You okay with that?"

"Yeah. Why wouldn't I be?"

That was the million-dollar question. Me, on a date with another guy. *Why wouldn't you be okay with that, Adam?* But I didn't want to fight with him, so I left the question unanswered.

"It'll be fun," he said lazily. "I'm glad you're getting out more. And Danial seems like a great guy." He yawned again. "Why don't you get Mike and Warren and some of the other kids to mix it up some too? They're good actors. They'd do anything for you. And the collective impact—"

"What's that on your neck?"

Adam touched his fingers to the bandage. "Ah shit. I should have taken this off last night." He lifted an edge of the tape and ripped it off.

"You got a tattoo," I said, and not in a wow-you-got-a-tattoo kind of way, but more in a you've-got-to-be-kidding-me kind of way.

He smiled sheepishly. "It seemed like a good idea at the time."

"You got a tattoo," I said again, looking more closely at the screen. The skin on his neck was red. Inked in script, one word: *Wicked.*

"It's not even one of the plays we're doing, but we all thought it would be cool."

"We?"

He hesitated, seeming to catch my innuendo and not knowing quite what to do with it. "Yeah. About six of us. Alec, Jeremy . . ."

"And?"

"I don't know. I don't even remember who all—"

"Was Justin there?"

He got a pissed-off look on his face. "Yes, we were all there."

"You and Justin have matching tattoos. On your fucking necks."

Adam folded his arms on the desk, then looked away from the screen for a moment. A muscle in his jaw twitched. He looked back. "It's no big deal, Nate. It's just a tattoo."

"Just a tattoo." I scoffed. "Why didn't you tell me?"

"I haven't even talked to you. I just did it yesterday afternoon, just before the power went out. I didn't know I had to check in with you over every god*damn* thing I do."

He did *not* just say that.

"Nate, shit," he said, ramming his fingers into his hair and gripping his head. "I didn't mean that."

"You don't have to check in with me, Adam. You can do any *fucking* thing you want."

He looked directly at the webcam. "Why are you acting like this?"

"Are you sleeping with him?"

"I can't believe you asked that! No, I'm not sleeping with him."

"Have you kissed him?"

He scrubbed his face.

"Simple question, Adam. Has any part of your lips touched any part of his?"

"He kissed me. Okay? Is that what you want to hear? He. Kissed. Me. I didn't ask for it. I didn't want it. It was nothing."

"How many times?"

"Don't do this, Nate."

"How. Many. *Times?*"

"A couple, I don't know."

I scoffed. Unbelievable. Un-*fucking*-believable. "So why did you tell me? If it was nothing, why didn't you just lie to me about it? Why not just leave it unsaid? I never would have known."

"I've never lied to you, and I'm not going to start now."

"You want to know what I think? I think you wanted me to know."

Now he scoffed. "You always want to believe the worst of me, Nate. Why is that? I'm tired of defending myself to you. And I'm just tired." He scrubbed his face again while I sat mute, silenced by the resentment in his voice. "I can't talk to you right now," he said after a moment. "I'm gonna hang up before one of us says something we're going to regret."

Too late for that, I thought.

Chapter 30

I read somewhere that people are mirrors, and that we only really know ourselves when we see ourselves in someone else's eyes. What did we know now? Adam hadn't called back. Not Sunday night. Not Monday. Not Tuesday. No text. No voice mail. No apology. Nothing. I hadn't called either. It wasn't the first time we'd gone days without communicating. It wasn't the first time we'd argued. But I sensed a shift in our relationship this time that hadn't been there before. I didn't even know who to blame.

Wednesday morning seven protestors lined up across the street from the school, each with their variations on the *God Hates Fags* signs we were growing accustomed to, along with a few new ones: *We pay your salaries. Keep our schools pure.* And *Keep homosexuality out of our schools.* To me, the new signs were even more insidious; it's one thing to have a bunch of crazies protesting outside the school, and quite another to have parents gnashing their teeth about the moral safety of their children.

Until this week, they'd stuck to Tuesday protests. Their presence today could mean only one thing. So it was no big surprise when the office request came second period.

I held back outside Mr. Thornton's office. I'd been here before. Last December. The week Adam and I went public. But I'd been doing a duet then. It was the first time I'd seen Adam lose his cool. Amidst threats that, according to Thornton, had been "flooding" into his office, we were being told to "take it down a peg." Incredible. Cargill and his goons bully a kid almost to death, but we hold hands and suddenly civilization as we know it is in peril. I'd seen fire in Adam's eyes that day.

"Keep your relationship to yourselves," Thornton had said. "There's no place for that in school anyway."

That lit Adam's fuse. "Last time I checked, holding hands was not against school rules," he'd said with a sarcasm I'd never heard from him.

"No, it's not."

"Then why are we being singled out? I have as much right to hold Nate's hand as any other kid in this school. And I intend to exercise that right."

"Look," Thornton had said, puffing out his chest in a me-administrator, you-student way that pissed us both off, "we can't keep you safe if you're going to flaunt this in everybody's face."

His concern for our well-being had been touching.

I was so looking forward to another round of his nurturing advice. But I was doing it solo this time. I drew in a deep breath and entered the administrators' area.

"Sit down, Mr. Schaper," he said as I stepped into his office. I took one of the two chairs facing his desk, the same one I'd sat in last spring. My butt had scarcely gotten acquainted with the upholstery when he got right to the point. "I hear you've been writing a blog."

I settled into my seat and met his eyes. "You heard right."

"Do you mind telling me what you've been writing about?"

"It sounds to me like you already know."

"What I know," he said, easing back into his chair, "is that you're stirring up some pretty serious opposition to your lifestyle, and it's starting to affect this school."

"Living like a bum on the beach is a lifestyle, Mr. Thornton. Green is a lifestyle. Gay is just what I am. It's my sexual orientation, and I can no more change that than I can change—"

"The color of your eyes. Yeah, I've heard it all before." The contempt is his voice was so thick I could have wrapped it around his neck and strangled him with it. "However—" He folded his arms across his chest and pushed against the back of his chair. It groaned in protest. And then he laughed. And it wasn't with humor. "There are plenty of folks out there, and many right here in this school, who do not believe that."

Mr. Wolf walked in and quietly pulled the other chair off to the side and sat down. I was so angry I barely registered his presence.

"There are people who don't believe the Holocaust ever happened either," I said, "but that doesn't change the facts."

He sprang forward and pointed a finger at me. "Young man, I've been very patient with you in light of what happened last school year, but—"

"Yeah. About that. You knew Andrew Cargill was a loaded gun. You knew long before he bullied Jake Winfield into—"

"Andrew never told Jake to hang himself."

The willful ignorance of his statement was like pouring gasoline on an already smoldering fire. I sprang up and knock his finger out of my face before I even knew I was going to do it. "You knew Andrew had it in for me long before he kicked in my skull and—" I couldn't finish. I was starting to sweat. Mr. Wolf leaned forward, his elbows on his knees and his chin planted on his clasped fists. But he didn't intervene.

Thornton settled back in his chair. "I had no idea—"

"You knew. But you did nothing. You don't scare me. I have rights, and I intend to exercise them. I don't need your approval or anyone else's."

"We are not having a gay homecoming dance."

"Maybe not. But if you're having a dance, I'll be there, and I'll dance with whomever I damn well please."

"I'll cancel the dance."

"No, you won't. Because if you try, I'll have the ACLU and the media all over you so fast you'll wish you'd stayed a lousy junior high social studies teacher."

Thornton's face reddened. "If you insist on pushing people like this, I can't guarantee someone won't get hurt."

The statement was so absurd I laughed.

"Why are you doing this?" he said. "I assume you're still seeing Mr. Jefferies? He's not even a student at this school anymore. Why don't you just cool it with the gay until you graduate? Then you can do whatever you want."

"Cool it with the gay?" I laughed. "I spent two and half years at this school scared to death that someone would find out about me, terrified what that would mean. Do you have any idea how that feels? Do you? But I'm not that same kid anymore. And it doesn't surprise me one bit that you're not willing to stand up to the bigots and the other small minds in this community. You never have. But I will. There are other kids like me out there. And until they feel safe being who they are, then I'll gladly take one for the team, *flaunt* it as you so eloquently put it last year."

"The protestors aren't going away."

I hoped not. They were the best advertisement for gay rights I'd seen. And they worked cheap.

Mr. Wolf caught me in the hallway before I could get back to class.

"You might want to cool it a bit, Nate," he said, stopping me with a hand on my arm.

I shrugged off his hand. "Fuck you."

"Whoa." He held up his hands. "I didn't mean it that way. You know me better than that."

"You didn't say anything in there."

"It didn't look to me like you needed any help."

I stuffed my hands deep in my pockets, reminding myself that he was one of the good guys. At the end of the hall, two girls came out of the bathroom laughing and talking loudly. When they saw Mr. Wolf, they lowered their voices and skittered off around the corner.

Mr. Wolf studied me for a moment, then he laughed and shook his head. *"Whomever?"*

"What?" I said, confused.

"You said you'd dance with whomever you pleased. You've been paying attention in English class."

"You want to talk to me about my grammar? Unbelievable."

"Well, it is good, but no. Look, things are changing around

here, even if Mr. Thornton doesn't want to admit it. The tide of sentiment toward our LGBT students is turning, and for the better. There are still a number of people who don't like it. And they're going to fight you. But their numbers are manageable. I just wanted you to know that."

I walked away thinking how badly I wished Adam had been here to hear that.

Chapter 31

I'm Queer. Get Over It.
Friends with benefits
By Nate Schaper on Oct. 8.
(Not what you think. Get your minds out of the gutter. LOL.)
Gays at the homecoming dance? OMG! Bar the door.
Ha-ha. That's right. Woodland Park High School is going progressive—perhaps not willingly, but that's beside the point. Yes, it's true. Danial and I are dancing together at the homecoming dance. Yes, yes, I know. Danial is straight, and yes, I may be the only actual gay there, but the point is two guys will be dancing together, and that hasn't happened in the history of this school. And that's progress.

Comments:

HappyBoy
Oct. 8, at 4:00 P.M.
   You're so lucky to have Danial.
GodChild223
Oct. 8, at 4:06 P.M.
   Stop trying to queer our schools. We don't need you and your

kind corrupting our kids. If I find out where you live, I'm going to take you down. [DELETE]

Xyz123

Oct. 8, at 6:32 P.M.

My dad hates that I play clarinet. He thinks I'm a pussy because I like to blow on a long wooden stick. LOL. How dumb is that?

PakistaniPal

Oct. 8, at 6:45 P.M.

Ahem.

Brett2010

Oct. 8, at 7:01 P.M.

A lot of my friends think that gay guys want to jump every other guy they see. Dumb. Thanks for proving that a gay and straight guy can be friends.

Despite my melancholy, I couldn't help laughing at Danial's comment when I approved it.

It was almost seven thirty now. I'd put off calling Adam as long as I could stand it. I'd tried to imagine all the possible ways the phone call could go. Sexy? Not likely. Not today. It was much more likely to fall on the other end of the spectrum where most of our calls seemed to fall lately—angry, hurt. Where it actually fell was somewhere in the dead middle, the place of no passion. The worst place of all.

"No show today?" I asked.

"No."

"How'd you spend your day?"

"Just hanging out." I waited, but he didn't elaborate.

"How was school?" he asked.

"It was okay." I didn't elaborate.

We talked the talk of strangers for a few minutes longer. I don't even know who hung up first. It had been four days since the incident in the parking garage, and I hadn't even told him about it. It didn't seem important anymore.

There wasn't much about those earlier two conversations—the last five months, even, if I was being honest—that I didn't regret by

Saturday morning. As someone had so ineloquently phrased it in English class earlier in the semester, I had buttered my bread, and now I had to lie in it. I felt like I was being punished. I felt like I was doing the punishing.

I called; he was in the shower.

When he called back a few hours later, I was in a piano lesson. I wondered if he'd waited, saying to himself all those things he didn't want to later regret, saying them to himself so he didn't have to say them to me.

When I was free, I called back; his phone was off.

He called again later in the afternoon; I was in the shower. He left a voice mail. His voice was quiet and, I wanted to believe, sad: "I've got a show tonight. The last one for this run. I'll try you again later." He paused, then, "I'm glad you're going to the dance tonight. I hope you have a good time. I do mean that."

A thin coat of dust had left the piano keys gritty. I brushed my fingers across them, thinking it had been too long since I'd played just for myself. I pressed a random key to test the tuning, then another. Not bad. Using a piece of sheet music, I fanned the dust off the bench and sat down, careful to let the hem of my suit jacket hang loose so I didn't wrinkle it because looking gay and good seemed like an important part of the evening. My hands, seemingly of their own accord, played "Heart and Soul."

Chapter 32

Last September 17
Falling in love

"Juliet told me you play." Adam laid his fingers on the keys and started a basic chord progression for "Heart and Soul." "Come on, let's see what you got."

Oh, I definitely wanted to show him what I got. But he was Juliet's best friend, just here to pick up some clothes he'd loaned me after that spontaneous swim in his pool.

I picked up the melody, basic at first, but then with a little more sass.

"Heart and soul, I fell in love with you."

He was singing? I looked at him, amazed. "There're lyrics to this thing?"

He laughed. "Didn't you see *Stuart Little?*" I'd made him miss a couple of lines, but he picked up on the next one. And then without warning, he switched from F to G. I followed easily. He sang the next verse, singing, "Na-na, na-na, na-na," when he forgot the lyrics, then switched keys again. The key of A this time. I ad-libbed a little more with the melody. And for the first time, he stumbled over the chords.

"Oh crap! Too many black keys."

I laughed. "Come on, you can do it."

I finished with a big flourish, playing both the bass and the melody.

When it was over, we both sat staring at the keys, stupid grins on our faces. "You play," I said.

" 'Heart and Soul' in three keys and a mean 'Chopsticks' in one." Then he shoved me playfully. "You're pretty good."

I blushed. "I still can't believe you knew the lyrics."

"If you had any idea how many karaoke parties I've been to, that wouldn't surprise you."

"You sing 'Heart and Soul' karaoke?"

"Busted." He laughed. "No, not really, but if there's a piano around, someone's going to play it. So we learned the lyrics. It's a geeky drama thing."

Applause erupted behind us. "Very nice, boys," Grandma said.

I watched as Grandma fawned all over Adam for a while, asking him a million questions about school, his family, his interests, and whether or not he'd had voice lessons. Somewhere in between stuffing peanut butter cookies in his mouth and casting confusing sideways glances at me, he told Grandma all about the fall musical and made her promise we'd be there opening night.

When he was done charming the pants off her, I walked him out to his car. After three straight days of rain, the air was steamy and the toads were carrying on in the small drainage ditches that ran along the streets in our neighborhood.

"You've got a real fan in there," I told him.

"I kinda hoped I had more than one."

My heart thumped. I didn't know how to respond, so I didn't say anything.

He tossed his things in the front seat but didn't get in right away. He leaned against the side of the car and folded his arms, his face serious. Then he glanced over his shoulder at the ditch. "Are those frogs always this loud?"

I laughed. "They're toads. And yeah, sometimes, when it rains a lot. They like burrowing down in the mud. I think that croaking is some kind of mating call. When they're this loud, they're pretty easy to spot. You wanna go look?"

"Watch frogs have sex?"

"Toads. And yeah, it's kind of interesting."

He screwed up his face. "Pass."

I laughed again.

"You know Juliet's crazy about you, don't you?" he asked out of the blue.

"I know."

"You're all she talks about now." He scrubbed his face with his hands.

The sun was losing its battle with the horizon and dusk was setting in. Adam looked toward the fading light and then back toward the croaking toads. "I really need to get going."

He didn't look like he wanted to leave, though.

"Uh, yeah, sure," I said, looking down at my feet.

"Oh, here." He reached into his pocket and drew out a folded piece of notebook paper and handed it to me. "I forgot to give this to you earlier."

I unfolded it. "My Thomas Paine response." The essay had been our first assignment in government, and Adam had asked to read it on our way out of class one day. Even then it had been hard to deny him anything.

"If the whole music thing doesn't work out for you, you might consider becoming a writer."

I folded the paper and moved to put it in my pocket.

"Uh, I know this will sound kind of stupid, but . . . can I keep that?" he said, nodding toward my hand.

"This?" I held up the paper.

He grinned sheepishly. "You might be a famous writer slash pianist some day. I could sell it on eBay for a gazillion dollars and buy an island in the Caribbean or something."

"Right." I handed it to him and he closed his fist around not just the paper, but my fingers holding the paper. It was as if someone had slammed on the brakes and time had entered a long screeching skid. My eyes dropped to my hand in his, his hand on mine, our hands together. Skin on skin, touching. And when I slid my eyes back up to his, I knew, and I knew he knew.

* * *

In that moment Adam and I had become a plural—a *we,* an *us.* What were we now?

Mom came in and draped her arms over my shoulders and watched me play.

"You're on your way to a dance," she said after a while. "You should be playing a happier tune." I didn't even realize I had changed songs. When I didn't respond, she tried again. "You look very handsome." She brushed a piece of imaginary lint from my shoulder, then licked her thumb and rubbed a spot of dried blood off my cheek. I leaned away a little until she stopped fussing over me.

"Nathan, is everything okay between you and Adam?" Okay? That word again. It had been more than two months since I'd seen Adam, since I'd been able to hold him, to touch him, to talk to him while looking in his eyes and not through the creepy webcam at the top of my computer screen. And now here I was, all dressed up, about to go out on a date with another guy. There was nothing *okay* about this.

"Why would you ask that?" I said.

"Because," she said, "the only time you play that *Shrek* song is when you're upset."

So I stopped right after *It's a cold and it's a broken hallelujah,* and just to be pissy, I launched into "I Kissed a Girl."

She slammed the keyboard cover down. I yanked my fingers out just in time to save them and said, "You don't like 'Hallelujah.' You don't like 'I Kissed a Girl.' Why don't you just request something, then?" I was taking out my funk on her, and it wasn't fair. But then, there wasn't much that was fair in my life right then.

"Is there something going on between you and Danial?"

I laughed. "Mom, Danial's straight as an arrow."

She sat down next to me and chewed on the inside of her mouth. "You know, I get why you're doing this. I do. But it scares me. I'll be honest with you about that, Nathan. But I get it. What I don't get, though, is why Danial's doing this?"

I'd wondered the same thing. Danial had to know that hanging out with me marked him as gay too. He didn't seem to care. At all. In fact, it was like a game for him. A dare. He got away with it because he was big and good-looking and confident. He was like Adam in that way, except Adam's force shield was his charm and cool factor. It was average guys like me who seemed to draw all the fire. I shrugged.

"Is Adam upset that you're going to a dance with Danial?"

I wished. No, Adam wasn't upset, at least not about that. Maybe if he were, we wouldn't be in this horrible limbo right now. Adam had been great, happy—happy that I was getting out, happy that I'd found a great friend in Danial, happy that I was doing so great without him. There'd been so much fucking happiness I wanted to scream.

A knock on the door saved me from answering Mom's question. "Showtime," I said, getting up.

Danial looked good. His dark skin glowed against his crisp white shirt. His jacket was slung over one shoulder and held by a single finger hooked under the collar.

"Wow," I said.

He rolled his eyes.

Mom grinned and gave Danial a hug. "You boys both look exceedingly handsome. The girls are going to love you."

I shifted around uncomfortably until she realized what she'd said. She squinched her eyes shut. "Sorry. You know what I mean."

Danial laughed. "Here. I brought you something," he said to me.

With an amused clearing of his throat, he brandished a triple homecoming mum the size of a hubcap under my nose. From the cardboard backing hung enough blue and silver ribbons, bells, and other junk to strike envy in the heart of any homecoming queen. And from the center of the gaudy flower blob, a mocha-furred teddy bear reached out its stubby arms and legs to me.

"Oh, hell no," I said.

"Oh, come on. It's a tradition. If we're going to do this, we're going to do this right." The blue and silver monstrosity had a rope strong enough to tether a small yacht stapled to the back so it could be worn around the neck. It was far too big and heavy to pin on. He snickered as he slipped it over my head. "Juliet made it."

"Oh, please remind me to thank her," I said sarcastically. "Maybe I should go slip into a dress."

"Suit yourself," he said with a wicked grin. "You might want to shave your legs while you're at it. I'll wait."

"Danial! My, don't you look handsome," Grandma said, coming into the room. "I made something for you b—Oh. *Oh,*" she said again as she took in the thing hanging around my neck. "That's . . . that's . . . that's the ugliest thing I've ever seen. Sorry, Danial."

Danial laughed and gave my grandmother a hug that completely engulfed her. For a few seconds, she practically disappeared before our eyes.

"Here. I made these for you boys." Grandma handed us each a garter with a single, small chrysanthemum. There were still streamers attached, but they were fewer and, thank God, much shorter. In the middle of each flower, secured with hot glue, was a plastic, glittery rainbow.

"Grandma, these are awesome," I said, taking one. "Stick your arm out, Danial."

"Does this mean you're not wearing the mum I brought you?"

"I'll wear it for you later if that turns you on."

Mom blushed, but Grandma didn't flinch. Instead, she produced a camera.

It was dark outside. The protestors—a larger group by at least another three or four now—huddled under a street light, spitting their poison as cars filed into the school parking lot.

"I believe your fan base is growing," Danial said. He slowed the car to a stop behind a line of cars waiting to turn in. Then he rolled his window down and stuck out his arm, giving the group the finger. One of the men made a very un-Christian-like comment and approached the car.

"Roll up the window," I told Danial sternly.

He ignored me.

The man was middle-aged and balding, his enormous gut hanging over his relaxed-fit jeans. And I use *fit* loosely because if it weren't for that stomach clamping them on, those pants would've been bunched around his ankles. That wasn't a sight I wanted to see. He stooped to peer in the car at us, gripping the top edge of the window with his Pillsbury hands. He looked at me in the passenger seat, then back at Danial. "Are you boys the homos?" He spat the last word out as if the word itself tasted bad in his mouth.

Danial smiled broadly. "This boy's mine, asshole. Get your own." He rolled up the window, forcing the man to move his fingers or lose them, but not before the self-appointed guardian of the pearly gates informed us of our fiery destination following our departure from planet Earth, a departure I think he would have liked to hasten.

"God, people can be so ignorant." Danial shook his head, then slammed the heel of his hand into the steering wheel. I looked at him, puzzled. When it came to narrow-minded, sanctimonious assholes like this guy and the lady at the music store, Danial usually dealt with them with sarcasm and humor. But there was this edge, this anger just below the surface that rose up every now and then.

The commons was already buzzing when we got there. The music was loud, the kind that made you want to dance, the kind you could feel in your bone marrow. We'd planned to arrive fashionably late, dance half a dozen dances or so to make our point, and leave. I saw a group of drama kids standing at the edge of the dance floor. I caught Juliet's eye just as a slow song started up. She grinned and grabbed Gaby by the elbow. Gaby looked and waved. The two of them moved onto the dance floor. I hoped some of the guys would follow, but whether they did or not, this was going to happen.

Danial looked over at me. "Well, cupcake, I believe they're playing our song." He winked.

I took a deep breath and hoped this evening wouldn't end in another visit to the ER. I'd seen all I wanted to of the inside of a hospital my junior year.

Danial surprised me by grabbing my hand and pulling me onto the dance floor. I saw a few surprised looks, but I was determined to *not* act like the star of some homo freak show.

Danial cleared his throat and palmed the back of his neck and looked like he hadn't a clue what to do now that he had me on the floor. I rolled my eyes and put my arms around his neck. He hesitated a moment before putting his arms awkwardly around my waist. "Good grief," I said. "Loosen up."

"Hey, give me a minute to warm up here. I've never danced with a guy before."

"Just pretend like I'm a girl." I wrapped my arms more tightly around his neck and pressed into him. Then I laid my head on his shoulder and closed my eyes. "You smell good," I said.

"Quit smelling me."

"I'm just saying."

He laughed in my ear. "You pop a boner, and this dance is over."

"Don't flatter yourself."

"You want me. Admit it."

My face flushed. Holding him was nothing like holding Adam. Adam was tall and lithe, and when he held me, it was like he never wanted to let me go. Danial was more solid, more like a linebacker to Adam's quarterback. It was different, but it wasn't bad. In fact, it was nice.

Danial cleared his throat. "I was kidding."

I decided to ignore the comment. Dancing with Danial was freaking me out in a way I hadn't expected. I needed to focus or this statement we were making was going to be over before it got started. "Are we being watched?" I asked, refusing to open my eyes.

Danial chuckled. "Oh, yeah."

"Thornton?"

"Looks jealous."

"Right. Wolf?"

"Working the crowd, sniffing out potential trouble. You want me to squeeze your ass and give them something to talk about."

"I'm not stopping you."

"Nah. That might send you over the edge, and we've got a few dances to go yet."

I was disappointed, and then I was ashamed. Some boyfriend I was. Then again, all Adam had had to say was no and I'd have happily stayed home and spent my evening texting sexy messages to him. Would it have killed him to be a little jealous? Would it have killed me to be a little not?

I asked Danial if the others were dancing, and he said, "I guess you could call it that. Warren and Mike look like they're terrified of letting their man parts get too close. It's pathetic really. They look like a couple from *Night of the Living Dead* dancing together. They're not doing your kind any favors, trust me on this."

"At least they're trying."

"That's being generous." He cleared his throat again. "Quit doing that."

"Doing what?"

"Breathing on my neck. You are enjoying this way too much."

The song ended and I stepped back and rolled my eyes.

"Okay, that wasn't half bad," Danial said. "No awkward sword fighting, no one was struck by lightning."

The next couple of songs were fast ones. We migrated toward the drama kids and all danced together. I was reminded what good dancers these kids were. Not so much Danial. But Juliet stepped in and showed him some steps. I glanced at Mike dancing nearby. He watched Juliet with Danial, his eyes narrowed. Juliet was oblivious. When the music switched to a slow song, she slipped her arms around Danial.

And there went my date, and Mike's.

I was heading off the dance floor for a soda when a kid stepped in front of me and asked me to dance. He looked familiar. And then I remembered—he was the kid Danial had pointed out in the hallway right after school started, the one he thought was checking me out.

His eyes lit up when I said okay. After all, that was the point. He was a guy. I was a guy. The simple fact that this stranger had asked me to dance at a school dance was something of a victory already.

He was almost exactly the same height I was, but younger by maybe a year, maybe two. I introduced myself, to which he said, "I know who you are. I'm Luke Chesser. I read your blog."

It only took an instant to put two and two together and come up with four. "You're Xyz123?"

He grinned, obviously pleased that I'd made the connection. "Yeah. And I think you're amazing."

Warning bells went off in my head, but he looked so sincere and hopeful standing there fidgeting with his tie and then awkwardly reaching an arm around my waist that I couldn't help but smile back. "Wow. This is a big step for you. You're not out, are you?"

He shook his head and looked around nervously. "Other guys were dancing together, so I thought . . ."

He thought our little statement would provide sufficient cover for him. He could be gay for a short time without actually copping to being gay, which would have been funny if it weren't so wrong. I had news for him. The way he was looking at me with such un-abashed adoration, adoration that I neither deserved nor wanted, at least not from him, and the way he was digging his fingers into my back as we danced—he wasn't fooling anyone.

"Have you told anyone, Luke?"

"Just you."

"Do you have some close friends you could confide in?"

He shook his head. "They wouldn't understand." His face screwed up, and for a moment I thought he might break down.

Shit. I caught Danial's eye as he and Juliet danced close by. "What the fuck?" he mouthed.

I flashed him a panicked look. I didn't know how to deal with this, but this is exactly what I'd been sticking myself out there for—getting kids out of the closet.

"It's okay," I said. "You've got friends here." Almost as an afterthought, and really without much thought at all, I added, "I have to work tomorrow until about four. Do you want to get together after that? I could meet you somewhere and we could talk."

"That would be awesome!" He smiled and planted his face in my neck.

For the rest of the evening, Luke was like one of those sucker fishes that cling to whales. I couldn't shake him. And I didn't want to hurt him. Here he was on the cusp of embracing his identity but highly vulnerable to any assault on his self-esteem, and I was going to brush him off? I didn't have the heart.

When he excused himself to go to the men's room, I got Danial to go with him, covertly. There were plenty of kids there who were not on board with this boy-on-boy thing, and I was afraid to let Luke go alone. Before he followed Luke, Danial leaned into me. "I think you're just trying to make me jealous now."

"Riiight," I said, thinking how much more I enjoyed dancing with Danial than with Luke. He did smell amazing.

Danial grinned and winked at me, then followed Luke to the bathroom, covertly.

Gaby grabbed me while the boys were away. I was tired, not so much physically tired as emotionally drained, but Gaby was a friend. And a good one, despite our rocky start. She'd been Adam's leading lady last spring. Juliet hadn't liked her. Maybe none of the kids had, and that's why they'd let her make a fool of herself flirting with Adam. It wasn't until he kissed me in front of her over burgers that the farce ended. She took it well though, distracted by the sudden realization that I was Nate, "*Nate* Nate," as she'd put it.

She had hammered me with questions about the assault, each one more insensitive than the last, not even waiting for me to respond, but supplying her own answers from her cache of hearsay. I was reeling with humiliation and shame when Juliet accidentally on purpose dumped an entire Coke in her lap, shutting her down cold. Despite all that, Gaby had given up a trip to South Padre to be there for me at the trial. She'd been a steady, if sometimes clueless, ally ever since. I could give her a dance, even if she was wearing a dress. "Hey, pretty girl," I said.

"Hey, handsome. Does Adam know you're stepping out with all these good-looking guys?"

"He knows. Not that he cares much one way or the other."

"Wait. Are we talking about the same guy here? Six-two, sexy, black hair, and a major hard-on for you."

I huffed. "So, how're things with you and Warren?"

"Uh-uh, baby. I know what you're doing. Spit it out."

I furrowed my brow like I didn't know what she was talking about. "Can we just dance, Gaby?"

"Talk to me, Nate. What's going on with that hot boyfriend of yours?"

He was hot all right, but all that heat, I feared, was warming someone else right now, and I was getting sick of hearing about what a saint he was. I didn't want to talk about it, but Gaby wouldn't leave it alone. She needled and prodded me with question after question until I broke down.

"He's just a little too okay with this," I blurted out, angry now.

"With what?"

"This," I said, gesturing around the room. "I mean, I'm on a date with another guy."

"Uh, hello. A straight guy."

"Yeah, whatever. Still, it makes me wonder, you know."

"No, I don't know. Oh my God, Nate. Have you lost your ever lovin' mind? The way he looks at you, like you're the only two people in the world. He adores you. We all know he's crazy about you."

"Then why doesn't my hanging out with Danial bother him? And why is he kissing other guys?"

"He's kissing other guys? Really? I mean, I figured he'd have to beat off those pretty New York boys with a stick, but you know . . ."

"I know what?"

She looked uncomfortable. "I mean, you know, he *would* beat them off. Right?"

Wrong thing to say. I looked off across the dance floor for some distraction, for someone to rescue me from this unwelcomed question.

"Come on, Nate," she continued. "It's Adam we're talking about. So what if he has to sow his wild oats in New York. He'll come back—"

"Wild oats? Who said anything about sowing his wild oats?" The song was over, and my voice carried over the din.

"I just meant—"

I let go and backed away from her. She reached for me, but I held my hands up.

Danial and Juliet and Luke stared at me from the edge of the crowd. Luke's eyes were wide as he took a step toward me, but Danial restrained him with a hand on his arm. I turned and hit the door.

* * *

I didn't know where I was going, but anywhere was better than there, with all their eyes on me. Two of the protestors were still huddled under the streetlamp with their sad little signs. I headed for them.

"Fuck you, motherfuckers!" I shouted, crossing into the road.

Danial grabbed my arm from behind. I tried to shake him loose, but his hand was like a vice. A car approached, its high beams blinding me for a second. Danial yanked me back to the shoulder.

"God will judge you for your sins," the fat man said.

"You ignorant excuse for a human being," I shouted.

"Come on," Danial said, practically dragging me back toward the car.

"He'll destroy your kind the same way he did Sodom and Gomorrah."

"How do you people sleep at night with all that hate inside you?"

He spat something else at me, but I'd pressed my hands to my ears and didn't hear a word.

Danial got me back to the car and shoved me in.

"What was that?" he said as he pulled out of the parking lot. He left by a back entrance so we didn't have to pass the homophobes on the corner.

I was too wound up to answer. And the truth was, I didn't know what *that* was.

He raced through a yellow light, then coasted down to the speed limit on a dark stretch of road before glancing back over at me. "Were you really going to beat up a middle-aged guy wearing black crew socks with sandals in October?"

"That was the plan."

He grinned and looked back at the road ahead, shaking his head. "I'm taking you to my house. I want to show you something."

Chapter 33

Danial's house backed up to a golf course, and that something he wanted to show me turned out to be an enormous telescope stored in a study in his house. I helped him wheel it to a small deck at the edge of his backyard overlooking the fairway. He set it up and trained it on the near full moon.

After making some adjustments with the knobs, he stepped back and pulled a joint from his pocket, gesturing toward the eyepiece with his other hand. "I don't know about you, but I plan to get fucked up and look at some celestial bodies tonight." He lit the tip with a match he'd fished out of another pocket, then sucked in deeply.

"Man, I didn't know you were such a pothead," I said with more disapproval than I really felt.

He laughed and coughed out the smoke. "You screw guys, and you're going to go all Sister Mary Catherine on me for smoking a joint?"

He had a point, sort of, except for the *guys* part. Just one guy. My nose burned. I stuffed the thought back down and stepped to the eyepiece.

The moon was huge. I pulled back and looked at it with my naked eye, then bent to the eyepiece to look again. Amazing. The moon looked just like it did in library books I'd looked through, only it had a luminescence that didn't translate in photographs.

"Pretty cool, isn't it?" Danial said in that tight voice that meant he was holding the smoke in his lungs.

"It's incredible. I didn't know you were into astronomy."

"This was my brother's telescope." He handed me the joint and took my place at the eyepiece.

I watched him make some more adjustments and thought about the big brother that looked so much like him. Danial hadn't told me anything about him, but I could tell from his voice every time he mentioned him that his death was still an open wound.

I rolled the joint between my fingers, then not knowing what else to do with it, I took a drag. The smoke caught in my throat, and I fell into a coughing fit.

Danial laughed without taking his eyes from the eyepiece. "Inhale more slowly, little bits until you get used to it."

I tried again. I wanted to cough the instant the smoke hit my lungs, but I fought the urge and managed to hold it for a few seconds before coughing it out. I handed the joint back.

He took it and stepped aside. I moved back to the eyepiece. "How did your brother die?"

"He was murdered."

My head snapped to him.

Danial inhaled deeply. I watched him for a moment before turning back to the telescope, but I wasn't looking. I was listening.

"It was a random attack. He shouldn't have even been there. He should have been at UT, studying for exams, eating ramen noodles, sleeping with his boyfriend."

I glanced back at him again and wrapped my hand around the telescope to steady myself. I thought I knew where this was going.

"My parents didn't know. When he brought Keenan home one weekend, they totally lost it. Threw him out of the house. Cut off all support. David had to drop out of school. He moved in with some friends in Houston, then one night about six months later, Keenan came down to spend the weekend with him, and some ass-holes jumped them. They'd just seen a movie. They were just walking down the sidewalk about ten o'clock at night toward Keenan's car." He huffed. "David was in a coma for two weeks before he died. Keenan didn't even make it to the hospital." He shook his head. "What a waste."

I sucked in a sharp breath. *Oh, Danial.* Suddenly everything was so clear to me. "Is that why I've never met your parents? You're protecting them from memories."

He laughed and drew deeply on the joint. "I'm not protecting them from you, Nate." He exhaled. "I'm protecting you from them."

I stared at him.

"They blamed his 'lifestyle' for what happened to him." He used little finger quotes when he said the word *lifestyle,* causing an ash to drop at this feet. He shook his head. "Man, that's so fucked up. They kicked him out. Then some redneck motherfuckers beat him to a pulp, and they blame him. The night he left..." He paused and laughed a little without humor. "The night they threw him out, my dad told him, 'You're dead to me.' And now he is."

"Just because he was gay?" I was thinking how very fortunate Adam and I had been that our parents had reacted so differently. Adam's parents had been more amused and relieved than anything, although his mom was kinda freaked out about the sex thing and was the one who insisted on condoms. Mom was getting used to it. She liked Adam. Who didn't? I think Grandma was just a fag hag. But Dad, he really wasn't so different, was he? He hadn't kicked me out. He didn't have that power anymore. But he had deleted me from his life as surely as I deleted the disgusting comments on my blog.

Danial went on, "We're Pakistani...Muslim. It's a hard religion, Nate. Sometimes I'm surprised my dad didn't kill him himself." He shrugged. "He didn't want to have a gay son, and now he doesn't."

Our dads had that much in common. The last time I'd seen Dad was right after we'd returned from Key West. He'd invited Adam and me to dinner. I suppose I had to give him points for trying. But in the end, he couldn't do it.

Last June 14
Stood up

I used my forefinger to twist the rubber bracelet tightly around my wrist. When I realized what I was doing, I forced myself to stop, only to find myself tugging on an earring, or twirling the votives that flickered in a shallow bowl of water in the center of the small table. Dad was late.

"Nervous?" Adam said.

"Yeah. A little."

"You know, this time yesterday we were eating conch soup on the beach and playing footsies barefoot under the table with sand between our toes."

"Me likey conch soup."

"Me likey playing footsies." To prove it, he slipped his foot out of his loafer and wiggled it a couple of inches up my pant leg.

I laughed. "You're such a tease."

"Not teasing," he said, taking my hand and pulling it to his lips. A man seated at the bar whispered something to the woman next to him and she laughed loudly. I wondered if the day would come when we could be affectionate with each other in public and not be objects of ridicule or even note. But I had no intention of waiting.

A movement at the hostess's desk caught my eye, and I looked over just in time to catch my dad's back retreating through the oversized restaurant door. *Shit.* I told Adam I'd be right back and hurried after him.

"Dad. *Dad.*" I caught up with him just as he stepped off the curb to cross the street. He stepped back up on the sidewalk and shoved his hands deep in his pockets but didn't say anything.

"This was your idea," I said.

"I can't do this, Nate," he said after a moment, looking everywhere, anywhere, but at me. "I thought I could, but I can't."

"You can't or you won't?"

"Does it matter?" He shook his head and smirked. "For twenty years I've worked my ass off turning boys into men on that football field. All those boys who came to me weak and uncertain. I pushed them. I took those boys, and I turned them into men. But I couldn't do that with my own son. I failed you, and for that I am profoundly sorry."

"This has nothing to do with me being a man."

"You were sitting at that table, earrings in your ears, that stupid amoeba thing hanging around your neck." He flicked my pendant with his thick fingers. "Your hands all over some—"

"My hands weren't all over anybody."

"Tell me you're not shoving your dick up his ass. *Tell me*."

I didn't say anything, and he gave a disgusted laugh. "You don't have to tell me. I heard it all in that courtroom."

"You're making me sick."

"Yeah? Well, now you know how that feels."

With that, he'd stepped into the street. I watched him go with a mixture of anger and despair. The despair was not for myself, I realized, but for a man who had just thrown away his only son.

We didn't talk a lot during dinner. Adam seemed to know that I needed to be alone with my thoughts. I hadn't realized how important this dinner was to me until it was. I'd never been the kid my dad wanted me to be, but I was his kid. I'd hoped that trumped everything. It didn't. He was who he was, and I was who I was, and who we were prevented us from bridging the chasm that existed between us.

Adam excused himself while I paid the tab. I tucked some bills into the leather folder and laid it back on the table and got up. The couple was still at the bar, a little drunker, a little louder. The man had his hand on the woman's thigh. He leaned in and slid his fingers just under the edge of her skirt.

I rubbed my thumb along the letters stamped on my rubber bracelet—WWND—and glanced around. At another table a young woman whispered in her dinner date's ear. He laughed and whispered something back. Across the room a man ushered a woman to their table, his hand placed firmly on her ass. And no one paid them any attention. And what's more, they took no note of anyone around them either. Not one furtive scan of the room. Not one fucking sideways glance.

I hooked my fingers around the edge of the bracelet and tugged it over my hand. *What would Nate do?* It had been my reminder and my talisman for all these months. I looked at it a moment, then held the rubber ring over the leather folder and let it drop.

Adam appeared behind me and placed his hands on my shoulders "Ready?" he asked.

"Yeah, I'm ready."

I considered telling Danial about that evening, but it seemed wrong somehow. This moment belonged to his loss, not mine.

Danial handed me the joint. I carefully drew in a deep lungful and held it as long as I could. He gestured toward the telescope. "Go on. Look."

My heart was breaking for him, but I looked through the eyepiece again. "Saturn," I said softly.

"You're looking at something eight hundred, nine hundred million miles away."

"Wow. It really does have rings."

He laughed. "Yeah. They weren't just making that up."

I took my eye away from the telescope again and looked at the black sky, trying to figure out which pinpoint of light was Saturn.

"It's that one," Danial said, close behind me. "It's pretty bright, kind of yellowish, about thirty degrees off the horizon. Do you see it?"

There were so many stars out tonight. The sky never looked like this in my neighborhood. Too many lights. It was darker here. I easily picked out the light he pointed to.

"If we stayed out here a couple more hours, you'd see Jupiter rise in the east. Now that's an impressive planet. The brightest thing in the sky outside of the moon and the sun."

I looked through the eyepiece again. "Does Saturn have a moon?"

"Can you see it? Cool. That's probably Titan. Some books say Saturn has eighteen moons, but it's actually more like sixty-one, plus some moonlets that have their own rings. Titan is the biggest. It's kind of weird, isn't it? No matter how many pictures I see of Saturn, it's still kind of startling to look through a telescope and realize it really exists, rings and all."

It was so clear. I felt like I could almost reach out and touch it.

The telescope was amazing. Not the kind of thing you'd run down and pick up at Best Buy. When I asked Danial about it, he told me his dad was an astrophysicist. He'd worked at NASA until his brother was killed. After that, they left Clear Lake and bought this house. His dad retired from NASA and took a job teaching at the community college.

"I'll never understand why some people can't just let others live their lives, you know," Danial said. "You don't have to understand. You don't have to agree. Just leave people alone. When I look at the moon and planets and stars, all that narrow-mindedness and hate seem so petty. The universe is such a big place. One hundred thousand light years just from one end of the Milky Way to the other. One hundred. Thousand. Light years. In the time it's taken for light to travel from one end of our galaxy to the other, thousands of generations have passed. It really makes you realize how small we are, doesn't it? How short our time on earth is."

He stepped back to the telescope and handed me the joint again. I made room for him, but just barely, and took another drag. "Let me show you something else," he said.

His hip brushed against mine as he adjusted the scope. I thought about what he'd said. How short our time on earth was. I reached out and laid my hand on his back. He had taken off his dress shirt before we came out. He was warm through his white T-shirt. I'd never noticed just how broad his back was before. I let my hand slide down along his spine, pressing my fingers in to feel the ridges of each vertebra. Bump. Bump. Bump. Bump. Bump.

He looked over his shoulder. "Nate, get your hand off my ass."

I smiled to myself.

Danial straightened up and turned to me. When I fuzzed out my eyes, I could almost believe he was Adam. I kissed him. His mouth was hard and needed some softening up, so I kissed him again.

Danial cleared his throat. "Uh, Nate. I'm not kissing you back."

I pressed into him and slid my hand down the front of his jeans.

"Okay," he said, grabbing my wrist. "Now you've got your hand on my dick."

"You like it. You can't hide that."

"Oh, please. I'm a guy. My dick gets hard in a stiff wind."

He was lying. There wasn't even a breeze tonight. I tried to free my wrist and get my mouth on his again, but he was playing hard to get, or at least hard to get to. "I'm not kissing you, Nate. You are stoned, man, and you're totally going to regret this in the morning."

I looked off into the night sky, the muscles in my chin twitching.

"Dammit, Nate." He wrapped his big arms around me and held me tight. "My brother was gay. But I'm not. You're like a brother to me now, kiddo. And besides, I'm not the one you really want."

We stayed that way for a while. I sniffed, and then Danial sniffed, and that made me sniff again.

"I'm so sorry about your brother," I said.

"I think you would have liked each other."

If he was anything like Danial, I knew I would have too.

"Hungry?" he said.

"Like a fox."

"I'll make some popcorn and we'll eat it under the stars." He put his mouth close to my ear. "It'll give you something to do with your mouth besides slobber all over me."

I shoved him away, but he just laughed and promised to take me home when he was sober enough.

Chapter 34

Danial and I lay on our backs in the dark and tossed popcorn kernels into the air and tried to catch them in our mouths—a little trick I couldn't have accomplished in broad daylight, my brain was so sluggish. Pleasantly so, but sluggish all the same.

When my cell phone rang a while later, I ignored it.

"You gonna answer that?" Danial asked. And I said, "Nope," and he said, "Why not?" and I giggled and said, "I don't know," and he said, "Is it Adam?" and I said, "Probably."

The ringing stopped. A moment later it started again.

Danial rolled over and reached for the phone in my pocket. "Give me that."

"No," I said, still giggling. We wrestled for the phone, but he managed to grab it and push the answer button on the last ring.

I stared at the pinpricks of light in the black sky.

"Yeah, this is Danial," he said into the phone. "He's right here." He handed me the phone, but I tucked my hands under my back. He put his thumb over the microphone hole. "Take the damn phone and talk to your boyfriend."

Instead, I got up and walked off down the fairway.

* * *

I could hear him behind me, talking in a low voice, but I couldn't make out the words. I fought the urge to just lie down again and close my eyes. I focused, instead, on placing one foot in front of the other.

Left. Right.
Left. Right.
Left.
Left.
Left my wife
with forty-nine kids
at home in bed
with nothing to eat
but a can of sardines.

I giggled again. I could see the green just ahead. I hated golf. Golf was for sedentary, middle-aged men. Like Mr. Stanford, my seventh grade social studies teacher. I wasn't sure he even played golf, but he was the type. I always hated the way he sat on the edge of his desk, one leg hiked up, his dick clearly outlined down the right side of his leg. That thing was massive and those polyester pants did nothing to disguise it. The sight was almost enough to knock the gay out of me. Almost.

Left. Right.

Didn't the president play golf? He was middle-aged, true. But not the sedentary type. He really did look good without his shirt. He was a basketball jock. I wondered if Adam had ever played basketball? He wasn't a jock type. More of a dancer. But, oh, that body.

Right. Left.

I thought about the first time we were together, the way he'd let me just look at him. All the shame from years of wanting something others said I shouldn't want dissolving in one perfect evening. God, he was so beautiful. And then I remembered that somebody else was looking at that body now.

Danial caught up with me and matched his steps to mine. I stumbled and he caught me by the arm and just held on. "He seems like a pretty decent guy," he said after a while. "What's he like? Is he a flamer?"

"Adam? A flamer?" I huffed. "Adam a flamer." I laughed at the idea. We had polished each other's toenails one time. I smiled at the memory. God, I missed being with him.

Last December 8th
The second time

We couldn't get our clothes off fast enough this time. Coming out to Adam's parents had its disadvantages—no more pretending we were just hanging out in his room when we closed the door, which, of course, we were no longer allowed to do. We hadn't dared try my house, and parking was out of the question. It had been a week and a half, and we were crazy for each other.

And then an opportunity had presented itself. It was the night of Natalie's Christmas party, even though it was still two and a half weeks until Christmas. Mom had taken Grandma to visit her sister. The house was empty.

"Wait," Adam had said, already breathless. From the pocket of his crumpled jeans just inside the front door, he fished out two small packets.

"Condoms?"

He chuckled. "A little gift from Mom."

"Why don't you just kill me now?"

He tore a packet open and draped the condom over his forefinger, wiggling it to make it spin. "Just think of it as playing dress up."

I groaned.

Some time later, after the pounding in my chest slowed, I rolled into Adam and propped up on my elbow. My fingers traced a line through the light sheen of sweat on his smooth chest, down his hard, slick belly, and then over the softer areas. He shivered. "You've got goose bumps," I said.

He smiled. "I like you touching me."

I smiled back. "Good, because I plan on doing a lot more of it."

"Could you do it in your room? I'm freezing."

It was the first time he'd been in my room. I wasn't sure what he would think. I leaned against my headboard, shirtless, the top button of my jeans still undone, and nervously watched him scout around.

He stopped to look at a movie poster. "*Walk the Line,* huh?" He glanced over at me, an amused glint in his eyes. "I wouldn't have pegged you as a Johnny Cash fan."

I rolled my eyes. "My mom. She totally digs that movie. She liked the whole guitar-slung-over-the-back thing. She wanted me to hang it on my wall for inspiration." I chuckled. "I don't know how inspiring Johnny Cash is, but, you know, I have to admit Joaquin Phoenix is kind of cute, or at least he was until he went all wacko with that weird rap persona."

He flashed a grin my direction, then trailed his fingers along my desk. "No books?" he said, looking at my sparse bookshelf.

"No books. Public library."

I took a book from the drawer in my bedside table and tossed it to him. He caught it one-handed—nice reflexes—and studied the cover, then turned the book over and scanned the description on the back, shaking his head. "I'm shocked, Mr. Schaper," he said with mock severity. "Does your mom know you read gay literature?"

"There are a lot of things my mom doesn't know about me."

He flashed me another grin, then became thoughtful and placed the book on a shelf, facedown. He continued his exploration, examining each framed photo, a smile tugging at the corners of his mouth. He picked up last year's football picture. In it, I was down on one knee, a football tucked under my arm, number seventy-seven emblazoned on my jersey, the pads making me look much bigger and tougher than I really was. "Cute," he said. "Can I keep this?"

I rolled my eyes.

He tucked it under his arm and continued around the room.

"Juliet told me you played," he said, setting down the picture and picking up my guitar.

I shrugged.

He handed it to me and stretched out on his stomach at my feet, his cheek resting on his folded arms. I strummed some chords, stopping here and there to correct the tuning.

"Tell me about your parents," he said after a while.

"There's not much to tell. They divorced when I was six and my mom's raised me ever since."

"Do you see your dad much?"

"Used to. Not so much anymore."

I picked out a tune on the strings. "When I was, like, twelve, I wanted to take piano lessons. He and my mom had this huge fight. I was at his house—it was his weekend—and I told him about the lessons. I was really stoked." I shook my head, remembering. "He totally freaked out. He called my mom and started yelling at her. He said he was sick of her trying to turn me into a sissy. After he hung up on her, he came into my room and gave me this big lecture about becoming a man and how I needed to act tougher and a bunch of crap like that." I played a short, hard riff, then stilled the strings with the palm of my hand. "Anyway, he finally agreed to let me take lessons, but in return I had to play football."

He grinned. "I'd never pictured myself dating a football player."

I looked up at him and smiled. "Sorry to disappoint you. I quit. I only played because I had to. And then I realized I was selling out every time I put on that uniform. I decided I wasn't doing it anymore."

"How did your dad take it?"

I bit my lip and sucked in a deep breath. "Not so good. We haven't really talked since. He's been pretty unavailable."

I stretched out my leg and rubbed my foot against the side of his face.

He rolled back over onto his stomach and took my foot in his hands. He pressed his thumbs into the arch and slowly slid them up to my toes. "How do you think he'll react when he finds out about me?" He moved his thumbs back down and repeated the slow slide.

"It doesn't matter what he thinks."

"It matters. I can see that in your eyes. But he's the one missing out, Nate." He stared at me until I met his eyes. "You're a beautiful person just like you are." He pressed his lips to my toes one at a time. "Some day he'll figure that out."

His cell phone rang and he slid it from his pocket with a groan. "Mom," he mouthed as he brought it to his ear. "Hi, Mom. Yeah, I'm a Nate's. We're doing our nails."

"What?" I mouthed.

He grinned. "I'll be home in a couple of hours. Yes, I will. All right, Mom. Bye."

"Doing our nails?" I said.

"Should I have told her what we've really been doing?"

We did polish each other's toenails that night. Adam thought it was high time I flamed a little, embraced my inner queen, as he put it. But that simple act was almost as intimate as anything else we'd done together.

We used to be so close. I fingered my tattoo through my dress shirt—*Regret is forever*.

Danial knocked on my head with his free hand. "What?"

"Where'd you go? I lost you for a few minutes there."

I grasped around my head for the thread of the conversation we were having. "Flamer. No. He's just a regular guy. Except, there's really nothing regular about him. He's always been, I don't know, amazing. Gorgeous, funny, playful, sweet, talented, smart—"

"Okay, okay. Jeez. Almost sorry I asked."

I yanked my arm away from him. He let me go.

"Okay, he's cornered the market on all the good adjectives," he said. "So what's the problem?"

I wanted to be a little pissed at Danial, but I couldn't be. I leaned into him, and he wrapped an arm around my shoulder. "I feel like I'm losing him."

"We're talking about the same guy, right? Mr. I-want-to-feel-you-inside-of-me?"

He laughed, but his words just made me want to curl up in a ball and cry. He quit laughing and gripped me tighter.

"You weren't there for the late show," I said. "It wasn't pretty, and it damn sure wasn't sexy. We got into this big fight."

"About?"

"Nothing. Everything. I don't even know anymore. Sometimes I feel like I'm ninety percent carbonation, and everything about his life there just shakes me up so when I talk to him I can't help but spew. He's just, I don't know, different—his hair, he's got this tattoo on his neck I didn't know anything about. I mean, what the fuck is that? He gets a tattoo and doesn't even tell me? He's distracted. He's out all the time. He's living in a gay community with lots of beautiful men. I can't compete with all that. I'm a fucking high school student living in Texas."

"Who says you have to compete?"

"One of his roommates kissed him, Danial. More than once."

"Big deal. You kissed me. Not that I'm not flattered, but, you know, I didn't exactly feel the earth move."

I pulled away from him and stumbled. He caught me and held on and I let him. "Look," he said, "you either trust him or you don't. Some things you just have to let go."

"He says I always think the worst of him. Then he hung up before we could, as he put it, say something we'd regret. We haven't really spoken to each other since. He's not even a little jealous about me being out with you tonight. It's like he wants me to find someone else."

"Oh, you are mental. He wouldn't be calling you and sounding worried half to death if he didn't care about you."

"He thinks I'm fragile. He's always been my protector. He was the one who held me together when everything fell apart. I couldn't have done it without him. I tried not to be such a burden on him, Danial, but I just couldn't help myself, you know. He was always the strong one. I wasn't. I needed him. I still need him."

I wiped my eyes with the collar of my shirt and sniffed. "I can't blame him. He deserves a whole person."

"You're not the pathetic, needy person you're making yourself out to be."

"You don't know what I put him through."

"No, I don't. Tell me."

We walked the entire length of the golf course. I talked. Danial listened, stopping me here and there to ask questions, but otherwise letting me talk without commentary. I told him about the New

Year's Eve party, the brutal assault that was still so vivid in my mind, the weeks in the hospital healing physically, and the months that followed when I struggled so hard to heal emotionally. Dodging calls from my therapist, trying desperately to pretend everything was okay when it was anything but. Facing my dad and my classmates and their stupid, flippant, inconsiderate comments that sucked the soul out of me. Being deposed by my attorney about the most intimate details of my relationship with Adam in front of my mom. And then the trial. God, the trial. That had broken me.

Chapter 35

Last March 17
The trial

In the fourth-floor hallway of the criminal courthouse, on the northern edge of downtown Houston, I huddled with Adam and a small group of friends. Adam held firmly to the back of my neck, kneading the muscles there with his thumb, trying to relax me as Mike urged me to stay strong. Beyond that, no one seemed to have much to say.

My mom reached an arm into our circle to get my attention. "The prosecutor needs to meet with us."

"Okay." I took a ragged breath and stood tall. "I guess this is it." I acknowledged their pats on the shoulder with a wan smile and turned to go. That's when I saw my dad. What little courage I had managed to amass from our group bonding ran down my leg.

"Nate," he said stonily. He nodded his head once, but there was no encouraging hand on the shoulder, no hug, no nothing that would connect this man to me beyond a mere acknowledgment of my existence. His eyes flicked to Adam's tight grip on my hand as the others melted into the background.

I swallowed hard. "Dad, this is Adam."

"I know who he is."

Adam stayed with me, always with a steadying hand on my elbow or my shoulder or my knee, until the bailiff called for everyone to rise and announced the judge. Only then did he take his seat behind me in the gallery.

Andrew Cargill was seated with his attorney at the table across the aisle, dressed in a suit like some kind of choir boy. I avoided looking at him, opting instead to keep my head down and my eyes on my hands, trembling in my lap. My stomach turned over. Mr. Maldonado, my attorney, looked over his notes, then leaned over to speak to me in a low voice. "Relax, Nate. It will be hours before you have to take the stand."

But those hours that followed were like a nightmare I couldn't wake up from. Witnesses were called and questioned. My face burned with shame when friends testified as to what they saw that night in the moments immediately following the attack.

But it wasn't until the defense attorney questioned Adam that the most intimate details of our lives were laid bare for everyone to gawk at. I was grateful that my family and friends were sitting behind me. I could feel my dad's humiliation and disgust mounting. I didn't have to look at his face to know it was there.

Adam answered every question with a calm and confidence that I envied. When the prosecutor asked him to describe his relationship with me, he looked at me and smiled before answering. "I love Nate," he said simply. The defense attorney tried to twist the details of our relationship and make it seem perverted. He tried to twist the events of that night to make us look like consensual partners in the crime. But Adam dismissed all as nonsense and repeatedly laid out the facts as if he were talking to a mentally challenged child.

When the judge dismissed Adam, I was sure the worst was behind me. What was left to say?

But I was wrong. Sensing I was the weak one, the defense attorney had saved his best for me. He hammered me with questions about our sex life. When did I last have sex? How many times? Where? Did I enjoy anal sex? Did we ever insert objects into each other's anuses? Had I ever looked at gay porn? He was relentless with his questions. Maldonado objected repeatedly, but the questions were allowed more often than not. The more the prosecutor pushed, the more I stammered and fumbled my way through near incoherent answers. It was everything Maldonado had tried to prepare me for, and more, and while I knew Adam was right, I wasn't on trial here, it didn't feel that way. I shook so hard my teeth chattered. Maldonado, seeing what was happening, made a motion for a recess.

The judge granted us fifteen minutes, and I fled the courtroom.

The hallway spun as I stumbled toward the stairwell past people on cell phones and attorneys speaking to clients in tense little huddles. I slammed into the bar on the door, releasing the latching mechanism, and fell onto the landing inside. From there I made my way quickly down the three flights of stairs to the lobby below, then out into the city. I expected someone to grab my elbow at any second or to suddenly block my path, but no one did, and once I was free of the claustrophobia of the courthouse, I just kept going. I yanked the knot loose on my tie and trailed it on the sidewalk, then abandoned it altogether. When my cell phone vibrated in my pocket, I turned it off.

I wandered for hours, maybe. No plan. I was completely lost in the city, and soon I was, literally, completely lost. Not that I noticed or cared. When I was too tired to walk anymore, I slid down the wall of a brick building in what appeared to be an older part of the city—a building that seemed to be held up by only the collection of homeless men leaning against it. I closed my eyes. What I couldn't do in my own bed without pills anymore, I did well holding up that wall. I slept. Or maybe I just passed out.

"Are you Nathan Schaper?"

I opened my eyes. On the sidewalk in front of me was a pair of shiny black shoes. I closed my eyes again, confused and too tired to care. He repeated the question, and this time when I opened my eyes the police officer was stooped down in front of me. I nodded my assent and realized my cheek was resting on the concrete.

"Your family's pretty worried about you, son. Are you okay?"

I sat up, and answered him dully.

"Let's go," he said, standing and offering me his hand. "I'm going to take you home."

I didn't get all the pieces put together until we were in the police cruiser and well on our way. The policeman was talking to someone on his radio. I searched my pants pockets for my phone, but it was gone. In fact, my suit jacket was gone as well. Mom was going to be pissed. Without warning, tears blurred my vision and spilled down my grimy cheeks.

"Rough day?" the cop said, passing a travel pack of tissues through the bars that protected him from nut jobs in his backseat.

I took the tissues without answering.

It was dark when he pulled up in front of my house. The front door opened before he got the car in park, and Adam sprinted out, Mom and Grandma right on his heels. He pulled me from the car and crushed me to him and the tears started all over again. He let me go long enough for Mom and Grandma to check me over.

"Let me talk to him," Adam said to Mom in a low voice when she finally let me go.

She nodded and turned her attention to the police officer, and Adam ushered me inside.

I don't know what I expected, but I didn't expect to be roughed up. Still, that's what it felt like when Adam pulled out a dining room chair and none too gently told me to sit. I sat. He pulled out a second chair and turned it to face me and sat down. He propped his elbows on his knees, fisted his hands together, and pressed his chin into them. When his eyes met mine, they were hard. He didn't say anything, just looked at me for a long time, and when I couldn't stand it anymore, I started babbling.

"I know you're mad," I said wearily. I tried to explain that I just needed to get out of there, that I didn't know what the protocol was and that maybe I'd have to go to jail, or maybe they'd declare a mistrial, but I did what I had to do and then my cell phone—I patted my pockets. No phone—no harm was done and—

He cut me off midsentence. "Shut up. Just SHUT UP."

I winced and shut up.

He scrubbed his face with his hands and then resumed his chin-to-fist position. I braced myself for whatever was coming.

"This ends right here, right now, Nate. You have an appointment with Dr. Parkerson tomorrow morning and—"

"No."

"You're going if I have to drag your ass there kicking and screaming," he said angrily. And then almost to himself, "God, I blame myself for this."

"You didn't—"

"You have to deal with this, Nate. I've tried to respect your feelings, but this isn't going to just go away or get better on its own. I can see that now. I should have seen it a long time ago. Do you have any idea how scared I was when we didn't know where you were? How scared we all were? Anything could have happened out there. Anything! I won't lose you." His voice cracked and he paused a moment to compose himself. "You're going, and I'm going with you. And you're going to keep going, as often and as long as necessary, until you beat back this thing that's eating you up. Do you understand me?"

His right eye was slightly swollen, the skin around it purple. How did I not notice that before?

"Who hit you?"

"Your dad," he said offhandedly. "He coldcocked me when I tried to follow you out of the courtroom."

"My dad?" I pondered that a moment, then felt heat rising in my veins. "Did you hit him back?"

He shook his head slightly. "Your mom beat me to it."

"Mom?"

He smiled a little, but his eyes still flashed with resolve. "She used some words that made me blush. Man, she's got a right hook. She could really give you some lessons."

"Mom?"

"It took two of the guards to pull her off your dad."

I tried to imagine my mom as a fighter, the look on my dad's face when his passive ex turned grizzly. "Where is he now . . . my dad?"

"I don't know."

He damn sure wasn't here, I noted.

"Look," he said, taking my hands in both of his and gripping so tightly my knuckles ground together, "you don't have to do this alone, but you do have to do this. And you will, or I swear to God . . ."

He didn't finish, and I had no idea what he was swearing to do, but whatever it was, I believed him. He talked for a while, and I half listened, but mostly I just watched his face contort as he struggled to tell me what this was doing to him and everyone else who loved me. Mom and Grandma came in sometime during his speech, and he gave them a "He's going to be okay," and I knew a lot had been discussed while I was on the lam. When Mom placed a bowl of tomato soup and a grilled cheese sandwich on the table next to me, I pushed it away, but Adam pushed it right back and told me to eat. When I said I wasn't hungry, he picked up a wedge and practically forced it into my mouth with an "Eat, goddammit." I took it from him and choked down a few bites.

"Is this your idea of tough love?" I asked, dunking the wedge into the soup to prolong having to actually eat it.

"Any way you want it, baby."

When I'd managed to eat half the sandwich and a few bites of soup, Adam hustled me up the stairs and turned on the shower, but I was too tired to do anything more than curl up on the bed. "Not yet," he said, dragging me to my feet again. "You smell like a homeless person."

Chapter 36

I didn't tell Danial that when I'd protested, Adam had stripped me down himself and told me to get in. I didn't tell Danial that when I did and hugged the wall, Adam had muttered something, then got undressed and climbed in with me. I didn't tell Danial that Adam had peeled me off the wall, and when my eyes drifted over him, had said, "Don't even think about it."

"I can't look at you naked and *not* think about it," I'd said.

Adam had rolled his eyes, and the corners of his mouth twitched up just slightly. "Then don't look." He spun me around and the shower spray hit me in the face. I adjusted the showerhead, then braced my forearms against the wet tile and rested my forehead against my arms, allowing the spray to clear my head and pound into my shoulders as Adam got busy with the shower gel. It smelled like mango and oranges, and when I closed my eyes, the scent and Adam's hands moving over my body and the hot water began to loosen the knots in my muscles. By the time he toweled me off and got me into some sleep pants, I was ready to collapse. From the bed, I watched him pull on a pair of my boxers and then turn off the light.

"Scooch over, handsome," he said in the dark.

"You're staying? Mom—"

"It was your mom's idea."

I thought about that as he rolled me to the wall and wrapped himself around me. "You're my warden?"

"Yep."

"I don't suppose it would be ethical for the warden to cavort with the prisoner?"

"Nope."

"I promise I won't tell," I'd said sleepily.

He'd scoffed, and the last thing I remembered was him saying, "Not tonight, baby. You need your sleep."

I held on to Danial, but I kept that memory to myself. There were some things that belonged to Adam and me alone.

Adam called again during our walk, but Danial assured him I was okay and that I'd call back soon. I couldn't explain why I wouldn't take the phone. I just knew I needed him, and he wasn't here.

"I'd heard things, but I never knew the whole story," Danial said quietly as we sat on an arched stone bridge that traversed a small stream between the fairway and the green. He looked at me with such pity it made me squirm.

"Quit looking at me. You're freaking me out."

He smiled a little, but I could still see the pity. I didn't want pity. I'd had enough of pity. He reached over and fished the pendant out of my shirt. "You never take this off." He turned it over and rubbed his thumb across the engraving of Adam's name. "Did he give it to you?"

"Yeah. He has the other half with my name on it. It was a Christmas gift last year."

Danial dropped the pendant, and I tucked it back in my shirt. It was warm from his hands.

"Call him."

I shook my head.

"You're not going to straighten things out by running away. If you don't call him, I will."

"Don't. Promise you won't. He'll just want to come rescue me. Because that's what he does."

"What's wrong with that?"

"That's not what a relationship should be about."

"Can I just make an observation here?"

Would it have mattered if I'd said no?

"For such a smart guy, you're quite a dumbass. Life is too damn short to be playing these games. Tell him how you feel."

"Like you tell Jules?"

"That's different."

"Not so much. She likes you too, you know."

He drew in a deep breath. "I'm not moving in on some other guy's girl. Now quit changing the subject. Come on." He stood up and pulled me to my feet. "I'm taking you home, and when you're all alone and in your jammies and feeling all gooey again, call him. I know you love him. That's so obnoxiously obvious. What's the worst that could happen? Somebody gets hurt? But you gotta think about all the great things you could miss out on if you don't take a chance. And if worse comes to worst, you can always come on to me again. Who knows? Maybe I've got some deep gay tendencies that just haven't surfaced yet."

I laughed. "Yeah, right. Trust me, if you had any gay tendencies, we'd be rolling in the grass right now."

"Would you really have done that?"

I watched a lone cloud make its way across the face of the moon, slowly blotting out the bright moonlight, and realized how chilly it had gotten. I shivered from the cold and then I shivered again because I didn't like my answer to that question.

"Never mind," he said. "You didn't."

I could feel the muscles in my chin start to twitch again.

"Stop it," Danial said, forcing me to look at him. "You didn't. That's all that matters. Don't beat yourself up." He gave me a big hug and took me home.

Danial was right—Adam and I, we needed to talk. To really talk, without suspicion and jealousy and anger. On the drive home, I made myself a promise. I would be honest with him. Completely, no-holds-barred honest. About why I'd pushed him to go to New York, about how desperately I hadn't wanted him to go, about my fears and my flaws and the source of all the pettiness I'd subjected him to. And about how proud I was of him, about what a hero he'd always been for me. He would reassure me, and this time, I would believe him.

It was just past midnight. (One A.M. New York time.) Late. But he was probably still up, I told myself, somewhat sarcastically, and then remembered I wasn't going to think that way. The plan: I would text, and if he was up, I would call. But then, I decided to check Skype first. While I waited for my computer to boot up, I undressed and tossed my suit on the back of my desk chair. Mom would freak when she saw the grass stain on my slacks. I sat down in my jammies as Danial called them, then decided *what the hell* and yanked them off. I settled in in my boxers just as Skype loaded. I was only marginally surprised to see Adam's name with a little green check mark next to it. I clicked the call button thinking I might catch him in his briefs and we could turn on the webcam, and after we talked, maybe we could have one of those sexy conversations that had become all too infrequent.

A familiar voice, not Adam's, answered, no video. "This must be Nate," the voice said without even a hello, and I knew instantly I was talking to Justin.

"Where's Adam?"

"You've got some nerve. I don't know what kind of game you're playing—"

"I want to talk to him."

"He's tired. Verrry tired. Tired, tired, tired," he said, clearly suggesting that he, Justin, had something to do with that. "And he's sleeping like a baby now."

"Wake him up."

Justin laughed, the sound slippery like a slick of oil on the roadway. "He's had quite enough of your angst and silliness. Why don't you go back to your playpen and leave him alone. I'll take care of him from now on." He paused a moment, then chuckled. "The way I took care of him tonight."

"I don't believe you." And I didn't.

"Don't. It doesn't matter to me one way or the other. You don't understand him at all."

"And you do?"

"Oh yeah. I know exactly what he needs. Go play with your little high school friends and leave the big boys alone."

"You know what? Forget it. I'll just call him."

I was determined not to let him get to me. I was reaching to disconnect when he said, "Those boys fucked you up in more ways than one, didn't they, Nate?" I froze, my hand on the mouse. He scoffed. "He's not a psychologist. He's not Superman. You want a hero, Nate? Go catch a matinee. You need your head shrunk? Go see your Dr. Parkerson. But leave Adam alone. You don't deserve him. Oh, and just to set the record straight, he kissed me back."

With that, he disconnected, and I watched Adam's name ghost on the screen.

Chapter 37

I'm Queer. Get Over It.
Mission accomplished
By Nate Schaper on Oct. 12
We came, we danced, and nobody died or got arrested or beat up
or sent to detention.
Oh, and when life gives you a lemon ... suck it.

Comments:

HappyBoy
Oct. 12, at 12:40 A.M.
    What happened to Adam?
GodChild223
Oct. 12, at 12:43 A.M.
    [DELETE]
Xyz123
Oct. 12, at 12:52 A.M.
    Nate, why did you leave??
PakistaniPal

Oct. 12, at 1:00 A.M.

Sounds like somebody needs an intervention . . . again.

Brett2010

Oct. 12, at 2:15 A.M.

Wow! Really? You danced together at a school dance? Boy on boy? Wow. I mean, WOW. You Texas boys really know how to put it out there.

Chapter 38

There was a text waiting when I woke up the next morning.

Hey, baby. You shld have woken me up. Meet you for lunch at 11:00.

There were three things I knew. (1.) The text hadn't been meant for me. (2.) I hadn't been his first thought that morning. And (3.) He was calling someone else baby now.

I didn't turn on my computer. Half an hour later, I watched the screen on my phone light up. *Adam calling.* I didn't answer.

"You look like crap," Danial said, handing me a Starbucks cup over the counter.

Crap suggested feeling. All I felt was a horrible numbness or a numbing horribleness.

"What are you doing here? It's Sunday."

"I was in the neighborhood."

"Yeah, right. Any arsenic in here?" I asked, setting the cup on the counter.

"They weren't taking special orders this morning. You're cranky. I take it the phone call didn't go so well."

"Why would you think that?"

"Hmm," he said. "Wild guess."

A woman came into the music store just then, setting the new bells on the door jangling. Danial stepped aside while I used a mouthpiece puller to remove the stuck mouthpiece from her son's trombone. I glanced up when the bell rang again and was surprised to see Luke walk into the shop. Danial raised his eyebrows and smirked.

Luke waved and tugged on his ear, then wandered over to the music rack and shuffled through the sheet music.

I glanced back at Danial and shrugged. I finished with the customer and walked over to Luke. "This is a surprise," I said.

He wrinkled his forehead and dug the toe of his athletic shoe into the carpet. His mop of blond hair fell forward into his eyes. I had to resist the temptation to brush it back. "Hope you don't mind," he said. "Juliet, the redheaded girl, told me you worked here. After you left last night. Why did you leave? Weren't you having a good time?"

He was so transparent. It didn't take a linguist to see the embedded question in the question. Because what he really wanted to know was, was I having a good time with him. "Uh, yeah. I had a great time. I just, uh, I just needed some air."

He nodded his head. "Yeah. It gets really hot when you're dancing."

I nodded my head back, thinking . . . *okay*.

"So . . . what are you drinking?" he asked, nodding down to my hand.

"I don't know. I haven't tried it yet. Probably a latte. Danial brought it."

"You and Danial, you're . . ."

"Dating? No. We're just good friends."

"There's that other guy you write about sometimes."

That other guy. My nose burned. I was uncomfortable with the way he was looking at me, just waiting for something. I decided to change the direction of the conversation. "Is there something you needed today, or did you just stop by to say hi?"

He looked around the room, watched Mr. Ratliff through the plate-glass window in his office for a moment, then Danial, still leaning against the counter (Luke waved). "We talked last night about getting together after you got off work today. Remember? I thought maybe you'd like to meet for pizza or something."

He looked so eager I almost laughed. But I knew from his comments to my blog posts that he was terrified of coming out, and yet here he was. And he'd danced with me last night in front of all those kids. He reminded me so much of myself, the way I drew courage from Adam to do things I never would have considered before. Maybe I was his Adam. I couldn't think about that right now. His eyes were doing this melty thing, and it made me nervous to think this cute kid was falling for me.

It's just pizza, I told myself.

"Uh, sure," I said. We made plans then shuffled around awkwardly until Mr. Ratliff stuck his head out and asked me for some help. I was only in Mr. Ratliff's office for a moment when I heard the jangle of the bell. I looked up and saw Luke slipping out the door.

"You gonna tell me what happened?" Danial asked when I finished with Mr. Ratliff.

"With Luke?"

"Him too, but first, you talked to Adam. Well?"

I slammed the cash drawer. Danial's eyebrows shot up. He watched me turn the page in the appointment book. "Next week?" I asked.

"This is just a crazy observation, but you seem kind of upset."

"Okay, next week," I said, starting to make a notation in the book. The pencil lead snapped. I tossed it aside and looked around the desk for another one. Where were all the damn pencils? Danial pulled one from his pocket and handed it to me.

"Thanks," I mumbled. I started to make a notation.

"I already have a lesson scheduled for next week."

I flipped the pencil over and scrubbed out the marks I'd just made, then tapped the pencil on the page, looking for something, anything that needed marking or erasing.

"Quit stalling," Danial said. "What happened? You two break up?"

"Yeah, something like that."

"No, you didn't."

I looked at him, and then I glanced at Mr. Ratliff in his office, then back at Danial. "Yeah, we did."

His mouth dropped open, then snapped shut again. I handed him his pencil and went to the workroom. Danial picked up my drink from the counter and followed me.

"Whoa, whoa, whoa, whoa," he said, grabbing my arm.

"I didn't talk to Adam. And I don't want to talk to Adam. And I damn sure don't want to talk *about* Adam."

"Why?"

I looked at the gadgets hanging from the pegboard on the wall as if I might find an answer to that question dangling from a hook somewhere. I pulled my cell phone from my pocket and opened my inbox and held it out to him. He took it and read the text. "So?"

"*So?*" I took the phone back and jammed it in my pocket.

Danial rolled his eyes, which pissed me off because he didn't know the whole story. So I told him about my "conversation" with Justin the night before.

Danial took a deep breath and blew it out. "He called repeatedly last night because he was worried about you. Doesn't that count for something?"

"Yeah. He worries about me. Big fucking deal. He told that creep about me, Danial. And then that *creep* mocked me."

"So, that's it, huh?" Danial said. "You're not even going to give Adam a chance to defend himself? You're just going to take the word of some two-bit actor over—"

"Adam told me he was tired of defending himself to me. Tired of it. T-I-R-E-D. And you know what, whether he kissed Justin back or not, it doesn't matter. He told him about what happened to me. Why would he do that? Huh? He knows how I feel about Justin. I'm just one big *fucking* joke in New York."

"I think you both need to be committed." He grabbed the phone out of my pocket before I knew what was happening and shoved it in my face. "Call him and fix this."

I grabbed for the phone, but he tucked it behind his back. "Are you gonna call him?"

I dropped my head back and closed my eyes and focused on

breathing. "It's none of your business, Danial. Now give me the god*damn* PHONE."

He handed it over without another word. "Can we please talk about something else?" I said, shoving the phone back in my pocket with a trembling hand. I cast for something, anything. "What do you think about Luke? He wants to get together this evening for pizza."

"Are you going?"

"Yeah. Why not?" I said, dully. "He could use some support."

"Yeah. Well, I think he wants more than support from you."

"And maybe he'll get it."

He seemed to think about that for a moment, then said, "Just be careful. The only person I know who is more vulnerable than that kid right now is you."

I looked away and fought the burning in my nose.

He stood up, drank the rest of the latte, set the empty cup on the counter, and sighed heavily. "Want to get stoned later?"

I huffed. "I've got a date, remember?"

"Yeah. Stop by after if you want. My parents won't be back until late."

"Sure."

"Where's Juliet?"

"I wondered when you'd get around to asking."

He sneered.

When Adam called again late that afternoon, I was only too happy to answer.

"Why didn't you take my calls last night?" he asked without even a hello.

"I was on a date. Or did you forget?"

He sighed heavily and audibly into the phone. "Nate, I don't want to fight with you."

"Good. Because I don't want to fight with you either. I have to change. I'm meeting someone for pizza."

"Someone? Who?"

"Someone I met at the homecoming dance."

He was quiet for a moment, then, "Is this some kind of date?"

I almost choked on the question. I took a deep breath. "Maybe it is, maybe it isn't. I guess we'll just have to see what happens."

"Why are you doing this?"

"Because I'm hungry."

He ignored my sarcasm. "So, is this what you want? To see other guys? Or is this some kind of punishment because some guy kissed me or because I have a fucking tattoo on my neck?"

Oh, it's for a reason much worse than a kiss or a fucking tattoo, Adam. But I didn't tell him that. He knew what he'd done. Instead, as coldly as I could muster, I threw his words back at him. "It's no big deal."

"No big deal, huh? Great. Fine. You know what? Maybe we do need a break from each other. Maybe I'll see you at Thanksgiving."

Inside I was raging, but I answered him with a calm, "Yeah. Thanksgiving. Sure."

Luke was already in a booth in a far corner, his back to the door. His table choice spoke volumes about where he was—that place between excitement about embracing his authentic self and being found out. His soda glass was empty when I got there. Since I was right on time, that meant Luke had gotten there at least ten or fifteen minutes early. I could see his leg jiggling under the table. He was nervous. Cute.

I stayed back and watched him for a minute, remembering other times I'd sat with Adam in that same booth. I mentally probed about for the pain I was sure would overtake me and send me running for the bathroom, clutching my stomach. But all I found was an emptiness. A profound emptiness that screamed to be filled.

I sucked in a deep breath and headed over to the table. "Hey," I said, sliding in across from him. His face lit up immediately.

"Hey!" he said, sitting up straighter and smiling broadly. "You came. I mean, I wasn't sure you'd really come because, you know. But, you came."

I laughed. "A Coke, please," I said to the waitress who'd approached our booth. "And I'm sure he'll have another." I gestured to Luke's empty glass.

"Yes, please." He grinned at her.

When she asked if we wanted to order, Luke said, "Have you ever tried their chicken fajita pizza?"

"Nope. But I'm game." I looked back to the waitress. "A large, please."

Luke beamed. Why did I feel like this was Christmas morning, and I was the big gift from Santa? I cleared my throat and leaned my elbows on the table. "Did you have fun at the homecoming dance last night?"

"I had a blast!" He glanced around quickly before he continued in a lower voice. "I've never danced with another guy before."

I laughed again. "Was it everything you hoped it'd be?"

"Even better."

I knew the feeling. I shook off the memories before they could take hold. It was Luke's turn, and I wasn't going to spoil it for him. "You know, everybody's journey is different, but one thing I think I can say for sure, you won't regret it." At least, I hoped not, thinking briefly back to the older Qasimi brother. But Luke wasn't Muslim, I told myself. But then, neither was I.

"I know you said you're not with Danial. Does that mean you're still with Adam?"

"How do you know about Adam?"

"You blogged about him. But you haven't mentioned him much in the past few weeks. So, I mean, I was thinking you were with Danial, but if you aren't, then are you still with—"

I cut him off. "We've decided to see other people." I picked up the parmesan cheese shaker and shook some into my hand, then put a pinch in my mouth.

"You looked kinda sad when you said that."

The waitress set our drinks on the table and told us our pizza would be right out.

I smiled at her, then looked at Luke. He had blue eyes, just like Adam's, only lighter. And that wild blond hair. Again I felt the urge to reach over and brush it out of his eyes. He waited, a puzzled look on his face.

"Yeah," I said finally. "It wasn't one of the happier moments in my life."

He nodded. "I'm really sorry."

I looked at his serious expression and decided I wanted to see more of the happy Luke.

"Tell me about you. Other than reading my blog, what do you do with your time?"

"I play in the marching band."

"A band geek?" I said, surprised.

His face darkened. "Just because we play in the band doesn't mean we're geeks."

"Oh, no. No, no. I didn't mean it that way." I grinned at him. "I totally love the band. I would much rather have played with the band than play football."

"You play football?"

"I quit right before my junior year. I never liked it. It was something my dad made me do in exchange for piano lessons. What do you play?"

"Clarinet."

"That's cool."

"You want to come watch me play? We have a really awesome halftime performance. I think you'd like it. We have a game next Friday night. It starts at seven. It'll be the first time we do all three movements of our show performance. Can you come?" He was speaking fast, as if in speaking the words more slowly he might not get them all out before someone cut him off.

"Would you really want me to come?"

"Yeah. I mean . . ." He seemed embarrassed. "Nobody knows, you know, but that's okay."

Yeah, right. I decided it was time for a reality check. "Luke, you can't dance with me the way you did last night and not have people talk."

"But, those other kids were dancing together too, and they're not gay, are they?"

"No, they're not gay. But that doesn't mean there won't be talk about them too. The difference is, those guys have nothing to hide, they have each other, and they just don't care what other people say."

"Are you saying that people are really going to know I'm . . . you know?" He looked a little panicked, and when he took a sip of his soda, he sloshed a bit on his shirt.

I tried to give him an encouraging smile. "Would that really be so bad?"

"I don't think I'm ready for this."

"None of us are ever really ready." I laughed. I reached across the table for his hand. He looked around nervously, pulled it away, and then put it in his lap. I withdrew my hand and took a sip of my soda.

He smiled apologetically. "How did you do it?"

"Come out?"

He nodded.

I smiled, thinking about how we'd inadvertently outed ourselves. "Adam and I, we couldn't keep our eyes or our hands off each other. Juliet was the first to notice. She's the redhead Danial danced with."

"The one who told me where you worked. She seems nice."

"She's great. She really stood with us. Then we accidentally outed ourselves to Adam's mom."

"How?"

I grinned. "Let's just say she caught us in a compromising position."

"Were you, you know?"

I scratched my head. I wasn't one to kiss and tell, but then I realized that wasn't true. I was, and I would, and when Luke leaned across the table, his eyes flashing, and said, "What's it like? Please, please, please tell me," I did.

An abridged version to be sure. Not the more tender moments, the memories that hurt now, the ones that I'd replayed over and over in mind on lonely nights. Instead, I told him about the more embarrassing moments, the ones we laughed about now, or had laughed about, like the cop knocking on our window that night we went parking in Ridgewood Park and the morning after that first night I'd "crashed" at Adam's house, the morning we were caught in aforesaid compromising position.

Chapter 39

Last November 21
Caught in a compromising position

A small prodding on my backside. Adam's naked body under me, warm, soft, and hard at the same time. Eyes still closed, I pressed my mouth into his shoulder and allowed myself to drift happily back to sleep. Another small prod. Lazily I opened my eyes.

"Mea!"

I yanked the sheet up to my waist.

Adam was instantly awake. I rolled off him as he bolted upright. "Mea! How did you get in here?"

"Your door was locked, so I used a pixie stick. See." She proudly held up a thin green plastic stick.

"Mea?" Adam's mom called out from the top of the stairwell.

"Oh my God," I gasped in panic.

The door was wide open.

Before either of us could move a fraction of an inch to something that resembled an appropriate sleeping arrangement for two teenage boys, his mom was in the doorway.

"Mea!" she scolded.

The shock registered on her face before the last syllable faded. It took only a second for her to take it all in. She sucked in a sharp breath and went pale. "Oh, shit." She averted her eyes. "Mea! Out of this room right now, young lady."

"Okay," Mea sang out. She skipped out of the room, oblivious to the fact that she had just outed her big brother with that cursed pixie stick.

Adam's mom quickly closed the door behind her.

"Guess what, Mommy," we heard Mea say through the door. "Nate doesn't have a tattoo on his ass like Adam does."

"Mea Jefferies, where on earth did you learn that kind of language? What tattoo? We have to talk, young lady."

"Oh, God," I groaned when I was sure they were gone. I banged my head back against the headboard, hard. "Just kill me now." The jolt of adrenaline that shot through me when I woke had left my fingers numb. I thought if I tried to stand, I'd pass out.

Adam ran his finger up my arm. "You're pretty cute when you're mortified." He chuckled.

"You're laughing? I can't believe you're *laughing*. I mean, oh my God, look at this room." Actually, the room was every bit as neat as it had been the night before, but the bed, oh, Jesus, the bed was a fucking mess. The sheets were rumpled and damp, the bottom corners had come loose, and the comforter was nowhere to be seen. The air mattress his mom had left, apparently while we were "watching" a movie, was still tightly packed, still sitting on the chair, completely and obviously untouched.

"Hmmm . . ." Adam sat up next to me and surveyed the bed with that wicked smile I had come to love and dread. "Looks like somebody—or should I say some bodies—had a good time last night."

I groaned and flipped over, burying my face in the pillow.

Adam brushed his lips against the back of my neck. He traced a line down my spine with his tongue, inching the sheet down as he went. My body responded, and my breath caught in my throat. This was just wrong.

I flipped over. "Have you lost your ever lovin' mind? Your mom . . . oh, God . . . oh my God, your stepdad too . . ."

He grinned. "We wanted to come out." He gestured at the bed. "Well, we're out! And what's done can't be undone."

He was doing that Shakespeare thing again. I groaned and

pulled the pillow over my face. "I would have preferred something a little more subtle."

He pulled the pillow off, flung it across the room, and kissed me. "Ah, come on. Where's your sense of danger and fun?"

"I think it just ran down my leg."

He chuckled. He seemed to be considering something. I was afraid I might know what that something was too.

"No!"

He laughed.

Suddenly he stopped and looked toward the door. "Do you smell that?"

"What?"

"Bacon."

I glared at him. "Oh, hell no."

"Oh, hell yes," he said, grabbing my arm, laughing. "A quick shower and then it's time to put your big-boy pants on."

"We can't take a shower together!"

He cracked up. "Well, we certainly can't show up at the breakfast table like this." He nuzzled my neck and drew in a deep breath, then let out a loud sigh. "My parents know the smell of indiscretion."

We took a shower. It wasn't all that quick.

Adam's mom and stepdad sat across the bar from each other, leaning on the counter and talking in low voices when we finally dragged ourselves into the kitchen.

Actually, I was the only one dragging. Adam was buoyant. I was astounded at how cavalier he was behaving, as if we'd just performed some life-saving surgery rather than unspeakable acts of passion on each other.

His mom turned away when she saw us and busied herself with Mea, who was watching a cartoon at the other end of the bar, but Ben greeted us with a cheery, "Good morning."

I wanted to die right there. I couldn't even meet his eyes. Why hadn't I bolted when I had the chance? I was keenly aware that Adam and I were both freshly scrubbed, our hair still wet from the shower. My face burned. Parts of me were pleasantly sore and thankfully behaving for the moment. That was something, I guess.

Ben cleared his throat. "Hungry?"

"Starved," Adam said, accepting a plate and handing it to me. He took the next one for himself.

Starved? *Starved?* Oh God. I was going to throw up or hyperventilate or stroke out right there on the kitchen floor.

Adam pushed out a bar stool for me with his bare foot. I sat, still not trusting myself to look up. His stepdad slid a platter piled with bacon and eggs and toast over to us. Adam dished up our plates.

"So," Ben said, a hint of mischief in his voice, "did you boys sleep well?"

His mom shot her husband a look over her shoulder.

I choked on my orange juice and Adam patted my back until I could stop coughing long enough to catch my breath.

"Great," Adam said. "You okay?" he asked me.

Uh. Let me check. No. "Fine."

His stepdad nodded his head, a curious smile on his face.

His mom ran out of things to do for Mea and returned to her stool, embarrassment, shock, mortification all written on her face. My heart pounded as I waited for whatever was coming next. Whatever it was, it wouldn't be good. Next to me, Adam was shoveling in the eggs with gusto. I wanted to kick him. *Have the decency to at least look contrite!*

She looked at Adam. "You have a tattoo?"

"A dragon!" Mea said brightly.

Adam winked at his little sister, then looked back at his mom. "Do you want to see it?" He could have been talking about a haircut for all the pure driven snow in his voice.

"Not right now."

Adam shrugged. "Okay." He got up and crossed to the refrigerator. "Nate, you want some more orange juice?"

I glanced up. "Sure," I mumbled. His mom fussed with Mea's braids. She turned back suddenly and caught me watching her. We both dropped our eyes. I knew then she was as nervous as we were . . . or rather as I was because Adam seemed to be enjoying the whole thing.

Ben cleared his throat and they exchanged a look. "Adam, come sit down," he said.

His mom looked like she might hyperventilate. "Maybe we should talk about this later?"

"Talk about what?" Adam asked all innocent like.

He was going to make her say it! I wondered, not for the first time since I'd met him, if a person could die of embarrassment. I forced myself to take a small bite of toast and kicked Adam under the bar when he sat down. He grinned and squeezed my thigh.

She took a steadying breath, got a nod from Ben, and jumped in. "Nate, you seem like a nice young man."

"He's a very nice young man, Mom."

Thanks you for defending my honor, but no thanks. Would you please shut up! I couldn't believe he was toying with her.

She raised her eyebrows as if to say, *Are you done?*

Adam gestured that she should continue.

She put her hands over Mea's ears and cut to the chase. "I don't like the idea of you boys having sex. I think you're too young."

This time I choked on a bite of egg and just avoided spraying it all over the counter. We were *not* having this conversation!

Adam patted me on the back. "I'm eighteen," he said. He crunched on a piece of bacon.

"I know you're eighteen. I was there when you were born."

Ben folded his arms on the counter, clearly enjoying the show. I noticed the conversation hadn't killed his appetite any more than it had Adam's. I couldn't say the same for mine or his mom's.

She tried appealing to me. "Nate, when you came to spend the night last night, I had no idea—"

"Is Nate Adam's boyfriend?" Mea asked out of the blue.

The room went completely and utterly silent. Even the auto-drip coffeemaker seemed to be holding back its gurgle. Adam looked at me. I looked at him. His mom looked at us both. His stepdad leaned back on his stool, a smile stretching across his face, and waited. Adam reached under the bar and took my hand, never taking his eyes from mine.

"Yes, honey," she said. "I think he is."

"Good. 'Cause he's really cute."

Adam leaned over and kissed me on the cheek. The effect of that simple public gesture was incredible. My face grew warm with pride this time. My heart expanded in my chest with gratitude for what I believed was their acceptance. I suddenly realized there was at least one place in this world where we could be a couple.

His mom cleared her throat.

Adam pulled away and winked at me.

She sucked in a breath and blew it out, causing her lips to flutter, and shook her head. "I never thought I'd have to say this to you boys. House rules. No more sleepovers and doors stay open. Got it?"

Adam grinned and took a swig of orange juice. "Sure, Mom. Whatever you say."

"Yes, ma'am," I muttered.

"And, as the only adult in this room"—she gave her husband a look that said, *Thanks for nothing*—"I feel I have to say something."

"Okay," Adam said, shrugging. "Shoot."

I held my breath.

"I wasn't born yesterday. I know that you boys are going to do what you're going to do no matter what I say. And I can't say that I approve. But, look, I . . . uh . . . I guess I need to know that you're being safe."

That again.

Adam laid down his fork and leaned toward his mom. "I promise, Mom," he said in a sober tone, *finally,* "if Nate gets knocked up, I'll do the right thing by him."

Ben choked back a laugh.

"Don't be a smart ass," she said.

"You said *ass*," Mea said in a small, singsong voice.

Ben pinched his lips, but it wasn't enough. He snorted. Adam dipped his chin and laughed into his chest. As embarrassed as I was by the entire conversation, my funny bone had been tickled too. His mom's mouth twitched with the effort to stay serious. In the end she lost it.

"Out of the mouth of babes," Adam joked. We broke into a collective fit of hysteria. Just when it seemed the laughter might calm, it ramped back up again until we all had tears in our eyes.

I doubt Mea understood even half of what was going on, but she giggled along with the rest of us.

Finally we calmed down. "Seriously, Mom, you don't have to worry. Nate told me if you don't suit up, you don't get in the game."

I did not! I kicked him under the bar. I'd kill him later.

His mom looked embarrassed behind the smile that tugged at her unwilling lips.

But the walls were down and the anxiety washed away with the tears streaming down our faces. What was left was a kind of euphoria I'd never experienced, a moment in which it seemed like everything in the universe had finally lined up and locked into place. I would never have guessed that giving up my deepest secrets would feel so empowering. I doubted his parents understood what that moment meant to me. There would be many times down the road that I would reflect on how good it felt to bask in their acceptance and love. Perhaps it was naïve, but I was beginning to think my fears had all been for nothing.

His mom was slowly shaking her head. "I knew it."

Adam and I exchanged another look. We knew what *it* was.

"I think I've known since you were probably twelve."

"Why didn't you say something?" Adam asked, his eyes on her.

"Because I wasn't absolutely certain. I hoped you'd tell me when you were ready. If you were gay, I wanted it to come from you." She reached across the bar and took his hand.

For a while the talk turned to who knew what, when, and how. As it turned out, there was a lot about Adam she never knew, some of which brought her to tears, some of which brought Adam to tears. I admired Ben for asking questions too and for encouraging Adam to be completely open and for accepting him just as he was. Adam held my hand in a vice grip on top of the bar. With small glances my way for affirmation, he told them how we met, how our relationship had grown, and how much we meant to each other. For all his earlier cutting up, I could see how important this conversation was to him, and my heart was glad.

"Nate," she said, looking at me after the story had unfolded, "do your parents know?"

"No, ma'am, they don't."

"Maybe you should tell them."

I wasn't sure I could ever have that discussion with my parents. But I promised I'd think about it.

His mom pointed her spoon at us. "No more sleepovers. Got it?"

Chapter 40

God, what had happened to us? How was it possible for two people to be so close, to share so much, and then nothing?

Luke sat back in his seat, his eyes wide and glassy, bright splashes of color on his cheeks, and I realized I was really starting to like him. He was so easy to read, so innocent and full of wonder.

"Okay, we're not talking about that anymore," I said and changed the subject. "You're going to need some support. You're part of us now—me, Danial, Juliet, Gaby, Mike, Warren. They're like a big gay support group. They'll be yours too if you let them."

He nodded.

"What about your parents?" I asked.

"Do you think I should tell them?"

"If you think they can handle it, yes. It helps to have your parents behind you. But if you think they'll go ballistic, no. Not until you're older. I know that sucks, but . . ."

I was thinking about Danial's brother again. Maybe he'd still be alive if he'd waited to introduce his boyfriend to his parents. If he'd finished school first and been independent, maybe he'd be doing great things now instead of lying cold in a grave somewhere. But then I thought how great Adam's parents were, and how much I needed my mom when my world fell apart. She hadn't dealt with it so well at first, but eventually she did come to terms with it. My dad, not so much.

"I'll think about it," Luke said.

Over pizza we talked about school, movies, just stuff—my new guitar I was picking up next week, his fear of bugs, looking at the moon through Danial's telescope.

"Who's your favorite music artist?" he asked.

"I don't know. It depends on my mood. Who's your favorite?"

"Taylor Swift," he said, without hesitation. Ouch. "At band camp last summer we used to blast 'You Belong to Me' from someone's car stereo and dance in the street behind the band hall during our lunch break."

I smiled at the image in my mind. "You and Adam would get along great," I said, then instantly regretted it.

He smiled back, sheepishly. "I taped the *Sexy Bitch* T-shirt to your locker."

"I know."

Later I walked him to his car. He'd parked in the farthest corner of the lot. It was darker there than the rest of the lot, and I didn't want him going alone. I leaned against his car as he unlocked the door with the key. He held up the remote. "Battery's dead," he said, grinning. Instead of opening his door, he turned back to me and shuffled his feet, looking up at me from under his eyelashes. "That was fun," he said.

"Yeah. It was," I said and meant it.

"I've never kissed another guy before."

Well, that was direct. I was amused by the way he got right to the point. I wasn't sure if his words were an invitation or an assumption, but I guess it was all the same in the end. He stepped toward me, closed his eyes, and pursed his lips. I fought the urge to laugh. I brushed my thumb across his lips. "Just relax your lips," I said softly.

He opened his eyes and relaxed his lips. I hated myself for it, but I couldn't help thinking, *This one's for you, Adam.* I leaned in and brushed my mouth against his. His eyes closed and he moaned, making me grin despite the flash of heat I'd just felt. I pulled away.

"Did I do it wrong?" he said, his eyes snapping open.

I tried to draw my grin back in, but it just wouldn't go. "No, you're doing fine." He was so eager that I decided to give him something worthy of a first kiss. I leaned in and kissed him gently at first and then with a bit more bite. He tasted like cilantro and garlic. It wasn't bad, but my body didn't sizzle with electricity the way it did when I kissed Adam. Anytime my lips got anywhere near Adam, I wanted to lose myself in him, meld my lips, my body to his, crawl inside his skin. Just one more time I wanted to hold him to me. But that just wasn't going to happen.

I wanted desperately to walk away from Luke, to get in my car, call Adam, and say what? *Hey, you totally betrayed me to that creep, but I forgive you.* No. The Adam I knew wasn't coming back to me. This was Luke's moment.

I wrapped my arms more tightly around Luke, and he responded by pressing into me. He was moaning again, getting into it. Kissing him was pleasant enough, I guess, but I had a feeling he was enjoying it a bit more than I was. I could feel his growing excitement and pushed away.

"No. Don't stop," he said, breathless, and attached himself to me again.

I laughed a little. "Pace yourself, Luke," I said and pushed him away again. I felt a stab in my heart remembering a time when Adam had said the same thing to me. I spun Luke around and hustled him into his car.

He looked up at me with his big blue eyes melting in their sockets. "You'll come Friday?"

I smiled. "I'll be there."

"Nate?"

"Luke?"

He smiled at that. "Do you believe in love at first sight?"

I didn't answer. Because I did. And this wasn't it.

I picked up my phone and lit up the screen, then set it back on the bathroom counter, then picked it up again, then put it down.

I don't know who I am without you anymore. I need to find out.

That's what I'd told him in Key West.

It was only half true. I didn't need to find out. I didn't want to find out. He had to have known that. But I guess I had anyway. In fact, I guess we'd both learned a few things—about who we were, about what we wanted. I wondered if he felt free finally. I wondered what he'd see when he looked in the mirror tonight. I know I didn't much like the person I saw. *Mirror, mirror, on the wall . . .* I closed my eyes and grimaced at the images running through my mind. Me kissing Danial. Me kissing Luke. They were like pictures I drew as a kid. All the parts were there, but they weren't art. They weren't beautiful. Kissing Adam. That was beautiful. Did he think so anymore?

My hand found its way to the leather strap around my neck. I held it for a moment, and then fished out the pendant and slipped the strap from around my neck and stared at the engraving on the back. I ran my thumb along each letter, spelling out his name forward and backward, forward and backward, forward and backward. Then I clutched the pendant tightly in my fist, feeling it bite into my palm, and without looking at it again, I stuffed it in the back of a drawer.

Then I took off his earring. I held it in the palm of my hand and rolled it around with my finger, allowing my heart the luxury of shattering one last time.

They took my earrings.

He'd lifted himself from my hospital bed just long enough to remove one of his studs, and then slipped it into my own ear. *It looks good on you.*

Maybe he could pretend we never happened, but I couldn't. I stuck the earring back in my ear.

Chapter 41

I didn't go to the game Friday. I stayed home, in my room, alone, wallowing in my hurt. When I bumped into Luke in the hallway Monday morning, he looked so disappointed that I bought him a soda after school. I didn't have the heart to stand him up again the next Friday. I brought Danial with me.

I hadn't been to a football game since I played varsity my sophomore year, hadn't wanted to go, but I'd promised Luke. When we got there, the band was already in the stands warming up the crowd with "The Horse." Luke was easy to spot, standing at least half a head taller than the other kids in his section. I pointed him out to Danial as we made our way past the seats several rows back.

"He plays clarinet?" Danial said. "Jeez, why doesn't he just wear a sign?"

"Knock it off."

He laughed. "They look like toy soldiers, don't they?"

"It's kinda cute."

Danial nudged me in the back. "Of course, you would think so."

I rolled my eyes and sat down.

Now that I didn't actually have to play the game, I was surprised to find that I was looking forward to watching it. I scanned the field for familiar numbers. When the players removed their helmets for the national anthem, I noticed a lot of new faces, but I picked out Liam and Brett and a couple other guys I used to hang out with before I became the school homo. We hadn't exchanged two words since that day in the cafeteria when they made it clear our friendship was O-V-E-R. That was F-I-N-E with me. Real friendship was never something I'd had with them. Real friendship was sitting on the bleachers next to me.

After the school song, the drums struck up a cadence I remembered from my team days. I looked over at Luke as the players lined up for the kickoff. The kids, with the exception of the drummers, were doing this head banging thing that reminded me of Beavis and Butt-head doing Judas Priest—*Breaking the law, breaking the law*. He had one arm draped over the shoulder of the girl to his left. The guy to his right had his arm over Luke's shoulder. And they all had one rock hand in the air. Luke had just enough hair to make it fly. "Looks like fun," I said to Danial.

He looked at me and raised his brows.

"Oh, lighten up, Qasimi."

When the band was done breaking the law, Luke stretched to see over the heads of the other kids (he didn't have to stretch much) and looked around. I assumed for me. Someone caught his attention a few rows in front of us. I followed his eyes to a woman with the same straight blond hair holding a camera. She snapped Luke's picture and waved to him. Then she sat next to a stocky man in a white button-up shirt. His hair matched his face—gray. On the other side of the woman was a younger version of Luke, but with glasses. He was absorbed in a video game on a handheld system and looked like he couldn't have cared less about the game or the band.

Luke continued his search. When he found me, he broke into a wide grin and punched his clarinet in the air. I smiled back and shook my head.

"He's got it bad for you," Danial said.

"Maybe I've got it bad for him too."

"Right. You got it bad all right, but not for him. You're gonna break that kid's heart one day. You know that, don't you?"

I winced. "Why does everything have to be so serious? I like him. We had fun together."

"He looks at you like you're the fucking messiah. Haven't you noticed?"

Of course I had. "I can't help that. I'm the only other gay person he knows. He doesn't even know what it's like to *be* gay."

"So, what, you're teaching him?"

"No. Of course not."

He looked at me. "You're lying. Please tell me you have not had sex with that kid."

"Oh, come on," I said, shocked at the thought. "You know me better than that. I hardly know him. We ate pizza, we talked, I kissed him. Okay? That was it."

Danial groaned. "If I'd known you needed to be kissed that damn bad, I'd have kissed you back that night."

I rolled my eyes. "I didn't do it for myself."

"Oh, what, now you're making out with some kid as a public service? You got some kind of martyr complex? That's even worse. He's pretty vulnerable right now, you know. Don't fuck with his head."

"I'm not fucking with his head. I won't hurt him."

"You won't be able to stop it." He paused a moment. "You know what that's like. Dammit, Nate. You're just as vulnerable as he is right now. Why don't you just give it a rest for a while? Get your head together. Leave this kid alone."

Danial didn't know what he was talking about. Luke needed me. And I planned to be there for him. I could live only one day at a time.

A couple of people were headed up the row toward us. "Don't let anyone have that seat," I said to Danial.

"Why?"

"Juliet's coming as soon as she's done with dress rehearsal."

His eyes lit up. "Why didn't you tell me? I would have showered or something."

"Oh, please. You always smell amazing."

He grinned. "You are so gay."

"Yes, I am."

The teams were evenly matched and it looked like the game might be a close one. Jeff Bowers was quarterbacking. Early in the second quarter, he snatched the ball and fell back, looking for a receiver. Liam opened up and we all stood just as he caught the ball at the twenty before the cornerback could take him out.

"Do you miss it?" Danial asked when we sat back down.

"Nope."

Coach Carr called a time-out. I stretched out my legs and looked over at Luke. He was looking back at me and grinned when my eyes met his. The girl next to him nudged him and he turned back to the front. Beside me, Danial checked his watch again. I cleared my throat.

"What?" he said.

The crowd was suddenly on their feet and screaming. I stood and looked down the field. The referee had his arms straight in the air. Touchdown. I'd missed it. The band launched into the school fight song and suddenly Juliet's arms were around my waist. Surprised, I twisted around to give her a hug. "Hey, gorgeous," she said, squeezing me a little tighter and a little longer than was appropriate for a friendly, platonic greeting. But then, we had a history. And then she was done with me. "Hey, dance partner!" She slipped her arms around Danial's neck and hugged him too. He looked at me over her shoulder. I raised my eyebrows.

He moved down a seat so Juliet could sit between us. "So, you want to tell me why we're here at a football game?"

The band was filing into the aisles and heading down to the field for their halftime performance. I knew Luke was facing our way and would be watching us. I flicked the briefest glance his way. Juliet followed the direction of my eyes and saw Luke smiling at me like he was about to detonate from sheer happiness.

Juliet looked back at me. "Nate?"

I looked at her but quickly cast my eyes down out of guilt.

"What's going on?

When I didn't answer, she looked over at Danial. He shrugged.

I glanced back up at Luke. He was just stepping into the aisle. His smile was gone and he looked worried. I smiled encouragingly at him and watched the relief spread across his features. He smiled back. He cast a glance toward his parents. His mom gave him a thumbs-up; his dad was staring at his iPhone. Then Luke turned and bounded down the steps toward the field.

I leaned forward and planted my elbows on my knees and watched the kickoff, but I could feel Juliet's eyes on me.

"Shit," she said after another moment. "That explains the text Adam sent me."

My eyes snapped up to hers.

"He asked me to keep an eye on you. But when I called him back, he wouldn't say anything more." She paused a moment. I could see in her eyes the gears turning and locking into place. "That's the kid you were dancing with at homecoming. What's going on? You're not . . ."

I thought about denying it, but it was just a matter of time—perhaps seconds—before she figured it out anyway. "We're, uh, dating, I guess, sort of."

"Come again? Because I just thought I heard you say you're dating that kid."

"We broke up, Jules. It's over."

Her eyes bugged out of her head.

I closed my eyes, forcing myself to breathe. "I don't—can we talk about this later?" I leaned over her to Danial. "I'm gonna go get us some sodas." I squeezed Juliet's hand and fled down the stairs to the concession area.

I walked around awhile before I got the drinks, my hands stuffed deep in my pockets, my thoughts whirling around in my head. I wasn't sure if I felt good that Adam was still worrying about me, or irritated that he still thought I needed looking after. I chose irritated; it was easier that way. Needy Nate. Needy fucked-up Nate. I laughed humorlessly to myself. My nose burned, and I blinked back the tears pooling in my eyes.

Suddenly Luke was in front of me, a plume sticking out of the top of his hat that hadn't been there when he left the stands. "What are you doing here?" I said, pretending my eyes weren't wet. "Aren't you supposed to be on the field?"

"I have to go to the bathroom. Are you okay? What are you doing here?"

"I'm fine. I just came down to get some drinks." I blinked a few times, then gave up trying to pretend I hadn't been crying and dragged a sleeve across my eyes.

Luke politely pretended not to notice. "Here. Hold this for me." He handed me his clarinet and tugged off his gloves, handing those to me also. Then his hat. His hair was stuffed up into a stretchy sheer black cap. Then he turned. "I need you to unzip me."

I tugged down the zipper on the back of his jacket, wondering if he planned to strip down right there in front of everyone. He tugged off his jacket and handed that over too. The black pants he wore were actually black overalls. Underneath the overalls he wore a blue WPHS band T-shirt. "I gotta hurry. Do you want to come with me?"

"Uh, no." I laughed, feeling a little better.

He winked. "I'll be right back."

I watched him go, his tall, lean frame looking pretty darn cute in his uniform.

I hardly had time to squeak a note out on his instrument before he was back again. I helped him back into his jacket, then handed over, one by one, his gloves, then his hat, then his clarinet. "How do I look?" he asked when he was finally dressed.

"Like a toy soldier."

He smiled. "Then I guess I did it right." He started to leave, then turned back. "You'll pick me up at the band hall after the game?"

"I'll be there."

He beamed, then hurried away.

I had drinks and popcorn and was back at my seat just as the band took the field. Danial and Juliet were deep in conversation when I stepped into our row. Immediately the conversation came to an end, and I knew they'd been talking about me. I sat back and scoured the band, trying to spot Luke. It was impossible. They all looked alike. I gave up and relaxed, enjoying the music. They were really good, I thought. A jazzy band with lots of quick stepping and dancing around. It actually looked like something I might have enjoyed if I hadn't wasted all those years pretending to be some kind of football stud.

Juliet kept stealing little looks at me, so when the performance was over and the band marched off the field to a drum tap, I looked over at her. "All right. Let's hear it."

She put her drink on the ground and folded her arms tightly across her chest. "I can't believe how stupid you are both being. If there were ever two people in this world who were meant for each other, it's the two of you. Get on the phone with him." She dug in my pocket and pulled out my phone and handed it to me. "Work this out. This is insane. I cannot stand the thought of the two of you apart. I could kick you both." Then she growled at me, causing Danial's eyebrows to go up in surprise.

I took my phone, and as calmly as I could, stuck it back in my pocket. "There's nothing to talk about, Jules. It's over."

"Bullshit." I didn't respond. She looked to Danial for backup. He just gave his head a miniscule shake. She looked back at me, biting her lip, then wrapped her arms around me. I was aware of people around us looking. "Jules," I whispered. "Please don't do this. I'm begging you, okay. Let it go."

She sniffed in my ear and pulled away, brushing a tear from her cheek with her little finger. I struggled not to cry again. The band was filing back into the stands, so I focused on locating Luke. I spotted him at the bottom of the steps. His hat was off. He tugged off the sheer cap and shook out his shaggy blond hair. His cheeks were flushed. He winked at me when he got to his row. I watched as he stripped down to his overalls and hoped I wasn't making a mistake.

I leaned against the car in the dark lane behind the school and watched Luke bounce out of the band hall with a couple of the other players. He searched the row of cars and waved when he saw me. He slapped one of the guys on the back, then jogged out to meet me.

"Hi," he said, breathless. I wasn't sure if it was the jog or me making him pant.

"All ready?" I asked.

"Yeah."

We stowed his stuff in the trunk and got in. I turned the key in the ignition, but he placed his hand on mine before I could shift into drive. "Wait," he said, watching out the window. He waited while a couple of kids passed by our car, then scrambled over the console, grabbed my face between his hands, and crushed his lips on mine. "I've been waiting almost two weeks to do that again," he said when he finally pulled away. He settled back into his seat. "Okay. I think I'm good now."

I scratched my head, still a little stunned. "Okay, then."

I noticed the grasshopper climbing up the inside of the windshield just as I pulled onto the street. I hoped Luke wouldn't notice, remembering what he'd said about being afraid of bugs. As he chatted away about the performance, I watched the grasshopper climb higher up the windshield and closer to Luke. Technically, grasshoppers weren't bugs, but I didn't think Luke was the kind to fuss over that distinction. It had spiny legs, an exoskeleton. It was a bug. I was approaching a traffic light thinking how I was going to deal with his bug phobia if it came to that when his eyes landed on the bug/not-bug and he screamed and started pawing at his seat belt latch, trying desperately to unlock it and then, succeeding, proceeded to scrambled over the console and into the back.

"Jeez, calm down." I said. "It's just a grasshopper. I'll get it. Calm down."

I pulled to a stop at the light and rolled down my window. Then I took the car manual from the storage compartment, and trying not to laugh at Luke halfway in the backseat now and gasping, I brushed the grasshopper onto it. It was one of those big yellow and brown flying grasshoppers. I'd collected them in boxes when I was a kid, like they were pets.

"Come on, little fellow," I said, carefully carrying him on his magic manual carpet to the window, where I tossed him out. I never actually saw him fall out the window, but I was pretty sure he did.

I rolled up my window and looked back at Luke and laughed. "Boy, you weren't kidding about being afraid of bugs."

"They creep me out," he said, still looking nervously around the car as if he expected an entire swarm to materialize any second. He settled back into his seat and snapped the seat belt into place.

The light turned green and I pulled into the intersection. And that's when I felt its spiny legs on my neck. I screamed and Luke screamed. I brushed frantically at my neck and Luke huddled up against the car door, whimpering. I managed to get the car on the shoulder of the road and jumped out. The poor grasshopper flew away, and my screaming gave way to hysterical laughter. I flopped back into the car and slammed the door. My sides ached from laughing. Then Luke was laughing too, albeit a little shakily. "Dammit," I said. "That scared me half to death."

"Me too. I think I peed my pants."

I said, "Seriously?" because, I mean, he had to be kidding.

"Uh, yeah. Seriously."

I buckled my seat belt and smiled. "You're lying."

"Not lying," he said sheepishly.

I cast a sideways glance at him and he indicated the wet spot on the front of his shorts. I don't know why I found that so endearing.

Luke's parents had gone out to dinner after the game and the house was empty, so I came in and looked around his room while he took a quick shower. If I'd had any doubt whatsoever about his geek quotient, it was gone now. His room was like a shrine to the god of marching bands. He had trophies on his shelf dating back five or six years—WISD Freshman Honor Band, Fifth Grade Concert Band, Third Chair Region Band. I laughed at one that read "Most Likely to Drive Band Directors Crazy." That was Luke. Above his headboard was a poster of the University of Texas Longhorn Band. The picture was a close-up of a trombone player in the ugliest uniform I'd ever seen—a suit like the Lone Ranger might have worn on a date if Howdy Doody had dressed him. It was just all kinds of wrong—orange, with white fringe across the shoulders and bric-a-brac running down the length of the pant legs, a white cowboy hat, white shoes. Next to that poster was the front line of the Fightin' Texas Aggie Band. I liked the knee boots, but the overall military thing just didn't do it for me. I pegged Luke as more of a bric-a-brac guy.

I was fingering through some music on a music stand in the corner when he came back into the room and slipped his arms around me from behind. He was warm and still damp from the shower. He laid his wet head on my shoulder.

I hugged his arms to me. "You're getting my shirt wet."

"Wet T-shirt. I like the sound of that."

I rolled my eyes at him over my shoulder.

"Do you want to see me naked?" he breathed in my ear.

Okay. This was happening way too fast. I twisted around in his arms and thanked God he was still wearing a towel around his waist.

He reached for his towel, but I caught his hands in mine.

"I know this is all really exciting, Luke, but don't be in such a hurry to experience it all."

"Why not?"

Because you're sixteen. Because your parents could come home at any second and kill me. Because I love someone else.

"Just don't. Okay?"

"Did you feel crazy like this with your first boyfriend?"

I winced. Then I realized, just like that, I had become Luke's de facto boyfriend. There was no more Adam and Nate. There was just Nate and Luke, whether I liked it or not. Whether I wanted it or not. Whether I could stand it or not. It was what it was, and no amount of heartbreak on my part could change that. I held Luke to me for a moment and breathed in the clean peppermint smell on his skin, then went and waited in the car.

Chapter 42

Luke wanted to go to Market Street and hang out outside Starbucks where a lot of the band kids were getting together.

"We can't hold hands or anything, though. I mean, you know. They just . . . they wouldn't . . ."

"I understand," I assured him. "Coming out is a really personal decision, Luke." I pulled up at a red light and look over at him. "You'll do it when you're ready. I'm cool with that. Around other people, we're just a couple of guys hanging out." I play punched him in the shoulder.

"You're not mad?"

"No, I am most definitely not mad."

Relieved maybe. But mad, no. Not even a little.

But I was worried that Luke was playing with fire, and he was going to get burned.

The light changed and I turned onto Market Street. "You know, Luke, I *am* out. Your friends, at least some of them, are gonna know I'm gay. And they're gonna guess you are too."

He looked out the window at the crowds already gathering and thought about that for a minute. "Call your friend Danial."

"Danial?"

"Yeah. Make him come too." He turned to me, excited now.

"They already think you're a couple. Then we could be together, but it would look like you're with Danial."

I struggled to wrap my brain around that. So I was going to act like the straight guy was my boyfriend, and the gay guy wasn't. That was just stupid enough that it might work.

I told Luke I didn't know if he'd do it, but of course I knew he would. He was my self-appointed bodyguard, a role he took almost too seriously. By association, he'd become Luke's too. That, and I think he just liked to watch me squirm. I was sure he'd arrange to shock the band nerds with our "gayness." Oh well, I didn't go through everything I'd gone through to be a shrinking violet now. We circle around Market Street and headed back to Danial's. I called on the way.

I found a spot in the parking garage and pulled in. Danial got out of the back. Just as I reached to pull my door handle, Luke grabbed my arm. He ducked down and glanced out my window at Danial then back at me. "Will you kiss me before we go?" he said in a low voice. "A really good one. One that will last me at least a couple of hours?"

I laughed. "I don't know if you're incorrigible or just insatiable. But come here." I pulled him to me and kissed him, and kept kissing him, letting him be the one to pull away. It occurred to me somewhere between the kissing and the kept kissing that Danial was right. I was performing a public service. I decided then and there that if that's the way it was, then I'd perform a damn good public service. Luke deserved that at least.

"Dayum," he said, breathless. He reached down to adjust himself, looking a little embarrassed.

I laughed. "I'm glad you enjoyed it. Come on. My *boyfriend* is getting impatient."

Luke ducked down and looked out the window at Danial again. "Are you sure he's not gay?"

"Yep. I'm pretty sure."

Danial held the door for me as I got out. "I think I just threw up a little in my mouth," he said in a low voice, a disgusted look on his face.

"Maybe you should try it sometime."

"Uh, pass."

I laughed and pinched his cheek.

Kids were sitting at small tables and spilling out into the alley outside Starbucks as we approached. I could see that Luke was nervous. He'd pulled a baseball cap on as we got out of the car and he kept adjusting it and readjusting it.

"Take it easy, Luke. It's gonna be okay."

"Yeah. I know," he said, his voice betraying his anxiety. "Maybe you could hold hands or something so, you know, they'll know you're together."

"Yeah, Nate, maybe we should hold hands . . . or something."

"Don't encourage him, Luke," I said.

Danial grinned and grabbed my hand.

Luke looked at our hands and frowned. "You don't have to look so happy about it," he said to Danial, his voice tight.

"Can't have it both ways, Lukey," Danial said. He let go of my hand and flung his arm over my shoulder, pulling me to him.

"He's just trying to torment you, Luke. Ignore him."

Luke glared at Danial. "Don't try anything."

Danial held up two fingers on his free hand. "Scout's honor," he said, with a mock straight face. When Luke looked way, Danial dropped his arm from around my shoulder and pinched my ass.

I looked at him and rolled my eyes. Luke shot a look back at him, and Danial shrugged.

"There are some of the guys," Luke said, pointing.

We followed him through the crowd, drawing some stares. Most of the kids had seen me with Danial or with Adam before and only registered mild surprise.

"This isn't going to work," Danial said in my ear. "You know that, don't you? I mean, he's not fooling anybody. How's he going to explain hanging out with a couple of gay guys?"

Danial was right, of course, but I wasn't sure there was much else to do but let the train wreck happen and then try to clean up the twisted metal afterward. It was just a matter of time anyway. Luke had already gotten a taste of living an authentic life. He wasn't going to settle for less much longer. I wasn't too worried about the kids here. They'd get used to it soon enough, and Luke seemed pretty resilient.

It was the parents. You could never be absolutely certain how they'd respond. If they flipped out, they could damage his spirit irreparably, not to mention his very existence. The only thing I knew for absolute certain right then was that whatever happened, Danial and I would be there for him.

Luke stepped into a circle of friends and stuck his hands in his pockets. He glanced back at us and seemed a little uncertain what to do.

"Let's get a cappuccino," Danial said.

I winked at Luke and followed Danial inside. "How can you drink that stuff? It'll put hair on your chest."

He hooked a finger into the V at the top of my shirt and pulled it out, pretending to look down at my chest. "Then maybe you need to drink more."

I started to sneer, but then snorted a laugh. "Make mine a latte, caveman. And you're buying. You owe me anyway."

He ordered.

"Should we get one for Luke?" I asked before the barista could get away.

"Maybe we should just stick a sandwich board on him—*I play with boys.*"

"Yeah, I guess you're right."

We got our drinks and went back out to the alley. Luke was watching and snaked through the crowd to get to us. "Did you bring me something?"

I shot Danial a look and handed him my drink. "Latte?"

"Great. Where's yours?"

"I didn't want anything."

"We can share."

I smiled. "Sure."

He took a sip then handed me back his / my drink. "Hold this. I'll be right back. I gotta pee."

Danial stepped on my toe as I took the drink.

"Oh good Lord," he said after Luke was out of hearing range. "Being gay is the least of that boy's problems."

"Give him a break. He's just nervous. I was a basket case when I came out."

"But he's not coming out. At least, not intentionally. Do you see how gay he's acting?" Danial said.

"He is gay, but yeah, I know what you mean. He's a little nerdy, a little naïve, but that's part of his charm." I grabbed his cappuccino and took a sip. "Ugh. That's nasty." I shook my head and handed it back, then pretended to check for any new sprouting hairs on my chest.

Danial laughed.

I got rid of the taste with Luke's / my latte. "Why don't you go talk to him," I said.

"Me?"

"Yeah. You're like the Rosetta Stone of gay-straight relations. You can explain it to him from a straight guy's perspective."

He palmed the back of his neck and gave a heavy sigh.

I walked around and watched the crowd while I waited. Market Street was actually a long oval, bracketed on one end by an H-E-B Market and on the other end by an indoor mall. In between were restaurants, shops, a movie theater, and a bookstore, all anchored by a park green in the center and made somewhat urban with benches and a fountain. The park was just around the corner from Starbucks, so I wandered over. Some older kids were tossing around a Frisbee. Three younger ones were playing in the fountain while their parents watched from a nearby bench. They looked so carefree, so innocent, so happy, so not me.

"Nate?"

My head snapped around at the familiar voice.

"It is you." Adam's mom gave me a kiss on the cheek. "We've missed you."

I hadn't seen his mom and stepdad since I'd picked up my phone after taking Adam to the airport two months earlier. Had it really been only two months? Seeing them now was like stepping into a time warp. I felt disoriented.

Ben reached out to shake my hand. For a moment I just looked at it, not sure what do. Then I clasped his hand and let him pull me in for a hug. "What are you doing out here?" I said. My voice sounded rough, like I hadn't used it in a while.

"We just got out of the movie theater. Date night." She smiled at her husband.

"Uh, great. How's Mea?" *Keep it simple.*

"Oh, you know Mea. More precocious than any seven-year-old has a right to be."

I smiled, not sure what else to say.

Mrs. Jefferies—no, it was Jensen now—just looked at me, a pained expression fleeting across her face. I looked down at my feet and dug the toe of my shoe into the sidewalk. "Honey," she said to her husband, "do you mind if I talk to Nate alone for a minute?"

"Come on, let's sit down," she said. The benches were all taken, so we sat on a concrete wall that ringed the fountain. She studied my face while I studied my shoe, then she took my hand and dipped her head to capture my eyes with her own. It was hard, but I looked at her.

"How've you been?" she asked softly.

"Okay," I answered, my voice noncommittal but still rough. I cleared my throat.

She nodded her head and tried again. "I don't know what's happened between you and Adam. I know something has happened, but he won't tell us what."

I nodded but didn't offer anything more.

She wrapped her other hand around mine as well. "You know we think of you as our son. And you know you can talk to us about anything, don't you?"

From the corner of my eye, I saw Danial and Luke approaching. *Shit, shit, shit, shit.* "I know," I said, trying to remain calm. "Thanks." I looked back at her and forced a small smile.

"Hi," Luke said, drawing up in front of us, Danial just steps behind him.

I stood up, then almost sat back down when my knees acted like the hinges that held the top part of my leg to the bottom had broken. "Mrs. Jefferies, I want you to meet some friends of mine. This is Luke Chesser and Danial Qasimi."

I realized too late that I'd screwed up her name again, but she didn't correct me. Instead, she shook their hands as I introduced them. "Danial, Adam's told me about you."

Before Danial could respond, Luke cut in. "You're Adam's mom?" He took a step closer to me and slipped his hand in mine. Suddenly that seemed to be all anyone could look at—those two hands, his and mine, clasped together, guy skin touching guy skin, not Adam's skin, but Luke's skin touching Nate's skin.

Part of me was glad—now Adam would know what it's like to have someone you love move on, assuming he still loved me, which, to be honest, wasn't really clear anymore. But part of me was screaming, *No, this is too final.*

Don't tell Adam. Please don't tell Adam.

It had to be mere seconds but seemed much longer before Mrs. Jefferies—Jensen—overcame her shock. She squeezed my arm and smiled sadly. "I better go." She kissed me on the cheek again, nodded her head to Danial and Luke, and left.

I dropped Luke's hand and walked away in the opposite direction.

Luke followed me. I knew he would. I stuck my hands in my pockets. He fell into step beside me and we walked, not speaking for a while.

"Nate?" he said hesitantly.

I looked up at the night sky. There were so many streetlights on Market Street that it was hard to make out many stars. I tried to recapture that feeling I had in Danial's backyard of time being so short and problems so insignificant in the greater universe. Why couldn't I just be happy in the now?

"Did I do something wrong?" Luke asked.

I pulled my hand from my pocket and entwined my fingers with his. Despite all the people standing around, he didn't pull away. I glanced at him. His face was a mixture of worry and relief. "You didn't do anything wrong," I said finally.

"You still care about him, don't you?"

I winced. "Why do you say that?"

"Because every time someone says his name, you look like—like you're in physical pain."

I didn't answer. I couldn't.

"He really hurt you, didn't he?" Luke continued.

I drew in a shuddering breath and struggled to maintain control, but seeing Adam's parents had been too much. I rubbed at my eyes with the heel of my hand.

"Oh, Nate," Luke said with such tenderness that I broke down. He pulled me over to a dark corner of the street and we sat on the curb, his arms around me, my face planted against his shoulder.

He murmured to me over and over. "I love you, Nate. I won't ever hurt you. It's okay."

After a while I was able to get control. I wiped my eyes with the neck of my T-shirt and sniffed. "I think some of your friends saw you holding my hand."

"Doesn't matter. I'd do it again in a heartbeat."

I fixed my eyes on his. "That's really sweet."

He smiled. "Danial told me people were talking, but I didn't believe him. Then some kid said something to me, and Danial got all in his face and called him an ignorant jerk and told him if he ever heard him or even heard about him talking to or about me like that again, he'd kick his ignorant homophobic ass all over Texas."

"That's Danial, all right." I laughed, then felt another tear roll down my cheek.

"He's pretty cool."

"Yeah," I agreed.

I sniffed and swiped at my eyes again. "Adam gave me this bracelet once. He had it made in a kiosk in the mall. It was one of those rubber bracelets like people wear that are stamped with WWJD. Only this one was stamped with WWND."

"What would Nate do?"

"Yeah. I used to wear it all the time. It was a reminder to be true to myself. To live my life honestly. To love who I am."

"But you don't wear it anymore."

I smiled a little. "I did for a long time. It took a while, but I finally got the message. The closet is bullshit, Luke. Even with all that crap people are going to say about how you're a sinner or a perversion, you're gonna find that it's still better just being you." I pushed a lock of blond hair out of his eyes. "God made you just the way you are. Don't ever forget that."

A sweet smile spread across his lips. "I love you, Nate." There it was again.

I squinched my eyes up. "Luke—"

"You don't have to love me back right now. You don't have to say anything. I just wanted you to know."

I ruffled his hair with my hand. "What am I going to do with you?"

"I could name a few things."

"Yeah, I bet you could." I wrapped my arms around him.

He slid his arms around my waist. "I'll make you forget. I promise."

I was counting on that.

For the first time in five weeks, no protestors showed up for T-shirt Tuesday. Word was that the day before a female algebra teacher at the other high school had taped to her file cabinet a photo of herself kissing her partner at a friend's wedding, thus potentially damning the souls of her 125 or so freshmen students. They had to be saved, I supposed.

Chapter 43

I did *not* think trick-or-treating with Luke's little brother was a good idea.

"Oh, come on," Luke pleaded on the phone. "He's ten years old. What does he know? We'll just be hangers-on anyway. Guard dogs for him and his friends so they don't get lost or picked off by some Jason with a thing for little boys in creepy costumes carrying pillowcases full of candy."

I growled. "I'm not dressing up."

He laughed. He'd won and he knew it. The outcome had been inevitable. Luke just didn't take no for an answer. He was like a little puppy—eager and persistent and totally oblivious to any dangers lurking around him. How could I say no?

"Come over about seven."

Come over? Uh-uh. "I'll just meet you somewhere."

Mom stepped into the open doorway and leaned against the facing.

"No. Please. Come on. You've got to meet my parents sometime. Besides, I already told them a buddy from school was coming over. Now you have to come."

I started to argue, but there was no point. "All right. No costumes."

He laughed again and hung up. I thumbed the End button and set my phone on my desk.

"Are you going somewhere with Danial tonight?" Mom asked.

"Nah. He doesn't do Halloween." I didn't offer any more information and the silence just hung there for a moment.

"Soooo . . . are you going somewhere with Juliet?"

"She's going to a Halloween party with some of the kids. I didn't want to go." I hadn't told Mom yet about Adam. Maybe I was hoping I'd wake up and this would all be a really fucked-up dream. But I hadn't, and it wasn't.

"So, who were you talking to?"

All right, Mom. Game over. "I'm going trick-or-treating with Luke and his little brother." She just looked at me, her face squinching up. I scratched the back of my head. "I mean, we're taking his little brother and some of his friends. He's ten."

"Who's Luke?"

I leaned back in my chair and covered my face with my hands, then let them slide down. "He's a guy I've been seeing."

"What?" Her face blanched. "But you and Adam—" Her mouth clamped shut as the full force of what I'd said hit her. She sat on my bed and waited for me to explain. Instead, I broke down.

I had not wanted to start this again, and for sure not in front of Mom, but the tears came anyway. She pulled me over to the bed next to her and put her arms around me like she did when I was a little boy. "He's found somebody else," I said in between sobs I just couldn't hold back anymore. I'd thought I was done with this on Market Street. In fact, each time I broke down, I thought that was it. But I was like a pressure cooker. Each time the pressure built up beyond a psi I could tolerate, it had to be released in a noisy, messy burst. Then things quieted down for a while, but the pressure built up again, and it was only a matter of time before it had to be released. The only thing that would stop the cycle was to turn off the flame. I didn't know how to do that.

She patted me on the back and tried to soothe me with a string of *Oh, baby*s. It wasn't working. If the pressure wasn't released, I'd self-destruct. I'd be done when I was done.

I feared sometimes I'd never be done.

"Maybe it's for the best, honey," Mom said when I calmed down some. "You two got close awfully fast. Too fast."

This was *not* what I wanted to hear. I pulled away and dried my face with the neck of my T-shirt. It was a typical parentlike platitude. I knew what was coming before she even said it.

"I love Adam," she said, undeterred by my sudden coolness. "You know I do. But, Nathan, you're young. You're going to meet a lot of guys, and maybe even some girls—"

"Girls?" I made a disgusted noise in the back of my throat and shook my head. *That again.* Jeez. Why was gay so hard for straight people to get?

"I don't want to hear this, Mom." I could see she was determined to reduce my feelings for Adam to a schoolboy crush. It was much more than that and she knew it. She had to know it. I was feeling stupid enough for thinking that our love was something epic, the kind of love people wrote songs and novels about. I didn't need her to treat me like my feelings weren't real.

Mom was still trying to patch my broken heart, but I'd quit listening. I didn't want to be fixed up. I didn't want to get over it. What I wanted was to hit rewind and go back to a happy place with Adam. A place where he still loved me. A place where there was no Luke and no Justin. Then I felt guilty. Luke didn't deserve that. Justin did. But not Luke.

It was still too early to go to Luke's, so I drove over to Adam's house. I parked across the street and a few houses down, just in case his parents looked out the window. He wasn't there. I didn't know why I was. Except maybe being there connected me to him in some small way.

A jack-o'-lantern glowed on the front porch. Some early trick-or-treaters made their way to the door and knocked. I sat up in my seat. What was I hoping to see? Adam? Handing out candy to little monsters and ghouls?

I wished that Danial were there with his little stick of brain fuzz. I could've used a hit right then. I felt drained, numb. I really just wanted to go home and crawl into bed and wait for this nightmare to be over. I damn sure didn't want to go trick-or-treating. I wasn't thrilled about spending the evening with Luke either. I examined that thought for a moment, turning it this way and that. On the one hand, there was something about Luke. He was adorable, naïve and blunt and, Danial was right, completely fan girly around me. I smiled in spite of my broken heart. He was so easy to like. He'd be so easy to love.

Someone opened the door. Ben, I think, my not future father-in-law. It only took seconds for him to hand out the candy, and then the kids were bounding down the sidewalk again and the door closed.

I didn't want to love Luke, at least not in the same way I loved Adam. It wasn't Luke. It was me. That sounded like some pathetic break-up line, but in truth, I'd have rather wallowed in my misery than have fun with him. As much as I liked him, he wasn't The One. He could never be The One. The One was doing God knows what sixteen hundred miles away in New York. I'd googled the distance. In fact, like some crazed stalker, I'd googled and Google Earthed everything about his new life. I knew what his apartment building looked like (kinda dingy and worn down) and the name of the deli on the corner (Bert's). I even knew a few things about his slutty new roommates (like the fact that Alec had a thing for bad wigs when he performed with his band, Bad to the Bone, and Jeremy tweeted incessantly about stupid shit like whether he should have cream cheese or butter on his bagel and how nasty it is to have to pull a string out of your cat's butt).

Mom thought I was too young to know what love was, that I was too young to be committed to one person. She was wrong.

I ran my thumb across the keys on my phone. The screen lit up. No texts, no voice mails, no missed calls. My inboxes were as empty as I felt. I desperately wanted to hear his voice. I didn't give myself a chance to think about it; I speed-dialed his number and held my breath while the phone rang. After four rings, the call rolled over to voice mail. "It's Adam. You know what to do." I wished I did.

I considered hanging up, but my number would show up on his missed-calls list. No point in pretending I didn't call. But I didn't want him thinking I was sitting around like some pitiful jilted lover just waiting for him to turn his countenance my way and make my heart flutter for a moment. Although I would have almost settled for that.

I gave my vocal chords a quick pep talk before I opened my mouth—*Sound happy, or at least okay.* "Hey, Adam. It's Nate. I just wanted to wish you a happy Halloween." I paused for a moment. There was so much more I wanted to say. I wanted to beg him to come home. Beg him to love just me. Beg him to be the Adam who'd told me we were two parts of a whole.

Before I could commit one way or the other, he called me back. I switched over to the incoming call. I could barely separate out Adam's voice from all the noise in the background. It sounded like another party, or maybe he was at a bar already. I glanced at the time. Six forty (Seven forty New York time). *Not wasting any time living it up, are you, Adam?* Apparently he couldn't hear me either. He kept repeating, "Hold on. Don't hang up," until finally the background noise muffled.

"Where are you?" I asked. Even I could hear the edge in my voice.

He didn't answer immediately.

"Nate, is something wrong? Are you okay?"

Is something wrong? Is something *wrong?* What wasn't wrong with this? "No, nothing's wrong."

And then there was someone else's voice—"Hey, baby. What are you doing out here?"—so clear and breathy that I knew the voice's face had to be close to Adam's. "Are you waiting for me?"

Stupid. Stupid. Stupid. "I have to go," I said abruptly. "I have a . . . I have a date."

"With Luke?"

He knew about Luke? Good. Maybe he was a little jealous too. I didn't want to ask, but I couldn't help myself. "Is that Justin?"

He didn't answer. Instead, he asked, "Why did you call?"

"I don't know. I guess I just wanted to say happy Halloween."

"Thanks. You too."

And then that awful silence again. I bit back a fresh onslaught of tears and hung up.

* * *

Luke swung the door open before I could knock. His smile was huge as he took me in standing in a narrow path between mounds of leaves piled up on the porch, cobwebs hanging low around my head and shoulders. He looked like he was fighting the urge to pounce on me like an eager puppy. He stepped out onto the porch in his bare feet and pulled the door slightly to.

A black-and-white cat pressed up against my leg. Luke laughed and reached down to pick it up. "This is Justin," he said, holding it up for me to pet.

"Justin?"

"Yeah. I named him after Justin Timberlake. That's on the DL, though, so keep that to yourself."

Justin was a dumbass name for a cat, I thought. Even dumber-asser for a New York boyfriend. I gritted my teeth and petted the cat.

"You're just a buddy from school, okay?" he said in a low voice. "No touching, no, you know, looking at me. Stuff like that."

I almost laughed out loud. *Oh, Luke.* "Got it," I said.

He pulled the door closed a little more and stepped even closer to me. I shoved my hands in my pockets in a show of restraint, but after a quick glance around, Luke leaned over dumbass-name-Justin-cat and kissed me on the lips. Hello. Porch lights!

But as always, Luke seemed totally oblivious. He reminded me of a little kid who put a blanket over his head during hide-and-seek and thought no one could see him, despite the fact that four-fifths of his body was completely exposed. I feared that exposed part was going to get him into trouble one day. He just didn't get it. But that was part of his charm.

"Come on in," he said stepping back and opening the door wide. He set Justin (grrr) down on the porch as I stepped past him. My phone vibrated in my pocket. As much as I wanted to take the call, I didn't.

The Chessers seemed like okay people. Not too warm, not too cold. Luke introduced me as a friend, but I hardly seemed to register on their radar screens as they continued whatever the suburban walking dead did with their time. *God.* What was wrong with me? I was getting more cynical by the day.

Little brother—Matthew, aka Road Kill—was another life-form entirely. I wondered for a moment if the boys were adopted. I met Matthew in the bathroom, where he was gluing more gore junk to his cheeks and throat and then soaking them with fake blood. He looked so much like Luke, except for the wire-framed glasses and the gore. I took in his shredded duds. "Nice costume."

"Thanks," he said, glancing up at me in the mirror.

I sat on the toilet while Luke helped him bloody up the back of his head. And then his dad was looming in the doorway. "So, Nate, what instrument do you play in the band?"

Before I could tell him I wasn't in the band, Luke piped in. "Trombone."

I resisted the urge to show surprise or look at Luke.

"A brass player," his dad said. "Good. Trombone is a nice manly instrument. I've been trying to get Luke to switch over to brass. Clarinet is a girl's instrument."

I shot a quick look at Luke in the mirror and caught him rolling his eyes at his dad's comment. I tried to see hurt, but all I saw was boredom. Luke had clearly heard all this before and wasn't affected by it. Yay, Luke.

"I think his first-year band director was just trying to fill out the band, and Luke looked like an easy mark," his dad continued. "Luke said he asked to play one of the bigger brass instruments like baritone, but the director refused."

I doubted very much that Luke had done any such thing. Another quick glance at him in the mirror confirmed that.

"If I'd been on the school board then, he sure wouldn't be playing a wussy clarinet now."

"I like clarinet," Luke said.

It was clear that his dad most definitely did *not* like his son playing clarinet any more than my dad had liked me trading music for football. But at least his dad was here. Mine had long since become too busy to make our every-other-weekend father/son bonding crap. Not that I'd missed the incessant insults and jabs to be something I wasn't. Still, the rejection, the understanding that his love was conditional, had hurt. Still hurt. It wasn't supposed to be that way.

I followed Luke up to his room.

"Trombone?"

He laughed as he dug around in his closet for something. "Yeah. Hope you don't mind. Band kids hang out with band kids. Mostly just because we spend so much time together. It's easier if he believes you're with the band, you know."

"You don't think he'll notice I'm MIA at games and stuff?"

"Are you kidding? There're over two hundred kids in the band and fourteen trombone players." He found what he was looking for. "Here they are!"

"Pink capes?" I said when he shook them out. "You really are gay, aren't you?" I laughed and held one up to myself. "Normally I don't do costumes. But I would so wear this."

He grinned and pulled on a hoodie. "I thought you might. Here. Tuck it under your jacket until we get outside."

"Why do you have pink capes in your closet?"

"Hero day at school. A bunch of us band kids wear them. It's fun."

I was liking band more and more.

Two of Matthew's friends were waiting in the front yard when we left the house—Road Kill #2 and Road Kill #3. It quickly became obvious that they didn't need or want our babysitting services, which was totally cool with me. Luke and I trailed along behind them, hanging out at the curb as the boys cut across lawns in their shortest-distance-between-two-front-doors dash for candy.

A little ways down the street we came to a section where the preceding and forthcoming street lights failed to overlap and illuminate. The sky was cloudy, so no moonlight filled in the gap. Luke took advantage of the darkness by slipping his hand in mine. He moved in close to me so anyone with cat vision would still find it difficult to see that our fingers were intertwined.

"God, I want to kiss you," he said, looking up at me in the darkness. He made a quick assessment of the street activity. Ghouls and princesses and caped crusaders roamed the street, but none were in our little patch of darkness. Emboldened, Luke let go of my hand and slid his arm under my hoodie and around my waist. It was unusually cold for Halloween, and his fingers felt icy when he pressed them into my back. I shivered, a response he immediately misinterpreted.

"I know, I know. Me too," he said, slipping his fingers under my shirt. I almost gasped, but I didn't want to send him over the brink so I forced myself to stay still.

"Let's just keep our eyes open. If either one of us pulls away, then the other will know there's someone coming. Okay?"

I almost laughed out loud at his subterfuge. Instead I just said, "Okay."

And then we were kissing. Eyes wide open. Kinda weird.

I had to admit, Luke could kiss. Being the expert on kissing now, I'd coached him well. I'd learned from the best. I stuffed that thought down and closed my eyes for just a second, letting myself experience his lips and the play of his tongue against mine. His fingers were warming up, along with everything else.

"Oh, shit!" Luke pulled away suddenly and folded his hands under his arms. A cluster of costumed preschoolers and their parents made their way past us. Neither of us spoke until they were out of hearing range.

"I closed my eyes," Luke confessed, a little breathless. "Sorry."

I grinned and draped my arm around his shoulders. Then I planted a kiss on his temple.

He looked up at me sheepishly. "No harm done, right?"

I looked around me. "Not that I can see."

"Man, Nate. You're like nuclear sexy when you do that. I need some dampening rods or something when I get around you. You're gonna get me in trouble."

"Dampening rods?"

He moved back in close to me. "Yeah."

I laughed and nudged him down the street. "Come on, before I get you in real trouble. Speaking of trouble, where's your brother?"

"We'll catch up with them eventually."

We walked with our hands in our pockets, out of step and bumping into each other because of it. We caught up with the boys at the end-of-the-street *Texas Chainsaw Massacre* display. A man in the neighborhood was dressed up like the gruesome killer in a little scene between two houses. Kids were gathered around and screamed every time he swung the bloodied chainsaw in their direction. We stopped and watched until the neighbor across the street, Ms. Strohm, shanghaied Luke into lighting all the luminaries along her driveway and sidewalk.

I watched from the street as Luke lit each of the candles in the sand-filled bags, my fingers wrapped tightly around the phone in my pocket. I debated with myself over whether or not I really wanted to listen to my voice mail, assuming there was voice mail.

Finally I slid the phone out of my pocket. One missed call. My heart thudded as I hit the button to view, but then sank when I saw the call had been from Danial. Why was it so hard to let go?

"Are you and my brother dating?"

Matt was standing next to me, peering up at me from behind his wire-framed glasses. He held out a Twizzlers. I took it and looked around for his friends. I didn't see them.

"Alex said you're that gay guy from the high school."

That gay guy from the high school. Yeah, I guess I was.

"His sisters are freshmen. They know all about you."

I was still trying to decide how to respond to his first question, but he didn't give me a chance. "So, my brother's really gay," he said. He seemed to turn that thought over in his head for a moment.

I felt like I should say something. I went for the Dr. Phil response. "How do you feel about that?"

He shrugged. "It explains why he's always looking at pictures of naked guys on the Internet. Don't tell him, though. He doesn't know I know. He's not nearly as sneaky as he thinks he is."

Yeah, that was Luke. I fought the smile creeping its way across my mouth. I was pretty sure Luke and my grandmother were going to get along great.

"He's still my bro, though, right?"

I nodded.

"It's okay if you like my brother. Don't tell my parents, though. My dad hates gay people." He started to walk away, but then stopped and turned back. "And, it's not as dark out here as you think." He grinned and I grinned back and told him I'd remember that.

I unwrapped the Twizzlers and took a bite, watching him walk away. When Luke came back a minute later, I offered him the candy. Instead of taking it, he just bit off a hunk.

Chapter 44

A week later, I watched Luke, sprawled out across my bed, sound asleep, his mouth slightly ajar. On the table next to me, a glass of blue Powerade sat in a puddle of condensation, untouched. I'd only left the room for a few minutes to pour the drink for him. Mom had accosted me in the kitchen with that look. "Nate, he's awfully young. Do you know what you're doing?"

I'd screwed the lid back on the bottle and shoved it back in the refrigerator, then picked up the glass and met her eyes. "I'm bringing him a drink. He's thirsty. That's all."

By the time I'd returned, he'd passed out. It had been a long day for him—a four A.M. wake-up call, at the band hall by five thirty A.M., on the bus at six, a two-hour drive, run-through, performance, preliminary contest results, another performance, then back on the bus for a two-hour drive back. I'd picked him up at ten and tried to take him straight home from the band hall, but he'd insisted on doing the Cinderella thing and staying out until the absolute stroke of midnight, his curfew.

I flipped my cell phone around in my hand, stopping occasionally to run my fingers over the keypad. It was already ten fifty, eleven fifty New York time. If I was going to wish Adam a happy birthday, I had to do it now.

It was just a text. *Hope you had a great birthday.* Or maybe just *Happy Birthday.* He deserved at least that. He'd been there for me, even when—especially when—I was hard to be with. Like that first day home from the hospital.

I'd been euphoric at first, like I'd been sprung from a long prison term of bland food and constant hovering, not of guards, but of doctors, and nurses, and Mom. My room felt unfamiliar when I entered it, but Juliet and Mike showed up a few minutes later, and their chatter soon bridged the gap between before and after, and the alienness of my room dissolved.

It was great to hang around with friends and talk about normal stuff—music, homework, teachers, cars, movies, anything . . . anything but the other. To wear real clothes and sit on a bed without rails. And to look at my walls and see posters instead of white boards with orders scribbled on them. We laughed about nothing, and we laughed about everything. When the conversation reached a quiet, comfortable place, I picked up my guitar and played some familiar riffs.

I was home.

I lost myself in the rhythm for a while, relishing the bite of the strings on my fingertips and feeling my heart stir in ways that became increasingly uncomfortable. When I looked up again, Juliet had fat tears streaming down her face. I leaned the guitar carefully against the wall and got up, then slung my duffel bag onto the bed. "I'm tired," I said abruptly. "Can you guys go."

It wasn't a question. She and Adam exchanged a look. I could see the confusion and hurt in her eyes, but I didn't really give a fuck. I unzipped the bag, fighting the impulse to scream, but they hesitated a moment too long. "Everybody, just *go,*" I said, pressing my fingers to my temples.

I busied myself unpacking my bag, trying to uncoil the tight anger in my chest while Adam walked them to the landing and said good-bye. When he came back in, he sat on the edge of the bed and watched me. We were alone, finally, the kind of alone where you could lock the door, but neither of us made a move to do so.

"What's wrong?" he asked.

I shook my head and gritted my teeth. The silence stretched out until he said, "Nate."

"*Nothing* . . . is wrong."

"Nate." He reached out for my hand, and everything I'd been holding back exploded in a white-hot flash. "Why does everybody act like there's something wrong? Just because I'm a fucking walking cliché." I yanked the zipper closed on the empty bag and kicked it in the general direction of my closet.

"You're not a cliché."

"Gay boy gets butt fucked with—"

"Stop it." He reached again for my hand, but I spun away from him.

"No, you stop it. You tell me how that's *not* a cliché. I'm fucking sick of the pity. I can't stand the way they look at me. I can't stand the way you look at me."

"Nobody's—"

"Yes, they are." I pressed my hands to my pounding head again. "I just want to go back to the way things were. I just want to go back. . . . *Dammit!* Can't people just let this go? Why can't they just let me . . ." I couldn't finish. I didn't know how to finish. I grabbed the desk chair and flung it as hard as I could at the door. When that wasn't enough, I swept my desk clean with my arm. A snarl clawed its way out of my gut. I kicked my guitar into the wall and then stomped it to splinters. Then Adam was behind me, pinning my arms to my side and forcing me to the bed. He held me firmly while I thrashed and clawed at him.

"Nathan?" my mom said, alarmed. She stood in the doorway, her face white.

"It's okay, Ms. Schaper," Adam told her.

That's what he said to me too—"It's okay"—over and over again until finally, my anger spent, I slumped against the mattress, breathing hard and sweating. My head pounded.

"I just. Want. To move. On."

"Okay," he said gently. "Okay."

He undressed me and tucked the covers snugly around me. And then he lay next to me, shaping his body to mine, stroking my hair and my neck. I pressed my face into the pillow to muffle the sobs.

Later I reached for his fingers and held them to my cheek. "Don't let me go," I'd whispered.

"I won't."

And he hadn't. Not for a long time. No matter what had happened between us since, I couldn't let this day go unmarked.

I sat on the bed and dragged my fingers along Luke's smooth jaw. His lips drew back in a small smile, then relaxed again as he drifted back into a deep sleep.

I sat up and hit a key to light up the screen. I thought for a minute, then thumbed out a message. *Happy Birthday, Adam. I didn't forget.* I swallowed hard. That wasn't right. I tried again. *Happy B'Day! Thinking of you.* My eyes burned. I cleared the words and tried one more time. *Happy Birthday, Adam.* I let out a ragged breath and pushed Send.

After a few moments, the screen went black. I stared at it, willing it to light up. A few minutes later it did. *Thank you.*

That was it.

I waited, hoping that maybe there'd be another text. Some declaration, some something that would make sense out of all this pain. But there was nothing.

The screen stayed black, and after a while I took a deep breath and set the phone on my bedside table. I lay down on the bed next to Luke and brushed my fingers across his cheek. His eyes flickered, then opened, and he smiled at me sleepily. "What time is it?" he asked hoarsely.

"About eleven," I whispered back, my eyes pleading with him to make me forget the way he'd promised.

He studied my face for a minute, then scooted close to me and slid his knee up between my legs and rolled into me. He kissed me and I kissed him, and we didn't stop until we were sweaty and sticky and gasping for air.

It would be the first time Luke missed curfew.

Luke's flimsy excuse that the band had gotten in late was derailed before he even got it out of his mouth. His dad's phone call to the band hall earlier had killed that one. So he said he and some of the guys had gone for burgers afterward and then one of them dropped him off. He was still grounded for a week, but it was a price he gladly paid for getting closer to me.

He'd managed to dodge his parents' questions so far, but according to Luke, they were starting to act a little suspicious. That worried me. I didn't know Luke's parents at all except for that brief meeting on Halloween and what I'd seen in the stands at the game. I could tell Luke was his mom's pride and joy, what with all the photos she was taking. But was her love big enough to wrap around a gay son? And what if it wasn't? And what was with his dad and that face that looked slightly put out? And those cracks about manly instruments? Luke was so pure and innocent. I couldn't stand the thought of him being hurt. And I admit, I was a little obsessed with the thought. I felt like I'd earned that right.

He was sprung from his punishment just in time for the fall musical the second week in November. Danial had been like a little kid about seeing Juliet direct the play. She was still seeing Mike, but anybody with eyes could see she and Danial had it bad for each other. I wondered how much longer they could pretend otherwise. And I wondered how much longer I could pretend that Adam's coming home in eleven days didn't matter to me. I had planned to take Luke to the musical, but when it came time to get in the car, I just couldn't do it. Luke knew that all things Adam still cut too deeply, and he didn't push. Instead he came over and we played corny duets, him on the clarinet, me on the piano. He was attentive and funny, trying hard to keep me distracted, to keep me from thinking too much. It was Mom and Grandma's first chance to really get to know Luke. They warmed up to him easily. It was hard not to.

Adam didn't come home for Thanksgiving. I had driven by his house a few times after dark. A single light shone through the glass in the front door, but there was no way I could tell for sure if he was there. His bedroom, the one with all the lava lamps, faced the back. I tried to sound casual when I called Juliet Thursday night, but she knew.

"Have you seen Adam?" I asked, without preamble. It was hard enough to get those words out without my voice cracking.

"I'm sorry, Nate," she said quietly into the phone. "He stayed in New York. His parents and Mea flew up there for the holiday. I'm really sorry, baby."

I hadn't expected that to sting so much. "It's okay," I said. "It's no big deal. I was just wondering." It was over, but I guess somewhere in the back of my mind I'd been hoping that maybe it wasn't.

Luke tried, but there wasn't much he could do to pull me out of my funk.

"You don't deserve this, Luke. I just need time to mourn, I guess. Every time I think I'm really over it"—I shook my head—"I'm just not."

We were sitting on the trunk of my car in the driveway. He held my hand, examining my palm and each of my fingers in turn as if he'd find some hint of our future there.

"I hate him," he said simply.

"Don't."

He scrunched up his brow. "What if he came back right now and wanted you back?"

"That's not going to happen."

"But what if he did?" He looked up at me, real fear in his eyes.

"I'm not going anywhere, Luke." And that was the saddest truth of all.

Chapter 45

"You guys have got to come tonight," Juliet pleaded. "Natalie's Christmas party won't be the same without you there." She was perched on the front counter in the music store, twisting her hair into a loose ponytail over her right shoulder, a flirty move she made a lot around Danial, and one that clearly charmed him.

I busied myself hanging the new stock of instrument ornaments on a small tree beside the counter and ignored her.

She growled in frustration. "Come on. Where's your Christmas spirit?"

I gave her a look that I hoped conveyed how much I resented that particular question. Danial just shrugged. "I've still got twelve days to choke up some Christmas spirit," I said sullenly.

She breathed a heavy sigh. "Come on, Danial. It'll be fun. And you," she said, looking at me. "You already stood me up once. And you hardly ever go anywhere with Luke. Let the poor kid out of the closet. He's a nice guy. We want to be his friends too."

I tossed the empty box into a recycle bin and grabbed my new guitar by the neck. I whacked Danial in the hip with it. "Let's go."

"Won't you at least think about it?" Juliet said as I hustled Danial toward the lesson room.

Without turning back, I gave her a peace sign over my shoulder.

"I'll take that as a yes," she yelled as we disappeared inside.

"What've you and Gary been working on?" I asked, settling into one of the two metal chairs and pushing the door closed with my foot.

"Let's just play. You lead. I'll try to follow." I chose a simple riff, five chords. Danial watched my fingers and caught the chords here and there until he got the hang of it. Once he got the riff down, I played around a little.

I watched his fingers. "That's good," I said, nodding. He was a natural guitar player. His hands were broad, his fingers nimble, his fingertips toughening up, his reflexes quick. I bobbed my head to the beat. "You've definitely improved."

"Yeah, well, I have a lot of time to practice." He stopped playing and leaned back, then propped his feet up on the edge of my chair. "So, why don't you want to go to the party?"

His feet were crowding me, so I knocked them off. "Too many memories. You're paying for this lesson. Play."

"Good memories or bad memories?"

"Hmph. Good, I guess, but even the good memories are bad memories now, you know. Natalie's party last year, that was the first time Adam and I appeared together in public. Wouldn't you agree that showing up there with Luke tonight would be just a little weird?"

"I don't know. Depends on the party? Is it one of those awkward stand-around-and-pretend-like-you-actually-enjoy-small-talk-while-you-stuff-your-face-with-chips-just-to-give-your-hands-something-to-do parties?"

I laughed a little. "No. It's karaoke. Dancing. It's actually kind of fun."

"Then go. Maybe Juliet's right. Maybe you'd have a good time."

"Why don't *you* go?"

He shrugged and placed his fingers back on the strings. I picked up a new riff, something a little simpler. He watched my fingers and matched me chord for chord, responding more quickly to changes this time.

I looked up at him as I played. "They broke up you know."

"Who?"

I grinned, knowing I was about to make his day. "Juliet and Mike." He dropped the next chord, and my grin broadened. "Last weekend. It was a mutual thing. They've never been more than just really good friends anyway." I waited for him to react. He tried to feign indifference, but his hands gave him away, screwing up chord after chord. Finally, I dipped my head low to catch his eyes. "Sooo, caveman, you going to the party now?"

He rolled his eyes up to me and matched my grin. "I'd say the odds are definitely improving."

I laughed. "I'd sure put money on that horse."

"Hmph. So how are things going with your fan girly boyfriend?"

My laughter died in my throat and I focused on the strings. Luke. Luke was kind of fan girly, and I liked that about him. But it was one thing for him to think of us as boyfriends, and quite an other for anyone else to think that. I shrugged. "It's okay."

"Are you two making the beast with two backs?"

I winced. Shakespeare. *Othello*. Iago had said that: "I am one, sir, that comes to tell you your daughter and the Moor are now making the beast with two backs." It's exactly the kind of thing that Adam would say. Adam. No, not Adam. I had to quit thinking that. Luke. He was the one I had to focus on now. He deserved that. I thought about Danial's question and answered it the only way I knew how: "I'm not sure how to answer that."

It was his turn to raise his eyebrows. "Uh, Nate, do we need to have a little biology lesson here?"

"No. We do not," I said sarcastically. "We, uh, haven't gotten naked together."

He nodded his head slowly. "Okay."

"But we have, uh—"

"Whoa. Okay. You don't have to paint a picture. I got it." He shivered, a reaction that drove away the blues, and I laughed.

"Hey. You had your shot."

"Has he taken you home to meet mommy and daddy?"

"Yeah. I've met them." But I didn't much like them. At least not his dad.

* * *

Juliet won. I called Luke after Danial left. I think he would have squealed when I asked him if he wanted to go if he were the squealing kind. Thankfully, he wasn't, but his excitement was palpable and infectious. By the time I left the music store at four o'clock, I was actually looking forward to the party. Luke wanted to drive to avoid the awkward questions at home, and I wholeheartedly agreed, but he was so keyed up over the party—not the party itself but the fact that he was going as my date—that I insisted he leave his car at my house. I didn't trust him not to run a red light and T-bone somebody on the way. He was that distracted. It would be the first time we'd actually appeared at an event as a couple. The irony of that wasn't lost on me as we stood together on Natalie's front porch several hours later.

Last December 8
Another Christmas party, another date

I felt conspicuous under the bright porch light. From somewhere inside the house, someone, not Joan Jett, was loving rock and roll. I bounced up and down nervously on my heels. "How do I look?"

Adam stepped back just long enough to give me an appreciative once-over. He took a deep breath and groaned a little. "Good enough to eat," he murmured in my ear, then bit my earlobe.

I laughed. "Down, boy. This is going to be hard enough without you making me blush every time I turn around."

He made a little X over his heart with his finger in the tight space between our two bodies. "My best behavior. Promise."

"Yeah." I chuckled. "That's what scares me." I tucked a piece of hair behind his ear. "How can you be so calm?"

"Who says I'm calm?"

I glanced out to the curb to make sure Juliet was in position. She was leaning against her car and gave me a little finger wave and a thumbs-up. I took a deep breath.

"Here we go." Adam pressed the doorbell, then reached for my hand, intertwined his fingers with mine, and squeezed. "Fortune rewards the brave," he said under his breath.

"Shakespeare?"

"Paula Abdul."

Mike Rutgers opened the door. I recognized him as one of the cast members. He stopped short when he saw us together, holding hands. "Whoa." He paused a second to take it all in. "I was going to say, what's new, dude, but I guess I know." He looked at Adam and then at me, a goofy look on his face. "Does that mean Juliet's available?"

Juliet pushed past us. "Yes, that means Juliet is available," she said, grabbing him by the hand and pulling him into the house. "Come on, lover boy, you're with me tonight."

A large woman appeared in the doorway. "Adam!" She held her arms out and he scooped her up and spun her around.

"Put me down." She laughed. "You're going to hurt yourself."

"Promise you'll dance with me tonight?"

She blushed. "No, because you never behave yourself, and I am a married woman." He pouted and she laughed. "Besides, there are too many pretty girls here waiting for that honor." Then looking around Adam at me, she said, "I don't believe we've met."

"This is Nate Schaper," he said, releasing her. He wrapped both arms around my waist and planted a kiss on my cheek just as Mrs. Maguire, Natalie's mother, reached to shake my hand.

Her eyes widen and her mouth stopped in mid "Nice to meet you." Her features contorted slightly as she seemed to deconstruct and then reconstruct everything she thought she knew about Adam. "Nate. Wow. Nate and Adam. Adam and Nate. Wow. You are certainly full of surprises, young man," she said to Adam. Then she focused her attention on me. "And you," she said conspiratorially, "are a very lucky fellow." She winked at Adam.

He laughed and let go of me to embrace her again.

She whispered something in his ear, then pushed him away. "Go on, you two. The karaoke machine is out back. I hope you brought warmed-up vocal chords."

"I love Joan Jett," Adam said. "Come on." He dragged me out

the French doors. Chloe and Amanda were already on the make-shift stage. Adam grabbed my face, planted a quick kiss on my lips, and hopped up onto the stage with the girls.

I blushed. At least half a dozen kids had to have seen that kiss. Chloe's jaw dropped. She looked at Adam and then back at me and then back at Adam again. And then back at me.

He ignored her look and grabbed a spare microphone. Chloe looked at Amanda and mouthed "Oh. My. God." Amanda shrugged and giggled.

What followed was an uninhibited, raunchy, and totally awesome version of Joan Jett's famous chorus. His voice was amazing, but his body oozed sex appeal.

And I wasn't the only one appreciating it.

He gave love a bad name and left his heart on the dance floor, all the while treating us to hip rolls and thrusts and crotch grabs and shimmies and all kinds of wiggling. I had no idea his body could move like that. It was when he hurt so good that I had to walk away for a minute out of sheer red-faced embarrassment and a wee bit of memory-induced excitement.

Juliet shoved a Smirnoff Ice in my hand. "Keep it on the down low," she shouted in my ear.

I took a sip from the bottle.

She hooked an arm around my neck. "Dance with me," she pleaded.

"What happened to Mike?" I mouthed.

She rolled her eyes and moved against me. "So?"

"So what?"

"You did it. You're out and nobody died."

I grinned. "But I'm here and he's up there, so I'm not sure we've fully tested that outcome."

"Well, you're about to now."

From behind me, Adam slipped his arms around my waist. "This dance is mine," he said in my ear.

Juliet let go, a little reluctantly, I thought, and disappeared into the crowd. Adam moved into the empty place she'd left and wrapped his arms around my neck and drew me so close to him there was no breathing room between us. He took a sip of my drink, then sang quietly but passionately in my ear about being the meaning and inspiration in his life, about wanting to have me near him, about no one needing me more than he needed me. On the stage, someone else was doing the Chicago cover, but Adam sang to me like he'd written the song himself. We swayed and stepped to the music, both loose and hungry for each other. And when his lips found mine, his mouth cool and lemony from the Smirnoff, everything else faded into the background, and there was just him and me, two satellites orbiting the same need, alone together in the vast expanse of the cosmos, until Juliet danced close and nudged me with her elbow.

"Uh, boys, you might want to get a room."

"Eeewww. Gross," a female voice said, one I didn't recognize.

My face reddened, but Adam chuckled. "She's just jealous because we have two penises and she has none." I grinned into his hair. He finally contented himself with laying his head on my shoulder. I closed my eyes and enjoyed the feel of my body moving with his. I refused to let that ignorant comment spoil our moment, not then, and not later at my house, where there was no need to lock the door this time.

Luke bounced on the balls of his feet. "How do I look?"

Good enough to eat.

"Like you're about to wet your pants again," I teased.

"I am."

"Don't."

Luke grinned, and I put my heartache over what Adam and I'd had and what could have been out of my mind and allowed Luke's enthusiasm to suck me in. I straightened the hood on his hoodie. "Here we go," I said and knocked on the door.

Unlike the night Adam showed up with me in tow, no one was surprised to see me with Luke. We slipped in without fanfare, for which I was grateful. Karaoke was already going strong. Danial showed up right behind us. We walked around and said hi to everyone. Luke held tight to my hand as I introduced him around, but Danial was too busy casing the room to give anything more than a cursory nod to my other friends.

"Relax," I told him. "She's here . . . somewhere."

"What are y'all whispering about?" Luke asked, looking like he didn't much appreciate being left out.

"You came!" Juliet squealed, appearing out of nowhere and throwing her arms and legs around Danial. He staggered back a few steps in surprise.

"That's what we were whispering about," I said in Luke's ear.

"Oh." He looked embarrassed.

I cleared my throat loudly. Juliet dropped her feet to the floor and gave me a quick hug and a kiss, and then after just a moment's hesitation, she gave Luke a hug too. Done with that, she grabbed for Danial's hand. "Come on. Dance with me."

We followed them out to the patio where couples were slow dancing in the low light. "Your eyes are doing that thing again," I said to Luke, grinning. He was looking at me with that raw adoration I had neither earned nor deserved.

"What thing?"

"They're getting all melty."

"Is that bad?"

"Come here, you." I pulled him to me and we danced. He held me close and planted his mouth in the hollow below my ear, not kissing me, just breathing. It felt good.

"I could stay just like this forever," he whispered in my ear.

I smiled and kissed him on the forehead. "There's a lot you'd miss out on if you did."

He pulled away and looked at me. I winked at him. His eyes slid down to my lips. "Tonight?" he said, his voice pleading.

"Luke."

"You don't have to do anything. I'll do everything."

I laughed. "My mom and my grandmother are home."

"We can lock your door." I gently pushed his head back to a place beneath my jaw.

"We'll see."

He pressed a kiss on my earlobe. "I love you," he whispered, then clutched at me so tightly I could hardly breathe.

I smiled into his hair. He was so easy to please. He just wanted me, near him, with him, proud of him, loving him. It was all so simple. Maybe I *could* let go of the past and embrace the future. What did I have to lose? If you can't be with the one you love, love the one you're with. Isn't that what the song said?

Maybe it was time to let go. I kissed his hair. "I love you too, Luke."

With the reflex of one who had been waiting for just such a declaration, he tightened his arms around me again, making it impossible for my lungs to expand. "I can't breathe," I whispered in his ear.

He pulled back, his eyes bright and happy. "Oh, what the hell," I said, wrapping my arms back around him. "Squeeze me as tight as you want. Who needs air?"

After the song, we went to the cooler next to the patio table for sodas. Luke was moving about in such an obvious state of bliss that I had to laugh. I shoveled ice into two plastic cups and filled them with Coke from a bottle and handed one to him. Natalie had stocked the cooler with wine coolers, but I was afraid of how alcohol might affect my boyfriend. I laughed to myself. Danial was right. He really was fan girly. But I had to admit, his adoration was flattering. He wasn't slobbering just yet, and I wanted to make sure he didn't start. So no alcohol for Luke.

Danial joined us. I handed him my soda and poured another. He took that one too. "Thanks, bro. I'd love to hang out with you two girls, but—"

"Go," I said, grinning. "Far be it for me to get in the way of lust." I winked at him and tipped the bottle again.

Warren and a couple of the other guys were just starting a new song. "Come on," I said, taking Luke's hand. "Let's go watch."

We found a spot in the group gathered around the makeshift stage. I stood behind Luke and wrapped my arms around him, careful not to slosh him with my soda.

The guys were singing an Eagles song about wanting to touch somebody, even if it took all night. Luke looked back at me and raised his eyebrows. I grinned and shook my head. But the smile faded when the chorus promised a heartache tonight. I was glad I was standing behind him.

Almost directly across from us, Juliet and Danial were nuzzling each other. He whispered something in her ear and she giggled. It made me happy seeing them together.

And then her face fell, her eyes focused on something near the house. She whispered to Danial. He looked over his shoulder. I followed their eyes. Standing in the sliding glass doorway was Adam. He searched the crowd. My breath caught in my throat and my knees buckled. I looked back frantically at Juliet and Danial.

Luke felt the change in my posture. He turned his head to me, his eyes full of worry. "Nate?" I tried to act like nothing was wrong, but I couldn't help looking back at Adam. Luke's eyes followed mine. "Nate?" he said again, fear creeping into his voice.

I tore my eyes away and looked at Luke's sweet face, only realizing then that I'd sloshed him with Coke after all. "Oh shit, Luke, I'm sorry."

He ignored the soda dripping from his hoodie. His eyes darted back at Adam. "Is that who I think it is?" His voice had lost its confidence. He sounded like a little boy afraid of the monster in the closet.

I forced myself to smile at him. "It's okay, Luke. You don't have anything to be worried about." I knew it was a lie even as I said it. Out of the corner of my eye, I could see kids surrounding Adam. Someone had plugged the speakers into their MP3 player and Jay Sean was taunting me with lyrics about being my only.

"Why is he here?" Luke asked.

I pulled him into my arms to dance. He was trembling, or maybe it was me trembling. It was hard to tell. "I don't know," I said. I held him to me more closely, reassuring him with my presence. "But it doesn't matter. We're okay. Okay?"

"Okay," he said, but I could tell he wasn't convinced.

I wasn't convinced either.

I was desperate to look at Adam, but I forced myself *not* to look anywhere but right at the top of Luke's head. I considered how we were going to make our exit. We couldn't stay. This had been a mistake. And yet, I'd gotten to see him, and now I wished he'd leave because seeing him meant wanting to touch him and wanting wasn't getting.

I was so focused on not looking around that I was startled when I turned Luke and bumped right into Adam.

"Do you mind if I cut in?" he asked politely.

Luke's head snapped up and his eyes darkened. "Actually, I do mind." He tightened his hold on me, and I found myself fighting to expand my lungs again.

I caught Danial's eye. I had no idea what to do. If I had the power to disappear, I would have invoked it right then. Danial headed my way.

Adam looked from Luke to me. Luke tried to turn me away, but my feet felt like they'd been cast in concrete and wouldn't budge, and the moving and the not moving almost sent us tumbling to the ground.

"I just want to talk, that's all," Adam said.

I glared at him, then turned to Luke and forced my face to relax. "Luke, it's okay. It'll just be a minute. Why don't you go get us some wine coolers?" I handed him my cup. I was going to need a drink after this. Maybe Danial had a joint in his pocket. *Shit.*

Luke didn't want to go, and for a few awkward, unbalanced seconds, I didn't think he would. I smiled reassuringly, and finally he went with one last pleading look over his shoulder.

Adam stepped into his place. He took one of my hands in his, but when he moved to put the other around my waist, I turned and stalked off, off the patio and into a corner of the yard, as far away from everyone else as I could get without actually being alone with him. He followed. I hooked the cuffs of my sweater with my fingers and folded my arms tightly against my chest because I no longer trusted any of my limbs. Finally I allowed my eyes to meet his. His look was so intense I could hold it for only a moment. I glanced toward Luke. He watched us from the patio table. Hope and guilt sparked equally in my chest. I looked at my feet.

Adam drew slightly closer, and I tried to slow the hammering in my chest. I looked back at Luke, and Adam's eyes followed mine. "So that's Luke, huh? He looks kinda young."

"He's not," I spat back. "Why are you here?"

He looked back at me and bit his lower lip. "I guess I just had to see it for myself."

I huffed. "Kind of like coming to a funeral and gawking in the open casket. Just making sure everything's nice and dead before you throw dirt on top."

He wrinkled his brow like he was fighting a sudden, sharp pain. I knew the feeling. "Yeah, something like that," he said quietly.

"You came, you saw, go home. I'm sure you have an early flight to catch in the morning."

"No flight, Nate."

I scoffed. "Did you and Justin have a little tiff?"

He rolled his eyes to the sky. "What is your obsession with Justin?"

"I could ask you the same thing. Did you bring him home with you? Is that it? Is he out waiting in the car? Bring him in. We can have a big ol' *fucking* gay party right here."

"What are you talking about?"

I had had enough of these stupid games. I struggled to get my cell phone out of my pocket, then scanned through my text inbox until I found his errant text and shoved the phone in his face. "This is what I'm talking about."

He took the phone and studied the screen.

"You should be more careful before you press Send."

He looked confused for a moment, then met my eyes. "Is that what this is all about? A stupid text?"

"Did you think I wouldn't find out?" I sneered. "I talked to Justin."

"What do you mean, you talked to Justin? What are you talking about?"

"The night of the homecoming dance. Surely you remember that night, Adam. Did you feel the earth move beneath you? Because apparently your boyfriend did."

"I have no idea what you're talking about, Nate, but you're about to piss me off."

I laughed. "I'm about to piss *you* off? Oh, that's good." Just as quickly as it came, the laughter went. "Don't you dare talk to me like I'm stupid. I Skyped you. You seem to be a little technology challenged these days. You left your computer on. And your boyfriend was all too happy to have a little chat with me."

"What did he say to you?"

"Plenty." I looked back at the patio and found Luke. He looked like he wanted to kill Adam, rip his throat out, and I would gladly have let him, but Danial kept a hand on his arm, talking to him.

Adam watched me watch Luke, then repeated his question: "Nate, what did he say to you?"

I swallowed hard and willed myself not to cry before I turned back. "I trusted you, Adam, with everything. My heart, my body, my secrets. I believed in you. He told me about the two of you."

"He lied."

"And then he told me about me." I let that sink in a moment. "He couldn't have known the things he knew if you hadn't told him. And then he laughed at me. It was like he shot me right through the heart, and you gave him the bullet."

"I didn't, Nate. I swear to you."

"I can never forgive you for that." I turned to leave, but he grabbed my arm.

"Baby—"

I whipped back around and got in his face. "Don't you EVER call me that again."

He looked down at my clenched fists. "You want to hit me, Nate, then hit me, beat the crap out of me if it makes you feel better, but you are going to listen to me. That text—"

"I don't want to hear it."

"Well, you're gonna hear it. Just STOP for a goddamn minute."

"So you can lie to me again?"

He sighed heavily. "Nate, I have never, not once, lied to you. Never. Please, just hear me out. And then if you want to walk away, God help me, I'll let you go."

When I hesitated, he said quietly, "What do you have to lose, Nate?"

I didn't answer, but I didn't leave either.

He took a deep breath and let it out in one huff. "I can't even believe I have to say this, but there is nothing going on between me and any of my roommates, not now, not ever. You are the only one I love, the only one I want to love. Have a little faith in me, Nate."

"You kissed him."

"He kissed me. It's a game for him. After that last night the power went out, I completely swore off drinking. I wasn't about to ever let that happen again." He tugged down his turtleneck. *Wicked* still marked him, but the skin around it was red, the ink slightly faded. "Laser removal. Two treatments. It'll take another three or four, but it'll be gone, completely."

"He knew—"

"I don't know how he knew. Yes, I have talked about you, to Alec, not to Justin. If you want to hate me, hate me for that. But things had been so bad between us. Alec's been through some rough times himself, and he's a good listener. He's on your side, Nate, on our side. I guess Justin overheard us."

"The text—"

"The text. It was meant for Alec. I was hurt and upset and angry when you wouldn't take my calls that night. We walked the streets of the city well into the morning hours and just talked. He convinced me that there was a lot of subtext in your words, things you were feeling, but not saying. He reminded me of how much you've been through, and how if you seemed needy it was—"

"Needy? NEEDY? No. No. Don't you dare tell me you came back because you feel sorry for me."

"I don't feel sorry for you. I've never felt sorry for you." He paused and seemed to grapple for words. "I didn't come back for you. I came back for me."

I closed my eyes and focused on breathing. I could feel him move in closer, and then his hand touched my ear.

"You're still wearing my earring," he said softly.

I couldn't help myself. His hand touching me. I pressed my wet cheek into his fist and felt that spark of hope ignite.

"This is not over between us, Nate. I could see it in your face when you first saw me tonight. I can see it in the tears in your eyes. God, how did we let this happen?" He pulled me to him and I went. "We're two parts of a whole," he whispered in my ear. "The yin and the yang. How could you have ever doubted that?" He sniffed and tightened his hold on me, and after a moment, I clasped him back and felt my breath catch in my throat. "Come home with me. There's so much more we need to talk about. Heart-to-heart, face-to-face, just me and you."

Just me and you. No, not just me and you. "Luke." I pulled away from him and looked anxiously around the patio. A few kids remained and the music played on, but Luke was gone. So were Danial and Juliet.

"It doesn't matter what you've done," he said, clearly misunderstanding. "All that matters is that you're here with me now. I don't care about anything that happened before. I don't care about Luke."

I looked back at him, my heart in my throat, and took a few steps back. "I care."

"Nate, don't."

I held my arms out, then let them drop limply to my sides and shook my head, vaguely aware that I was crying openly now. "I can't. Luke doesn't deserve this. He's was there for me when you weren't." I looked back at the door, then back to Adam and whispered, "I'm sorry."

His face fell and he looked away.

Chapter 46

"Where is he?"

The conversation around us ground to an awkward stop. For once, I didn't care. Juliet took in my face, and when it looked like she wasn't going to tell me, I put a little force behind my words: "Where *is* he?"

"Danial took him to his house," she said quietly. She glanced over my shoulder, and I knew Adam had come in the back door. I could see the apology in her expression. I brushed past her, and she grabbed my arm. "You can't do this, Nate."

I lifted my eyes to Adam and tried to convey all my regrets in those few brief seconds. When I spoke to Juliet again, it was with a voice heavy with emotion. "I can't not do this, Jules."

I barely saw the road as I made my way to Danial's.

No one answered the door. I found them in the backyard, Danial stretched out on the ground, looking up at the sky and smoking a joint, farther out in the yard, Luke with his eye pressed to the telescope eyepiece.

I sat next to Danial and took the joint, careful to inhale slowly. "How is he?"

Danial propped himself up on his elbows and watched Luke for a moment. "He's okay." He took the joint back from me and sucked in deeply, then blew out the smoke and studied me.

"Why are you here?"

I didn't respond.

He huffed. "Let him go, Nate. You can't choose who you fall in love with. You just do. And I know you're trying to be noble and all, but you're not doing Luke any favors by leading him on. You know he's not the one." He paused for a moment. "He knows that too."

I felt the tears well up in my eyes again and wondered when I'd become such a crybaby. I hadn't come here to let Luke go. I hadn't even considered it. And now it seemed a foregone decision. "I never meant to hurt him."

"He knows that."

I looked at Danial.

"We talked," he said.

I took the joint and another drag, then handed it back to him. "You have to hate me right now."

"I don't hate you, Nate. And Luke, he doesn't hate you either. But I promise, if you continue this farce—and it is a farce; I know that, and you know that—one day you're going to wake up and you're going to hate him. You think he's hurting now? You do that to him and I *will* kick your gay ass all over this county. We both saw what went on between you and Adam tonight." He laughed a little. "The whole world saw."

"I want you to meet him."

He looked at me for a moment, then looked back at Luke. "Luke's not the only one losing you tonight." He took another drag and handed the joint back to me.

"Nobody's losing me tonight." I flicked the ash off the end the way I'd seen him do. "What do I say to him?"

"The truth. He's tougher than you think. And you owe him that."

"The truth. I don't even know what that is anymore."

"You know."

I looked back at Danial. He smiled a little then slapped me lightly on the shoulder. I got up and headed down to Luke, thinking about what he'd said. I knew Luke heard me approach, but he didn't look up from the telescope.

I touched his hair and felt him twitch, but otherwise he didn't respond. "See anything good up there?"

"I've never seen the moon this close up. It's amazing."

"Yeah, it is," I said, stroking his hair.

"It makes everything down here feel so different, you know?"

I smiled and leaned my chin on his shoulder. "Yeah, I do know."

He was quiet for a minute while I kneaded his arms. "You're going back to him, aren't you?"

He glanced over his shoulder and I nodded.

"I always kind of knew this night would happen," he said after a moment. "I saw that picture of the two of you, the one on the beach? I found it in your desk drawer while you were in the bathroom."

I laughed a little and sniffed. "You snooped in my desk drawers?"

"I just wanted to know you, everything about you. You always held things back about Adam. You looked happy in that picture." He turned then and looked at me, his eyes visibly puffy even in the darkness. "I knew when he came back, I'd lose you."

We pressed our foreheads together. "You haven't lost me, Luke. I've hurt you, and that's something I never wanted to do." He twitched again as if his muscles were tensed up and beginning to spasm. "But I'm not sorry that we got close."

"I'm not sorry either. Can I ask you something?"

"What?"

"Did you say you loved me just to make me happy?"

I rolled the question around in my mind for a moment. It just wasn't that simple. Yes, I had said it to make him happy. I'd done a lot of things to make Luke happy over the past few months. Was that so wrong? He had needed validation, companionship. I gave him that. And he'd been a salve for my wounded heart, caffeine for my flagging ego. I ran my fingers down his cheek. But I did love him.

"No," I said finally. "I didn't say it just to make you happy."

"It's not the same way you love Adam, though, is it?"

I shook my head.

I expected more emotion from him, but he just nodded and looked over at Danial for a moment. "Danial told me about all you'd been through together. I don't want to like him—Adam—you know, but he's been really good to you."

"What else did Danial tell you?"

"He told me that now that you have Adam back, he's gonna need a new best friend."

I smiled. "Watch out for that one." Luke met my smile with one of his own. "He's the best," I said. "But don't ever try to kiss him. He's just not into boys."

"You kissed Danial?"

"I tried."

Luke cracked up. "Oh, man, I wish I'd been there to see that."

"Trust me. It wasn't one of my prouder moments."

He grinned again, and then without warning, his grin turned into a grimace, and I pulled him to me and held him tight while he got it all out. The temperature had dropped, and his ear against my cheek was cold. I pulled his hood up over his head.

"This is good-bye, isn't it?" he choked out when the tears finally subsided.

"No. Not good-bye."

The drive back to my house was quiet, save for the phone call to his parents. It was already 12:05; Luke had missed his curfew. His dad's voice, loud and angry, carried across the console, cutting through the rush of warm air from the heater.

I looked at Luke with sympathy and worry. "He sounded pretty mad."

"Yeah." He shrugged. "It's okay. I'm not going anywhere anyway."

His words stung.

I followed him home to make sure he got there safely. His dad was standing on the front porch when Luke pulled into the driveway, his arms folded across his chest. Even from this distance, I could see his eyes follow my car as I circled the cul-de-sac and headed back. I wanted to hang around and make sure Luke was okay, but I was afraid I'd just make things worse for him.

No lights burned at Adam's house. But in the wash of the street-light I could see him sitting on the front porch, hunched over his knees. When I pulled up to the curb, he stood. I got out and made my way to him. His face, even in the dim light, was a fusion of pain and hope so tender I could hardly bear not reaching out to him. I grabbed the cuffs of my sweater again and folded my arms tightly against my chest, in part because I was cold, and in part to stop me from doing something I wanted to do so desperately that I had to physically restrain myself. I cleared my throat and struggled to find my voice. "I just broke someone's heart that I care about very much. And I have to know if I did the right thing."

"I'll tell you anything you want, Nate," he said quietly.

"You said you came home for you," I said in a voice still heavy with emotion. "What does that mean?"

"Come on. Let's sit. We should have done this a long time ago."

We sat close to each other on the cold flagstone. From behind him, Adam grabbed a blanket I hadn't noticed and settled it around our shoulders, then clasped my hand tightly, intertwining his fingers with mine. I gripped his back.

He let out a long, slow breath, visible in the night air. "When I thought I'd lost you, I knew I couldn't stay." He turned my face to his. "I could never be happy in New York knowing what it cost me. The person I love most in this world. New York was only good as long as I had you here, believing in me, waiting for me to come home. All the long hours, the parties, someone was always sticking a drink in my hand, the blatant come-ons—it was never me. But you were my anchor. You kept me grounded."

"And yet, it took you two more months to come home."

"Two months and one day, to *get* home, Nate. There's a differ-ence." A shiver rattled through me and he moved even closer, drawing the blanket across me and grasping it with his free hand. "Can I ask *you* a question? Why didn't you tell me about that

Skype with Justin? After everything we've been through together, why is it still so hard for you to trust me?"

It was a good question. And one I wasn't sure I could answer, and yet, somehow I knew it had to be answered. For me as much as for him. An old memory surfaced, something my grandmother had told me years ago, before she'd moved in with us, before my parents had split up. Back when I was small enough to spank and when my dad could still look at me with something other than disgust. He'd spanked me over some infraction I no longer remembered. But I did remember hating him for it. Grandma found me in my room, wailing at the door with my bare feet. She hauled me onto the bed and told me about this show she used to watch when she was a kid. *Family Affair.* I'd never seen the show, but the name had stuck with me all these years. It was a sitcom about these kids, Buffy and Jody and an older sister, who lived with their uncle, a father figure so gentle that all the kids of her generation dreamed of growing up with an Uncle Bill. One day Jody sees his friend get a spanking. The kid's dad tells Jody that he spanks his son out of love. Jody gets it into his head that maybe Uncle Bill doesn't really love him, or at least not enough to punish him physically. So he starts getting into trouble just for that spanking that would prove he was loved. After Grandma told me that story, I didn't resent the spankings so much. And when they stopped, so ended the only physical evidence I thought I had that my dad loved me.

The analogy wasn't quite right, but it was the closest I could get to what I was feeling.

We sat quietly while Adam mulled it over. "You wanted me to spank you?"

I choked out a laugh.

"I'm not really into S and M, Nate, but if that's what it takes to make you feel safe and loved, then I'm your guy."

"You'd spank me?" I looked back at him, still grinning.

"It would be an affront to my inner pacifist, but yeah, I'd spank you."

"I don't want to be spanked."

"That's a relief." He brought my hand to his mouth and kissed it. "It's really good to see you smile again," he said softly. Then, "Keep talking, Nate. I want to understand."

I pressed my lips together and looked off at the quiet street. A gray cat ambled down the center. Somewhere a dog barked, and the cat froze, then perceiving no threat, sat and groomed himself. "It's hard to explain," I said. "And it all seems so stupid now when I'm sitting here with you."

"Not stupid. Nothing you feel is stupid. Tell me what's been going on in that pretty head of yours."

God, where to start. "Have you ever wondered, even for a minute, if I was attracted to Danial?"

"Are you?"

"That's not the point." I ground my teeth and grappled for a way to explain something I barely understood myself. "The point is, you being around other guys always makes me a little crazy."

He smiled. "I've noticed."

I didn't smile back. "But it's not that way for you. Whatever I do, whoever I hang out with, whoever you find sitting at my desk, everything is just a little too okay with you. Like it doesn't matter. Like I don't matter."

"Everything you do matters to me."

"Then why do I feel so shitty all the time? You didn't even know Danial."

"I knew *you*."

"I kissed him."

Adam grew still beside me, his only reaction, a mild grinding of my knuckles together. The cat got to its feet and moved on down the street. When it disappeared into the shadows, I turned back to Adam.

"Now you are getting a spanking," he said with mock seriousness. When I didn't laugh, he sighed and went on. "Nate, Danial is straight. He's no threat to me, to us. But I am curious. Why?"

"When I fuzzed out my eyes, he looked like you."

Adam's eyebrows shot up.

"It was nothing. I made a complete fool of myself, but Danial was a good sport about it. He knew how much I missed you."

"Is that why you hooked up with Luke? To make me jealous?"

"I didn't hook up with Luke." It wasn't the whole truth, but I saw a brief flicker of relief in his eyes, and I knew it was truth enough. It was all the truth we could take right now. "And I wasn't trying to make you jealous," I continued. "I hung out with him because he needed me. I only told you we were dating to hurt you, the way I hurt. Maybe I just wanted a reaction. I wanted you to stop me. To claim me." What came next was the part that still ate at me. "But you didn't fight for me. You just let me go."

"Oh, Nate." He scrubbed his face with his free hand. "If you'd only known how much that tore me up inside. There was this wall between us that I didn't know how to get past. I tried to back off, give you the space you needed to figure things out. And then Juliet saw you together, and my mom and Ben. And then you called me on Halloween, and I felt like you were just rubbing salt in the wound."

"That's not why I called. But when you answered, there was all this noise and voices in the background." *Are you waiting for me?* I tried to clear the voice from my head. "It was like you'd just moved on."

"I hadn't moved on. I was just going through the motions, doing what everyone expected of me, but barely getting by day to day. We started another four weeks of rehearsals for the next show. I threw myself into it, but it wasn't any good anymore. By the time you texted me on my birthday, I was so steeped in hurt and anger . . . I guess it was after that that I just kind of fell apart. The show opened the next weekend. I got through it, but I hardly remember any of it. By Thanksgiving I was ready to just walk away from everything."

"Why didn't you?"

"When I told Mom and Ben, they pulled Mea out of school early and flew up. Believe me, they never wanted me to go to New York, but they didn't want me doing anything rash either. I stayed in the hotel room with them. We talked about my future; we talked about you. Friday after Thanksgiving Ben negotiated my way out of both my contract and my sublease. I had to agree to stay until the show run ended last night, and in return they released me from any further commitments. We shipped my stuff home. I've been living pretty much with a couple changes of clothes and a toothbrush since."

Suddenly I understood what he was saying, what he'd been trying to say all night. "You're not going back?"

"I'm not going back. I doubt I would have gone in the first place if you hadn't pushed me with that cockamamy bullshit about needing to know who you are without me. That was bullshit, wasn't it?"

"You're not going back?" I said again, still trying to grasp what that meant.

He reached up and touched my face and shook his head. "Acting and singing and dancing, that's all fun, but it isn't my life. My life is right here. With you. Ben pulled some strings and got me an eleventh-hour admission to UT for the spring semester. I'll be in Austin, but I'll be home every weekend."

I dropped my head back and closed my eyes, feeling the tight knot of anxiety unravel in my chest and wanting to cry like a baby at the release. He let go of my hand and pulled me to him. "Call your mom and tell her you're staying with me tonight," he said huskily.

I already had.

Chapter 47

My ringtone woke me. I squinted at the window and the early day-light seeping around the edges of the blinds as I slid out from under Adam and fumbled for the phone on the bedside table.

"Mom?" I answered, my voice groggy. Adam stirred next to me. I smiled to myself and walked my fingers through the valley between his shoulder blades. He groaned pleasantly.

"Nate. I need you to come home."

The terseness in her voice got my attention and my fingers froze in their trek. "Is everything okay?"

Adam rolled to his side and nudged his knee up between my legs and opened his eyes.

"Baby, it's Luke."

I sat up. "Luke?"

"He's here, Nate. I found him on the front porch when I went out for the paper this morning. I think he was there all night. He's really upset. It sounds like he had a fight with his dad."

Adam propped himself up on one elbow, watching me, his face etched in concern.

"Don't let him leave. I'll be right there."

*   *   *

Adam came with me. From the car, I called Danial, waking him up. When he heard Luke's name, though, he was alert and getting dressed before I even hung up the phone. I filled Adam in on the drive over. Until then, I'd told him almost nothing about Luke, except that he needed me. In the five minutes it took to get from his house to mine, I told him why.

I burst in the door and Mom got to her feet and headed for me. On the couch, Luke nervously picked at his cuticles, his elbows on his knees, a blanket thrown over his shoulders. He didn't look up. "I called his dad," Mom said in a low voice. "He knows he's here. He's not happy about it. He's on his way to pick him up." Then she embraced Adam. "It's so good to see you."

I went and sat next to Luke. I took his hands in mine and held them still. They were ice cold. It hurt to think about him sitting all alone on my porch all night while I was wrapped in Adam's warm arms. He wasn't wearing his hoodie, just a thin, faded band T-shirt, and the night had been chilly. My heart broke for him, and I couldn't help feeling like I had done this.

"Tell me what happened," I said gently.

He took in a shuddering breath. "I told him," he said in a barely there voice.

I didn't have to ask what. I knew. Instantly.

He sniffed and pulled one hand free to swipe at his eyes. "Oh, Luke." I let go of his hands and pulled him to me. He gasped and arched his back. I released him and searched his face. He turned his head away and wouldn't look at me, even when I said his name again and eased the blanket from his shoulders and let it drop to the couch. His blue shirt was speckled darker blue randomly across his back. I tried to pull it up, but he stopped me. "It's okay," I said quietly. When I lifted it again, he resisted, then quit, dropping his head in shame.

The shirt was stuck to his back at the speckled points, and I had to tug gently to release it. Vicious welts, maybe six of them, sprayed across his back. The skin had split on some of them and had leaked blood, already dry and crusted along the raised lines, but bleeding again where the scabs had stuck to his shirt. *What the hell?* I looked back at Adam, his face red with fury. Mom stood frozen, her hand to her mouth, her eyes wide. "I'll get something to put on that," she said when she got over the initial shock, then hurried out of the room.

Adam let Danial in when he knocked a moment later. Danial crossed the room in six long strides and took the armchair my mom had been sitting in when I got home. He pulled it up close to Luke, taking in the sight of his back, his face tense.

He looked at me. "He came out to his dad last night," I said.

Danial grabbed Luke's chin and turned his face to him. "Did your dad do this to you?"

Luke nodded.

"What happened?"

As Luke began to tell his story, Mom brought in a refrigerator-chilled bottle of aloe vera burn relief. This was no sunburn, but I knew the aloe vera had antiseptic and analgesic properties. It would help. She offered to put it on his back, but I wanted to do it myself. I took the bottle and squeezed some of the green gel into my hand and squished it around some to warm it.

"I didn't think he'd get so pissed," Luke was saying. "He wouldn't stop yelling at me. Finally I just gave up trying to explain things to him and went up to my room."

He winced as I dabbed the still-cold aloe vera onto his welts.

"But then he followed me. I was brushing my teeth in my bathroom and he was yelling at me, calling me all kinds of awful names, and his face was all red."

He winced again and I backed off for a moment. I noticed Danial had Luke's hands now, holding his eyes steady with his own.

"He just totally lost it. I've never seen him like that before. He grabbed this toy arrow that my brother had left in my room and just started hitting me with it. He cornered me in the bathroom and I couldn't get out."

"What about your mom?" Danial asked.

"She's out of town. At her annual zit conference." I remembered that Luke's mom was a dermatologist. I wondered how she'd react to both his news and his dad's reaction. I didn't have time to think much beyond that when I saw Adam glance out the front window. He looked back at me, his face worried, and I knew Luke's dad was here.

My mom handed me a couple of ibuprofen and a glass of water. Danial took them out of my hand and coaxed Luke into taking them.

Adam opened the door before Luke's dad had a chance to knock. All eyes locked on him. He was dressed in a suit. *A suit?* I thought, wryly. He'd just beaten the crap out of his son, then didn't know where he was for hours, and he was dressed for church?

"I'm here to get my son," he announced tightly.

Adam pushed the door open a little wider, and Luke's dad took in the scene in the living room. Luke's shirt was still off while the aloe vera dried. I was still sitting close to him, my hand cupped on the back of his neck. Danial was still across from him, still holding his hands tight in his own.

"Get away from my son, you perverts." He took a threatening step toward us. "If I ever catch you anywhere near him again, I will tear you apart limb by limb."

"My son is not a pervert," my mom said, drawing herself up and claiming every inch of her five foot four frame. "And neither is yours. Don't you *ever* threaten my son again. And how *dare* you strike this boy." Her face was angry, and she was breathing heavily through her nose. I had never seen my mom so riled up.

"Mind your own business, lady." Mr. Chesser looked like he might punctuate that demeaning line with a wad of spit on the floor, but Danial was on his feet and in the suited man's face before the last word was out of his mouth. He shoved him, hard, and Luke's dad stumbled back into the door.

Adam stepped in front of Danial, and placed his hands on his tensed arms.

"Don't," Luke croaked. He grabbed his shirt, pulling it over his head. "I'll go."

He tried to stand, but I grabbed his wrist and held him back. "You don't have to go with him, Luke. You can stay here, with me." I darted a look at Mom. She nodded her head and I mouthed a thank you.

He tried to get up again. "I can't stay."

"Luke, don't." I was panicking now because I didn't know what this angry man would do to this sweet boy, and I didn't want to find out.

"You're not fucking my kid anymore, faggot," his dad spat.

Danial lunged at him again, but Adam held him back, urging him to stay calm in a low voice. Nobody thought to hold my mom back though. She crossed the distance between them and slapped Luke's dad in the face so hard it left a red handprint.

He looked stunned and then seemed ready to retaliate, but Adam and Danial were both poised, fists clenched, ready to take him down if he made one move toward my mom.

"Luke is spending the day with us," Grandma announced from the kitchen doorway. Her sudden appearance, her matter-of-fact attitude, and the fact that she was old seemed to take the heat in the room down a notch.

"I'll bring him home myself," Mom said, her rage barely contained, "when he's feeling better and after I've had a chance to take some pictures of his back. In the meantime, I suggest you calm down unless you want to spend some time in jail."

"That's my son and I will deal with him however I see fit."

Mom pointed at Luke. "That boy has done nothing wrong. And he doesn't deserve to be treated like this. Get over it, or I swear to God I'll see to it you're arrested for abuse."

My heart swelled with pride for both of the women in my life.

There was a tense moment when I had no idea what would happen next. Then Mr. Wolf was at the doorway, and I knew immediately by the calm look on his face as he took in the defensive postures in the room that Mom had called him.

He smiled at my mom, then turned to Luke's dad. "John, let's talk outside."

Luke's dad stood taller and yanked down on his jacket to straighten it. Then with a huff and a dark, threatening look, he followed Mr. Wolf outside.

I hadn't realized I was holding my breath until he left. I exhaled and squeezed Luke's arm.

"Adam, this is Danial."

The two clasped each other's hands and then Adam surprised me by pulling Danial in for a hug. The two embraced for a long moment. Adam only let go when Danial patted him on the back.

"And this is Luke."

Adam settled into the chair opposite Luke and took his hand. He smiled at him and then surprised me by kissing the top of his head. They looked at each other for a while, and I felt like some secret understanding was passing between the two of them. The tiniest of smiles tugged at the corners of Luke's mouth. I breathed a sigh of relief.

"I'm going to help your grandmother make some coffee," Mom said, getting up. She followed Grandma to the kitchen, leaving the four of us alone to start figuring out these new bonds we were forming with each other.

Danial sat on the arm of the couch on the other side of Luke.

Luke looked up at him and then at me. "This is kind of embarrassing," he said.

Danial laughed. "Nate stoned—that's embarrassing. This is nothing."

Luke smiled sheepishly. "Nate told me he tried to kiss you."

"Tried?" Danial said, his eyebrows raised.

Adam looked at me, his brow furrowed, not because kissing Danial was news, but perhaps because telling Luke about it was. Danial nudged Adam's knee with his foot. "He was stoned. Give him a break."

"I didn't know you smoked," Adam said to me.

"He doesn't," Danial said. I wanted to tell him to shut up, but he just kept running his mouth. "Well, he did, twice. Does that mean he smokes? Or he just smoked, but he doesn't 'smoke.'" He made those stupid finger quotes when he said the word *smoke*.

Adam just looked at him like he was cracked in the head, but that didn't deter Danial. Why wasn't I surprised?

"But I have to say, Adam," Danial continued, "you're a lucky guy. Nate's a pretty good kisser."

"Yeah, he is," Luke said innocently.

I groaned. I was going to kill Danial later. But then I got the feeling he was baiting Adam, testing the waters to see if our relationship was really big enough and strong enough to allow other friendships like his and Luke's.

Adam glared at him. "You may have gotten a sample, but the dish belongs to me."

I stared at him, shocked at such an un-Adam-like statement. And then I realized he was trying to be the jealous boyfriend I'd wanted. Not exactly a verbal spanking, but close enough, and I loved him for it, but I still cracked up at the intense expression on his face.

I couldn't stop the giggles, and tears were soon leaking from my eyes. Adam looked at me, a grin spreading across his face. "Was that too much?" he asked.

"You'll have to forgive him," I said, swiping at my eyes with the heels of my hand. And then I cracked up again. Luke was laughing too. Danial just shook his head and rolled his eyes, but the smile gave him away. Adam had passed the test.

Mr. Wolf must have thought we'd all lost our minds when he came back in a few seconds later. We knew he had serious business to talk about, but it still took a few more minutes of hysterical laughter before we got control of ourselves. It was cathartic laughter though, and when it finally calmed down, I think we all felt a little more capable of dealing with the crap that had just hit the fan.

Mom came in with a tray holding six mugs of fresh coffee along with spoons and cream and sugar. Mr. Wolf took it from her. They exchanged a brief but meaningful look. How long had that been going on? I knew they'd had dinner together a couple of times, but I'd been too wrapped up in my own crises to pay much attention to her love life. It was hard not to approve. Mr. Wolf was what I'd always wanted my own dad to be—open, gentle, willing to hold his own prejudices up to scrutiny when they were challenged, willing to stand up for what was right even when it went against all he had believed to be true, willing to change and to love. It occurred to me that Mr. Wolf was very much like Jody's Uncle Bill. He set the tray on an end table, and we all helped ourselves.

Mr. Wolf pulled up a chair, and we waited expectantly for him to tell us what had happened outside with Luke's dad.

He took a sip of his coffee, then set it down, clasping his hands in front of him. "Your dad's been on the school board for quite a few years, Luke. We go back a ways."

Luke nodded, but this was news to me. I wasn't sure yet if it was good news or bad news, though.

"He's very upset about your revelation last night. He feels like your friends"—he gestured to us—"have brainwashed you, and that you're throwing your life away."

"Throwing my life away? Are you kidding me? What does my being gay have to do with my success or failure in life?"

"You're preaching to the choir here, son. If there's one thing I've learned in the past year, it's not to judge people who are different from me. I don't know a nicer, more compassionate, more genuine person than Nate."

I blushed. He winked at me and kept talking. "I didn't get it at first either, but as I've gotten to know him and to know his mom"—now Mom blushed—"I just came to understand things differently. Give him some time. Maybe your dad will too."

"And what if he doesn't," I said. "My dad still doesn't get it. We haven't spoken since he stood me up for dinner last summer. He wanted me to choose between having a father and being gay." I laughed without humor. "As if that were possible."

Adam's eyes softened as he looked at me, and I wondered again how I ever doubted him. He knew how sad it made me to have my dad throw me away just because I fell in love with someone who peed standing up like me.

Luke looked at me now too with such kindness and sympathy that I felt guilty. Here he was in the throes of one of the most horrible things that can happen to a kid, and he was feeling sympathy for me. I pulled his head to me, careful still not to touch his back, and kissed him on the temple.

"Your dad understands that hitting you was wrong," Mr. Wolf continued. "He feels bad, and he has assured me it won't happen again."

"You believe him?" I said, astounded, feeling quite certain that the angry-faced man who'd stood not ten feet from me half an hour ago was more than capable of striking Luke again.

Instead of answering me, Mr. Wolf addressed Luke. "Son, has your dad ever lost control like that before?"

Luke looked at me before answering, then dropped his eyes. "Not that bad," he said to Mr. Wolf. "At least not in a long time. Not since I told him I didn't want to be a Cub Scout anymore."

I almost smiled at the image forming in my mind of a younger Luke, looking much like his little brother, all wild blond hair and wire-framed glasses, wearing a blue scouting cap and khaki shorts cinched at the waist with a corded belt, a bandana tied around his neck. But as he told us about his dad kicking down the tent he couldn't quite get to stand right and stomping on the aluminum poles so they'd never support a tent again, all the while berating him in front of the other kids, who looked on in shock and sympathy, I thought about my own dad and similar moments on the football field. The almost-smile morphed into a familiar tightness in my throat.

Luke stopped and swiped at a tear. I fought the urge to do the same. "He's never hit me before."

Danial dropped his head back and closed his eyes. Luke laid his head on my shoulder and wiped his eyes with my shirt. "He's not going back home," I said. "He can live here with us."

"Nate, I know you're concerned, but until Luke turns seventeen, he cannot be legally emancipated in Texas. That means—"

"I know what it means. It means his dad can keep right on hurting him."

"It won't be that way. Luke's dad is not a bad man. He just did a bad thing."

I made a frustrated noise in the back of my throat. It made me insane how powerless kids were against the adults in their lives. It wasn't fair and it wasn't right that someone else's ignorance could stomp all over another's right to live free and be happy, not to mention safe.

"It's okay, Nate," Luke said, putting his hand on my knee. "I'm not afraid of my dad."

"He doesn't have to go home until tonight, right?" Danial asked.

Mr. Wolf nodded. "I'll talk to his dad and see if maybe he can even postpone it until tomorrow. Luke can stay with me. I can take him to school in the morning."

"He can stay with me," I said.

"No, Nate, he can't."

"You've got to be kidding me. Guys sleep over with guys all the time."

"You know this is different."

I knew, but I wasn't letting it go that easily. I was too pissed to let anything go right now. "What? You think that just because we're gay we can't keep our hands off each other? You think we're going to be rolling around fucking each other's brains out all night? You think that's what defines us." Wasn't that exactly what my own dad thought? God, he couldn't even accept that I had been brutalized by those thugs.

From the corner of my eye, I saw my mom wince. I didn't dare look at Adam.

But Mr. Wolf was not my dad, a fact he reminded me of when he said, "Nate, stop it. That's not fair. You know that's not what I think. I'm trying to help Luke here. Let me help him. I think his dad will agree to a little longer cooling-off period. But Luke would have to stay at my house. His dad will never agree to his staying here." When I balked, he said, "Come on, Nate, you have to look at it from his perspective. It doesn't matter if you and Luke are intimate or not. It's just not appropriate."

Luke collapsed on my bed, facedown, exhausted, and fell immediately to sleep, his mouth slack and drooling on my pillow. From the armchair, I watched his back rise and fall, covered now in a clean T-shirt, one of mine. I couldn't shake the guilt. Danial had warned me. But I didn't think either of us had considered just how badly things would turn out. Last evening Luke had been a giddy sixteen-year-old, his only worry that he'd wet his pants in all his excitement. And now . . . I wanted to save him. God, how I wanted to save him. I propped my bare feet up on the bed and quietly strummed my guitar. At my desk, Danial was showing Adam how to optimize a computer's performance by tweaking mine. I turned my attention to them as they got acquainted over caches and cookies and found myself almost surprised to see Adam there, as if the past twelve hours or so had merely existed in my head. But he was there.

As if he knew I was watching him, he glanced back at me and winked. He said something to Danial, then came over to me. "Scooch over."

I edged as close to the armrest as I could to make room for him. Not nearly enough, but he wedged himself in anyway, settling on one hip and facing me. I barricaded him in with the neck of the guitar.

He ran his fingers down the side of my face. "Every orifice in my body hurts right now," he said quietly. At the desk, Danial muttered, "Oh God." Adam grinned slyly at me and worked his lower jaw. I grinned back, flicked my eyebrows at him, then placed my fingertips on his temporomandibular joints and massaged them. "Hmph. How's your grip?"

Danial groaned. "I'm gonna throw up." Then more loudly, "I can hear everything you say, you know."

Adam winked at me again, groped me—"Strong"—kissed me on the mouth, and went back to the desk. He slapped Danial on the back. "Jealous?"

"Uh-huh."

When Mom showed up at the door with a tray of grilled cheese sandwiches cut into little triangles and stacked bowls of tomato soup—comfort food—Adam was on his feet again.

"I thought you boys"—she took in Luke's sleeping form on my bed and dropped her voice—"might be hungry." She handed Adam the tray. "You might want to wake him up. He'll never sleep tonight if you don't."

Adam set the tray next to the computer and followed Mom back downstairs for drinks so she wouldn't have to make the trip back up. Danial grabbed one of the bowls of soup, dunked a triangle in it, then popped it into his mouth.

I unfolded myself from the chair, but he got up and wiped his hands on his jeans. "I'll get him," he said through a full mouth. He grabbed Luke's bare foot and wiggled it. "Come on, sleeping beauty. Time to wake up."

Luke pulled his foot away and planted his face in the pillow. Danial grabbed the other foot and shook it more firmly. "Come on, stud. You can't spend your whole day in dreamland."

"Leave me alone," Luke groaned, kicking out at Danial.

I could empathize. I wanted to crawl into bed right next him. I hadn't had much sleep myself the night before. My eyes were scratchy and my brain slightly lethargic. The rest of me, like Adam, apparently, was pleasantly sore.

"What are you smiling at?" Danial asked, shifting his gaze to me. He rolled his eyes. "Figures. Come on. Help me get this boy out of the sack."

Between the two of us, we managed to cajole and taunt Luke into wakefulness by the time Adam got back with drinks.

It was one of those perfect mid-December days in the Gulf Coast area of Texas, the kind that almost made you forget the stifling, heavy summer heat. The sky was a deep blue, the breeze blowing in through my open window crisp and cool. We took turns looking longingly out the window as we ate.

When the sandwiches were gone, I grabbed a football out of the back of my closet and tossed it to Danial. He caught it easily. Adam groaned. "No."

"You're kidding, right?" Luke said.

Danial laughed. Not a one of them was much into sports, but the desire to stretch our limbs and do something to slough off the multiple frustrations of the last twenty-four hours finally overcame their aversion and we walked to the park half a mile or so from my house.

Before we left I dabbed some more aloe vera on Luke's welts and gave him a few more ibuprofen, hoping that would allow him to enjoy the day without his back bothering him too much. He was stiff, but I could tell he felt better.

After a little instruction—this is a football; this is how you hold a football; this is how you throw a football; this is how you catch a football; this is how you [fill in the blank] a football—we ran some plays. I learned one thing quickly—while they might not be into sports, they were natural athletes. Adam was lithe and quick and would have made a great quarterback. Plus he liked being the center of attention. Danial was big and tough and fearless—perfect for a linebacker. And Luke, well, okay, maybe they weren't all natural athletes. But when it came to the *touch* part of touch football, he was certainly motivated. When I teased him about that, he grinned and smacked me on the ass. "See what I mean." I laughed.

As we warmed up we shed our sweatshirts and hoodies and then chucked our shirts altogether. Luke kept his on, but gave us a good laugh when he looked us over and announced, "God, I think I've died and gone to heaven."

"Two on two," I said, still chuckling. I pointed to one end of the field. "Me and Adam against you guys."

We attracted a small group of female fans who giggled and watched from the sidelines. I snapped the ball to Adam. He fell back and tossed it to me before Danial could grab him. I dodged Luke and went in for a touchdown. Adam jogged over, bumped my fist, and pulled me in for a one-arm hug. Then, because Adam was never one to shy away from a good PDA, he grabbed my face in his hands and kissed the hell out of me.

One of the girls said, "Eew, gross," and they left.

"Okay, knock it off, guys," Luke shouted from the other side of our field. "You're making me horny." A couple riding by on their bikes peddled faster.

"Keep it up, you three," Danial said, "and we'll have the park all to ourselves pretty soon."

Adam ignored them. I ignored them. The world around us seemed to fall away, and for a few needful moments, there was just him and me again, bare chest to bare chest, loose and hungry, not thinking.

"Come on, guys," Luke yelled again. "If you're not sharing, you're not pairing."

That cracked us up and I pulled away, feeling slightly drunk, but underneath a little ashamed too at being so inconsiderate of Luke's feelings. Adam lifted his eyebrow in a silent communication that I understood perfectly. We ran for Luke. Careful not to hurt his back, we assaulted him, in a good way. He wrinkled his nose. "Okay, okay. You can stop now." He laughed.

Danial picked up the ball, planted it on his hip, and groaned. "Oh, God. I'm in homo hell."

We walked home, laughing, tossing the ball around, and cutting up with each other like we'd been friends forever, until we saw Mr. Wolf's car in the driveway. Luke's face screwed up, and I cupped my hand behind his neck. I shifted my gaze over his shoulder to Adam and Danial. They seemed to move infinitesimally closer to Luke, as if to protect him from whatever was to come. We were quiet as we crossed my yard to the front door.

"I tried, Luke," Mr. Wolf said. "Your dad won't allow you to stay at my house tonight. He wants you home."

I glared at the assistant principal. He could have done better than that. I felt like he'd betrayed Luke, betrayed me. "He's not going," I said.

"Yes, Nate, he is. That's his dad. He has rights too."

"Yeah, well, as far as I'm concerned, he gave up those rights when he picked up that arrow."

"You're overreacting. It's over. Let it go." I held his eyes for a moment, trying to convey with everything I had that I could not, would not, Let It Go. I knew he got the message when he said my name and shook his head. Then he turned to Luke. "Are you okay with that?"

Luke nodded.

This wasn't over. He'd seen Luke's back. His dad hadn't hit him just once. He'd hit him over and over and over again. He'd been out of control. And then he'd had plenty of time to work up some regret before Mom called him, but that was not a repentant man who showed up on our doorstep. My teeth ached from clenching my jaw. Adam put a hand on my arm to calm me. It wasn't working, not this time. I hated feeling so powerless.

Luke turned the football round and round in his hands, then handed it to me. "I'll see you at school in the morning. Maybe you could wear the T-shirt I gave you."

I nodded and bit my lip to keep from screaming. "Give me your phone," I choked out finally.

He looked puzzled but handed it over. My number was already programmed in. I added Danial's and Adam's and set them to speed dial. I showed him which buttons called whom. "You call us if you need anything, if you're afraid, or if you just need to talk. Okay?"

"Okay."

I made him promise. We watched as they drove away, and I realized that Mom hadn't taken any pictures. I hoped we wouldn't have an occasion to regret that.

Adam went home to sleep, but Danial hung around, both of us silently hoping Luke would call. Finally around nine I couldn't stand it anymore and called his number. The call went immediately to voice mail. I didn't know what that meant, but it scared the hell out of me.

I looked at Danial. "Will you drive by his house on your way home?"

He called me later to report absolutely nothing. The house was dark. As tired as I was, I slept little that night.

Chapter 48

Adam drove me to school the next morning, hoping to see Luke too. He said he'd worry all day until he knew he was okay. Adam was technically a visitor now and no longer allowed to roam the hallways, so we sat on the steps outside the school and watched for Luke's car. I was surprised when his dad pulled up to the curb and Luke got out.

I stood up. His dad glared at me. He said something to Luke, forcing him to stick his head back into the car for a minute. Then Luke slammed the door. His dad didn't move until the car behind him honked its horn. He pulled out, but not without one last backward glance.

I rubbed my hand up and down Luke's arm and studied his face.

He gave me a weak smile. "I'm okay."

"I called. You didn't answer your phone last night."

Luke huffed and shook his head. "He took away my phone, my computer, my car keys. He hits me and I'm the one grounded."

Adam fished his phone out of his pocket and handed it to Luke. "Take mine. It already has Nate's and Danial's phone numbers in it."

I looked at him. He had Danial's phone number programmed in his phone?

"Keep it on silent, okay? And don't let your dad see it."

Luke took the phone. He stared at it for a minute and looked up at Adam from under his lashes. "Thanks."

Adam smiled, then jumped to his feet. "I've gotta go, and you two need to get to class. You take care of this sexy bitch for me, Luke," he said, winking at him.

I pulled my jacket wide so Luke could see I was wearing the T-shirt he'd given me. "You did ask me to wear it." I laughed.

Luke smiled back and I felt a whole lot better.

Mr. Thornton caught me as I entered the front door and insisted on inspecting my shirt. Just to be pissy, I handed him my backpack. He took it—a knee-jerk response—then clearly regretted it almost immediately and dropped it to the floor. I yanked off my jacket, then my shirt, turned it inside out, and tugged it back on, holding his eyes with mine the entire time. Without a word, I picked up my jacket and backpack, grabbed Luke's hand, and walked off.

I'll flaunt it if I want to, Mr. Thornton.

"Nice," Danial said. He'd been waiting for us in the main hallway and caught the whole thing.

"I don't like him."

"I can see that."

I had Luke repeat what he'd told us outside. I added the way his dad had acted when he saw me waiting and how Adam had given Luke his phone.

Luke was carrying his backpack by the handle, instead of over his shoulder like he usually did. Danial noticed and took his backpack and slung it over his own free shoulder. "If you need me, you call me," he told Luke. "I don't care what time it is. I'll be there. And you keep that phone hidden."

"I will."

We tried to spend as much time with Luke as we could during the day. But he was a sophomore and we were seniors, so our paths didn't cross too often. At the end of the day, we waited with him until his dad got there. I hated letting him out of my sight. His dad glared at me again, just the way he had that morning. It creeped me out.

* * *

After school, Adam came over and hung out with me while I attempted to study for finals. I kicked back on my bed and struggled through some notes, scanning page after page with no idea whatsoever what I'd just read. Eventually, I gave up and turned my attention to Adam. He was seated at my desk, clicking around on the University of Texas Web site. I watched for a while. Then I found myself thinking about Luke again, what he was doing, if he was okay. His dad had taken his computer. Petty. Why didn't he call? I thought about his little brother, Matt, and I was glad he had at least one ally in the house. Did his mom know yet? Was she friend or foe? Questions, but no answers. I returned to the notes and tried to focus. Four more days and it would be Christmas vacation, and that meant not seeing Luke. I had a bad feeling and couldn't shake it.

"You're staring at nothing again," Adam said.

"This is impossible." I tossed my spiral to the side. "Did you see the look his dad gave me?"

"Yeah, I know."

I stared at the ceiling and he climbed onto the bed next to me and took the notes. "You want me to quiz you?"

"I want to call him so bad, you know, just to know he's okay."

He shuffled through my notes. "Chemistry. God, I hated this stuff."

"I just feel so guilty being here with you, and he's there all alone. It's just so damn unfair."

"Okay, no chemistry." He dropped the notes on the floor and linked his fingers with mine. "Can I ask you something?"

"What?"

"Do you wish you were with him right now?"

That stopped me. Because that's exactly what I was wishing. Not in the way Adam was suggesting, but the wish was there. I knew what it was like to have your spirit crushed. I'd been there, more times than I could count.

You're gonna march your ass into that counselor's office tomorrow first thing and change your schedule back, or you can forget your fucking piano lessons.

I'm done with you.

Adam didn't understand. How could he? I bled for Luke. That was all.

"No," I said.

"You hesitated."

"No, I didn't."

"Yes, you did." He let go of my hand and slung his arm over his forehead. "Nate, if you have feelings for him—"

"I don't."

My cell phone woke me. I'd dozed off. I couldn't have been asleep more than half an hour. It was still daylight outside. Adam got my phone from the bedside table and looked at the screen. "It's Luke."

I sat up and grabbed the phone, answering the call even as I cleared my throat. "Luke? Are you okay?"

He spoke in a whisper. "Don't wait for me outside tomorrow, Nate. My dad says if he sees you with me again, he'll get a restraining order against you. And then he'll have you arrested if you get anywhere near me. Please, just meet me at my locker tomorrow."

"Okay, Luke. It's okay."

"I have to go. I'm in the bathroom. He took my bedroom door off. Can you believe that?"

"Oh, Luke."

"I'll see you in the morning. I've got to go. I love you, Nate."

"I love—" But he'd already hung up. I ended the call, avoiding Adam's eyes.

Chapter 49

The first bell had already rung and still no Luke. I kicked his locker. Danial looked irritated that he hadn't kicked it first.

"He's not coming," I growled, kicking the locker again. "That bastard's done something to him."

Danial rubbed his forehead with the heel of his hand. "Let's give him another minute. If we're late to class, so what."

I leaned back against the locker above Luke's and banged my head on the metal door. "We never should have let him go home."

"We didn't have a lot of choice, Nate."

"We always have a choice."

And then Luke was hurrying around the corner, dragging his backpack, his face flushed.

I met him halfway. "You had us worried half to death," I said, taking his backpack and carrying it the rest of the way to his locker.

Luke spun the lock. "My dad's doing this on purpose. He's getting me here late so I can't hang out with you." He yanked on the lock, but it refused to release. He slammed the heel of his hand against the locker.

I watched him spin the dial again and knew there was something he wasn't telling us. He yanked, but the lock held firm. "Dammit," he growled, banging the locker again.

"Here, let me do it," Danial said. They switched places and Luke gave him the combination.

"What's going on, Luke?" I asked.

Danial released the lock and opened Luke's locker for him. Luke dug what he needed out of his backpack and shoved the rest into his locker. He stood up and looked at us, his face glum, defeated. "We're moving."

I had expected bruises, something broken or bleeding; I hadn't expected that. I huffed and ran my hands through my hair, looking wildly at Danial. He pinched his eyes closed and let out an angry breath.

"He can't move you because you're gay," I said to Luke, knowing good and well that his dad could do just that.

"He's not," Luke said. He stared at his feet. "He's been commuting to Odessa for months. Mom wants to keep our family together. She's already turned her practice over to her partners. We already have a house and—"

"What? Yours isn't even up for sale," I said. And then it clicked. This wasn't something his parents had cooked up in the middle of the night to punish him. This move had been planned. And he'd known. For how long?

He sniffed. "Mom didn't want the Realtors showing it until after we moved. Dad's company is selling it. The movers come the day after Christmas." He said the last in a small, little-boy voice, and then as if the revelation had emptied him of any substance, he slid down the lockers and sat heavily on the floor, then looked up at me. "I don't want to go."

Danial sat down next to him. I felt like all the air had gone out of me and I sat too. "Why didn't you tell us?"

Luke's face was flushed. He tugged at the collar of his hoodie some, then pulled it over his head and wadded it up next to him. "I didn't want to mess things up. I kept hoping Dad would hate Odessa and change his mind about the transfer, or that Mom would hate Odessa and tell him she wouldn't go." He hugged his knees to his chest and slumped over them.

I wanted to say something, anything to make things okay, but all I could think was Odessa. An image presented itself in my mind, an image of cowboys and pickup trucks and oil rigs and dirty men in orange jumpsuits and hardhats. Nowhere in that picture could I place Luke. Nowhere.

"Gentlemen, get to class. You're already late." I looked up to see Mr. Wolf standing at the end of the hallway. There were only a handful of students around, all of them hurrying to class. I hadn't even heard the tardy bell ring.

Danial reached out to give Luke a hand up. "Come on, bro," he said.

I followed behind, shouldering Wolf as I passed him. "Nate," he said, grabbing my arm, but I shrugged him off and continued down the hallway.

It had been impossible to spend more than a few minutes with Luke each day, and the isolation seemed to be draining him of life. And me, I had been blowing my finals, and I knew it, but no matter how hard Adam had tried to keep me on track, I couldn't concentrate. I stared at my blog, sometimes for an hour at a time, but I didn't have the heart to write anything—hadn't in weeks. I found myself pouring over Luke's comments, seeing them in a whole new way now, though I couldn't say exactly in what way. Just that they felt different in light of everything that had happened. Adam was quieter than usual, something that registered with me in a distant way, like driving down the highway, getting from point A to point B, but not really aware of anything in between, of the road, the traffic, the exits. Just going through the motions, stopping, starting, changing lanes, all as if on autopilot. He'd been all I could think about when he was in New York, but now, with him safely here, all I could think about was someone else. I knew Adam wanted more of me; I could feel it in the way he looked at me sometimes, or kneaded my shoulders or my bare feet, or the way he fingered the pendant I was wearing again, rubbing his thumb across his name as if to remind me he was there. Or when he locked the door and dropped to his knees in front of me. I wanted to give myself to him, but I hung limp in his hands and in his mouth, unable to respond to him for the first time ever, unable to let go of the feeling that this time belonged to Luke, that I owed Luke that. He only had a few days. There would be time for Adam and locked doors later.

As the week unraveled, so did Luke. On Wednesday, pale and with bruised-looking skin under his eyes, he said he wasn't allowed to be alone with his little brother anymore. All doors in his house, except for the bathroom doors, had to remain open at all times. That pissed me off more than anything his dad had done so far. Even hitting Luke had been done on impulse. This was something far uglier. When his mom got back Wednesday evening, I'd had hopes that things would improve for Luke, but on Thursday he reported that nothing had really changed—still no computer, no cell phone, no door. His mom earned double what his dad earned, and allowing him to discipline the boys without interference must have been her way of letting him protect his pathetic masculinity. I thought it was a copout of the worst sort, and I didn't much like her after that. But Luke defended her. "She doesn't know about me, or what happened, and I'm not telling her." Matt had promised to keep his mouth shut too. I thought he was wrong, they were both wrong, but I could no more control their relationships than I could control the one between myself and my own dad.

We ended the week with a holiday program in the auditorium. The band played, but Luke didn't play with them, as if he were already gone. Danial and I saved a seat for him, both of us acutely aware that this might be the last time we'd see him. It was sixth period, and in another hour and a half we'd be dismissed for a two-week break. Luke looked frighteningly bleak when he came in and collapsed into the seat between us. I reached over and took his hand. It was hot. He closed his eyes and just breathed.

I looked across him at Danial. He shook his head and shrugged, a worried crease deepening between his eyes.

Juliet wiggled into the seat on the other side of Danial just as Mr. Thornton began blathering onstage about appropriate concert behavior, as if we were going to jump on our seats and throw popcorn during the performance like those gremlins in the movie. *Get on with it already,* I thought.

Luke's hand twitched in mine, the flush in his face extending all the way down his neck giving him color, but in the wrong way. I could see the muscle in his jaw working as if he were grinding his teeth. "I have to go to the bathroom," he said suddenly. He got up and stumbled over Danial, Juliet, and several other students to get to the aisle, and lurched from the auditorium. Danial started to get up. "I'll go," I said.

Luke was already puking his guts up when I got to the bathroom. I got a wad of paper towels and wet them in the sink. I flushed the toilet when he was done, gave him some wet towels for his mouth and held the others to his forehead.

"Damn, Luke, you're really hot. You've got a fever, man."

He gagged again and emptied his stomach of whatever bile was left. I pressed the wet towels to the back of his neck while he drooled and spit in the toilet. "Sorry," he sputtered.

I flushed again and helped him get cleaned up. "Let's get you down to Ms. Ellingson's office. You need to go home."

Even as I said it, I knew that was the last place Luke needed to go. I wanted desperately to put him in my car and take him home with me where Mom and Grandma and I could take care of him. But that wasn't going to happen.

The nurse's office was located in the main hallway, just across from the registrar. Luke was weak and starting to tremble all over when we left the bathroom. I put his arm over my shoulder and supported him around the waist.

"How long have you had this fever?" I asked as we made our way to the main hallway.

"I don't know. I wasn't feeling so great this morning when I got here." He folded himself into me a little more. "I'm so cold." I tightened my arm around his waist, trying to transfer some warmth to his feverish body.

"What the hell?"

Startled, I looked up to see Luke's dad and Mr. Wolf just outside the registrar's office.

"Get away from my son." He crossed the distance between us in three long strides and yanked Luke by the arm. Luke stumbled into a bench along the wall and sat down hard. Then his dad was in my face, his fists balled up at his sides. "I warned you to stay away from him," he spat at me, so close to my face I could smell the garlic he'd had for lunch. My own fists clenched. All I needed was a reason and an opportunity. It seemed I had both.

Mr. Wolf wedge himself between us, his back to me, his palms up in a defensive position. "Calm down, John."

"It's your job to protect my son." Mr. Chesser punctuated each of the last three words with a jab in Mr. Wolf's chest.

And then Luke was up and at his dad's side, wobbly but holding his own. "Nate was just walking me to the nurse's office."

Luke's dad turned on him and held up a forefinger in his face. "Stay out of this. I'll deal with you later."

But Luke didn't stay out of it. "Why are you here anyway?" he asked, visibly angry.

"Withdrawing *you*. Now *sit* down!" his father shouted in his face.

I still hadn't said a word, but I saw Luke swoon and lunged for him. The second I was out from behind Mr. Wolf, his dad was on me. He shoved me hard, sending me sprawling into one of the tin knights that decorated the school. It clattered to the ground. Mr. Wolf was on one knee with Luke, his radio out. It squawked, and he called for another administrator. As I got to my feet, the nurse opened her door, then hurried toward Luke. The school reception-ist and librarian had stepped out too. Both looked shocked and un-certain what to do. The receptionist ducked back into her office.

I barely registered Danial and Juliet at the end of the hallway as I threw myself at Luke's dad, propelled by years of secrecy and shame and fear and anger. He stumbled back in surprise and I drew my fist back. I wanted to smash his face. I wanted him to pay for every stripe he'd laid on his son's back, for every insult he'd ever carelessly thrown at him, and maybe I wanted him to pay for what my dad had done too. I didn't know. I only knew I wanted to hit someone just then. Before I could throw my fist, Danial was there, checking my arm and holding me back. My chest heaved. "You bastard," I spit.

"You queers are not getting my son," he said coldly. He ran his fingers through his thinning gray hair, smoothing it back into its tight-ass style, then straightened his tie. I hated him.

Mr. Thornton was stalking toward us, heaving with the exertion and his own anger. "Get him out of here," he shouted. I shrugged off Danial, and then shrugged off Mr. Wolf when he tried to lead me away to his office. I could get there on my own. Danial followed. At the end of the hall, we both stopped and looked back one last time at Luke. He was still on the ground, the nurse's back shielding his face from us. I turned away and walked on.

Neither Danial nor I heard from Luke that night or the next. Adam tried to get me to go shopping on Market Street. The tree was up in the green, lights were strung across the streets, holiday music was playing through speakers, and it was finally cold enough for heavier jackets and scarves. But I just couldn't generate any holiday spirit. Christmas was four days away, and I couldn't have cared less.

Finally, Luke called. It was Monday night, late. I knew from his whispering that he was calling from the bathroom again. I told him how worried I'd been and he explained that he'd spent Friday night in the hospital with a high fever and an IV in his arm. He'd tested positive for swine flu, but the worst seemed to be behind him now.

"I wish I could have come to see you," I said.

"It's okay. Mostly I just slept."

We were quiet for a minute. There was so much I wanted to say that I couldn't say anything, kind of like those people who'd tried to flee the fire in that nightclub and got all smushed up in the doorway and no one could get out. They'd died. I felt like if I couldn't squeeze a word through soon, they'd be lost forever too.

"I wish I could be there with you right now," I said, finally.

"Me too." His voice was so soft I could barely hear him.

"Does your new school have a marching band?"

He didn't answer right away. When he did, his voice was choked with emotion. "Yeah."

I swallowed hard and tried to make my words come forth steady and hopeful. "It's gonna be okay, Luke," I lied. "You're gonna make new friends, you're gonna—"

"I'll have to go back in the closet, Nate," he whimpered. "I don't want to."

Chapter 50

Christmas Eve limped in cold and rainy. I was so depressed I stayed in bed until my head pounded from being in a prone position so long. Finally I got up. I started to take some ibuprofen for my headache but decided I wanted to feel the pain. It was a small tribute to Luke.

I brushed my teeth, but I didn't bother doing anything with my hair or changing out of the T-shirt and soft flannel pants I'd slept in. Maybe I'd just wear them for the rest of the school holiday. What did I care?

Mom handed me something to eat downstairs, but I wasn't hungry. She watched me play with my food for a while. "He's going to be okay, Nate."

I looked at her dully and shook my head. "Mom, he's moving to the redneck capital of the world. He won't stand a chance there."

She chewed on her lip. "He'll be okay, Nate. In another couple of years, he'll go to college, and everything will be different."

I huffed. "You don't know Luke. He's just no good at acting straight. They'll peg him in a heartbeat. I'm so afraid they're gonna hurt him." I knew something about hurt, and I couldn't bear the thought of sweet Luke going through anything like I had.

Mom came around the counter and put her arms around me. "Then we'll pray for him to be safe."

I spent the early afternoon sorting through my feelings in a blog post, the first in a long time. Adam was shopping with his mom. I was glad to be alone.

I'm Queer. Get Over It.
For Luke
By Nate Schaper on Dec. 24.
I don't know if you'll ever read this, Luke. I hope you do. I want to say how very sorry I am for everything that has happened. If I could take it all away and make you happy again, I'd do it. I just want you to know that I'll think of you every day. You aren't alone, even when you feel like you are. Call me. Write. I'll be here.
Love, Nate

Comments:

HappyBoy
Dec. 24, at 2:32 P.M.
   Merry Christmas Eve! What's going on? I just read there's going to be some national hand-holding day or something in January. Google it.
PakistaniPal
Dec. 24, at 2:45 P.M.
   Answer your damn phone.

"What?" I said when Danial picked up.
"What are you doing?"
I could tell from the tone of his voice that he wasn't asking about my current activity. It was more like an accusation. I knew he'd read the post. When I didn't answer, he said, "You gotta let this go, Nate. You can't help Luke anymore, but there's somebody else who needs you right now."
"I don't need you to tell me how to deal with Adam."

"I think maybe you do. Let him go."

"I can't. Don't you understand that? I can't."

"Delete it, or I will. I know your password."

I knew he was right. Adam had been more patient with me than I'd ever been with him, and at a time when we were just finding each other again. I reached for my phone to call him, just to say *I love you,* but remembered that Luke still had his phone, and I put mine back on the bedside table. I'd go to him later, after the mall closed. Take my backpack with me. Stay the night. I'd make it up to him, every miserable moment he'd spent with me the past week or so. And we'd wake up together on Christmas morning, and Santa Nate would open his bag of goodies and ply him with gifts until he screamed in delicious agony.

But as for the post, I couldn't bring myself to delete it. Not yet.

Then late afternoon Luke showed up on our doorstep. I heard the jingle bells on the door first and then my mom's surprised voice. My immediate thought was that his dad had hit him again. But he met me halfway up the stairs, soaking wet, his hair plastered to his face and a sheepish grin tugging at the corners of his lips.

I scooped him up and almost sent both of us sprawling down the stairs. "What are you doing here? You're sick. You should be home." I held him back where I could size him up and squeezed his arms to prove to myself that he was really here. He was out of breath and soggy but otherwise looked okay.

"My dad flew to Odessa this morning," he said, still breathing hard as he peeled off his wet hoodie and damp shirt and took the dry shirt I offered him. "His plane won't be in until about seven, and my mom had to take my little brother for a dental cleaning. So I just left. And here I am."

"And here you are," I repeated. I smiled over my shoulder and tossed him a pair of flannel pants similar to the ones I was wearing, then busied myself refolding some underwear. When he'd changed, I left him to amuse himself in my room while I took his clothes downstairs and tossed them in the dryer. If possible, I'd get him back home before his mom got back and no one had to know he'd snuck out.

It was weird, really. Unexpected. As glad as I was to see him, I was strangely disappointed too. It was kind of like finding out your dog is going to die, and you spend all this emotional energy preparing yourself, saying good-bye, and then it doesn't, and you feel kinda like you've been cheated. I didn't want to feel that way. But not wanting didn't make the feeling go away. I turned the dryer on high heat and headed back up to my room.

He was towel drying his hair when I came back in. "You know, I don't think I've ever seen you in your jammies," he said.

I cracked a weak grin. "I've never seen you in my jammies either."

His smile faded suddenly, and he looked like he might cry.

"Oh, Luke," I said. I took him in my arms and just held him, trying to memorize the feel of him, that peppermint smell that always wafted from his skin, the mop of blond hair that was always falling down in his eyes.

He swallowed hard. "Nate." He paused before continuing, as if trying to muster up some courage. "Will you do something for me before I go?"

"Anything," I said. "Just name it."

He tossed the towel to the side and took one of my hands in his, kissing my knuckles first, then pushed my hand beneath the waistband of his / my flannel pants.

I stiffened and drew in a sharp breath. "Luke, not that," I whispered, pulling my hand back out.

"Please don't say no," Luke breathed. "I'm going back in the closet, Nate. I accept that. But I don't want to go back without really knowing what this is all about."

"Luke—"

"What if something happens, and I never get to experience this?"

"Nothing is going to happen."

"I want this, Nate. And I want this with you. Please don't tell me no."

His eyes were huge, puppy-dog eyes, pleading, begging eyes. "I can't," I whispered.

"He doesn't have to know. *Nobody* has to know. In two days I'll be gone. Gone and you and Adam will have the rest of your lives together. And I'll have no one. I'm not asking for much. We don't have to have real sex. Just this one thing. Just this one thing, Nate. *Please.*"

"You have lots of time for this, Luke." I was the one pleading now. *Don't make me hurt you. Don't make me hurt him.*

"I don't have any time." He hiccupped it out, like he was going to cry, then eased the waistband of his pants over his hips. The flannel puddled on the floor. I looked away, at the wall, at Adam's lava lamp sitting next to my phone on the bedside table, at the bed we'd made love in so many times. I knew I was being manipulated; I could feel it as surely as I could feel the prod of his penis as he stepped closer.

"No one has to know," he said again softly, taking my hand and wrapping it around him. *No one has to know,* I repeated to myself. Just this, and then, I swore to myself, I *would* let him go. I pulled my hand away and locked the door.

I felt Adam coming up the stairs two at a time seconds before I heard him. He tried the doorknob. "Nate? Your door's locked."

"Don't open it," Luke whispered desperately. He gripped my arm.

I closed my eyes. There'd be no hiding what we'd done. Even if we straightened the rumpled bed and got rid of the wet washcloth on the bedside table, there was still the locked door and the two of us, flushed and disheveled.

"I have to open the door, Luke," I said, pulling on my clothes. It was like we were in a full-out skid on a wet road taking dead aim at a massive tree, and I was helpless to stop the collision. I only prayed we'd survive.

"Nate?" Adam's voiced sounded worried. He knocked again. "Are you okay?"

"I'm coming."

Luke looked at me, dressed now too, begging for forgiveness with his eyes. "It's okay," I mouthed and opened the door.

"Hey, why's the—" Adam stopped. He looked slowly from me to Luke to the bed, and back to me, the truth lining up like the tumblers on a combination lock. I stared at my feet. Adam stared at me until I looked up at him. I could see his jaw tensing and releasing, tensing and releasing. His face screwed up as he struggled with his emotions. I bit my lip in shame.

He drew in a ragged breath, but his eyes didn't leave mine.

I felt like time had come to a standstill, like we were waiting, bloodied and broken, for the emergency crew to get there and pull the bodies from the wreckage.

"I'm sorry," I whispered when I couldn't stand it any longer. I reached for his hand, but he flinched and took a step back. "Adam."

I took a step toward him, desperate to make this right, somehow, desperate to keep him here long enough for me to fix this. "I love you." I reached for him again.

"Don't," he said coldly.

Luke took a small step forward, looking scared. "It was my fault, Adam. I begged him. Don't be mad at him."

Adam looked over at him then. He closed his eyes for a moment and drew in a deep breath. "We're going to miss you, Luke," he choked out, and with one last wounded look at me, he turned to leave. I grabbed for his arm, but he whipped around and held his hands up in a don't-touch-me gesture, took two steps backward, then turned for the last time and hurried down the stairs.

Luke urged me to go after him, but I couldn't run out on him. I had a lifetime to make things up to Adam. He'd forgive me. Because that's what Adam did.

Up and down Luke's street, inflatable Santas and igloos and snowmen waited slumped over until timers released the juice and the motors brought them to life once again. It looked like the neighbors had made a run on the tacky Christmas display section at Walmart. The only decoration in Luke's yard was a piece of tinsel tied around the new For Sale sign near the curb. We sat in my car several houses down from his and waited for his mom to get home. The plan was for Luke to walk the few houses home after his mom got there and make it look like he'd just stepped out of the house for a minute. We didn't have to wait long.

She pulled into the drive just moments after we arrived. We

watched her get out. Luke chewed on his bottom lip. "You won't forget me, will you?"

I squinched up my face and promised him I wouldn't.

He reached into his pocket, pulled out Adam's phone, and handed it to me, but I shook my head and told him to keep it. "I can't keep it," he said. "Not now." He held it out until I finally took it. It was warm from being nestled in his pocket.

He got out and headed back up the street to his house, his head down and his hands shoved deep in his pockets. Halfway there, he turned around and walked backward for a few steps. I got out of the car and leaned on the roof and watched him go.

Chapter 51

Mrs. Jensen opened the door as I bounded onto the porch. "He's in his room," she said. I searched her face for a moment and knew it was bad. "Nate," she said, catching my arm as I passed her. I stopped. She pursed her lips but said nothing more. I squeezed her hand and headed for the stairs.

His door was closed but unlocked. I eased it open. The negative space caught me off guard. The lava lamps that lined the high shelf on the far side of his room were gone, the shelf an empty slab of painted wood. It was the first thing I noticed, then the box below the shelf, one of those document boxes with holes punched out of the sides for handholds. The lamps were there, piled high, upside down, willy-nilly, cords hanging over the sides like so much trash. A dark stain anchored the bottom of the box to the carpet, and I knew at least one of the lamps had cracked when he'd dumped them. A faucet opened up in the bathroom as I shifted my gaze around the room. A small Christmas tree rested on its side under the window, small gold stars still clinging to some of the branches, others scattered about. His drawers were open, all of them. On the table next to his bed, a flat box, maybe three inches by four, wrapped in shiny red paper, a silver bow secured to the top. I sat on the bed and picked through one of the two duffel bags lying there.

T-shirts, underwear, jeans, shorts, crammed into the unstructured space like stuffing in a pillow. I pulled a shirt out and held it to my face. In the bathroom, the water shut off. I lay the shirt in my lap and picked up the gift and turned it over.

I felt him in the bathroom doorway. "What do you want?" he said coldly.

I looked at him. The hair around his face was damp. In one hand he gripped a leather toiletry bag.

"Is this for me?" I asked quietly.

He stalked toward me, zipping the small bag closed, and snatched the package from my hands.

"What are you doing, Adam?" I said as he shoved the gift and the toiletry bag into one of the duffel bags.

"What does it look like I'm doing?" he muttered, then turned to the closet and viciously yanked the hangers across the rod. I took the package out again and released the tape on the back and sides, allowing the paper to drop to the floor. Inside was a DVD—*Family Affair*, Season 1, a handwritten note taped to the front: *Episode 12, so I never forget. Love, Adam.*

I stared at it. "It didn't mean anything," I said quietly.

In the closet the assault stilled. I turned my eyes to him. He was holding on to the rod with both fists, his head bowed down between his arms. "It meant something to me," he said angrily. "It meant everything to me."

"They were taking him away, Adam."

"So you fucked him. A little parting gift?"

"I didn't."

"That was mine and you just gave it away like it was nothing." He grabbed an armload of clothes, stalked back to the bed, then crammed the clothes, hangers and all, into the empty bag. "Did he suck you off? Or did you suck him off?" He leaned on the bag and looked at me with hard eyes. "Did he come in your mouth?"

"Don't."

"Did you fucking *swallow* it?"

I winced at the fury in his voice. I didn't know this Adam. "You're making me sick."

"Yeah?" He scoffed and zipped up one of the bags and flung it at the door. It bounced off and landed with a thud on the carpet. "Well, now you know how I feel." Those were almost the exact words my dad and I had exchanged standing outside the restaurant the night he stood me up. The irony of that wasn't lost on me.

He jerked the other bag toward him, but I grabbed his arm and stopped him from zipping it. "It didn't have anything to do with us," I said.

He closed his eyes and breathed in heavy, uneven breaths. "It had *everything* to do with us."

"It doesn't change the way I feel about y—"

He jerked his arm out of my grasp. "It changes the way *I* feel about *you*," he said, looking at me. The words had been slow and measured, as if we wanted to make sure I heard them loud and clear.

"Don't say that."

"How many times do you think you can drag my heart through the mud? I can't do this anymore, Nate. You don't deserve me."

"I know that."

He zipped up the bag and shouldered it, and it hit me that he was really going to leave. That this wasn't one of those hang-up-before-we-say-something-we're-going-to-regret leaving. The regret was already piled ankle deep. Forever regret. This was good-bye. "I love you," I said desperately.

He looked at the ceiling and blinked, his face a battleground of emotion, then swallowed hard and leveled his gaze at me, softer now. "I know you do, Nate," he said quietly. "That's the thing that really gets me, you know. The thing that hurts the most. I know you love me. But that wasn't enough, was it? To keep you loyal to me? It didn't seem to matter to you. But everything you did mattered to me. Who you kissed mattered to me. Who you *touched* mattered to me." He hitched in a breath. *"It mattered to me,"* he said, slamming his chest.

He was speaking in the past tense, like we were already over, and I didn't know how to respond, what words would get through to him.

"This has always been about you," he continued. "About what you needed. Well, what about me, Nate? I needed you too. Did you ever for one minute think about me?"

There's somebody else who needs you right now. Danial's words came back to me as clearly as if he'd been standing right there. It had never occurred to me that Adam truly needed me. I was the one who always needed. "Why didn't you ever tell me that?" I said, struggling to draw in a deep breath.

His face hardened again. He scoffed and turned toward the door.

I was up, the shirt sliding to the floor. I stepped in front of him and gripped his shoulders. "Don't walk away from me." I was finding it hard to catch my breath. "Yell at me, cuss me out, hit me, but don't walk away from me."

"I'm not playing these sick games with you anymore." He took the DVD from me and held it to my face. "You're not a little boy, Nate. And I'm not your Uncle Bill." He put his face close to mine. "And I don't want to be."

He flicked the DVD to the side and pushed past me, but I grabbed his arm. He tried to pull away, but I tightened my grip because now I was pissed. "You never would fight for me. Maybe you just never loved me enough." I was starting to twitch with the effort of not crying.

"Don't you *dare*. I loved you with everything I had. You *made* me leave. And then you just threw what we had away. You just *threw* it away, Nate. Like it was NOTHING. Well, it wasn't nothing to me. IT WASN'T NOTHING. I would have done anything for you."

"Anything but forgive me," I whispered.

His features contorted. "I can forgive you. I just can't ... I can't ..." He didn't finish.

In one step I closed the distance between us and grabbed his face in my hands. I pressed my mouth to his. I'd make him remember what we had, what we still had. He resisted at first, but then his lips softened. "Make love to me," I whispered.

He stiffened and grabbed my wrists and pulled my hands from his face.

He made a strangled noise in the back of his throat. "You can't make all the bad things go away with sex, Nate." He was hurting my wrists. "Not with Luke. And not with me. I don't even know who you are." He let go and reached for his other bag.

"Adam, don't do this."

He turned back and shoved me hard in the chest. "I didn't do this, Nate," he shouted in my face. "YOU DID." His face contorted. He was trying not to cry, and failing. "You did!" His voice broke and he turned again.

"You fucking coward!" I shouted at him. I grabbed his arm again. "Scream at me. Hit me. Make me pay. I don't care what you do to me, just don't leave." He tried to shake me off, but I moved in front of him and grabbed him by both arms, my face close to his. "Adam. I can't live without you."

He swiped at the tears on his face. "We both know that's not true. I wish to God it were. At least it might give me something to hold on to, some reason to stay."

I realized in that moment that he was right. I did know. This wasn't about needing anymore. This wasn't about surviving. This was about choosing.

"I want you."

"You don't know what you want."

He was wrong about that.

"This is not over between us," I said, echoing his words.

When he spoke, his voice was calm and cold. "It is for me. I'm going to Austin, and I'm not coming back." He pushed past me. His cell phone fell out of my pocket and thudded onto the carpet. He bumped it with his foot, then bent over, set down one of his bags, and picked it up, looked at it for a moment, and then flung it against the wall. The back snapped off and the battery popped out on impact. Then he pulled the leather strap from around his neck and locked eyes with me as he wadded it up in his hand along with the pendant bearing my name. He held his fist up to my face, then opened his fingers and let the pendant drop at his feet, as if my name didn't even warrant a good throw. He picked up the bag again, and without another word, opened his door and headed down the hallway.

I stepped into the hallway, barely registering his mom on the landing, drawn to our fight like a bug to a zapper. "Go ahead," I sneered after him. "Run away. *Forever* had a pretty fucking short run, didn't it? You and your stupid Sharpie and your stupid heart."

He spun around and in two long strides was back. And that's when he decked me. I stumbled into the door frame and went down hard on my ass.

I wiped the blood off my nose and watched him go.

Chapter 52

Ten years later

He had a megaphone gripped in his hand and wore glasses now. And he seemed taller. But the blond hair peeking out from the baseball cap was unmistakable.

He put the megaphone to his mouth. "Woodwinds! Your dance moves are just okay." A chorus of boos rang out from the kids in the lower half of the stands. He held up his hands and shrugged before putting the megaphone back to his mouth. "Brass! Your dance moves are *ex*-cellent." The kids in the top half of the stands shouted and shook their instruments in the air. Someone blew a random note.

I smiled to myself. Luke held up a ringed flip-book so the kids could see the next song.

The drum majors counted off the beat. As the band played, he climbed the steps, stopping to dance with the clarinets, then moving up to percussion and then the trumpets. A trombone waved his horn in the air. "Mr. Chesser, over here!" Luke waved back and continued making his way up the steps.

He still had those boyish good looks, and it made me happy to see that the kids loved him. I had to resist the urge to run down the steps and touch him to be sure he was real.

The darkening sky gave way to fat raindrops. Luke and a

woman I assumed was the head band director hurried the kids out of the stands and into the area below. I followed.

By the time they all got down there, the brass players, who were the last to get to cover, were damp and steamy, but that didn't dampen their fun. It was loud under the stands. The drummers kept the party going with cadence after cadence, while the kids jumped and spun and shouted out chants. I tried to remember if I'd had that much energy when I was a teenager.

Luke was talking to the other band director when an amorphous group of kids surrounded them, shouting and dancing. One kid in particular shimmied right up against Luke, so close it tweaked my gaydar. At first Luke ignored them and continued his conversation with the other band director. But then abruptly he threw his arms in the air and bounced with the kids for a few seconds. I grinned to myself and made my way through the crowd toward him.

I grabbed him by the elbow. He held up a finger behind him to indicate he needed just a minute to finish whatever he was saying. Then he turned to me, clearly expecting a student, but finding instead a twenty-eight-year-old man. He looked at me curiously for a moment and then he caught his breath. "Nate?"

I smiled and he threw his arms around me. I laughed into his ear. "It's been a long time." He pushed me away and looked at me. "I can't believe it's you!" The drummers had picked up a new beat and he had to shout to be heard. "What are you doing here?"

"I'm here visiting Mom and my grandmother. Juliet told me you were the new assistant band director."

"Weird, huh?" He grinned and mussed my hair. "You got shorter."

I shook my head and laughed lightly. "I think you got a little taller."

He grinned again, then looked around him. "I have got to run to the bathroom. Here, hold this." He lifted the megaphone from across his shoulder and handed it to me. "I'll be right back." He hesitated a moment, then winked at me. "You want to come?"

Oh, what the hell. I went with him.

With everyone just killing time until the rain stopped, the men's room was especially busy and there was no opportunity to catch up until we left. But I really just wanted to look at him. All those years of worrying about him, not knowing what had happened. He never called. Not once. He caught me looking at him in the bathroom mirror as he washed his hands. I didn't bother looking away. I handed him a paper towel and we walked out together.

"Are you happy?" he asked, taking the megaphone from me.

I nodded.

As we stood there looking at each other, a handsome young man slipped his arm around Luke's waist and kissed him on the cheek. The gesture wasn't lost on the band kids. Those who saw hooted and wolf whistled. Luke laughed and kissed him back on the lips. "Go, Mr. Chesser," someone shouted and then whistled again. A drummer struck up another beat and the frenzy started all over.

The newcomer had a megaphone draped over his shoulder too. I could see in Luke's eyes that this was someone special.

"Nate, I want you to meet my chief nemesis, keeper of my secrets, and, uh"—he glanced around, then leaned in closer and finished in a low voice—"the guy I wake up with every morning." He winked at megaphone guy. "This is Curtis. He's the band director for those goons on the other side."

"Yeah? Well, those goons are gonna make your little band of misfits look like a junior high kazoo club," Curtis said playfully, yanking down the bill of Luke's cap.

"We'll see about that," Luke said, reseating his cap and clearly enjoying the banter. He looked at me sheepishly. "Curtis was the drum major of our university band my freshman year. I actually met him two years before that. He was a field tech for the band. We've been together ever since. We're, um, getting married over Christmas." He held the back of his hand up to me and wiggled his fingers, showing off a shiny gold band. I watched Luke's eyes go all melty when he looked at Curtis and remembered a time when they went all melty over me. I was glad they had each other.

Curtis sized me up, then reached out his hand. "So, you're Nate." He gripped my hand, a smile on his face, but his hand tightened around mine in a knuckle-crushing warning. I met his eyes, my own smile faltering. It struck me that this right here, this small act of possession, was exactly the kind of thing I'd wanted from Adam all those years ago. I glanced at Luke, but he was still watching Curtis, and I could practically see little red Hallmark hearts springing from his eyes and floating into the steamy air. Curtis released my hand with a "Hmph."

The rain had stopped and the head band director was shepherding the kids back into the stands. "Showtime," Curtis said. He smacked Luke on the butt and glared at me before heading back to the other side of the stadium and his band.

Luke watched him go with obvious pride. "I have to go back up," he said.

My nose burned and my eyes stung. I hadn't expected to cry. But through the years I had thought about him, worried about him, even though I had resisted the sometimes painful urge to look him up. And now, seeing that he'd not just survived, but thrived, it was like someone had loosed a tight cord binding my heart and the muscle released in one great heave. I looked up at the concrete bottoms of the bleachers and swiped at my eyes with my fist.

"I know," he said quietly, understanding my sudden emotion. "It was better this way. You couldn't save me. And I couldn't destroy you." He squeezed my hand and I squeezed back. "Can we get together later? I'd really like you to get to know Curtis."

"Sure," I said, sniffing back the snot.

He grinned again, excited now. "Are you here alone?"

I shook my head.

"Come to the band hall after the game?"

I nodded and he bounded up the stairs after the kids.

Juliet was drying off my seat with some paper towels she must have snatched from the bathroom. "Did you talk to him?" she asked.

I nodded and looked across her at Danial. "He's good." I smiled. "He's really good. I met his fiancé." Danial dropped his head back and offered up a word of thanks. "He wants to get together after the game. You guys up for it?"

I rubbed Juliet's swollen belly.

"Hey, gay boy," Danial said. "Get your paws off my wife."

I laid a kiss on her inverted belly button. "Face it, Qasimi, she's always going to love me best."

"Uh-huh," he said, and rolled his eyes. Juliet giggled and kissed her husband.

I smiled at them, my heart full.

"Sorry we're late," a voice said over my shoulder.

I turned and scooped a curly redheaded toddler into my lap, then turned my eyes on my fiercely handsome husband. Adam dropped down in the seat next to me and raised a curious eyebrow, then laughed softly. "Your eyes are doing that thing again," he said and brushed my lips with his.

Danial cleared his throat. Loudly. "Come here, Lucy. Your daddies need a moment and I want a kiss from my best girl!"

Our daughter clamored over her mother and climbed into Danial's lap. I watched her go, and felt my throat tighten. "Thank you," I mouthed to Juliet for perhaps the thousandth time. Juliet winked. Lucy looked just like her mom, the same crazy red hair, the same spunky attitude, with just enough of me thrown in to make her unique. I was pretty sure it was my DNA in her cells, but we didn't know for sure. We planned it that way. Juliet had offered to "do it" the natural way, kidding of course, but we assured her a turkey baster had sufficient capacity for a two-daddy contribution. One thing I could say with absolute conviction—Lucy was conceived in love. Mine for Adam and his for me. Ours for Juliet and hers for us.

Our Lucy.

People thought we'd named her after another famous redhead, but we knew better.

It was impossible to focus on the football game. The truth is, none of us cared a bit. Instead we soaked up each other's company and watched Luke shine. Lucy ate her first pretzel and demonstrated that she had inherited some rhythm from someone, which made me question that whole DNA thing. At one point Luke looked around and saw us in the stands. Lucy was dancing, and Luke laughed and pointed at her, mimicking her moves with his own. She giggled and buried her head in my lap. Luke blew me a kiss and turned away.

Adam looked at me, eyes narrowed. I laughed—he tried so hard—and told him about Luke's fiancé and wanting to get together after the game. He grabbed my chin and rubbed his thumb over my lips. "Just so long as we don't stay out too late. We're sleeping in my old room tonight. And I have plans."

"Oh, brother," Danial groaned.

We brought Luke and Curtis back to Adam's parents' house. Juliet and Danial met us there. Mea, sixteen now and stunning, had lit the tiki lamps before we got there and turned on the lights that were still strung throughout the branches. Then she disappeared upstairs with a handful of friends. My in-laws took their granddaughter inside for ice cream and a movie.

We sat around, two by two by two, and drank margaritas, and it was like we'd been doing this forever. Curtis took to Adam right away, and that seemed to soften his stance toward me. I smiled to myself. I was no more a threat to Curtis than Danial had been to Adam, but I did wonder how much he knew.

I was glad that Luke was still close to his little brother, Matt, whom he described as a raging heterosexual with gay proclivities. When I asked him what the hell that meant, he laughed and told me he had no idea.

One thing was absolutely clear. Luke was oozing with happiness, even as he told us about those awful first months—the isolation, the seething anger toward his dad, the lack of privacy. All he had was band. So he poured his energy and passion and pain into that. His story got a little fuzzy after that, but Curtis took over and told how they'd met Luke's junior year at the high school he now directed for. Curtis said Luke stalked him for months before he finally gave in, and I thought that sounded about right. But something Curtis had said suddenly struck me and I looked at Luke.

"You came back?"

His eyes darted nervously to Curtis, then back to me. "Yeah. That summer. Different neighborhood. I was zoned to the other high school."

I hardly knew what to do with that bit of news. "Your dad?" I asked.

"He's coming to the wedding," he said.

I choked up. "That's good, Luke. That's really good." And then I got up to top off my drink and compose myself. No one stopped me. My own dad had made some feeble attempts to come to grips with who I was, but ultimately he demanded I choose. So I had. I chose myself. It still hurt thinking how he'd deleted me from his life. He hadn't responded to our wedding invitation. I thought having Lucy would change things. It hadn't.

Luke didn't ask what happened after that night, and I didn't tell. It was a story Adam and I kept to ourselves. It belonged to us, and somehow I knew it needed to stay that way.

It was a memory we still talked about sometimes, a reminder of a place we never wanted to be again—me, bleeding on the carpet in his bedroom doorway, my nose fractured. It was his mom who'd taken me to the emergency room where a resident straightened my nose, gave me some Tylenol, and told me to go home and stay out of fights. I spent Christmas day alone in my room, devastated, depressed, bruised. I watched episode twelve of *Family Affair* over and over again, hating that little sap Jody, the prime rib Grandma brought me cold and untouched on my bedside table, the gifts I wouldn't open still piled under the tree downstairs. I hadn't bought a gift for Adam. I'd been so caught up in Luke's plight that I hadn't even thought about it.

I found out later that Adam had spent Christmas day alone too, in his new dorm room having busted the lock to get in. No phone, no sheets on the bed. Just a broken guy with two duffel bags stuffed with wrinkled clothes. His mom and Ben and Mea drove up the next day to move him in properly.

When the swelling went down, I made my first weekend trek to Austin, something I'd do weekly for many months to come. I came armed with only my computer, a book or two, my toothbrush, and a longing heart. I slept in the hallway outside his dorm room— technically against dorm rules, but none of the guys complained. Those first few weeks I saw little of him, just the occasional sighting when he stepped over me on his way out somewhere. Except for the time he accidentally on purpose kicked me, he acted like I didn't exist. I wrote some and I read, but mostly I just waited. I didn't know until much later the torment that he was going through on the other side of the door, the times he pressed his ear to the crack, listening to me breathe and thrash around. The fourth weekend he opened the door long enough to hurl a blanket and a pillow at my head, then slammed it again. The fifth weekend he came out and sat in the hallway with me, his knees drawn to his chest, his elbows on his knees, and his forehead pressed into his fists. He didn't say a word. And when I scooted closer to him, he got up and went back to his room.

Before I drove up the sixth weekend, I got my second tattoo.

He let me in that night, but he didn't make it easy. In the weeks to come, he yelled a lot, and sometimes I yelled back. He called me a slut and a bleeding heart and some other pretty ugly names, and I called him a few. He told me my blog was banal and self-indulgent, which stung, but I didn't think he really meant it. And that my nose was crooked, even though it wasn't. And once when I caught him looking at his name inked on my bicep, he scoffed and told me it was unoriginal and that I'd find laser removal pretty painful. He made me sleep on the floor, even though his roommate went home on weekends and his bed was empty, and some mornings I'd wake up and he'd be curled up on the floor next to me, wrapped up like a burrito. He didn't sleep well, and often he'd step on me accidentally on purpose in the middle of the night on his way to the bathroom.

But he didn't throw me out, and he didn't leave, and when I showed up again at his door each Friday night, even though he acted like I was some smelly rodent a cat had abandoned in the hallway, he let me in. And then one night near the end of the semester, he nudged me in the small of my back with his bare foot and woke me up. And when I rolled over, he told me to get my sorry self off the floor because he was sick of tripping over me. And when I did and asked him where he wanted me to sleep, he just broke down. I gathered him to me as he sagged to the floor and held tight. He cried, great soul-shattering sobs, and my heart broke for the last time. And somewhere in all that brokenness we found our way back to each other, and we talked finally of things that really mattered, of hurt, of fear, of need, of trust, of loyalty, of forgiveness, and of love.

He was a lawyer with the ACLU now, and I was writing books, books that I'd first begun sketching out in those long hours in the dorm hallway. Danial promised to read my novels to his Language Arts students, as long as there wasn't too much sex in them. I told him I couldn't make any promises.

Chapter 53

I slipped my laptop out of my satchel and opened it on Adam's desk. The lava in the lamps had overheated and broken up into bits, leaving the water cloudy. The lamps were different now, ten of them, each one marking an anniversary, a year in our lives together since. We kept them here in his old room, the place where we'd first come together, the place where we'd shed our childish illusions of each other only to find something more real, more beautiful underneath. The screen added its own blue light to the room as the computer booted up. While I waited, I studied his sleeping form. He was on his stomach, his arms under the pillow, his shoulders exposed where the blanket had slipped. It was almost enough to make me shut down the computer and crawl back in bed beside him. I could wake him up. He wouldn't mind. He never minded. But there was something I needed to do first.

I'm Queer. Get Over It.
Closure and good-bye
By Nate Schaper on Oct. 2
Human beings seek closure. It's that tendency to fill in the gaps, connect the dots, and see complete figures where there are only

dots. When this human need to fill in the gaps is blocked, psychologists say we experience frustration and anxiety.

Today, I connected my dots.

This is not the same world it was when I started this blog more than ten years ago. It's still not perfect, and maybe perfection isn't all it's cut out to be anyway. But it's good. It's really good. They say you can't always get what you want. But sometimes you can, and you do, even when you don't deserve it.

Whoever you are, wherever you are—live. Love.

Peace,

Nate

I shut down my computer and the lava lamps and, in the darkness, found my way back to my man.

Don't Let Me Go

J. H. Trumble

About This Guide

The following discussion questions and playlist
are included to enhance your group's reading of
Don't Let Me Go.

Discussion Questions

1. Discuss the significance and alternate connotations of the title.

2. *Don't Let Me Go* depends on flashbacks to develop the early relationship between Nate and Adam. How might the feeling of the novel differ if the story unfolded in chronological order?

3. How does Nate's assault affect his relationship with Adam? With his mom? His dad? Juliet? How might these relationships have evolved differently if the assault had never happened?

4. Adam's Christmas gift to Nate (the Yang) suggests that they are two parts of a whole. Do you believe this is a healthy attitude toward a relationship? Why or why not?

5. Nate says that "even heroes grow weary lugging around the burdens of their heroism." Do you believe this is true? Can you think of any examples to illustrate that statement?

6. Adam explains that his dragon tattoo is his way of taking control of his body. In what other ways do teens assert their independence? In what ways did you assert your independence as a teenager?

7. Do you believe that Nate and Danial's friendship is realistic? Has their relationship affected the way you regard friendships between gays and straights of the same gender?

8. Discuss the similarities and differences between Nate's relationships with Adam and Luke. What are his roles in each, and how do you think the experiences influence each other?

9. When Luke shows up on Nate's doorstep Christmas Eve, Nate tries to describe his unexpected disappointment: "It was kind of like finding out your dog is going to die, and you spend all this emotional energy preparing yourself, saying good-bye, and then it doesn't, and you feel kinda like you've been cheated." Share a time when you felt something similar.

10. In Nate's final blog post, he writes about the importance of closure. Why do you think knowing what happened to Luke is so important to him? Has there ever been a time when you didn't get closure on something? How did that make you feel? Is Nate's closure a satisfying conclusion to *Don't Let Me Go*?

11. Talk about the coming-out process for Nate, Adam, and Luke. If you identify as LGBT, discuss your own coming out. Do you think the concept of "coming out" can apply to something other than sexuality?

12. Music plays an important role in Nate's life and in the emotional development of *Don't Let Me Go,* as you can see by the following playlist. Listen to the songs (or read the lyrics online) and talk about how each one is relevant to the story. Feel free to include any personal connections you might have and your response to the songs.

The *Don't Let Me Go* Playlist

Check it out on iTunes: http://t.co/Tqa0XC5, or, visit iTunes Ping and search J.H. Trumble.

Music plays an important role in Nate and Adam's relationship. They fall in love over "Heart and Soul." They hold each other close to Chicago's "You're the Inspiration." They get playful with Glen Campbell's "Wichita Lineman." And they say good-bye as Lynyrd Skynyrd's "Free Bird" plays in an endless loop in Nate's head. Nate often turns to his guitar or to the piano to express his emotions, as we see on the evening of the homecoming dance when he plays Rufus Wainwright's cover of "Hallclujah." These songs and others are woven through the fabric of their story. But there are others that define them as characters—their love, their longing, and their hurt. Songs they might very well have listened to on their MP3 players. These are those songs, presented in chronological order.

"Let Me Be Myself," 3 Doors Down
Nate's theme song as he pushes back against his father's expectations.

"It's My Life," Bon Jovi
Nate chooses Adam over his fear.

"I Love Rock 'n' Roll," Joan Jett
On top of the world—their first public appearance as a couple.

"You're the Inspiration," Chicago
Love grows.

"I'll Stand by You," Pretenders
Adam stands by Nate when Nate can't stand by himself.

"Come Back to Me," David Cook
Nate sets Adam free in Key West.

"Never Say Never," The Fray
The novel's theme song and inspiration for the title. This is also the song Adam flubs on the way to the airport.

"Not Afraid," Eminem
Nate starts his blog—out, proud, and angry.

"Battlefield," Jordin Sparks
Long-distance relationships are so hard to maintain.

"Hallelujah," Rufus Wainwright
Nate deals with the increasing fear that he's losing Adam. There are a lot of versions of the Leonard Cohen song, but this is Nate's favorite.

"What Hurts the Most," Rascal Flatts
It's over.

"Need You Now," Lady Antebellum
Trying and failing to get by without Adam, Nate resists the urge to call him.

"Heartache Tonight," Eagles
Knowing the one you're with is not the one you love.

"How to Save a Life," The Fray
It's not over: Adam and Nate struggle to find their way back to each other.

"Kryptonite," 3 Doors Down
Adam's song when Nate does the unforgiveable.

"I Don't Wanna Live Without Your Love," Chicago
Nate seeks forgiveness.